D0485020

MVFOL

MORE PRAISE FOR NATIONAL BESTSELLER *CHOCOLATE SANGRIA*

"The best of chick-lit . . . Price-Thompson doesn't serve up a light, sweet-talking love story but instead gives us a raw look at the bonds of friendship, sexuality and self-identity. The novel also offers a fable on the consequences of keeping secrets and betrayal. . . . A heart-wrenching tale of love and family."

—*USA Today*

"*Chocolate Sangria* is a wonderfully written novel that demands attention from page one. Tracy Price-Thompson delivers a powerful sophomore effort, proving she has a literary talent that will entertain readers for generations to come."

—Zane, bestselling author of *Nervous*

"Vivid, striking prose, heartfelt and authentic. *Chocolate Sangria* is a thought-provoking book that examines sensitive issues among people of color."

—Marcus Major, author of *4 Guys and Trouble*

PRAISE FOR THE NATIONAL BESTSELLER *BLACK COFFEE*

"A page-turner that explores the dangerous liaison between two soldiers."

—*Essence*

"A racy tale of romance and ambition in the military."

—*The Washington Post*

"Price-Thompson has set this novel among a seldom-written-about group, African Americans in the military. . . . An excellent job of showcasing a lifestyle not often glamorized by contemporary novelists."

—*Booklist*

"[*Chocolate Sangria*] puts a literal spin on the war between the sexes. . . . This is not a light-hearted, sweet-talking love story, but an energizing slice of ultracontemporary romance."

—*Publishers Weekly*

"*Black Coffee* keeps you awake as it takes you on a roller coaster ride in love, relationships, and pain all camouflaged in a military setting. . . . Tracy Price-Thompson's writing is remarkable."

—*Black Reign News*

Photo: © Stavra Kalina

TRACY PRICE-THOMPSON is the nationally bestselling author of *Black Coffee, A Woman's Worth,* and *Chocolate Sangria,* which was a Main Selection of the Black Expressions Book Club. She is a highly decorated Desert Storm veteran who graduated from Army Officer Candidate School after ten years as an enlisted soldier.

A Brooklyn, New York, native and retired Army engineer officer, Price-Thompson is a Ralph Bunche Graduate Fellow of Rutgers University who holds an undergraduate degree in business and a master's degree in social work. She lives in Hawaii with her husband and their children, where she is currently at work on her fourth novel. She can be reached at tracythomp@aol.com.

ALSO BY TRACY PRICE-THOMPSON

BLACK COFFEE
A WOMAN'S WORTH

CHOCOLATE SANGRIA

TRACY PRICE-THOMPSON

CHOCOLATE
SANGRIA

A NOVEL

ONE WORLD / BALLANTINE

This is a work of fiction. Names, characters, places, and incidents are the products of the author's imagination or are used fictitiously. Any resemblance to actual events, locales, or persons, living or dead, is entirely coincidental.

A Strivers Row Book
Published by The Random House Publishing Group

Copyright © 2003 by Tracy Price-Thompson
Reader's guide copyright © 2004 by Random House, Inc.

All rights reserved under International and Pan-American Copyright Conventions. Published in the United States by The Random House Publishing Group, a division of Random House, Inc., New York, and simultaneously in Canada by Random House of Canada Limited, Toronto.

STRIVERS ROW, BALLANTINE, and the Strivers Row colophon are registered trademarks of Random House, Inc.

www.striversrowbooks.com

Library of Congress Cataloging-in-Publication Data
Price-Thompson, Tracy.
Chocolate sangria: a novel / Tracy Price-Thompson.
p.   cm.
ISBN 0-375-75779-1
1. African American women—Fiction.   2. Puerto Ricans—New York
(State)—New York—Fiction.   3. Brooklyn (New York, N.Y.)—Fiction.
4. Racially mixed people—Fiction.   5. Social isolation—Fiction.
6. Race relations—Fiction.   7. Gay men—Fiction.   I. Title.
PS3616.R53 C48   2003   813'.6—dc21   2002069046

Book design by J. K. Lambert

Manufactured in the United States of America
4   6   8   10   9   7   5   3
First Edition: February 2003
First Trade Paperback Edition: January 2004

This work is dedicated

to the beautiful people who lived at 315 Livonia Avenue,

Tilden Houses, in the Brownsville section of Brooklyn,

New York, from 1960 to 1995, who helped teach me the art

of making something out of nothing, a way out of no way,

a dollar out of fifty-nine cents, and who continue

to love me as one of their own.

ACKNOWLEDGMENTS

I'd like to begin by giving all praise to God, the Merciful and Compassionate Creator, who continues to bless me in abundance and guide my life along paths of peace and balance.

It seems like just yesterday when I penned the acknowledgments to my debut novel, *Black Coffee*. Thanks to the love, support, and encouragement I received from readers, family, and friends, *Black Coffee* quickly became a national bestseller, and my gratitude and appreciation to each of you is eternal and everlasting.

While it may seem like I thanked everyone under the sun in *Black Coffee,* my appreciation has multiplied along with my blessings; therefore, some additional acknowledgments are in order here as well, and I do so graciously and from the heart.

To my husband, Greg Thompson, a mighty oak tree whose roots run deep and whose leaves span wide: bearing fruit when I hunger, casting shade when I swelter, and providing a place of rest when I falter. (YSAGTM!)

To our children, Kharim, Erica, Greg Jr., Kharel, Kharyse, and Khaliyah: the treasures of the world are within your reach. Aim high. May God guide you and may our love and support help sustain you.

To my sister, Michelle Carr, thanks for being there for me and mine exponentially, to the hundredth power. You are appreciated beyond words and measure. I love you.

To my nieces and nephews and godchildren, Toi, Damon, C.J.,

Mel, Eddie, L.B., Traci, Jerel, Courtney Rae, Janise, Courtney Mae, Angelle, Ciara, and Darius: I love you all!

Many thanks and much love to my peeps, Margaret Price, Darryl "Pebbles" Price, Tonya "Tee Cee Lou" Price, and Anthony "Lefty" Price, for having a sustaining love and an undying support for my children and me. Having you guys as family is a comforting, secure thing, and demonstrates the love and commitment that each of you has for other people's children. It's good to know my kids and I have open doors and open hearts within our reach. We love ya!

To all of my Thompson family in Michigan, thanks again for your love and support. Your showing up in the midst of a severe snowstorm just to see me was truly amazing! Much love and many blessings.

Much love to Bridgette Dingle, my hardworking sister-friend who does a wonderful job of holding it all together. It's been more than twenty years and you remain a friend and remain in my heart.

To my best friends Kim and Jimmy Kendrick (and your sweet little Kimma-Jimma), Tawanna Harrington, Yvette "No-No" Gogins Williams, and Roberta "Berta" James. Much love to Tricia "Patty" Brown, Kim Stanley, Carmelia Scott-Skillern, Sheryl Hinds, Tracey Williams, Rhonda Tatum, Phyllis Primus, Pat Houser, and my dear friends and former neighbors, Sophie and Preston Moore and Barbara and Bobby Pentecost. We miss you!

Thanks and love to Sister Barbara Wortman and her children Tahmir, Abdur-Rahman, Jakinah, Shamone, and Murad (Mookie Moo-Moo) for their love and support and for being neighbors and friends who can be depended upon without complaint or excuse at a moment's notice, twenty-four hours a day, seven days a week. We love you. Similar thanks to James and Patricia Head and their children Laura and James Michael, for always being there to lend a helping hand, a watchful eye, and an open door. Thanks to George McNeil for being a trusted neighbor and for stepping in to help whenever needed. Thanks to Gwen McNeil for the friendship, good food, and even better desserts. Love to Antonette and Keoki.

To Marita Golden and the members of the Zora Neale Hurston/ Richard Wright Foundation for providing recognition and opportunities for emerging and established authors to shine. As a proud member of the Hurston/Wright family, I thank each of you for the honor of your association.

To L. Peggy Hicks, a wonderfully efficient and effective publicist who makes each of her clients feel special and treasured.

To my good friend Sherrie L. Respass, who has worked hard and endured much during our travels promoting and selling *Black Coffee*. I could not have done half as good a job without your winning smile and guerrilla sales tactics! Keep snatching them up for me, sis. Much love to you and yours.

To Tonya Howard and Tanya Marie Lewis, whose tireless and self-less efforts on my behalf are simply astounding. Where there is smoke, there is fire. Thanks to both of you special sisters for enriching my life and fanning the flames of my work.

Big thanks to the many members of the military communities in the United States who turned out in droves to purchase *Black Coffee*. Wait until you see what I bring you in my next military novel! And much love to the sistah-soldiers whose loyal friendships sustained me during my military career. You know who you are. If I didn't call you by name in *Black Coffee*, please charge it to my head and not my heart.

To my wonderful author-friends whose creativity never ceases to amaze me. You know who you are. The literary world has become a more colorful arena due to your talents! To my tour partners and signing buddies, Gloria Mallette, Karen E. Quinones Miller, Rita Coburn Whack, Trevy McDonald, and Marlene Taylor.

To Christine Young-Robinson, my tour partner, my homegirl, my dear friend. Thank you for your kindness and patience and wonderful organization skills, and big thanks for taking such good care of me on tour. Much love to you and yours.

Thanks to those self-published authors who are striving to bring quality works to our readers. Big thanks to Zane for raising the bar on self-publishing and for showing the literary world that a creative, motivated, business-minded black woman is a dangerous thing. Keep on doing what you're doing, my sister, because it works!

To TaRessa Stovall, my dear friend and business partner in TnT Explosions. May we continue to create great collaborative projects and strive to bring them all to fruition.

To my Prolific family, whose works are becoming more recognized daily. You are a talented and supportive crew! Jamise Dames, Carla Canty, Theresa Matthews, Cherryl Floyd-Miller, Linda Dominique Grosvenor, Rena Finney, Earl Sewell, and many, many others.

To my newfound friends and readers Renna Wilkinson, Jackie McGuire, Kim Burney, Alfreada Kelly, Sandy Thompson, Monique Patterson. Jackie, thanks for your help and your company during the signing at Fort Meade! Many thanks to Tamecka Murray and the sisters of the Nubia Bookclub in Staten Island, New York. Your support is truly appreciated.

Thank you to Emma Rodgers and Shirley Johnson and all of the bookstores, libraries, and bookclubs who selected and supported *Black Coffee* and who eagerly awaited the release of *Chocolate Sangria*. My success was assured because of your energy and enthusiasm for my writing.

To my agent, Djana Pearson Morris, for building my career and encouraging me to explore the range of my writing, and to my editor, Melody Guy, for being sensitive and insightful and for wielding her velvet whip with care and consideration.

And finally, big thanks to the readers who blew up my e-mail account and flooded my mailbox with letters about *Black Coffee*. It was your word-of-mouth support that made the novel a success. It is for you that I write. It is for you that I create. I'd love to hear your thoughts on *Chocolate Sangria,* and as you know, I personally respond to every one of my letters. Hit me anytime at tracythomp@aol.com or P.O. Box 187, Fort Dix, NJ 08640. Visit my website at www.TracyPriceThompson.com.

Peace and balance,
TRACY

CHOCOLATE SANGRIA

PROLOGUE

//////////////////////////////

The evening shadows hitched a ride on the tails of a tulip-scented breeze, slipping unnoticed through the double-paned bay windows. For weeks, spring had been elbowing its way into summer, and today the heady waves of ivory petals mingled with the aroma of beef Wellington straying seductively from the industrial-size kitchen.

The shadows prowled like seasoned burglars, stealing along the wooden baseboards, shifting and squirming effortlessly before snaking around the blunt corners and crawling into the crowded dining room, where Hattie stood mute before the overturned goblet of Beringer Merlot; she stared dumbly as the vintage wine permanently stained miles and miles of the hand-laced ivory tablecloth and pooled like fresh blood on the creamy, high-napped carpet.

"Don't just stand there like a fool! Find that new girl and get it cleaned up!"

Silence swallowed the buzz of dinner conversation as the scorching words blazed from Leah Jacobson's thin lips. Overhead, crystal chandeliers in tiers of four glinted dangerously as miniature beads of humiliation dotted the bridge of Hattie's nose and trickled down to form a creek in the shallow crevice of her upper lip. A piercing glare from the Missus broke Hattie's paralysis and sent her scurrying from the room in search of Sallie, the newly hired maid.

Hattie raced along the wide corridors, the folds of her pleated skirt rocking to and fro, her ample weight rolling from heel to toe and leaving curious imprints in the lion-colored carpet that slurped at her feet like quicksand.

Searching for Sallie was akin to looking for a saint in a whorehouse. Futile. Hattie entered the master study, where the stench of decades-old cigars clung to the furniture and settled beneath the carpet. She waved her hands furiously before her nose, beating away the specter of pale men and old money that haunted the room and dwelled among the wood-paneled walls.

There was no sign of the dim-witted girl amid the high-backed paisley chairs and elegant ottomans facing the long row of leather-bound books and journals. She was not snuggled beneath the enormous claw-foot desk carved from a knotted oak tree and covered with thick wax worn into it by the hard labor and heavy strokes of black ass and elbow a hundred years past.

The chile was not behind the handcrafted oriental partitions covered with the painted faces of smiling Japanese whores wearing downcast eyes and sly grins as they fanned their slender, milk-white necks. Not inside the narrow hideaway closets where mounds of ledgers and tablets sat molding and rotting among forgotten artifacts from an era gone by.

Hattie snapped her fingers twice and padded from the room. The hollow sound echoed heavily against the walls before settling into a serene nothingness. She sighed and pressed deeper into the mansion. "That Sallie-gal gots to *go!*" she muttered, as thoughts of Missus Jacobson and the dripping red wine sent chills through her heart. She'd have to find the new maid quickly or there would surely be a price to pay. Although the Missus had instructed Hattie to cook and Sallie to serve, after setting out two courses—soup and salad—the half-baked girl had simply disappeared.

Hattie snorted. The gal was too nasty to be working around somebody's kitchen anyhow. If it were up to her the chile would never have been hired; any fool could see she didn't have sense enough to light a flame under a pot of water! Gal was put together so backward she wandered around the mansion with her crooked legs moving like scissors—bones so knocked it looked like one knee didn't trust the othern!

And her hands!

Hattie nearly gagged. She'd never seen hands so filthy on kitchen help. To make matters worse, Sallie had a disgusting habit of dragging her clammy fingers along the walls and leaving grimy stains on the pristine surfaces.

Hattie's brow collapsed into a series of linear frowns. There was no need to call for Sallie again. If'n the gal heard, she would only pretend like she hadn't. Besides, the Missus was wanting that spill cleaned right away, and anybody fool enough to keep Missus Jacobson waiting was just begging to get her hiney cut. *Don't that simple chile know? Ass don't grow back like fingernails do, but that's something Little Miss Sallie's just gonna have to learn on her own.*

After twelve years of cooking, cleaning, and keeping house at the Jacobson estate, Hattie was reluctant to make unnecessary waves, although she felt no loyalty toward the haughty couple who treated her with blatant contempt and downright disdain. Domestic jobs were plentiful along this stretch of Long Island, and Hattie could find other employment virtually overnight; but it was her love for the Jacobsons' sixteen-year-old daughter that kept her tethered to the mansion and doomed her to a life of toil and misery.

From the moment she'd laid eyes on the chubby green-eyed thumb-sucking child, Hattie was hooked, her heart seized in a grip of fierce protectiveness that could never be broken. It was her love for sweet little Lola that compelled Hattie to slip from bed at four each morning, leave the tidy apartment she shared with her older brother, Herbert, and catch two city buses and the Long Island Rail Road straight to hell each day.

With a toss of her salt-and-pepper curls, Hattie continued her search, baby-stepping down the halls with the balls of her feet burning as though she'd treaded too close to the sun. She fished for the skeleton key in her skirt pocket, then unlocked the small supply closet to the left of the winding stairs and stepped into the darkness.

The interior of the closet was brutal. Moist heat flanked her and attacked from all angles, causing her rising temper to leap a full notch. She reached for the light string dangling from the ceiling and yanked.

God-toe-mighty-no!

Flinging the eight inches of broken nylon cord to the floor, Hattie reached blindly atop a high shelf, her hands searching until she located a plastic jug of Heinz white vinegar. She squinted against the gloom of the closet as she rummaged around for a dark-colored cloth. Her fingers skimmed deftly over a stack of neatly folded white towels and kept right on moving. There was no way she'd use white rags to sop up red wine, only to have the Missus demand they be soaked in chlorine bleach until they were either bone white or disintegrating shreds!

She shrugged at the senselessness of it all and grabbed three brown towels normally used for dusting, then relocked the supply closet and turned to shuffle back the way she'd come. Suddenly her feet were rooted in place as a chorus of moans echoed from above. The eerie sound slithered down the winding staircase before dissipating into the still air. Hattie narrowed her eyes and craned her neck toward the balcony overhead.

Sallie?

Not hardly, she smirked. It was more'n likely one of Mr. Jacobson's golfing buddies, wearing out the springs on the guest bed. The air Hattie pushed from her nostrils was thick with disgust. This wouldn't be the first time she discovered drunken guests doing the hanky-panky during one of the Jacobson's parties. In fact, that little red-haired Jezebel sitting right next to the Missus and wearing a fake mole and a shy smile had mussed the sheets of dang-near every bed in the house! Just two months earlier Hattie had caught her and Mr. Jacobson slapping bellies up against a west-wing wall, a kiss of filtered moonlight blanketing their pale, hairless bodies. She cringed at the memory and took two hesitant steps forward.

Shrouded moans. Cries of passion.

Time froze.

Hattie peered up at the balcony as the whispers darted behind the heavy drapes and hid beneath the embroidered tapestry. No, she realized. She'd been wrong. Not furtive tunes of pleasure.

Animal groans of suffering. Melodies of deep pain.

Sallie? Hattie's heart ricocheted against her throat. *With one of them drunken fools?* Her lips trembled and a deadly chill crept down her spine. She'd lived in the projects long enough to know the difference between the sounds of a good time and of a good time gone bad. Hattie swung her head violently to obliterate the aching sounds that threatened to dance with the nightmare buried in her memory.

Snatches of leering faces and hovering naked bodies bubbled up from the recesses of her soul and she squeezed her eyes closed and swooned, her knees suddenly rubber as she fought to blot out the vision of that long-ago night. *You's a silly woman, Hattie Dell,* she chided herself. *This ain't Harlem of '42. Best leave that kinda pain resting right where it be.* Steeling herself, she clutched the towels and vinegar and gripped the polished mahogany banister. A deep, guttural groan of getting-ready-to-die agony exploded in the air as the whispers rose in crescendo and hammered at her ears.

Her feet nimble, Hattie skimmed the winding stairs. At the top of the landing she barreled down the corridor, chasing the animal-like wails and following the telltale finger streaks drying on the flat white walls.

Sallie!

The whimpers ripped through the air and the silver in Hattie's teeth cried out. In her mind's eye, she was blinded by images of young, defenseless black flesh; ravished, brutalized, molested by pale, drunken hands. She drew breath and her nostrils were flooded by the memory of cheap sangria riding on hot, murderous moans. As Hattie approached the west corridor, the tension in the air suddenly changed. The low grating cries became high-pitched anguished shrieks. Rushing past the guest suites and the Missus's reading room, she rounded a sharp corner, entered the wing leading to Lola's bedroom, and gasped in surprise.

Just ahead was the lost Sallie; nasty fingers molesting the walls, crisscrossed legs comically propelling her backward, away from the cluster of rooms belonging to sweet, green-eyed Lola.

Dear God! Hattie pressed her hands to her lips and stared.

Not Sallie! *Lola!*

"Fool!" Hattie caught the twisted girl in three long strides. Snatching Sallie by the front of her dress, Hattie ignored the tiny buttons that popped and flew at her face. "Whatchoo seen? Whatchoo done to her? Answer me, gal! What's wrong with my baby?"

Sallie's eyes were squeezed tighter than two sphincter muscles. Her breath snagged in her throat. Her jaw hung slack, and a necklace of saliva stretched from her chin to her breast.

"Wench, *move!*" Hattie threw herself against the brass handle and flung the door open wide. Pitiful whimpers and mews of anguish grated her senses as she clamped both hands over her ears. A powerful wave of fear and pain washed over her. In over fifty years of hard project living, Hattie had thought she'd seen her share and somebody else's, but nothing she'd ever encountered had prepared her for this.

"W-w-what in the *hell*? Oh, Lawd ha' *mercy*—sweet Jesus!"

There was no mistaking the gory exhibition. Naked from the waist down, Lola lay spread-eagle atop her frosted canopy bed, a mound of fluffy white pillows—now blood-soaked platforms—pushed beneath her writhing hips. Her knees were bent at a forty-five-degree angle and her chubby white legs were parted to reveal both her swollen vagina and the mighty force from within its folds that threatened to split her open like a sweet Georgia peach.

Kneeling at Lola's feet was Pierre, the Jacobsons' gardener: His smooth hazelnut skin was ashen, his terrified eyes begging Hattie for forgiveness, understanding, and assistance all at once. Hattie's own eyes darted back and forth between the wailing child on the bed and the panicked landscaper on the floor. Her bone-dry tongue snaked out and tore at her lips. The sour stench of blood, sweat, and fear stung her nostrils and brought water to her eyes.

"Please," Pierre whispered. "Please, Miss Hattie. Help her!" The quiet urgency in his voice released Hattie from her stupor. She pushed the fear and confusion to a remote corner of her mind and rushed to Lola's side.

The girl's hands were colder than January; her fingernails were torn and caked with her own drying blood. Hattie looked from Lola to Pierre and whispered, "Oh sweet baby, what he done to you?"

The gardener pressed his hands together as if in prayer and begged, "Miss Hattie, please—"

"Goddamn your soul! Now, scram!" Hattie positioned herself at the child's knees and shoved Pierre out of the way. There was only one reason the pretty Negro gardener was between poor Lola's legs and up to his elbows in blood.

He was responsible for this mess.

Pierre scampered to the side, his bloody hand prints leaving evidence in the white carpet where he'd knelt. Hattie squeezed Lola's hands.

"It's okay, sweetie." She smoothed tendrils of dark hair away from the girl's face. "Auntie Hattie's here, and I ain't gon' let nothing happen to you."

Panic and fear disappeared from Lola's dazzling green eyes and a small measure of calm entered their pools. Lola trusted her. Always had and always would.

Hattie planted herself between Lola's legs and spoke gently yet firmly. "Listen to my voice, sweet baby. You just listen to old Aunt Hattie and we gon' come through this-here mess just fine." She peered at the drama unfolding between the teenager's thighs. The baby's head pushed forward like a sausage being squeezed from its casing. Although Hattie had never in life seen an actual birth, her instincts told her exactly what to do.

She prepared to be the back-catcher.

She grabbed at the dusty brown towels and cursed herself for not choosing the clean white ones, then rolled the entire wad into a ball and shoved it against the mouth of Lola's womb. Then Hattie hit her knees and positioned each of Lola's bare feet upon her shoulders as she commanded the girl to bear down.

"Push, honey," Hattie urged, as she gritted her teeth and grasped Lola's thighs. "Brace yo' feets against my shoulders and *push that baby out*!"

Lola did as she was told, her eyes squeezed shut, her white-ringed lips turning a deep shade of violet. One . . . two . . . On the third push Hattie heard an audible rip, and without flinching or even batting an eye she praised the teenager's efforts.

"That were good, sweetie. That were real good."

Hattie peered in closely, then jumped back a country mile as the baby's head suddenly reappeared.

"*Push,* dabnabbit!!!"

Lola growled deep in her chest.

With each downward thrust, tiny ebony curls emerged more fully from their wet cavern, and Lola's mouth flew open as she shrieked and yelped in pain.

"Uh-uh. *Uh-uh!*" Hattie dug her fingers into the soft flesh of Lola's thighs. "Not no, but *hell* no. Ain't gon' be no screamin' up in here tonight! The time for holl'ren is *done.* 'Sides, you know your mama can hear a rat across the lawn pissin' on a cotton ball, so you'd best hush up!"

Lola showed her teeth like a cornered dog but swallowed her pain in one big gulp.

"That's right, sweetie. Now, use all of your energy to get this here baby born."

No sooner had Hattie said those words than Lola bore down, gave a mighty groan and a valiant thrust, and to Hattie's dry-mouthed amazement the girl's vagina first blossomed like a new rose, then spread wide enough to hug all of Texas.

"God-toe-mighty-*no!*"

From the warm darkness of Lola's womb emerged a tiny pink head covered with jet-black curly hair.

"Oh my sweet blessed *Jesus!*" Hattie held her palms beneath the infant's damp skull. The baby's eyes were sealed shut, its mouth folded up and over itself like an old man's without teeth. Suddenly Lola heaved again, and with a bit of pulling and tugging from Hattie, the infant's torso shot out of its mother's womb and fell into Hattie's waiting hands.

"It's a girl!"

Tendrils of steam rose from the tiny body, and Hattie, not sure what else to do, turned the baby over and popped it twice on its bottom. Wails of protest immediately filled the room, and for a second no one moved. Pierre found his feet and bolted to Lola's side.

"Lola . . . baby. Please, I'm sorry, baby . . . please . . ."

Hattie eyeballed the young man. Twenty-two years old, son of Haitian immigrants, skin of caramel and lips of sugar. She understood everything. He was one of them self-hating Negro men. One of them who felt low on account of they color. Damn fool! Climbin' them trees his ancestors hung from! How dare he mix business with a white gal when every hand that had ever fed, rocked, or protected him was at the end of a colored woman's arm? Hattie scowled and paced along the edge of the bed. If the gardener wanted to play house, it shoulda been with a grown woman who looked a lot more like him!

And Lola. Hattie's gaze turned tender. Looking for love in all the wrong places, the mixed-up chile had given in to the attentions of the older man.

As if she'd read Hattie's thoughts, Lola begged, "Aunt Hattie, it was my fault! *I* pressured *him*. I wanted him. I needed somebody besides you to love me."

Lola coughed as waves of tears slid from her sea-green eyes. Hattie bit her lip against her own tide of tears, and whatever judgments she had been prepared to pass were quietly tucked away.

There but for the grace of God go I.

She knew how it felt to be young and in need of love. The only real difference between her and Lola was that Hattie didn't have no baby. Couldn't have one. Daddy had seen to that. Hattie used a sewing scissor on the cord, then wrapped the pink infant in Lola's flannel bathrobe and handed the wailing baby girl to her father.

"Hush, sweet baby," Pierre murmured, and stuck his pinkie into the infant's mouth. Instantly, she was quiet.

Lola begged, "You've got to help me, Aunt Hattie. I don't have anyone except you."

Hattie turned to Lola, and then the tears did slip from her eyes. She would die for this child. No other human being except Puddin had ever needed her so much.

"I'm here, baby. Your Aunt Hattie is here for you." She squeezed Lola's hands and let her strength and courage fill the young girl's soul. "What you want I should do?"

Lola swallowed hard. "Take the baby, Auntie. I-I want you to take my baby." She clutched Hattie's hands in an icy grip desperate with need. "Take her as far away from this house as you can. Raise her as your own. Love her the way you've always loved me. Save my baby, Auntie. Please . . . save my baby."

Hattie snatched her hands away.

"A-ain't no way I kin raise no baby!" she stammered. "Chile, I don't know nothing 'bout birthing no babies, and even less about raising 'em!"

Hattie backed toward the door, refusing to accept the magnitude of Lola's request. She needed to catch up with Sallie and get downstairs and clean up the Missus's mess! But the feat she'd just performed had begun to sink in. Images of the wine-stained tablecloth and the blood-stained sheets merged in her mind, and Hattie bit the insides of her cheeks to keep herself from swooning.

"Aunt Hattie." Lola sat upright in the coagulated mess of the bed. "Please." Her face was sheet white. "I'm begging you. Begging you! I'm scared, Auntie. I'm scared."

Hattie didn't budge. "Honey, they gots all kinds of places and programs nowadays for a white gal who done broke her leg! I bet there's some real nice places! Trust me. They'll take the baby, too—."

"Aunt Hattie." Lola's voice could have melted dry ice. "My mother is going to kill me. She'll kill me and put my baby in a foundling home. She'll find a way to make me suffer for the rest of my life. For the rest of my life I'll have to pay for this one mistake." She whispered, "Please, Aunt Hattie. Please, won't you help me?"

Hattie groaned like a woman twice her age. She knew all about paying for mistakes. She too had incurred a mighty debt at an early age.

And she was still paying for it.

She looked over at Pierre, who held the beautiful child in his arms. His eyes beseeched her. "She's right, Miss Hattie. And there won't be a thing I can do to help her from a prison cell, 'cause that's exactly where I'll be. Just as sure as I am a black man, Missus Jacobson will see me rot for the rest of my days."

Hattie whimpered and bit down on her bottom lip until blood ran free. Pierre was right. Their daughter and a common gardener? Those same black hands hired to dig in the dirt molesting their lily-white child? The Missus would slit her own throat and slay her own mama before she'd let that little secret get out! Leah Jacobson would see to it that all three of these lives were damned and ruined.

Hattie buried her hands in her wiry hair, yanking at the roots.

Never before had she felt such a burden of responsibility. Not since the night of Puddin's trouble.

Measure up, Hattie Dell!

Hattie heard her grandmother's stern voice echoing through her mind.

Us Lucas wimmens got broad shoulders and strong backs!

"But I ain't got no money to be feeding no baby!" Hattie silently protested.

If you can feed two, you can feed three! was her grandmother's quick reply.

"I'm fifty-three, Big Momma! I'm getting on! I don't know if I can stand no baby. If'n I even knows how to handle one!"

Big Momma clucked.

Hattie Dell Lucas, you disbelieve! He won't give you more than you can safely bear!

"But where me and Herbie gon' go with a pure-white baby like that? Us live in the projects! Ain't nobody gonna believe she's none of me!"

Thass all right. She black. She just ain't got her true color yet. 'Sides, if you feed her long enough, she bound to look like you!

The two women continued their struggle, but despite Hattie's desperate protests, the legendary spirit of her grandmother won out. Eartha Lee Lucas's spunk and vigor flowed powerfully through her granddaughter's veins, and Hattie reluctantly submitted to her authority.

She reached out her arms to Pierre and pressed the warm bundle to her stout breast, rocking back and forth as she snuggled the wriggling infant close and stared into her magnetic green eyes. The baby immediately turned her head, rooting toward Hattie's breast.

"Uh-uh, baby," Hattie muttered. "I'se the wrong cow. Ain't nothing but dust in these old sacs." She readjusted the baby's position, nestling her upright near her shoulder and inhaling the sweet scent of birth cloaking the child. She pressed her lips to Lola's forehead then turned to glare at Pierre. "Go. Git yourself down them stairs and fetch my pocketbook." She held her glare on his retreating back.

Hattie handed the peaceful baby to Lola and allowed her to cuddle and kiss her daughter for the first and last time; then, clutching her pulsating bundle, she moved toward the door. "Auntie," Lola called softly. "Can you call her Juanita, please? After Pierre's mother. Please call her Juanita."

Five minutes later, with the grating voice of the Missus ringing throughout the halls and Sallie nowhere in sight, Hattie and her small bundle slipped down the back stairs and darted into a waiting limousine driven by Pierre.

"I'm going on faith, Lawd," Hattie whispered, as Pierre sped down the winding driveway and toward the wrought-iron gates of the Jacobson estate. "Faith, I say! 'Cause it shole ain't by sight!"

Her heart pounded as she gazed over her shoulder at the mansion fading into the lush countryside. The world might never know what demons rode the Jacobson family or the nasty secrets those brick-and-mortar walls protected but Hattie knew that was one doorway she'd never darken again.

He don't never close a door without opening a window, she remembered Big Momma once saying, and thus she was closing one chapter of her life and beginning another. As was her habit in times of great turmoil and hardship, Hattie pursed her lips and hummed her grandmother's favorite battle hymn:

> *Lord, don't move this mountain,*
> *Just give me the strength to climb.*
> *But* Lord, *if I can't make it . . .*
> *Then lead me on around!*

PART I

SAVIN'
SCOOTER

CHAPTER 1

/////////////////////////////

"That thar boy's got half a bag of sugar in his tank," Herbie Lucas declared upon setting eyes on Socrates for the very first time. He and his sister, Hattie, watched from their fifth-floor window as their neighbors Jeo and Dorothea Morrison stepped out of a camel-colored Brougham with their five-year-old grandson and his small cardboard suitcase in tow.

"Herbie, *hush!*" Hattie glanced over her shoulder and snapped her fingers twice. "You see Miss Nita setting over there pretending to fuss with that doll baby's hair when she really listening at us. You know she repeat everything she hear! Besides"—she tucked a strand of graying hair behind her ear, then turned back to the window and nodded toward the slender boy who shuffled down the pathway nestled between his grandparents—"the poor chile just saw his mama slit his daddy from neckbone to navel, then they make him ride all the way from Alabama to Brooklyn with that crazy-ass Jeo when everybody knows he's blind in one eye and can't see out the othern." She grunted. "And all you can talk about is how sweet he look."

"Ah-yeah." Herbie coughed and touched the corners of a starched white handkerchief to his lips. "I reckon old J.J. did go out and get hisself gutted like a fish, and I'm glad Jeo and that old struggle buggy didn't tear up the road none too bad, but that thar boy is sweet. Mark my words."

Hattie peered closely as the trio approached the entrance to the building. She studied Scooter's willowy walk and the way his lean body seemed to move naturally against the soft summer wind.

"Ain't sweet," she determined. "He small for his age is all. Look a bit like Diana Ross to me. With all that pretty peanut-brittle skin and them big ol' eyes, I thank he kinda cute. Plus, Nita got her somebody to play with now. Be good for her to be around another chile."

Herbie coughed again, this time hacking up a thick wad of phlegm. Leaning out the open window he pressed his index finger to the opening in his throat and hock-spit down into the littered grass below. He rasped, "Don't know 'bout that. They say the boy mute, too. Jeo say the po-lice found him sucking his fanger and settin' in four days' wurf of his own mess. I bet that's why he cain't talk. Stuff like that gotta do somethin' to a boy. Make him turn 'round inside hisself and ball up in his own shit."

Hattie stepped away from the window and loosened the tails of her apron. She draped it over the back of a kitchen chair before shaking her head. "You can set there and stare all you want, but I'ma go meet them at the elevator. After all that driving, they gots to be wore out." She lifted a tin pan from a cooling rack and covered it with a glimmering sheet of foil. Despite herself, she moved back to the window for another peek. "C'mon, Nita." She looked down at the pigtailed little girl who had squeezed herself between the two adults and now stood watching the new arrival in silence. "Let's carry one of these-here pecan pies to Sister Dot and help her put on some tea."

When the elevator opened its doors, Hattie stumbled against Juanita's small shoulder and nearly cried out. Dorothea Morrison had gone down home a spry woman of sixty who made regular visits to the salon to maintain her ebony hive of spiral-curled hair. The woman who stepped off the elevator clutching the hand of a thin boy with miles of eyelashes and a blank stare was stooped in the back and had a head full of snow-white strands.

Sitting in the neat kitchen decorated in tones of tangerine and lime,

Dorothea shook visibly as she spooned too much sugar into her teacup and accepted a slice of Hattie's pie. Her grandson, Socrates, had fallen into an exhausted heap in the first chair he'd come across, and Juanita stood hovering over him, her green eyes roaming his face with undisguised curiosity.

Hattie snapped her fingers. "Come 'way from him, Nita, afore you stare him awake." Then to Dorothea: "Dot, that baby shole look tired. Didn't he sleep any all that way up here?"

Dot nodded. "That all he do is sleep!"

"He talk any yet?"

Dot sighed and shook her head. She raked a few large crumbs from the table and into her open palm. "Ain't opened his mouth. Act like he trying to leave us. Doctors say his mind went so deep he won't never remember none of it, and when he gets older we should just tell him both his folks died in a car accident." She squeezed her hands into fists and her bottom lip quivered. "That damn demon oughtta die! Oughtta fry in the 'lectric chair!" she whispered. "Goddamn her wicked soul! Jeo Junior was my onliest son, Hattie! You hear me? My onliest son!"

Hattie stood and retrieved a stiff dishrag from a rack above the sink, then held it out to accept the pie crumbs. She patted her old friend's back and rocked her the way you would comfort a colicky baby. "Trust Jesus, Dot. He don't make no mistakes. 'Sides, you got that baby over there to worry about now. J.J. was a man, but that'n there is still a chile. You gots to concentrate on him."

Dottie nodded and wiped her hands on the dry cloth, sobbing softly as she reached into her dress pocket and blew her nose into a crumpled white handkerchief. "That's what the doctors say too. They say to leave him be and he'll quit sleeping and start talking when his mind and his heart is ready." A fresh wave of tears spilled down her cheeks and she let go of a quiet sob. "I just don't know if'n my poor little Scooter is gon' ever be ready."

/ / /

It took four-year-old Juanita Lucas three months to chip away the wall of silence surrounding Scooter Morrison. Precocious and determined, each morning after breakfast she marched two apartment doors down and, with her green eyes sparkling and flashing, announced to Dot Morrison, "I'm here to save Scooter."

And save him she did. Juanita pestered Scooter like a gnat, asking him a million questions and answering every one of them for him. She bossed him around like a prison warden, forced him to play with her dolls, fixed him peanut butter and cheese sandwiches, and demanded he lick his plate clean.

She had no mercy.

While the adults in the building clucked over Scooter, fed him candy drops, and called him "poor baby," Juanita harassed him like a hornet and left no room in his life for either sorrow or solitude. Every morning she jerked a narrow-toothed comb through his coarse hair, painfully tearing out patches and snapping it off at the roots, slathered his arms and legs with a stick of cocoa butter to get rid of his "skeeter-bites," and insisted he open his mouth and let her scrub his teeth and gums with wet baking soda and a frayed toothbrush.

After a typical morning of Juanita asking endless questions and then supplying Scooter with the answers, he'd finally had his fill. "Why is your bottom lip so much bigger than your top lip?" Juanita inquired, and just as innocently answered in a voice she assumed would sound like his. " 'Cause one day when I was down Souf, way back in Ally-bammy, I fell out of a pecan tree and bumped my lip on a rock. Then I sucked all of the blood out of it and filled it back up with tobacco juice and that's why I have such a big, fat liver lip!" With a burst of laughter she tossed her hair in his direction and leaned against the bright blue card table that was cluttered with finger paints and colorful sheets of construction paper.

Scooter lunged. A strangled cry tore from his throat and he extended his hands like claws. Crazed, he knocked over a child-size yellow chair and snatched ferociously at his green-eyed tormentor.

Bracing herself, Juanita sidestepped Scooter's assault, and with a heavy thrust sent him crashing into the card table before tumbling to the floor, landing flat on his tear-streaked face.

Scooter recovered swiftly. Oblivious to the mess of paints that splattered his clothing and colored his rage, he scrambled to his feet.

Leaping, he sailed forward and sank his nails into Juanita's face, clawing her left cheek. His skinny arms flailed wildly as he wind-milled into her and buried his hands in her tangles down to her scalp, swinging her around by her endless bulk of hair.

Recklessly, they tussled and scrapped and pinched and clawed, until a triumphant Scooter, with tears pouring from his eyes and a slice of red war paint streaking his chin, found himself sitting astride Juanita's heaving chest. As he stared down into her face he saw no malice and no fear. Whereas he was wild and crazed, Juanita seemed accepting and calm. He pulled back his tiny fist to smash those steady green eyes to Kalamazoo, and then hesitated. Instead of striking, Scooter peered at Juanita closely, tilting his head from one side to the other.

And then he uttered his first words in more than three months.

"You got a big green booger in your nose." He belched, then grinned. "It's even greener than your ugly, bugged-out kryptonite eyes!"

And with that, the fighting children burst into uncontrollable laughter, rolling and frolicking in the paint-and-litter chaos of the floor, Scooter's high-pitched peals ringing and blending with Juanita's childish chimes and both filling the air with the unabashed glee of two very small children who have suddenly discovered that life can be happy and carefree.

CHAPTER 2

FIVE YEARS LATER

"Trade you a squirrel nut." Scooter offered the gooey treat as he slurped on an orange jawbreaker. Using his tongue, he rolled the hard confection around the roof of his mouth, then crunched loudly, shattering it to bits between his back teeth.

" 'Kay. Gimme two sour apple Now and Laters."

He laughed. "Yo' eyes may shine and yo' teeth may grit, but none a' my Nah Laters shall you get!"

"C'mon, Scoot. Gimme one for now and one for later!"

The sun shimmered high in the late summer sky, the powder-blue landscape serene and unblemished by a single cloud. The rectangular play area was sectioned off from the main courtyard by a series of chain-linked ropes. The interior consisted of six multicolored concrete barrels, two of the eight original plastic swings, several vomit-colored wooden benches, and four slate-colored concrete table-and-stool sets that had long ago been anchored to the pavement. Juanita and Scooter were lounging across the top of a Crayola-colored concrete barrel, each clutching a tiny brown paper bag as they chowed down on a feast of sweets courtesy of Uncle Herbie and purchased from Miss Bea's Corner Store.

The scent of freshly cut grass tickled Juanita's nose as she rubbed her palms over the chipped layers of paint on the barrel's surface and licked sticky remnants from her lips. She cast a longing look toward the entrance of their project building, an area that brimmed with children playing heated games of hopscotch, skelly, red light green light, hot peas and butter, and Mother, May I?

Nearby, a large group of brown-skinned girls clad in halter tops and culottes faced one another in a straight line. Stomping their feet to accompany the upbeat tempo of their urban chants, they looked like daunting divas to Juanita as she mouthed the words while they sang:

> *Ahhh-beep-beep!*
> *Walking down the street!*
> *Ten times a week!*
> *Ungowah! Black Power!*
> *Destroy! White boy!*
> *I said it, I meant it,*
> *I'm here to represent it!*
> *I'm cool, I'm calm,*
> *I'm Soul Sister number nine,*
> *Sock it to me one more time!*
> *Unh-Unh Good God!*

Smiling as the girls slapped hands and collapsed in giggles at the end of the rhyme, Juanita continued to mime along as the soul sisters with the cornrowed hair rolled their hips, clapped their hands, and shuffled their feet, then broke into their next song:

> *My name is Peaches,*
> *Doo-da-bop!*
> *Supercool,*
> *Doo-da-bop!*
> *You mess wit' me,*
> *Doo-da-bop!*
> *You's a fool!*
> *I don't dig no biting,*
> *Doo-da-bop!*
> *That's no lie,*

Doo-da-bop!
You bite off me,
Doo-da-bop,
And I'll black your eye!

Enjoying the singsong cadence that threatened a peer-induced ass-whipping, Juanita visualized her own hips swiveling and rocking and moving in sync with their kind of natural rhythm and sensual finesse.

This the way we willow-bee, willow-bee, willow-bee,
This the way we willow-bee all night long!
Oh! Step back, Sally, Sally, Sally,
Step back, Sally, all night long!
I looked down the alley and what do I see?
I see a big fat lady from Tennessee!
She wears her dresses above the knee
And she can shake-shake-shake back to Tennessee!
And then she turns around,
And then she touched the ground,
She goes waaaay back,
I got a hump in my back,
She do the camel walk, and then she freaks!
And then she freaks, ah, and then she freaks!

Juanita could see herself out there with them. Arms crossed, legs popping, shoulders shaking . . . She became lost in her fantasy and nearly slid off the barrel when her name was yelled out.

"Hey, Needa!" It was ten-year-old Sheila Jenkins, standing at the end of the courtyard just beyond the chanting group of girls. "You wanna jump? You can get next after this game, Needa!"

"Need-ah," Scooter mimicked under his breath. "You need-ah tell that witch to climb on her broomstick and take the hell off!"

"Later for you, Scooter-Pooter!" Juanita bolted upright. "I'm nine and I can make my own decisions! You're just jealous because don't nobody ever ask you to play!"

Her statement rang true for both of them. Although there were enough children in their building to fill an entire yellow school bus, Scooter was the only person whom Juanita could even remotely call a friend. Every other child her age had ridiculed or threatened her because she was different.

Scooter was different, too. With his falsetto voice and his wiggling hips, he stood out like a kernel of corn in a can full of peas, and truth be told, he caught far more hell than she did.

"Ain't jealous." Scooter rolled his eyes and unwrapped a Blow Pop, slathering it from all angles. "Just smart. And you should be, too," he stated wisely. " 'Member the last time she asked you to play somethin'? You ended up flying out the window."

"That was an accident!"

Scooter sat up. "Like hell! How does 'Swing your legs around and slide your butt to the edge' come to be an accident?" He rolled his eyes again. "Shoot! You shoulda seen yourself sail out that window like somebody's damn kite. You lucky a sore ankle is all you got." He went back to licking his purple Blow Pop.

Juanita glanced warily across the courtyard. The girls had finished with the intimidation lyrics and picked up a different tune, this one with a slow, funky, sensuous beat:

> Oh, beansa, beansa, beansa . . .
> Beansa to my heart.
> I been eatin' beans until they make me wanna faaaart. . . .

Scooter had a point. Time had not erased the feel of Sheila's hands eagerly thrusting at the small of her back. Sheila and her crew were dangerous, and if she were smart she'd stay put atop the barrel with Scooter. But she admired these Nubian-looking girls with their rich chocolate skin and stylish hair. There was nothing ambiguous about their full lips and regal noses. They paraded around the neighborhood with swinging backsides and budding breasts like they owned the dirt they tread upon. She envied the easy way they referred to one another as "sister," "earth," and "queen," because in Juanita's eyes, that's exactly what they were. Sister girls. Beautiful queens of the earth, and she'd give anything to look just like them.

She shook her head.

Behind her, the chanting girls rocked their hips and rolled their pelvises in a dip-swing-dip motion.

Forty is my number,
Fifty is my age.
If you don't believe me you can
Kiss my little assssss. . . .

"Forget you, Scooter." She needed these girls, would give anything to be counted as one of them. Assimilation by association.

"No, Nita! Forget *you*! But don't forget 'bout that time they made you steal that money from Uncle Herbie's shoe! That money he was saving for your auntie's eyeglasses. You don't wanna forget *that* now, do you?"

Hot shame rose in Juanita's cheeks, staining them crimson. Uncle Herbie had torn his bedroom up looking for that twenty-dollar bill he'd folded until it was just a tiny square of green. He'd gone through every piece of clothing he owned, peered under every mattress and cushion in the house, and searched every nook and cranny small enough to hide a cockroach.

Juanita remembered hiding in bed with her head under the covers, breathing in the scent of her own disgrace and waiting for the police to arrive with handcuffs and a warrant. Finally, unable to contain her shame one moment longer, she boiled over and jumped from the bed screaming, "I did it! I did it! I took the money from the toe of your walking shoes!"

That night after her bath, Uncle Herbie had come in and hugged her and kissed her and listened as she told him about Sheila and her gang. Told him how they promised to jump on her if she didn't come up with some cash to purchase a shower gift for Kendra's new baby brother.

Aunt Hattie had come in next and hugged her and kissed her, too. And then she'd told her to take off all her clothes. She said, "I'ma cut your ass wit' my right hand till I hear the voice of Jesus at my elbow commanding me to quit . . . then I'ma switch hands and cut you wit' my left!"

Juanita whimpered, "But I was so scared, Auntie."

Aunt Hattie wound the leather strap twice around her meaty wrist and hissed, "Chile, you betta fear me more than you fear nary one of them ol' mannish gals out there in them streets!"

Kendra's baby brother had died shortly thereafter, but the flesh on Juanita's butt still stung from the memory of Aunt Hattie's strap. Yet, anxious to be accepted by the other girls, she allowed herself to hope that this time would be different. The girls chanted loudly:

> *Listen, sapsucker, let me get you straight!*
> *Your mother got a poo-poo like a two-forty-eight!*
> *Your father got a pee-pee like a two-forty-nine . . .*
> *So listen, sapsucker, don't you talk about mine!*

With a toss of her wild curls, Juanita slid down off the barrel and abandoned Scooter without another thought.

Smiling, she stepped over the chain-link rope that divided the small playground and gingerly approached the small group of girls who were swinging a typical ghetto gym: a plastic-coated length of telephone wire. Sheila, her caramel face shining under a thin coat of Vaseline and her comb-pressed hair box-braided with multicolored barrettes securing the long ends, stood waiting. Her hands were perched impatiently on pointy hips while she tapped her sneaker-clad size tens on the hot concrete and chewed a massive wad of strawberry bubble gum.

"She just taking her own sweet time," remarked Kendra, a ten-year-old early bloomer who wore a bra and already had her period but was still in the second grade. "Sashayin' over here like somebody got all day to be waitin' on her yellow ass."

Although Sheila could be downright mean, Kendra wasn't playing with a full deck. Rumor had it that she'd sprayed Raid insect killer in her newborn brother's face and tricked her parents into believing it was crib death, and even though her nasty comments sent Scooter's warning ringing through Juanita's brain, there was no way she was going to blow this opportunity. It wasn't every day a girl like her was invited to jump rope with Sheila and her crew, so Juanita smiled again and quickened her pace. She wasn't eager to rise to the top of any-body's shit list.

Especially Kendra's.

"Mosey on over here, Red!" Kendra commanded, and Juanita duti-fully ran the last few yards. She stopped in front of Kendra and offered another smile.

"Your turn," Kendra said, and passed off her end of the rope. "You'll get your jump when the next person gets out."

"Uh-uh! Like hell she will," yelled Mutter Jeffries, a loud nine-year-old, who came from a family of ten, all one year apart in age, and whose mama, Auntie Hattie said, needed to try something else until she got that rhythm method down pat. "I'm jumping next! I ain't been down here turning for my health," she declared, holding her end of the rope in the air.

"Yawl work that mess out later," drawled Sheila. "Right now, I'm ready to jump!"

Dutifully Juanita swung her end of the rope up and over in a per-fect arc, the clapping sound of plastic striking concrete meshing in perfect time to the singsong cadence.

"All! All! All! All in together, girls, how you like the weather, girls? January, February, March, April . . ."

The six girls jumped into the rope as one, then jumped out accord-ing to the month in which they were born. Over and over they played game after game, their natural curiosity and creativity lending color and flavor to the inner-city lyrics. *"Bosco, Bosco, I know it's good to drink! Oh yeah! My mother put some in my milk and tried to poison me! Oh yeah! But I fooled Mama and put some in her tea . . . and now I have no mama to try to poison me!"*

On and on they jumped until Juanita, who was gritting her teeth but still managing to swing a perfect arc, turn a perfect rope, thought her arm would fall off. Each time the last girl jumped clear of the swinging rope she prayed they'd stop for a short break, but each time Sheila gave an excited shout and led the troupe back in for more.

Finally, they were spent. The girls collapsed breathlessly to the ground, laughing and panting, clapping one another on the back and praising each other's skills.

A moment later Sheila was on her feet and raring to go again. "Okay, get up!" she commanded. "This time we gonna sing, 'Old King Moses Was the King of the Jews!' "

Juanita climbed to her feet. A low throbbing sprang from her right arm. She looked down and noticed the end of the rope still clutched tightly in her fist.

"Who gets this?" she asked with an uncertain smile, not wanting to risk anyone's wrath by deciding it was their turn.

Every eye fell on her. Her cheeks grew hot.

"Who gets what?" demanded Sheila. "My foot in they ass?"

"No," whispered Juanita, not sure if Sheila was joking and not eager to find out. "Who gets the rope?"

"*You* do!" Sheila's hand was back on her hip, and that telltale right foot was tapping up a storm. "You got a problem with that?"

"No," Juanita breathed quietly. But she did have a problem. A big problem. Her arm felt like Lou Piniella's must have felt when he pitched a doubleheader for the Yankees, but she knew better than to complain. Mutter switched off with her older sister Queenie, and Juanita remained holding her end of the rope in a trembling grip.

"Let's jump double Dutch!" Kendra suggested, and momentarily forgetting her fear, Juanita sucked her teeth and let out an audible groan.

"Oh, I *know* you ain't over there sucking yo' teets!" snapped Kendra. She spat on the ground near Juanita and sniffed. "You lucky we let yo' red ass play!"

Juanita let her gaze touch the ground in front of her and pretended to measure out two lengths of rope. Her submission was duly noted.

"Oh, I *thought* so!" Kendra laughed, and the other girls joined her as they took up positions for the new game.

After fifteen minutes of high jumping, the rope tangled itself around Sheila's calves, causing her to stumble and go down on one knee.

"Yawl heffahs can't turn worth a damn," she hissed. Juanita was doing her best, but the fibers in her arms were knotted in protest and her fingers felt like they were being jolted by tiny bursts of electricity.

"She the one double-handed!" panted Queenie. Juanita stared at her turning partner. A thin line of sweat streaked Queenie's temples and the sides of her faded tank top sported two large, wet stains.

"I'm not double-handed."

"What?"

"She said you a lie!" shouted Kendra. "She said she ain't double-handed, and that's just like saying you a lie!"

Taking advantage of an opportunity to get away from swinging the dreaded rope, Queenie let her end fall to the ground, and with her sisters, Mutter and Pig, on her heels, she approached Juanita.

"You calling me a lie?"

"No," Juanita managed to whisper around the lump in her throat. "I'm not calling you nothing. I just meant that I'm not double-handed, my arm is just tired and—"

"Tired?" yelled Kendra. "Tired? What she doin' tired when we did all the jumpin'? Just 'cause she got them nasty cat eyes and all that hair she think she too damn cute to turn! Naw, she ain't tired!"

The Jeffries sisters got up in her face. They were so close Juanita could smell the fried Spam sandwiches their mother had fixed for lunch. Like a pack of hounds, the other girls smelled blood. Canine-like, they formed a small huddle around the pair.

"I *said*," Queenie repeated, bopping her head from side to side, "is you calling me a lie?"

Juanita stuttered. "I-I . . ."

"C'mon, now! Tell me quick before I faint: Is I'm a lie, or is I'm ain't?"

Kendra swore. "Fuck this! That's zactly what she callin' you! A *goddamn* lie! She said you a lie, your feets stank, and you don't love Jesus!" She stepped up on Queenie and shoved her. Hard.

Queenie lurched forward, barreling over Juanita, who fell backward, crashing to the ground. A sharp crack split the air as her head struck the cement and her teeth closed down painfully on her tongue. Aligning themselves in a bloodthirsty semicircle, the other girls picked up a deadly chant:

A fight! A fight!
A nigger and a white!

If the nigger don't win,
THEN WE ALL JUMP IN!

Juanita stared up at the jeering crowd with tears streaming from her eyes. Their faces contorted with hatred, the young girls laughed and egged Queenie on with taunts ranging from "Stomp that white bitch 'cause she thinks she's cute" to "Choke that heffah with her own long hair."

"Look, yawl," Mutter pointed. "She cryin'."

Pig snorted. "The more she cry, the less she pee."

Juanita panted with terror. Her teary eyes danced from face to face as she searched for a hint of sympathy. Her gaze finally lit on Sheila, who had been strangely quiet throughout the ordeal. Standing by with her hands on her narrow hips and her right foot tapping out a tune to beat the band, a strange smile played along Sheila's thin lips.

Juanita's hope surged. The snarling girls would tear into her any minute, and since Sheila had been relatively nice to her, certainly nice enough to invite her over to jump, perhaps she'd step in and call off the pack.

Wordlessly, Sheila held one dark finger in the air. Immediately the taunts ceased. The crowd moved back a few paces and Juanita rose to a sitting position, fingering the lump rising on the back of her head. As she climbed shakily to her feet something slammed into the pit of her stomach and sent her tumbling back to the ground.

"Git back down, heffah!" Sheila snarled. Over and over, she swung her Pro-Ked-clad foot into Juanita's midsection, sending wind and spittle flying out of her wide-open mouth and causing her to choke on the thank-you she'd been fixing her lips to utter.

"Stand back, homeys." Sheila spread her arms wide and blocked the bloodthirsty girls as they moved in close, preparing for the kill. "Uh-uh, yawl, this bitch is mine!" She balled her fists and shook them high in the air.

"Her wide ass belongs to *me*! So don't yawl jump in it, 'cause I don't need no help! I said, I don't need no help, so yawl step the fuck back— 'cause she's half-ass white and she's too damn fat!"

Juanita felt her hair yanked as Sheila dragged and scraped and pulled her painfully across the hot tar. She yelped and cried out as the angry girl booted her in the rear, slapped her across her face, and yanked out handfuls of her curls.

Kendra hopped from foot to foot giggling with glee. "Snatch that bitch bald! Snatch that piss-colored bitch bald!"

The last thing Juanita remembered thinking before escaping inside of herself was *Sheila had better watch her ass.* The girl was losing her grip, losing control of her crew. They were very disobedient. Ignoring her deadly commands to keep back, every one of them had jumped right on in to help.

, , ,

"You got hair just like one a' them Porta Reekins."

Scooter stood in Juanita's pink-and-white bedroom, working his hands through the tangle of her hair as he slathered a golden glob of Sulfur 8 on the quarter-size bald patches glaring angrily from her skull.

"No I *don't*!" Juanita jerked away.

Undaunted, Scooter batted his eyes and reached for her again. "Well, if not a Porta Reekin, then for sure one of them Bay Ridge Eye-talians."

Juanita jumped to her feet, knocking over her wooden footstool. "Socrates Morrison, you take that back with your country-ass self! My hair is straight outta Africa—just like yours! It gets nappy when it's real hot outside and it can even take a warm comb, so you just better take that 'Porta Reekin' shit back or I'll put my foot in your skinny ass!" Her fists were clenched into beat-your-ass balls and her chest heaved with anger.

"You cussed me, Nita!" Scooter gasped in a high-pitched whine, his slender hand pressed to his chest. "Yes, you did! You cussed me! What I do to you? Huh? What I do? If'n anybody's ass needs kicking, it's Sheila's! She the one who started all this mess! Alls I did was try to grease your bald spots after she jerked a knot up in you and pulled out all your hair! Why ain't you cuss her? Huh? Why you cussin' me?"

Juanita sighed and unclenched her fists. She righted the small stool and sat down heavily, the thickness of her thighs causing the shellacked surface to all but disappear. Scooter was right. She knew better than to cuss at a friend. Especially when he was the only friend she had.

"Sorry." Resignation clouded her eyes. She glanced meekly at a still-pouting Scooter. "You were right about them. I shoulda beat Queenie with Kendra and choked Sheila with her own damn rope." She tried to smile. "You still my friend?"

Cutting his large eyes at her, Scooter placed his hands on his narrow hips. "Yeah, I'm your friend. And I'll keep right on greasing your bald spots, too, but next time," Scooter warned, stooped over like an old man swinging an imaginary cane, clearly imitating Uncle Herbie, "next time, you call me out like that, I gots ta cut ya!" He stood in the mirror and performed a perfect imitation of Juanita's uncle, whirling and posing as if he were a master swordsman fencing against an enemy army.

Chimes of laughter filled Juanita's bedroom as the friends collapsed in a joyous heap, all traces of their unhappiness evaporating in an instant. Scooter was something else. He was a regular actor. He could play anyone from Mike Tyson to Richard Pryor. He could even imitate Bill Cosby. But these days his favorite pastime, his all-time favorite, was imitating Juanita's sixty-three-year-old Uncle Herbie.

////////////////////////////////

CHAPTER 3

Later that evening just as the sun took its leave and the moon prepared to do its thing, Scooter quietly entered the fifth-floor stairwell and jogged up several flights. Tucked away was the money his grandmother had given him for shopping, while her detailed instructions were seared in his memory.

"Now, don't forget," Dot had said to him, "Brother Foster needs a quart of milk and be sure you get two percent 'cause that whole milk gives him gas, and Sister Louise wants a loaf of light bread and a pack of sweet cornmeal. Try to keep everybody's change separate and be sure t'make your rounds starting from the eighth floor and work your way back down." She shook her finger for emphasis. "And don't you tarry. Get yourself in and out with those lists and to the store and back. Did you ask Nita to walk with you?"

"Yes'm, but she's eating dinner and said she couldn't go."

"Well, gone by yourself then. It shouldn't take you more'n half an hour, so don't make me come up at the Big Sixx looking for you."

"Yes'm," Scooter replied. He'd been making the weekly store runs for the elders in the building for almost a month now, ever since his grandmother's diabetes had slowed her circulation and caused the soles of her feet to become painful and inflamed. He palmed the money and stuffed it into the small hidden pocket she'd sewn into each pair of his underwear.

After skipping up the stairs to the eighth floor, he waited patiently while Elder Pritchard found his grocery list, then gratefully moved on to Fat Lady Field's apartment. He was on his way downstairs, nearly halfway done making the rounds to the seven residents he shopped for, when he paused in the fourth-floor stairwell. "Now, what I'm doing on four?" he questioned himself with a sly grin, holding his breath against the odor of piss and fried chicken backs.

Miss Louise had already called his grandma on the telephone and put in her grocery order, and since she was the only saint on the floor he could have skipped the fourth floor altogether. But that new guy, Julian, had recently moved into 4-C, and if Scooter was lucky, Julian might just be taking his trash to the incinerator or perhaps running out to the store himself.

Scooter paused in the stairwell, just before the entrance to the hall. There weren't many boys like him in this neighborhood, boys who dreamed of becoming a Broadway dancer or maybe leaving New York City and becoming a Hollywood singer, maybe even a big-time movie star.

But Julian was similar to him. He could sense it. It wasn't anything the boy had said or done, rather some faraway look in his eyes. Julian had a certain surreal glow about him, and Scooter instinctively knew they were kindred souls.

He eased the heavy stairwell door open and listened for a moment before stepping into the hall. Heavy voices of older boys rushed at him from the direction of the hall window.

> *I'm a bad little nigger from a bad little town*
> *It takes forty-eight whiteys just to knock me down,*
> *I don't pick no apples from your apple tree*
> *I'm a full-blooded nigger—don't you mess wit' me!*

Scooter frowned as the acrid smell of marijuana stole into his nostrils and slid down the back of his throat. "Yeah, man," one teenager bragged in an excited semiwhisper. "I fucked that bitch so hard her pussy swelled up like a balloon!" Excited laughter bounced in hush tones as the boys smoked their weed and fabricated stories of violence and conquest, belittling nearly every girl in the building as they reached for a Mack Daddy reputation.

Scooter grimaced at the graphic descriptions detailing their every bump, thrust, and grind, reducing women to mere slabs of meat and portraying their own phalluses as debilitating weapons.

He knew he'd heard enough as soon as Juanita's name was mentioned.

"One day I'ma fuck that half-white ho till her eyes turn blue." One of the punks laughed.

"That's gonna be a whole lotta fucking!" declared another, " 'Cause them eyes is greener than grass!"

"You betnot mess wit' her," Scooter heard yet another voice warn. "She looks like a fat-assed Bigfoot! You'd have to wrestle that big ho down to get summa that stuff!"

That was it. Scooter turned away as hot bile rushed to his throat. Juanita had never hurt anybody! She was only nine and already they joked about doing it to her! He turned to scamper down the stairs and out of range of their terrible words, when a rough hand jerked him by the back of his shirt and flung him against the graffiti-splattered concrete wall.

"Where you goin', muthafucka?"

Scooter blinked and found himself face-to-face with Dante Coleman, a tall, muscular seventeen-year-old who lived with his mother and four younger brothers in apartment 4-F.

"I was . . . I was just going to see Miss Louise," Scooter stammered, cowering against the filthy wall.

"Nuh-uh, faggot! You wuz listenin' to our convo, wasn't you? Yeah you wuz!" Dante planted his large hand on Scooter's chest and pressed. "You wuz prob'ly tryin' to get off! I bet you got a little boner in them pants, don't you? Huh? Fuck that, lemme see for myself!"

He pushed one hand inside of Scooter's pants while using the other to hold him by the neck. Scooter twisted and flailed his arms at the older boy. Groping Scooter's testicles, Dante squeezed hard and Scooter saw black.

"You ain't even got enough to have a boner down here," he laughed, fondling Scooter's genitals. "But, wait! What's all a this?" Dante fumbled around in Scooter's underwear, then twisted his lips into a broad smile. He yanked out the crumpled wad of bills and gave a low whistle.

"Hey, yo!" Dante stepped away from Scooter and pushed the stairwell door open wide. "Hey, niggahs," he called out to his partners, who were still getting high and telling tall tales. "Yawl come see what the fuck I caught!"

He turned back to Scooter, whose eyes darted helter-skelter in search of escape.

"You ain't gone nowhere." Dante pocketed the ball of money with a sick grin. "So don't even think about it "

He unzipped his pants.

"I hear you like to sing, ain't that right?" His eyes clouded over as his boys burst through the exit door and crowded into the stairwell.

Dante exposed his semierect penis and gave it a few slow strokes.

"Well, come on over here," he said moving toward Scooter with a look of pure evil in his gaze, "and sing real pretty into this here microphone."

⸎ ⸎ ⸎

Juanita pushed the last fish stick into her mouth and chased it down with a gulp of red Kool-Aid. She wiped the crumbs from her hands and was immediately overcome by familiar twangs of guilt. She'd eaten far too many pieces of the breaded whitefish—nearly the entire box—but boredom and loneliness had a way of causing her stomach to feel bottomless.

She thought about Scooter, and additional waves of guilt washed over her. He'd sounded so pitiful when he'd called to ask her to walk with him to the store. For the last few Saturdays he'd been Miss Dot's substitute runner, and while the older residents praised him, the children in the building terrorized him unmercifully.

Suddenly she had an idea. It hadn't been very long since his call. If she hurried she could meet him at the Big Sixx and keep him company while he shopped. It would make up for the way she'd spoken to him after that fight with Sheila and her gang. Besides, she could use the exercise. Those fish were swimming laps in her stomach.

Juanita slipped into her red Pro-Keds and silently unlocked the front door. Uncle Herbie was in bed calling cows, hogs, and mules, but Aunt Hattie was in her bedroom reading the Bible.

They'd never miss her.

Juanita didn't have a key and worried about leaving the front door unlocked, but she wouldn't be gone long. She wouldn't even wait for the ancient elevator like she normally did. She'd get there a lot quicker if she simply held her breath and raced down the fetid stairs.

She eased the front door open and slipped outside. Pausing, she reached back in and grabbed Uncle Herbie's cast-iron walking stick from its brass holder near the door. Just in case she ran into that crazy-ass Sheila. She'd be ready this time. Uncle Herbie might be old and decrepit, but he'd taught her how to wield his walking cane like it was a samurai sword.

Juanita's cheeks grew red hot as she relived the shame and humiliation of her earlier beating. Just let Sheila, Kendra, or any of them try her this time, she thought angrily. This time, instead of cowering on the ground and praying to God, she'd slice off one of their stupid heads at the neck and send it soaring into kingdom come.

⁊ ⁊ ⁊

"Yeah," moaned Dante as he cupped his member in one large hand. "I got me a real live one, yawl. He's gonna like this shit damn near much as I do!"

"Yo, Dante," said Lindell, a stocky tenth grader whose mother had gone crazy the year before and could be seen up on the avenue collecting empty cans in her birthday suit, "that's some foul shit. I ain't down wit' no gay shit like that! Puttin' your jammy in a niggah's mouth!"

Lindell started down the stairs.

"Me neither," Calvin Douglas spoke up, following his friend's lead. Calvin did whatever Lindell said, and if Lindell wasn't down, then neither was he.

"And I gotta go eat," drawled Kelvin Bookman, dapping Jerald Drew and Reggie Moore a farewell. "We having pork chops tonight and you know a niggah gots ta get him one."

Reggie yelled, "Count me gone," and took the stairs two at a time. That left Dante, Jerald Drew, and a terrified Scooter.

"Fuck all a' yawl," Dante said in a thick voice as he continued to rub against the smaller boy. "Ere last one a yawl."

"Your nasty ass prob'ly would," Jerald snapped, as he galloped down the filthy stairs to catch up with his homies. "You sick, man," he called over his shoulder. "Just fuckin' sick!"

Dante ignored his friends, not the least bit disturbed by their departure or their disapproval. He pushed Scooter down on the stairs and rubbed his penis against the smaller boy's face.

Scooter fought back, twisting his head and clenching his teeth.

But Dante was stronger. And determined.

"Open up, muthafucka." He wrapped both hands around Scooter's neck and squeezed.

Pounding waves exploded in Scooter's brain. An icy band of pain encircled his throat and he was cut off from his next, most precious breath.

A kaleidoscope of multicolored spots swam before his eyes. He could not breathe. He clawed and heaved and bucked and lurched, but he was unable to treat his starving lungs to just one more gulp of urine-tinged air.

Flailing his fists through the fog, Scooter heard a familiar voice. Someone was calling his name. He opened his eyes and Dante's contorted face floated before him in a murderous purple haze. Over and over the voice called out to him until at last he recognized it.

I'm coming, Daddy, Scooter's four-year-old voice answered in his mind. His father reached out and took his hand.

Daddy's here, big boy. Your daddy's here.

The heat in J.J.'s hand seemed to warm Scooter's entire body. His muscles turned to liquid and he ceased his struggle. Surrendering to the haze, he discovered that letting go wasn't so bad at all. J.J. Morrison took a step, and his son followed him. He took two more, and Scooter hurried to keep up. J.J.'s stride became longer and faster, and just as Scooter raced to catch up, he was snatched back by an incredible force and his lungs were treated to heaving gasps of precious air.

"You dirty son of a bitch!" Scooter heard his father shout, but no, his befuddled brain reasoned, it couldn't be. There'd been a car accident and J.J. was gone. Long gone. Besides, this was the voice of a child.

A girl!

As if from a great distance, Scooter realized that Dante was no longer holding him. The big guy had let him go and was dancing with the person who'd called his mama out like a dog.

Swallowing what seemed like shards of glass splintered in his throat, Scooter willed himself to stand. He fought to focus his bloodshot eyes, and he nearly fell down again when he recognized his savior.

It was Juanita!

And she was doing Uncle Herbie proud!

Juanita brandished Uncle Herbie's cast-iron cane like a scalpel, slicing it through the air and cracking down on Dante's body from every possible angle. Again and again, she smashed him over the head, whacked him in the knees, jabbed him in the gut, until the battered teenager succumbed to her deadly blows and lay sprawled on the filthy concrete stairs.

Still her weapon found its mark.

Screaming obscenities and calling him Sheila, Kendra, Puddin, and everything except a child of God, she smashed him in the back of the head, thumped him solidly along his backbone, and whipped him mercilessly across his buttocks until bloody welts covered every exposed area of Dante's skin.

And still her weapon found its mark.

Scooter was amazed. Never had he seen her fury so raw and unleashed. It thrilled him.

"Go 'head, Nita!" he rasped. "Do that shit! You kick him, I'll scratch him!" Scooter leaped onto Dante's bloodied back and flailed his fists, punching with all his might.

In a bloodthirsty frenzy, the two friends gave Dante Coleman an ass-whipping he would never forget. They really put it on him, pounding him for old pains and new hurts and for sorrows yet to come in their torturous young lives.

Juanita and Scooter beat Dante into a stupor, and would have beaten him within an inch of his life if not for the voice of authority echoing from the top of the stairs.

"Who that down there makin' all that racket? I say, who that hoopin' and holl'ren on them stairs?"

The *scratch-slap* of house shoes dragging across concrete sent Juanita's wrath dissipating into the air.

"Is that you, Nita? Chile, did you run outta here and leave my door settin' wide open? Whatchoo doin' down there, I say? I say, whatchoo doin'?"

Juanita lowered her arms, spent. Uncle Herbie's cane slid from her damp fingers and struck the concrete with a deafening clang, claiming its rest in the shadows cast by Dante's unconscious body.

Wearily, Juanita lifted her arms and wrapped them around her one true friend. "Yes'm, Aunt Hattie," she called breathlessly up the flight of stairs. "Yes'm, it's me."

"Gal, what your fool tail doin' down there making all a' that noise and raising all a' that sand? Whatchoo doin' down there, I say?"

"I'm down here . . ." Juanita swallowed hard and glanced over her shoulder at the prone figure of Dante Coleman. She stared at him for a long moment before gathering her best friend in her arms and dragging him up the long flight of stairs. "I'm down here savin' Scooter."

PART II

CONQUERING
CONAN

////////////////////////////////

CHAPTER 4

TEN YEARS LATER

The early-morning sun filtered through the pink-laced curtains and danced along the perimeters of Juanita's world. The thundering roar of the iron horse galloping along the el track was but a faint echo in the backdrop of her consciousness. Like most residents of New York City's housing projects, she'd developed environmental deafness, and to her soul the clanking and clamor of the elevated train was as gentle and soothing as a lover's whisper.

Juanita swept her thick tresses away from her face and allowed her damp towel to slip to the floor. Naked, she caught a glimpse of her pear-shaped reflection illuminated in the chrome border of the shower door, and the wavy image startled her. Stealing a glance at herself was like eavesdropping on an utter stranger, and tiny shocks rippled through her as goose bumps rose on her flesh.

Ignoring her body's reaction, she padded across the worn linoleum, its sun-baked warmth heating the soles of her feet, and squinted into the slightly clouded mirror. She used the flat of her hand to wipe away at a thin patch of steam and stood back to examine the sight before her.

With an air of detachment, she bore into the emerald pools of her wide-set eyes and marveled at the stranger she found within. The smooth, wheat-field hue of her skin stretched across a face that she found too foreign and too fair. Her nose, small and upturned, seemed lost in the landscape created by her lips—kissing lips, she'd once been told—and the horizontal cleft in her chin was deep enough to snuggle the pit of a good-size cherry.

She leaned against the cool veneer of the sink. Small droplets of water leaked from the crumbling faucet and formed a steady stream along a rusted path of porcelain before disappearing into the dank darkness of the drain.

Juanita held her hair high above her head and studied her profile. The smooth line of her jawbone was cloaked in the shadow created by her curls, and from this angle her forehead appeared defiant, strong.

Most people had trouble determining her heritage. Sometimes she was mistaken for Hawaiian or Hispanic, and once, up in the Bronx, somebody had the nerve to call her a gypsy. She stared into her reflection and was saddened by the fire smoldering in her eyes. Eyes that held endless questions that had never been answered. Eyes so unlike her auntie's or her uncle's or any others she'd studied in the molding pages of her family album. Eyes so foreign she burned with a longing to discover their origin.

"Nita," a tired voice on the other side of the door rasped. "You best hurry, chile. Scooter is eatin' already and it won't be but a quick minute 'fore your breakfast gits cold."

"Yes'm." Juanita turned away and unscrewed the cap from a jar of Dixie Peach pomade. Beginning at the edge of her forest of curls, she smoothed small dabs around her hairline, then massaged them throughout the hair itself.

With a small frown, she brushed a young spider away from the toilet tank, opened an old Q-tip box, and extracted a circular nylon fastener. Her fingers were sure as she wrapped the black band around her ponytail and proceeded to twist the length of it into a twirl, and then wind it neatly around itself over and over until she was satisfied with the results.

Juanita squatted and searched the low cabinet beneath the sink until she found what she was looking for. Then she stood and turned her back to the sink, holding a cracked makeup mirror high above her head, allowing the larger mirror to reflect the back of her hair in the face of the smaller one. Instead of the flat, dry look that was common to those with her grade of hair, Juanita's tresses gleamed radiantly.

Damn, she was good. Not a single curl hung loose. She could have twisted the tight knot at the base of her neck in the dark with one hand tied behind her back. Averting her eyes from her nakedness, Juanita stared at the ceiling as she nestled her small breasts, with their tiny rose-colored nipples, into a strapless white bra. She slid her generous thighs into a pair of Hanes high-cut briefs and lifted a multicolored sundress from a hanger on a hook behind the door. She stepped into the thin dress and pulled it up, pausing to tie the yellow and orange straps behind her still-damp neck.

Shoeless, she padded across the chocolate-colored tiles and into the sparse but immaculate kitchen, where Scooter was already halfway finished his breakfast.

"Look what the roaches dragged in!" he joked, looking up from a huge plate of buttered grits, scrambled eggs, and deep-fried country ham. Like the ninety-pound weakling who suffered sand kicks at the beach, Scooter had barely filled out at all. At twenty, he was a tall drink of water, and except for the elegant mustache that clung to his upper lip and the two feet he'd grown in the last ten years, his well-groomed physique, youthful features, and high-pitched voice had remained unchanged.

Thankfully, his job paid decent money, and Scooter spent almost all of it on his wardrobe. Whereas Juanita's style was plain and over-simplified, Scooter stepped out clean, sharper than a tack. He worked part-time at Chase Manhattan Bank, and true to his dramatic form, Scooter had parlayed their strict dress code into a daily excuse to suit up like he was going to a photo shoot at *GQ* magazine.

Today he wore a short-sleeved light-gray silk shirt with wine-colored pinstripes and a pair of hand-tailored light-gray slacks. Burgundy wing-tip shoes complemented the total package, and his precision-cut hair hugged his scalp closer than the skin on a snake.

"Mornin'," Juanita grunted, ignoring Scooter and turning her nose up at the sight of the breakfast food. It was far too early for her to eat, and for the last two months she'd been starving herself throughout the day. Around evening she'd be ravenous, and by midnight she'd be crazed with hunger. Twinkies, pound cakes, Devil Dogs, and potato chips would disappear into her mouth as she tried to fill the hole in her pinching stomach. Engorged, she'd sit in her room surrounded by empty bags and wrinkled cellophane . . . and then she'd force herself to do it.

Juanita snapped her eyes shut, and when she reopened them her mind was clearer. The kitchen seemed brighter.

Uncle Herbie, who had just celebrated his seventy-third birthday, sat on a low stool by the kitchen window reading a copy of the *New York Post*. He placed a gnarled finger over the small opening in his neck.

" 'Mornin', Neet," he growled in his cigar-scarred voice.

Juanita embraced him, enjoying the comforting and familiar old-man smell of his wrinkled skin and carefully pressed work clothes. The tracheotomy had slowed his activities considerably, but each morning Herbie still rose with the sun and, before dressing in the clothes Hattie had ironed and set out for him the night before, did several minutes of light stretching and calisthenics before performing an hour's worth of fencing maneuvers with his forged metal walking stick. By the time Juanita awakened, he'd already showered, dressed, and walked to the corner bodega to purchase a copy of the local rag.

As she held him in her embrace, her uncle's walking stick caught her eye. There was a time when she and Scooter would practice fencing moves with Uncle Herbie each day, but now, tarnished and bowed, the cane leaned forlornly against the side of his chair and gave no hint to either its lethal power or its menacing past.

Ten years had passed since Juanita had nearly lammed Dante Coleman into a coma. Ten years since she'd saved Scooter for the second time. Juanita blushed at the memory. Hard to believe she'd resorted to such physical violence. These days, the only action the lackluster slice of metal saw was Uncle Herbie's morning routine. Even Scooter refused to touch it. His Uncle Herbie imitation act had ended the night he was attacked by Dante.

Juanita took a large coffee cup from a cabinet above the sink, filled it with cold tap water, and proceeded to swallow it in long, fast gulps.

"Nita!" Hattie wailed as she ladled spoonfuls of grits onto a large plate. "Gal, don't guzzle that water like that! When it goes down the wrong pipe and kills you, don't come runnin' telling me about it!"

"Yes'm," Juanita answered mechanically, and plopped down in one of the four warp-legged chairs framing the small dinette table.

"Here," Hattie said, "these hominies been on for over an hour. They should be perfect right about now."

Juanita sighed. Tired lines furrowed Hattie's brow, and she favored her right leg as she crossed the kitchen. She'd gone back to doing domestic work to help pay Juanita's college tuition, and twice a week she scrubbed floors, darned socks, and cooked meals for several white families on the far edges of Queens. Juanita knew it was the same type of work her aunt had done before she was born, but at Hattie's age, working, taking care of Uncle Herbie, and mothering Juanita were beginning to take their toll.

Yet Hattie seemed invincible. Two years earlier, Dot Morrison had died, leaving Scooter and Jeo to fend for themselves, and in addition to her volunteer work at the community center and her self-imposed responsibilities to the church, Aunt Hattie had also become a surrogate mother to Scooter. She cooked for the bedridden Jeo, made sure the bills were paid, and stuffed Scooter with food whenever he came within two feet of her kitchen table.

"Thank you, Auntie." Juanita accepted the outstretched plate and sighed. The grits on her plate teemed with melted butter, and the thick slabs of streak-o-lean were fried to perfection and begging to be bitten. Ordinarily, she would have inhaled the plateful of comfort, but years of Hattie's down-home love sopped up with buttered biscuits and smothered in grits and gravy had done a job on Juanita's figure. She wore steak and eggs around her hips, and slab bacon and pancakes were permanently plastered onto her thighs, and although she'd recently began experimenting with "getting rid of her food," so far she hadn't lost a single pound. Juanita pushed the congealing food from one side of the plate to the other, pretending to eat for her aunt's sake.

"Auntie," she sang out a few minutes later in her best little-girl voice, "can I borrow four dollars for lunch and bus fare? I'll pay you back on Wednesday, as soon as I cash my check."

"Chile," Hattie fussed mildly, "I know you don't make a whole lot workin' in that school lie-berry, but what you do with the little bit you do make I can't see neither!" Hattie shuffled into her bedroom to get her purse, her eyes sparkling despite her protests.

Juanita moved quickly, and with a practiced flick of her wrist the food on her plate went sailing into the large green trash can. Uncle Herbie looked up with questioning eyes, but Juanita pretended not to notice; she busied herself by gulping down yet another mug of cold water.

Wiping her mouth with the back of her hand, she turned to Scooter and commanded, "Let's go!" Purposely avoiding Uncle Herbie's stare, she stepped into her sandals and slipped her arms through the straps of her backpack. "Hurry up, Scooter, before she comes back and makes me swallow a whole platter of grits!"

Scooter laughed. "She makes me eat off two platters!"

Juanita rushed to meet Hattie at the doorway and accepted four crumpled one-dollar bills, pushing them into her wallet before kissing her auntie good-bye.

"Race ya?" she challenged Scooter, and took off running. Scooter bolted and they ran screaming down the narrow hallway, their laughter ringing much as it had when they were children.

"Y'all take care, ya hear?" Hattie yelled from the doorway, but there was no response. As usual, Juanita and Scooter were focused entirely on each other, barring everyone else from the sacred boundaries of their private world.

CHAPTER 5

"**P**ump-pump-pump, *pump it up!!*" Jorge Corona's hands were a staccato blur atop the overturned plastic trash can as he kept time to both the Latin beat blaring from the king-size stereo and the rhythmic swinging of Conan's muscular arms as his friend alternately lifted and lowered more than two hundred pounds of heavy metal.

"*Hombre!*" Jorge called, his Hispanic accent lilting, his handsome smile revealing impish dimples. He wore his sandy blond curls cut close to his scalp, and a large gold crucifix was suspended from his corded neck by one of several gold herringbone chains.

Jorge sauntered toward the boom box and flicked the power switch to Off. His Hugo Boss jeans fit nicely on his well-defined rear, and his Cinco de Mayo T-shirt failed to conceal the powerful muscles that rippled along his chest. "How long you gonna work out, my friend? The fuckin' bus gets here in fifteen minutes and if we're late today, man, both our asses are *fried*."

Perspiration hung from Conan's skin as he completed his final, most punishing set of arm curls. Mountainous stacks of Weider steel weights were clamped to the ends of the long cylinder bar, and his palms were marred with thick calluses sculpted by the bar's rough, irregular grooves.

"I'm ready, man." Conan panted and strained to carry the barbell over to a corner of the small bedroom. Thick veins on his forearms, shoulders, and biceps bulged, and his overworked muscles felt torn-down and depleted, near the point of total failure.

Conan was just past his twentieth birthday, and his dark good looks and easy charm were apparent to everyone except him. Bright flecks of Irish gray were prominent in his light-blue eyes. His wavy hair glistened coal black and lush, and his small mustache and neatly trimmed goatee highlighted the olive tan of his smooth skin. A long, jagged scar ran above his eye and along his right jaw, but instead of detracting from his rugged good looks it amplified the strength of his features.

Unlike the naturally brawny Jorge, Conan was muscular and solid, but he worked hard to maintain his sculpted physique. Ever since the accident he'd trained faithfully under the Weider system. Rising before dawn six days a week, he was almost brutal in his workouts, subjecting his body to harsher and more frequent punishment than many professional bodybuilders.

"*Tu sabes que tu te ves bien 'mano*—you lookin' good, my man," Jorge drawled, and stuffed his mouth with the remnants of a Twinkie.

"One day"—Conan dried himself off with a thick towel, then bent down and cuffed the bottoms of his FUBU jeans—"all that shit you eat is gonna turn into fat." He looked up and grinned. "And then how you gonna get the honeys?"

Jorge laughed and dodged the wet towel sailing toward him. "With this," he said, grabbing his crotch and pumping his privates. "With this!"

, , ,

Frederico Gomez backed down the hallway toward the top of the stairs, swirling his janitorial mop across the black-and-white tiled floors and singing pleasantly in a low baritone. At forty-two, he was graying at the temples and putting on weight, but quite content with his lot in life. He had a wonderful wife, a fulfilling job, and, as the founder of the Community of Colors Cultural Center, a deep sense of personal fulfillment and gratification.

There were four apartments on each floor of the three-story tenement where he worked and lived, and in exchange for rent and utilities, he and his wife shared a modest first-floor apartment and took care of the building's routine maintenance: mopping floors, shining windows, and polishing brass five mornings a week.

Behind him, Conan and Jorge bounced out of the Lopez apartment, the curls atop their contrasting heads still damp from their morning workout.

"What's the word, Rico?" Conan locked his door and pocketed the small key.

Splashing a pool of sudsy water from a wheeled metal bucket, Rico stopped whistling and looked up from his work. Leaning the mop against the wall, he ran his hand through his dark hair, then shook Conan's outstretched hand.

"One nation, Top Cat! How's it looking this morning?"

Conan enjoyed the feel of the rough palm grasping his. Rico was a man to be respected and emulated, the head honcho at CCCC and a major role model for the youths in their neighborhood. Every male child walking their streets was Rico's self-proclaimed son.

Conan frowned as Jorge pushed past, jostling the older man on his way toward the stairs. With a defiant backward glance, Jorge traveled like a slow-moving storm, deliberately tromping through the freshly mopped area, dragging his feet along the tiles, and smearing dirty brown streaks along the partially dried surfaces. He picked up the tune Rico had been singing and mimicked him in falsetto. *"My baby loves me, oh yes she doooo. I know she loves me, 'cause I love her toooo."*

Jorge's laughter came out bitter. "What kinda shit is that, Top Cat?" He stomped down the stairs, planting his feet loudly on each step. "The fuckin' building super is a wanna-be singer!"

Rico narrowed his eyes, staring at Jorge's retreating back with something close to pity. He nodded at Conan. "Hey, man. You need to bring your homey down to the center. Get him involved in the neighborhood. Help keep his mind focused on something besides himself."

Then his eyes softened. If the system had ever failed someone, if a child had ever been allowed to slip through the cracks, it was Jorge. Rico lived directly below Jorge's old second-floor apartment and knew exactly what the boy had suffered. On countless nights, unable to bear the boy's torturous screams, he would barge upstairs and bang on the door until the half-dressed, owl-eyed Bobby answered the door, his wild afro sticking out in all directions, high on lunacy and reeking of perverted sex and cheap wine. Rico had called the police on Jorge's stepfather more times than he could count, and each time they'd taken Bonita, Jorge's mother, into custody instead. She was the parent. She was the addict and the streetwalker. She was negligent. Leaving Jorge home alone with a known pedophile, subjecting the boy to his sick torture for days on end. And instead of Jorge appreciating Rico's concern, he'd blamed him. He was embarrassed, and he blamed Rico for having his mother locked up on Riker's Island, where she called home begging her son to panhandle the neighborhood for her bail money.

Rico shook his head and marveled at how much the boy had grown over the years. Physically, that was. But there was something very stunted about Jorge's mentality, and no matter how often Rico reached out, how much he invited him to get involved in programs at the neighborhood cultural center, Jorge shunned him, was often hostile toward him; and since the night of that horrible accident, he'd been outright disrespectful.

Conan nodded toward Jorge and grinned. "Don't pay him no mind, man. You know how he can be."

"Yeah, I know." Rico retrieved the mop and dipped it into the soapy water, swirling it around and dunking it beneath the white foam, propelling the scent of disinfectant and ammonia into the air. Easy silence stood between them as Rico completed his task, then lifted his bucket by the handles and followed Conan down the flight of stairs. On the second floor, he dipped the mop into the water again, and began his side-to-side soapy ministering outside of apartment 2-B.

"Have you seen them lately?" he asked Conan, angling his head to indicate the elderly mixed-raced couple who lived inside the apartment. "I wonder if that toilet is still giving them hell. I changed the ring washer and replaced a seal, but the fix is only temporary. They may need a whole new fixture."

Conan nodded. "They're okay. Just last night I helped Mrs. Andrews give Pushie a bath. Her eyes are really getting bad. She could hardly see well enough to get around inside the apartment. Neither one of them said anything about the toilet, but I'll ask about it when I get home from work. Pushie was too weak to sit up for long, so I promised I'd come back and cut his hair and give him a shave tonight."

Rico nodded and touched Conan on the shoulder. "Top Cat, it's a wonderful thing what you're doing for Pushie and Angelique. With no children and no family, and only a few sickly friends, thank God for people like you who don't mind giving back to the folks of this community."

"Nah." Conan blushed and backed away. "It was your idea to start the elderly shut-in program. Without you, none of us would even think about the old people who get stuck up in these hot apartments with no one to shop for them or even stop by to make sure they're alive."

"Maybe. But you've been taking care of Pushie for a long time, even before we began the program, so I'm doubly grateful to you for helping out in other areas. You coming to the center this afternoon?" Rico asked. He rested his hand atop the wooden mop handle and tried not to look too hopeful. "The early-childhood literacy program has really taken off, and the kids are looking forward to it. Four o'clock sharp. They know when it's time for the Top Cat to show up."

Conan nodded. "I'll be there, man. You know I will." He enjoyed the look of wonder and awe in the eyes of the preschoolers when he read them tales of adventure and exploration. He'd tried to get Jorge to come out and participate, but it was useless.

"Nobody ever gave a shit about me when I was a little kid," Jorge always complained, and reluctantly Conan had to agree. Until Jorge came to live in their building, Conan could only imagine what horrors his friend had experienced; but between him and Rico, they would never give up on Jorge. They'd never stop encouraging him to make the most of his life and get involved with others who had even less than he did.

"One nation, man!" Rico called as Conan sped down the last flight of stairs. "Try to get your homey to come out with you, no? It'll do him good to think about something besides himself!"

"One nation," Conan answered, and lifted his chin as he trotted out the building and headed toward the bus stop. Up ahead he could see Jorge standing at the corner of Dumont Avenue, pacing in the street, shielding his eyes and looking down the hill for an approaching bus. Even from this distance he saw the way Jorge stomped around, swinging his massive arms and glaring at passersby like he was an underfed beast. His whole presence personified rage and intimidation, and secretly Conan was glad his friend refused to participate when it came to old people and little kids.

He had a feeling neither group was safe from Jorge Corona.

⁄ ⁄ ⁄

"Is not!"

"Is too!"

"Man, look at her! What Latina you know got eyes like that? I'm telling you she's a fuckin' wop!"

"Bullshit!" Conan protested. "She's Rican."

Conan scanned the crowded bus. The majority of the morning riders on the B60 bus line were regulars, and he found many of the faces familiar. He'd been riding the 7:12 bus for almost a year, ever since he was hired as an entry-level machinist at Grayson Fields Plumbing.

Most mornings, instead of bickering with Jorge, Conan studied the commuters who seemed to gravitate toward the back of the bus. Playing a mental game, he fabricated personality traits and life situations he thought suited their appearances.

He checked out the young black guy who was dressed to the nines but wore mismatched socks each day. He carried a leather briefcase and kept his head buried in the morning paper during his entire trip, never looking up until he reached his stop at Eastern Parkway. Conan figured he was some big-time insurance salesman, or maybe he had gone to college and had a job in electronics.

And the candy-eating pregnant teenager with her two giggling friends. Chick-O-Sticks, Twizzlers, Jordan Almonds . . . Conan figured the young girl had gotten pregnant by some knucklehead and dropped out of regular school. She probably took the bus to some sort of alternative school for unwed mothers.

There was also the elderly Hispanic woman who muttered softly in Spanish, her tattered stockings secured tightly around her ankles with thick red rubberbands she'd probably taken off a bunch of collard greens. She sat clutching several empty plastic trash bags, and Conan figured she worked in the kitchen of some local restaurant and filled the bags with leftovers each evening to take home to her grandchildren. The possibilities were endless, Conan knew. Behind the masks of anonymity the strangers wore, their lives were surely colorful and diverse.

Today, the only unfamiliar face was that of a strange-looking white boy. Conan sized him up. Early twenties, five-ten, pasty skin, stringy, flaxen hair, and the filthiest Converses Conan had ever seen. The young man stood out like a hooker at a bachelor party, because for one, he was wearing a long black trench coat on a day hot enough to pop open the johnny pumps, and two, he had taken Conan's favorite spot; directly across from the rear exit doors.

Conan led a protesting Jorge (who thought they should just tell the *gringo* motherfucker to *move*) to an empty grip pole that was two seat-lengths to the rear of the back door. This spot was cool, he thought, soothing Jorge. He could still see her clearly, and for that he was grateful.

For the past few weeks Conan had studied the beautiful creature in the flowered dress. She looked about eighteen, had skin the color of a Hawaiian sunrise, charitable hips, humble breasts, and a breathtaking smile.

Classic Puerto Rican *mamacita*!

He couldn't quite put his finger on it, but there was something about the tilt of her chin and the set of her sensual lips that distracted him to no end. A dazed air of detachment. A total ignorance of her own beauty. Who was she? And why was she always jabbering with that skinny black kid who dressed up like the old dude on *Soul Train*? Conan was drawn to her. He studied her, his creativity no match for her mystique. The intensity of his gaze should have burned holes in her flesh, but she never even looked at him. Had never even blessed him with a hint of a smile. She was too busy catching every word that fell out of that black guy's mouth. Conan wondered briefly if the kid was boning her. Nah. From the way he swung his hand and chattered away like a little *chica,* he didn't seem to have the heart for it.

The way Conan figured, the two of them must board the B60 a few stops ahead of him, because by the time he and Jorge climbed on, the city bus was nearly full. Somehow the chattering pair always managed to have a seat, she on the left side of the bus next to the rear exit, and her skinny friend right beside her. And on the inside! Conan groaned. Didn't dude know a man should always let a female sit on the inside, walk on the inside, do *whatever* on the inside, just in case some crazy shit went down in a hurry?

Although Jorge was right—her wide eyes *were* unusually green—there was no doubt in Conan's mind that with her passionate strut and those rosy lips that begged to be kissed, this *cosita linda* was a steaming hot Latina!

"She's Rican, man," he repeated with finality, issuing a rare challenge to his old friend. "I can tell. Look at her lips. Those hips. *Arroz con pollo y habichuelas,* man. I just know it."

"Bullshit!" Jorge exploded. "*Amigo,* just look at her hair! She's a fuckin' greaseball! There's enough oil in her hair to fry a bucket of chicken wings! Damn! Not one of you Lopezes can see straight." He counted off on his fingers and spittle flew from his mouth. "Not you, not your mother, and not your raggedy-ass old man!" He shook his head. "Trust me, man. That chick ain't no Puerto Rican. Shit," he added, "how the hell would you know anyway? You're only half a Rican yourself!"

Conan stared. Other than Thor, there was no one he loved more, but Jorge's half-breed cracks were getting pretty old. Besides, what did it matter anyway? He knew who he was and was damned proud of it. He loved his mother, and the fact that she was Irish didn't detract from her beauty, character, or importance.

"Yo, I might only be half Puerto Rican," Conan finally answered. He thumped his chest with his fist. "But you better believe I'm one hundred percent *hombre!*"

"Lighten up," Jorge snapped. He jerked his head from side to side, popping his bronzed neck like Mike Tyson. "Get that fuckin' chick off your mind." The muscles in his neck coiled and roped like hot steel.

"She's a *gringa,* and that's all there is to it. Besides, what's so special about this greaseball? You been staring at her like she's the fuckin' Virgin Mary or something!" Suddenly he laughed and blew tiny kisses in Conan's direction. "You know the only girl you really need is me!"

Conan shoved his hands into his pockets. He stood with his legs apart and balanced himself in time to the swaying bus. He concentrated on maintaining his balance as Jorge's half-breed wisecrack aroused him to a slow burn. He was getting tired of making excuses for Jorge's shit-talking. Tired of taking his low blows with a good-natured grin. Lately, his friend came too close to crossing that line. Far too often.

The pair had been best friends since the second grade at P.S. 81, even though they were exact opposites. Whereas Jorge was impulsive and brash, Conan tended to be reflective, more sensitive, slower to react to new situations. They'd grown up in Brownsville, not far from the East New York border, in a lower-class neighborhood that still held traces of its original ethnical diversity but had spiraled in an economic decline.

Twelve years earlier, eight-year-old Jorge, his free-spirited mother, and her transient boyfriend had rented the apartment beneath the one occupied by Victor Lopez, his wife, Grace, and their seven-year-old twins, Conan and Thor. By the end of his first week, the hot-tempered Jorge—who had always been large for his age—had picked on and beaten up nearly every kid on the block. Except Conan. Instead of picking a fight with the amiable Conan, the wild, towheaded boy with a thousand curls seemed drawn to him.

Although they were in different classes in school—Jorge had been held back in the first grade and rode one of those short little school buses—they spent every spare moment together; spinning tops, shooting dice, rolling marbles, and even building model airplanes, which Conan enjoyed and Jorge was surprisingly good at. Jorge began spending so much time with Conan and Thor that quite naturally he began to take his meals with their family. There was never anything to eat at his house anyway, unless you counted the molding bread and the half-empty cases of malt liquor.

On the last day of fall in the third grade, Jorge arrived home from school and found his mother sprawled on the bathroom floor, her black boyfriend nowhere in sight and a hypodermic needle stuck in her arm. Jorge had been suspended for punching out a waif of a girl, and had been waiting for hours for his mother to pick him up from school. By the end of the day he'd placed twenty-seven calls from the principal's office, but with each call the phone just rang and rang. Jorge turned ten that year, and never once did he grieve. Never shed a single tear. He simply packed up his winter coat and old rubber boots, grabbed two grainy black-and-white photos of his grandmother holding his infant mother on her lap, and clutched the only thing he had from his biological father: a miniature flag of Puerto Rico taped in a clear plastic case. Everything else he owned had already found a niche upstairs in the small bedroom shared by Conan and Thor, and now their permanent new brother, Jorge.

After Jorge moved in, their days passed much the same as before, but whereas Conan and Thor had inherited their mother's dark hair, blue eyes, and even disposition, Jorge's blond curls raged and his temper ran high. He fought constantly, repeatedly angering Conan's father until, in a fit of rage, the man of the house ordered his wife to toss the young ruffian back out on the streets.

Grace refused. She saw past Jorge's tough exterior and into the bleeding walls of his broken heart. She understood his fear of abandonment and his reluctance to bond or conform. She nurtured him like he was a precious bird with a faulty wing, hoping and praying the day would come when love would heal his wounds and he'd be fit and whole and able to soar to great heights. Unfortunately, Jorge's wings failed to mend. Even Grace was not enough to fix what ailed him.

He became egotistical and arrogant, and clung to every shred of Hispanic culture and Puerto Rican nationalism he'd ever learned. It had only been twenty years since the Hispanic population boom in Brownsville and East New York, and while Conan's decidedly Brooklynese diction and dialect was shaped by his parents and their black, Jewish, and Italian neighbors, Jorge spoke with a practiced Hispanic inflection and was fiercely proud of his Latino heritage.

His favorite motto was "Life's too short not to be a Rican," and he even went as far as having a massive colorful slogan that read LOCO LATINO tattooed prominently on his right arm. And why not? He had the temperament of a bobcat with a toothache, and fed right into the media's stereotypical archetype of a hotheaded, quick-fisted Latino.

Twice already he'd been arrested; once for breaking the jaw of an old wino who called Conan's mother a *puta* after she refused to give him her spare change, and again six months later for flying into a mescaline-induced rage and breaking the plate-glass window of a local bodega when the black clerk refused to sell him a quart of beer for thirty-five cents.

"C'mon, *amigo*." Jorge was now bumping his hip against Conan as the bus swayed. "I'm your girl. Toot up!" He smacked his lips and batted his eyes, pushing against his friend for a mock kiss.

Conan's anger subsided. It was hard to stay mad at Jorge when he turned into a clown. Sometimes he was just too stupid to realize the impact of his words. Besides, years of experience taught him that when dealing with his peppery friend, sometimes it was best to let shit ride. But still, Conan hated losing face with him, hated to let Jorge think he was punking him.

And he hated the way Jorge treated girls. Didn't like the way he referred to them as chicks and bitches and ho's.

Especially this girl.

"Man, fuck you." Conan yanked his hands from his pockets and grabbed at a silver pole as the bus swerved to a sudden stop. He watched as the double doors opened to admit a mass of fresh commuters. The weird-looking white boy in the trench coat remained rooted to his spot, forcing the incoming passengers to stream around him. Sweat rolled down his face and dripped from his chin.

What a fuckin' weirdo.

Conan turned back to his friend and mock-punched Jorge's iron shoulder. "Just fuck you."

"No thanks, my man." Jorge gave a short laugh and elbowed his brother-friend playfully. "Sorry, *amigo*. You ain't got the right equipment."

CHAPTER 6

The B60 rolled down Rockaway Avenue, weaving with the erratic flow of traffic. Nearly every window had been pushed opened and the passengers were grateful for the small breeze, even if it was tinged with traces of exhaust fumes and rotting garbage.

Juanita sat in the end seat near the rear door, picking at her cuticles. It seemed as if every two blocks the bus pulled over to pick up another group of life-weary commuters. She glanced at her watch and frowned. She and Scooter were both completing their second year at Huntington Junior College, where Scooter, much to his grandfather's dismay, had opted to study theater arts with an emphasis in drama. Juanita had chosen elementary education because she loved children; she planned to eventually open her own child care center and surround herself with the wondrous creatures on a full-time basis.

Although Huntington hadn't been her first choice of schools, and her Aunt Hattie had made it clear that she was willing to scrape toast and scrub floors to send her niece to a prestigious university, it was really all that she, and even more so Scooter, could safely afford. Unlike her, Scooter was basically on his own. He took his meals with the Lucas family, but he paid his tuition, fees, and living expenses out of a modest insurance policy left to him from his grandmother's estate.

Juanita shifted the position of the bulky red knapsack leaning against her right foot. On a normal day she carried fewer books and couldn't care less about the flow of traffic, but this morning she had a tough test in her first class, Literary Masterpieces, and she planned to use the full two-hour period to formulate her answers and write up a tight, succinct essay. She felt confident and prepared; instead of staying up late to haunt the house gorging on cakes and chips, she'd spent most of the night studying, scrawling pertinent notes in the margin of the text in preparation for the open-book exam.

In addition to her part-time job in the school library, Juanita carried eighteen semester credits, including calculus and biology. There were so many facts and figures floating around in her head that she was anxious to complete her exams and then quickly purge her brain of all the extra information. *Purge.* The mere word made her uncomfortable. Her life was so emotional and frenzied she was constantly attempting to purge herself of one thing or another.

Her stomach growled and pinched, reminding her of the breakfast she'd thrown into the trash. She ignored the familiar pangs and tried instead to concentrate on what Scooter was saying.

"I said," he repeated, "do you see those two bow-wow-wows over there? Scooby-Doo and Scrappy-Doo? The fine-ass blond one wearing the dingy wife-beater and his buff sidekick standing there in those wrinkled-ass chinos?"

Juanita had seen the pair. Had been seeing them for weeks, although she'd never let on to Scooter. From the corner of her eye she'd caught several glimpses of the handsome duo; their tanned olive skin, rippling muscles, neatly trimmed goatees . . . The guy in the blue chinos was cute, but the one in the wife-beater! Was all of that damned gold necessary? Gold cross, gold medallion, gold earring, gold rings. Hell, she giggled inside. He probably shit gold-filled nuggets!

She turned to Scooter. "Nah," she lied. "I hadn't really noticed them."

It wasn't a total lie. Other than noticing the fact that one had overdosed on gold, she hadn't allowed herself to acknowledge them. Especially the dark-haired guy.

Today, the handsome pair were talking alternately in Spanish and English, but Juanita paid them no attention. Her mind was focused on

The Epic of Gilgamesh and *The Iliad*. She didn't have time to dip on their idle chatter. Couldn't understand most of it if she tried.

The bus was nearing Sutter Avenue, a congested area with heavy traffic. It was this portion of the trip Juanita hated most. Frenzied Brooklynites swarmed everywhere, darting out from between parked cars, jaywalking, and crossing against the traffic light. The traffic was so dense the bus was sometimes forced to inch along a few feet at a time.

Scooter spoke. "Pin your eyeballs on the Lone Ranger and Tonto. You might not have noticed them, but their shady-looking asses are sho nuff noticing you!"

Juanita sucked her teeth. "How do you know they're noticing me? All of these people on the bus? Why do they have to be noticing me?"

"Girl"—Scooter's eyelashes fluttered—" 'cause I heard them arguing about yo' azz, that's why! One saying you fine and the other saying you ain't! You know how them Porta Reekins are! They play that Poppy shit. Plus they like to do the nasty all the time—they probably over there talking about doin' it to you!"

"Shut up, Scooter!" Juanita smacked his arm. "The only thing you understand in Spanish is 'meeta bentay'!"

Scooter laughed. "And don't forget, 'sucka me beecho'! Hell, what else I need to understand? All the rest of that crap they talk just means, 'Yo, homey, get your knife.' " Scooter turned serious. "All jokes aside, Nita, I smell a rat. You better watch those two. A spic'll cut ya up in a New York minute."

"Scooter, please—"

A howling siren cut through the air as all hell broke loose. The forward momentum of the bus was jarringly redirected. Horns blared. Brakes squealed. Hydraulics hissed. Passengers lurched violently, scrambling to grab hold of straps, poles, and each other. Personal belongings tumbled to the ground and slid across the floor like honey on beeswax.

"Eeep!" Scooter screeched. Arms and legs akimbo, he went sailing across Juanita's lap, causing her to slam backward in her seat. She winced and clapped her hands over her ears.

"Who the fuck pulled the emergency brake?" the driver roared, as he fought to maintain control of the bus. His mammoth arms strained.

Angry veins bulged on his forehead and ballooned down his neck. Battling the bus with a maximum payload, he fought to cut a hard right, and fortunately for all, the bus rolled to a squealing stop.

There was a long moment of stillness. Several riders had toppled to the floor and lay sprawled atop newspapers and purses, intimately entangled with perfect strangers. The absence of clamor was deafening, painful even, as the acrid odor of burned rubber filled the air. With a tired hiss, the emergency system belatedly kicked in and both the front and rear doors popped open.

Scooter's falsetto was first to break the silence. "I'm suing the goddamn city!" he cried. "I got whiplash and I can't move my back!" A cacophony of similar complaints filled the air.

Dazed, Juanita lowered her hands from her ears and silenced him. "Shut up, Scoot." She rolled her eyes and bent down to find her bag. Her eye caught a snatch of red canvas a short distance away. Just as she reached to retrieve it, a white guy draped in a shabby black coat brushed past her. Beating her to the punch, he snatched the knapsack and sailed down the three short stairs, hurling himself off the stalled bus.

Juanita watched mutely as he hit the ground and took off sprinting, knocking startled pedestrians to the ground and ducking and dodging through the swarming mass of bodies.

"My bag!" she managed to yell as she jumped to her feet.

Scooter grabbed a handful of her yellow sundress and held her fast. The Hispanic guy in the wrinkled chinos plucked himself off the ground where he'd landed during the melee, and with a quick backward glance, pushed past his blond-haired friend and bolted down the steps and through the rear doors.

With her mouth a big wide O and her eyes the shape of Spanish olives, Juanita watched helplessly from the window as he made a mad dash behind the thief and quickly disappeared into the crowd of pedestrians.

"W-w-wait!" she tried to yell, but suddenly the doors closed and the bus was moving, continuing its journey down the avenue, the angry driver spewing curses, oblivious to the thievery that had just taken place on his watch.

Most of the passengers were busy righting themselves, brushing off their clothing, and retrieving their newspapers. Anything was liable to happen on a city bus or train; this minor snafu was taken lightly, all in a day's work.

But Juanita remained standing near the back door, her lips moved silently.

And they say black folks are trifling! She, a black woman, had just been robbed in a black neighborhood by a white dude! Not only did he get her wallet—he also got her books! How in the hell was she supposed to take an open-book exam without the text?

She gaped at the others on the bus. A few riders had witnessed the theft, but they remained seated impassively, averting their gazes and refusing to meet the questions in her eyes. This was New York; the natives weren't trying to get involved in other folks' drama.

Her blood boiling, she turned toward Scooter. "Now ain't that some shit?" She spoke loudly. "That white boy stole my damn books! *And* my purse!" Her eyes raked around the bus, challenging her fellow passengers. "And look at all of these so-called brothers riding the back of the bus!" She swept a pointed finger around in a semicircle. "Every one of them," she accused. "Every last one of them saw what he did, but nobody did shit about it!"

She turned to Scooter. Questioning lines appeared on her forehead. "Except . . ." Her voice faltered and suddenly her eyes widened. "Except that guy who jumped off—"

"Puh-leeze!" Scooter smirked. "Girl, you on dope or dog food? Can't you see they working together?" He pulled Juanita into his arms. "Nita." He stared into her eyes. "Don't tell me you believe that hype? They planned the whole thing! That guy was in on it from jump street!" Scooter pointed. "Him, too, with his Mr. T-lookin' azz."

Fighting tears, Juanita glanced across the aisle at the blond-haired guy with the colorful tattoo. LOCO LATINO. Crazy Puerto Rican. Both his hands gripped the overhead strap, and his perfectly chiseled body swayed to the rhythm of the moving bus. Could Scooter be right? The guy had seen the whole thing, so why was he still here? Why wasn't he out there trying to help his boy?

"Here, girl." Scooter reached in his pocket and passed her a used

Kleenex. "Dry your eyes—you look like a monkey with a migraine. Besides"—he offered her a smile—"you're leaking all over my silk shirt." He planted a quick kiss on Juanita's forehead. "Don't worry, Nita," he reassured her. "We'll go to the police station and file a report this afternoon. The Men in Blue will track down that wrinkled-up Chico and the sweaty-azz Man, and arrest both of their thieving asses for not only ripping off your shit but dressing up like Darth Vader in hundred-degree heat and losing a fight with a Black and Decker iron."

Juanita accepted the crumpled tissue and tried to smile at his feeble humor as she mopped at her eyes. Sniffling, she blew her nose noisily and glanced into the swaying crowd of passengers.

A shiver of fear trickled down her spine. Señor Goldilocks, with a shock of towhead curls gently grazing his perfectly bronzed brow, still stood across from her swinging merrily from the overhead strap. But now his dark eyes were boring deep into her soul. He was staring her down. And wearing a broad, sinister grin.

CHAPTER 7

That's exactly why females are supposed to sit on the inside!

Conan could have kicked the skinny kid's ass for letting the girl sit by the door. He could've kicked his own ass for jumping off the bus. What a bonehead thing to do! One minute he was arguing with Jorge, the next minute he'd been flung to his knees and was hugging the dirty runners on the B60 floor. And now he found himself darting and weaving through the jam-packed open market: pounding the blistering concrete, wheezing like a *maricon,* and chasing a skinny white boy who ran like Barry Sanders on a patented breakaway!

With the thief ahead by half a block, he chased him down Sutter Avenue and up toward Pitkin. Conan's heavy, flat-footed paces were clumsy and awkward in comparison to the smooth, elongated strides of the man he pursued. Storefronts and dilapidated buildings rushed past in his peripheral vision. Bounding from the sidewalk, the thief took it to the streets, skirting effortlessly amidst the sea of cars.

Block after block, Conan gave chase. Fire percolated in his chest as he strained for oxygen. His blood pumped in waves, pounding in his ears and obliterating the inner-city sounds. As they approached M. Slavin & Sons fish market the thief suddenly changed directions and darted down a shady side street lined with two-story apartments and a lumber warehouse. His arms windmilling, Conan skidded around the corner and slipped on a ragged cardboard box someone had used as a bed the night before; in a brief moment of panic, disappointment tugged at his heart. One moment the thief was in sight and the next moment he was gone.

Poof. Vanished.

Conan slowed to a stiff-legged jog, his heart banging against his ribs. He dropped to one knee in the middle of the sidewalk, his head bent low and spinning like an old forty-five, his perspiration-soaked T-shirt clinging to his heaving torso.

In a gush, he spewed up his breakfast, the pungent brown liquid pooling in the cuff of his navy jeans before splattering his Nike sneakers and dripping down to the filthy pavement.

Moments passed, and Conan staggered to his feet. He raised his damp shirt and mopped his face. Sickened by the odor of his own bile, he pushed away from the curdling mess and managed to drag himself over to a beat-up green Impala parked at the curb. He leaned against the grimy automobile until he was able to stand and breathe without pain.

Finally, he stepped back into the midst of pedestrians and began shuffling in the direction he'd last glimpsed the thief. No doubt he was long gone, probably someplace up in the Bronx—no, Yonkers—by now. Conan trekked the length of the city block with watchful, cautious steps. As he passed Osborn Street and neared the intersection of Thatford and Belmont, he paused. The line of demarcation was clear. Not a solitary soul walked or drove in this dead-end, dilapidated direction. He did an about-face, squinting as he scanned the Osborn Street crowd. His eyes skimmed the moving bodies, searching for one in particular. It was useless. He'd lost him.

A slight breeze drifted over Conan's bare arms and cooled the perspiration on his skin. Sailorlike, he held his right hand to his brow to shield his eyes from the sun. Yes, the empty streets confirmed it. The buck stopped on Belmont Avenue. There was no outlet; the street was littered with old trash and cardboard boxes, but otherwise empty.

Ahead on the right was the slaughterhouse, a live chicken market that supplied poultry to local food chains. To his left was an abandoned building, concrete gargoyles standing faithful guard, protecting the tombs whose windows and doorways had been long boarded and sealed. The remainder of the block consisted of overgrown fields of tall grass sprinkled with broken glass and trash. The stench of rotting chicken was overpowering in the heat, and up ahead he glimpsed several decaying carcasses smoldering under the hot sun.

There was no real reason to venture down this street; the white boy could have gone anywhere. He could be hiding several streets away or could have hopped on another bus. Besides, Conan was tired. He'd run himself into the ground for a total stranger, and for all he knew there was nothing important in her bag. And if there was, why wasn't her snazzy friend with the two-hundred-dollar alligator shoes out here humping his dogs and taking part in the hunt?

Kicking at an empty Shasta can, Conan turned and briskly headed back the way he'd come. He'd gone four or five steps before stealing an instinctive glance over his shoulder. He saw a slight figure slip out of the slaughterhouse and turn in the opposite direction, heading toward Watkins Street. Corn-colored hair grazed the man's shoulders. A long black coat hung loosely from his frame.

And he rummaged through a red knapsack.

Conan whirled, rushing forward with the speed of a running back, bursting into a sprint with his very first step.

His pounding footsteps alerted the thief to danger, and he spun around with his arm raised in defense. Conan sailed through the air like a cannon, landing solidly atop the scraggly boy. He flipped him over quickly before pinning him facedown on the ground.

They struggled, and although Conan outweighed him by nearly forty pounds, the thief was wiry and swift. Scrappy. With his forearm locked around the guy's neck, Conan tightened his bicep muscles and squeezed. The thief grunted and pressed his pelvis into the hard ground, his back bent and arched into a concave half-moon, with Conan riding high on his shoulders.

The backpack lay in the shadow of the thief's upper body, one strap still encircling his wrist. Conan faltered, then quickly regained his balance. He planted his knee midway between the thief's scrawny neck and the top of his wiry buttocks, then rolled his weight forward and pressed.

A stiff cry of anguish pierced the morning air.

"Gimme the goddamn bag!" Conan jerked his arm upward, and the thief strangled on his next breath. His arm still encircling the thief's neck, Conan ignored the dirty yellow strands clinging to his face and clawed beneath the boy's damp body.

"Give it up, asshole! Turn loose the goddamn strap!"

"I c-can't move. Breathe. P-p-please."

Conan loosened his grip and gave the thief enough slack to loosen the strap.

Wrong move.

A slice of metal glinted in the sunlight and a white-hot finger of pain pierced Conan's forearm. "Shit, goddamn *maricon*! You cut me!" He sprang to his feet, cradling his arm and pressing it to his chest.

The scrappy thief rose, the 007 in his outstretched hand dripping with Conan's dark blood. They panted and circled each other warily.

The thief spoke first. "C'mon, Jose." He crouched into a fighting stance; knees bent, arms outstretched. His eyes were wild and a clear fluid ran freely from his nose and hung from his upper lip. The knapsack swung like a pendulum from his knife arm.

"You a bad motherfucker, right? Chasing me like I did something to you! *Now* what the fuck you wanna do?" The thief kept the knife pointed at Conan but rummaged through the bag with his free hand. He came out with a dark-colored wallet. With grimy but agile fingers, he removed several dollar bills.

Conan didn't answer. His gaze was locked on the dripping knife as he pressed his torn arm to his chest. Damn! The knife blade looked even dirtier than the thief. Probably had lockjaw on it or some nasty shit like that! Wasn't no bag or no female worth all of that!

"Yo, man." Conan came out of his crouch and licked his lips. "I don't wanna do shit." He stole a quick glance toward the avenue, where cars whipped past in a steady stream. Here, not another soul was present. Cautiously, he backed up toward Belmont Avenue and civilization, his eyes pinned on the thief but chancing small peeks at the jagged slit in his forearm. He squeezed the edges of the wound together with trembling fingers. Thick blood welled up and spilled over his hand. If the dude didn't have a knife, Conan would have floored him again.

"You gon' fight or run, spic?" The thief took a few menacing steps forward, brandishing his knife. "You wanna do something?"

Do something? Conan shook his head and backed up even further. He knew a good run beat a bad stand any day, but there was no way in hell he would turn his back. The crackhead would probably chase him down and stab him in the back. *Do* something? Conan envisioned his fresh blood mingling with chicken shit and guts and running into the city gutters, and he frowned. "Nah, man." He'd save this for another day. His feet shifted into third gear. "Like I already said, I don't wanna do shit."

CHAPTER 8

Contrasting the morning sun looming in a sky of deep blue, the interior walls of Chase Manhattan Bank were painted a soft shade of evening rose. Magenta-hued carpet gave the spacious room an air of elegance, and the cherry wood desks and coconut-colored leather chairs were gracious and inviting.

"Peace, black man." Jesse Muhammad greeted Scooter at the entrance to the bank. The fifty-three-year-old security guard with the balding head and the Colgate smile dapped Scooter five, welcoming him warmly.

Scooter shook his head sadly. "Ain't no peace happening this morning, bro. My friend got her bag snatched a few minutes ago on the bus. I guess there ain't much peace to be found in the world these days."

Jesse held Scooter's hand in a vise grip and scolded, "Make your own peace, black man! Make your own peace!"

Scooter grinned. Jesse had been an elite Marine Corps sharpshooter back in Vietnam and boasted of bringing home two things from the war: his distrust of the white man and his inability to urinate at will. As part of his combat sniper training, Jesse had spent countless hours being indoctrinated under extreme conditions, and even more hours lying motionless and concentrating on enemy targets while concealed in dense shrubbery along high ridges and in the spurs of swampy valleys.

Jesse had become an expert marksman, one of the best in the Marine Corps, and he had countless awards and decorations to prove it. But in conjunction with the harsh training, his body had become conditioned to relieving itself only three times each day: once at 3:45 A.M., which is when his outfit rose to eat chow and begin their shifts, again at 1:45 P.M., when the XO called their first smoke break, and again at 8:45 in the evening, just before he retired for the night.

"Yeah, man," Jesse repeated. "Make your own damn peace!"

Scooter grinned. "How about some love, peace, and elbow grease!" He dapped Jesse the black-man-hand-thang. "I'ma start making all that and more!"

Scooter was still smiling as he headed toward the tellers' cage and approached his workstation. He perched upon a high leather stool and gazed out on the main banking floor, then frowned. The plastic nameplate glued to the front of the thick bulletproof glass surrounding his area read, SOCRATES MORRISON, HEAD TELLER, but on a day like today he'd be forced to wear several hats, including clearance clerk, administrative assistant, and payroll supervisor.

For the next two hours he busied himself preparing the weekly payroll for several major accounts, something he usually did with relative ease on Thursday mornings, since his classes were scheduled for late afternoon. However, two of the branch's most experienced customer-service assistants were out sick with a late spring bug, and the lead clearance teller was on maternity leave with her fifth child. The morning rush of white-collar workers with their hefty paychecks would place an enormous strain on the branch's personnel resources.

Scooter adjusted his position on the stool and sighed. The payday crowd was awesome, and instinctively he quickened his count. His lips moved in a silent rhythm as he slid the stacks of crisp twenty-dollar bills out of the paper holders and deftly transferred them from his left hand to his right, counting rapidly but with complete accuracy.

"Socrates." A soft, feminine voice rang out behind him. "Just wanted to remind you about the weekly cash count. Since Doug is out sick, Mr. Steinberg will be assisting you in the vault."

Distracted, Scooter turned to face Evelyn Lipswitch, a short, buxom white woman in her late sixties who served as the branch manager's personal secretary. He flashed a grin at the warmth in her smile and the twinkle in her china-blue eyes.

"'Kay, Evvie," he answered, his tone sweet and buttery. "Tell him as soon as I'm done with the payroll for Junior's, I'll head right down."

The matronly woman patted Scooter on the back. Although her appearance was as gracious and cozy as deep-dish apple pie, in her case appearances were exceptionally deceptive. Armed with a razor-like intellect, she'd given forty years of faithful service to Chase. Some said it was really she, not the stern-faced branch manager, Solomon Steinberg, who was responsible for the operational effectiveness of Branch 101.

Known as a walking code of banking laws and regulations, Evelyn was trusted by many and invaluable to all; there was never a transaction too complicated for her to handle. And she absolutely adored young Socrates Morrison. He was the only teller—in fact, the only employee, including Mr. Steinberg—who dared to address her by her first name.

She told him, "Well, don't keep him waiting too long. It's been a rough week without Jacob and Doug, and as you can see, his nerves are beginning to fray."

Scooter glanced across the room to where Mr. Steinberg stood. Two beats away from being handsome, the branch manager was instead rugged and well-built in his five-hundred-dollar navy pinstriped blazer and matching trousers. They watched together as the fifty-two-year-old manager engaged in a heated conversation with Mitchell Edwards, an international banking subordinate manager. Normally, Mr. Steinberg communicated a staunch air of indifference, a detached aloofness common in white men accustomed to power and authority, but right now he looked anything but in control.

Scooter marveled as his boss slammed his fist down hard on the desk. He pushed at the tangle of wavy hair at his crown, and instead of seating himself behind his desk, he towered above it, his body language speaking for itself.

"Okay," Scooter agreed, and shuddered. "He looks aggravated. I won't keep him waiting much longer. And if I do"—he winked at the older woman—"I'll be sure to tell him it was your fault."

Evelyn shook with laughter. Socrates was a regular guy, always cracking jokes and keeping things lively. And that was exactly what the branch needed. New life. Raw energy. Before Socrates had been hired, the days had seemed longer and employee morale was such a drag! Evelyn was glad she'd talked Mr. Steinberg into taking a chance and hiring the handsome black boy, although it had taken almost every ounce of her considerable influence to sway the hesitant manager.

"Are you saying you have a problem with minorities," she'd questioned when Steinberg revealed his plan to hire a young white male instead of the similarly qualified Socrates. The colored boy was no threat. He didn't carry a boom box or wear his pants riding low on his waist. This young man was a *student,* for Christ's sake! A Negro with the drive to better his situation. An *orphan,* for crying out loud!

"It is *not* just because he's black!" Steinberg had protested weakly.

"Well then, explain to me why, in the twenty years since you've been here, not one qualified black male, other than Jesse who guards the door, has ever been hired."

Steinberg stammered, "I-I can assure you that it's not because they were black. I'm not a racist. There's just something about this young man that . . . disturbs me, that's all."

Evelyn didn't buy his excuse. She shot back, "Disturbs you? Perhaps you see a bit of yourself in him, Sollie. Could that be the problem?"

His expression became uneasy. A contrite look crept into his eyes. "That boy and I have absolutely nothing in common," Steinberg denied, but Evelyn wasn't fooled. She'd seen quite a bit in her day, from the absurd to the obscene, and as a New York native she could spot a wolf wearing sheep's clothing. Besides, guilt rode high upon Solomon Steinberg's forehead and the way he shifted his eyes confirmed her long-standing suspicions, although he'd never admit it.

In the end, Evelyn had won, and to date Socrates had not disappointed her. Whereas Steinberg made great efforts to avoid the sweet young man, Evelyn loved his playful banter, his ready smile, and the effortless way he seemed to connect with the customers. It hadn't taken him long to distinguish himself and move up ahead of his peers. As the head teller, Socrates handled every situation with humor and poise, which was the main reason he'd been chosen over two more experienced tellers when the position became vacant.

Evelyn pinched Scooter lovingly on both cheeks. "Behave yourself, young man. And don't forget about Friday night. I'm preparing one of your favorites, chicken and dumplings!"

Scooter smiled. She reminded him of his grandmother. It made him feel good to know that this elderly white woman not only liked him, she trusted him in her home. Evvie had never had any children of her own, and her husband had been dead for ten years. This would be their second full month of shared Friday-night dinners, and while Hattie was getting suspicious, Evvie was actually a pretty good cook. Besides, he had never really been fond of deep-fried whitings or porgies, a Friday-night special in the Lucas household.

Scooter glanced again at the branch manager and decided the payroll could wait. It was obvious that Mr. Steinberg wasn't impressed with him, and getting on his bad side would be like cutting his wrists and then swimming with a hungry shark. He placed the blocks of twenties in a canvass money bag and secured the bag in his petty-cash safe. After spinning the lock several times, he checked his tie, rubbed the toe of each shoe on the back of his pants leg, and headed toward the main banking floor.

/ / /

Solomon Steinberg mopped his forehead and stuffed his silk handkerchief into his front trouser pocket. The bank's air conditioner was set at a comfortable seventy-two degrees, but his internal thermometer had spun out of whack.

He fidgeted in his seat, repeatedly opening and closing his desk drawer. For a man who was accustomed to controlling his environment, his world felt suddenly amiss. He massaged his neck. It was barely ten A.M., and already it had been a long day. Damn Doug and Jacob both! How dare they both call in sick on a Thursday. On cash count day. That meant he was obliged to go down into the main vault. To go down there with that black kid.

Socrates Morrison.

Steinberg fished in his jacket pocket for a Marlboro, then remembered he'd quit five years ago. Had acupuncture. Cost two hundred bucks and was probably the best thing he'd ever done for himself; his breathing had become less painful, his lung capacity had improved. He'd even returned to the gym, swimming several laps each morning before coming to work to face his growing frustrations.

He massaged the muscles in his neck. Even with the added exercise, he felt like a powder keg about to blow. His nerves were so frayed, his behavior so erratic, he'd actually argued with his employee and longtime friend Mitch Edwards right on the banking floor. Right at his desk! Anyone could have seen them.

Steinberg took a long, deep breath and exhaled slowly. In close to twenty years, he had never before lost control, had never raised his voice in exasperation while at work. Not even the time when that stupid blond chick sent the Department of Motor Vehicles a block of hundreds instead of twenties in their weekly payroll bag. When the error was discovered he'd simply contacted their finance and accounting officer, explained the mix-up, and fired the girl on the spot.

He hated blondes.

Perhaps he should have swum an extra lap or two this morning. Maybe then he would have been more prepared to face his demons.

He fingered a five-by-seven oak-framed photo that rested on his desk. The perfect couple. Blanche looked awestruck; her eyes wide and expectant, visions of bliss peeking from her smile, corn-colored hair fanned around her shoulders, the ends flipped upward in a slight curl.

He stared at his younger self. Traced the outline of his head, tilted slightly away from hers. He looked dumbstruck, as though he hadn't expected the picture to be taken, or wasn't sure why he was there. Actually, the photo had been snapped during his shotgun wedding and honeymoon in the Poconos, the day after his hasty marriage to longtime girlfriend Blanche Lovitz. Exactly a week after, his invisible life was made visible and his sexual escapades were broadcast to his devout Orthodox Jewish family and his Harvard upperclassmen.

Nigger lover, is what they'd called him. *Cocksucking nigger lover.* Even now, the shame of it sent rivulets of perspiration trickling from his armpits. Bill had escaped persecution through expulsion, but Steinberg was a white man and had been allowed to stay. To remain behind and face the humiliation and degradation that was an unbearable consequence of what society and his religion had deemed a deviant lifestyle. Moisture dripped from his chin and left stains like teardrops on the cherry veneer of his desk. He retrieved his handkerchief and mopped up as best he could, then, hands trembling, he pressed the damp cloth to his nose and blew hard.

The branch was a blur of activity. Customers shifted from foot to foot as they waited impatiently in the spiraling lines. Account reps scurried back and forth, placating the frustrated high-balance account holders. Across the banking floor, the boy stood behind the partitioned tellers' cage engaged in an animated conversation with Evelyn. He threw back his head and laughed heartily at something she said.

Steinberg watched, fascinated by the way his lips slid across his teeth when he smiled, the way they parted to reveal slender bits of his pink tongue.

His loins tightened.

Even from this distance he could see how the boy's eyebrows, lush and bushy, blended together above his nose almost in one straight line. How he held his shoulders and back erect. How the lean curve of his flanks jutted out in profile. Just like Bill's. Solomon would recognize an ass like that anywhere, and he was willing to bet it was the same exact shade of brown that Bill's had been . . . pecan brown. Like a paper grocery sack. And his hair. Steinberg had loved the abrasive feel of Bill's coarse, foreign pubic bush as it scraped back and forth against the most delicate parts of him.

As Steinberg watched, Evelyn pinched the boy's cheeks. He thought he saw the boy's nostrils flare. That had been the one thing he'd loved most about Bill. The way he closed his eyes and bit down on his lip, the way his nostrils pulsated just as he reached the point of no return. The way he arched his back and cried out right before he—

His eyes snapped open. He hadn't realized that he'd closed them. Hadn't realized he could slip so completely back into his other self. He needed to walk over to the water cooler to refresh himself, but he didn't dare. His daytime fantasies had worked him into a state of embarrassment. Lately, his nighttime dreams left his pajama bottoms slick with wasted love.

It had been more than thirty years since the last time he'd seen his first love, William "Bill" Jackson. Over thirty years since his carefree days at Harvard and their subsequent summer of love, deception, and unmasking. Thirty years and still he couldn't get the man out of his system. When he made love to Blanche it was really Bill, spread out in all his glory, whom he pounded and hammered from the rear. When he caressed her hips, thighs, and dimpled white ass, it was really Bill's lithe flanks that he massaged. And when Blanche headed south in what she perceived to be her distasteful albeit wifely duty, Steinberg still saw Bill, his face alight with pleasure, his smooth brown lips a sharp contrast to the milky white love-stick he gripped, his cheeks collapsing and expanding as he pumped and swallowed, his eyes smiling up at him with unrestrained love.

In the thirty-some-odd years since he'd married Blanche, in the thirty-some-odd years since he and Bill had been discovered in an unlocked room in a Harvard dorm sharing their love and creating their own private joy, Steinberg had never been with another man. Thirty-some-odd years of self-denial.

Of self-deprivation.

He'd allowed Blanche the obligatory indulgences: two kids, a minivan, a sprawling house in the suburbs complete with the dog and the white picket fence. But throughout it all he'd lived a shining lie. Masking his carnal desires behind a facade of a normalcy: loving father, devoted husband, astute businessman, pillar of his community.

During those long hard years he'd often dreamed about gay love. Ached for it. Cried for it. Twice he'd gone to bathhouses and actually come close to it. But never had he felt so utterly driven to cross that line again. Never. Until the day he laid his eyes on the young black boy who thirty years earlier could have been Bill's twin. Never. Until the morning, some 147 days ago, that Socrates Morrison strolled through the doors of Chase Manhattan Bank and caused his carefully constructed world to spiral out of control.

Steinberg rolled his chair closer to his desk. He reached down into his lap and squeezed himself hard. Flames of unfulfilled passion leaped up and licked at his loins. Moral weakness coursed through his veins. He closed his eyes and prayed. God help him if he had to go down into that vault. His thirst for the boy ran deep enough to parch his soul. It was time to start living for himself again. He couldn't let Bill get away a second time. He just couldn't.

God help him.

" dunno what's wrong with that lazy motherfucker, Mista Williams." Jorge shrugged as he stepped into a blue jumpsuit and pushed his thick arms through the sleeves. "I told him you wasn't taking no more bullshit. . . . I guess he didn't believe me."

Chance Williams gave Jorge a hard look. An amateur wrestler turned mechanical engineer, Chance was the only ethnic minority in the Grayson Fields supervisory chain. His bright-yellow GF shirt had been specially ordered to accommodate his broad shoulders and mammoth upper arms, and his dark-brown skin shone under the fluorescent lights.

Jorge was lucky, Chance thought. At Grayson Fields, blacks and Latinos were typically hired for low-paying positions of deliverymen and maintenance workers; but business was good, and because of the company's recent expansion and campaign of diversity in the work-place, several minority workers had been transferred to hydraulics and heavy machinery.

Of the fourteen men Chance supervised during his ten-hour shift, Jorge Corona was, thankfully, the exception rather than the rule. True, he was stronger than two John Henrys, and when he wanted to work it was like watching a steam engine, but who wanted a young hothead on their watch who kept up more internal calamity than Dennis Rodman and was more unpredictable than Mike Tyson?

But Jorge's friend Conan was a different matter altogether. Chance questioned, "Are you sure about that, Jorge?" His story seemed contrived. Difficult to believe. It was true that a zero-tolerance policy had been laid down earlier in the week, but it had been with employees like Jorge in mind. Conan was an excellent worker, maybe one of the best. In fact, Chance was considering him for an assistant shift supervisor position when Gary Johns took off for his back surgery in the fall. Chance glared at Jorge and massaged his own squat neck, suspicion narrowing his eyes. Conan and Jorge were as different as Janet Jackson and Whoopi Goldberg, yet they ran together thicker than thieves. He couldn't figure it out; one was straight up and responsible and seemed to have had a decent upbringing; the other was a renegade. A loudmouthed, shit-talking rebel without a cause.

Jorge read his doubting mind.

"I'm telling you, yo! I left his lazy ass laying in the bed with his prick in his hand. He wouldn't even get up to lock the goddamn door." Jorge grinned, rolling his sleeves up above his elbows. "But don't worry, my brother. I know how to run the heavy master puncher *and* throw the switches. I been watching him for a long time, and there ain't shit Conan can do that I can't do better."

"You're standing here asking me to hand you Conan's job, and you're supposed to be his best friend?"

"Friendship, bullshit! Didn't you say if anybody was late again this week, or if one of us just didn't show up, his ass was canned?" Jorge slipped a protective apron over his head and grabbed an overstuffed clipboard hanging from a peg. "Man, stick to your fuckin' word! I can do this shit. Look." He flipped through the dog-eared sheets of paper. "I can read the plans and operate the machines. You pay that joker five dollars more an hour than I make—I'll do an even better job for a raise of two-fifty."

Chance shook his head in disbelief. "Man, with a friend like you sliding it to him from the back, Conan better invest in some Vaseline. Grab a pair of safety goggles. I'll let you work the heavies today, and if you don't fuck around and lose an arm we'll see about putting you in there again tomorrow." He shook his head again, muttering in disgust as he left the dressing room. "Crazy asshole. Somebody better tell Conan to hire a goddamn bodyguard."

, , ,

Compare and contrast the role of women in Lysistrata *and* The Iliad. Now what kind of cockamamy question was that? Juanita scratched her scalp, and her fingers came back slick with hair grease. She glanced around the large, air-conditioned amphitheater. Scores of heads were bowed in concentration, the crackle of turning pages the only sound.

She grasped her borrowed number-two pencil and opened her booklet. Let's see. . . . *The role of women in* Lysistrata *differed from the role of women in* The Iliad *because the women in* The Iliad *were considered insignificant underlings who had no say-so in the day-to-day business of Greek life, and the women in* Lysistrata *were able to have a voice in their communities by withholding sex until their demands were met and yada yada yada* . . . The rest was pure filling. Fluff. She simply stated and restated the main points to the tune of four full blue-book pages, and was surprised that she'd been able to get that far.

She sat up in her chair and dug into her scalp once more, then used the sides of her dress to wipe the goo from her fingertips. A terrible sense of dread nestled in the pit of her stomach. A fear of failure. Her professor had been kind enough to lend her his personal copy of *The Norton Anthology of World Literature,* but of course his copy didn't contain any of the class notes, definitions, or terminology that she'd painstakingly scribbled in the margins of her own book. Juanita closed her eyes and sighed. It was useless. There was no way she could concentrate after her morning ordeal. And it just wasn't fair. After all of her studying she would probably walk away with a D, or a C at best.

She rested her chin in the palm of her hand and chewed her frayed fingernails. That white boy was the stupidest damn thief she'd ever seen. If he had to pick someone to rob, at least he should have been smart enough to pick someone who was likely to have some real money. Aside from her schoolbooks and plastic DMV identification card, the only cash she'd had was the four dollars donated by Aunt Hattie that she'd tucked behind an old snapshot of her and Scooter.

And that guy in the chinos, she wondered. What the hell was his game? What kind of petty thief planned a heist just to rip off a broke college student? Damn Puerto Ricans. She made a sucking sound with her teeth. Scooter was right. They'd probably been checking her out for a long time. Just waiting for the right opportunity to victimize her. And the blond-haired guy! She shuddered involuntarily. Something about him had sent terror straight through her bones. The way he'd looked at her; his amber eyes had been filled with a sick sort of evil. Almost the same look Scooter had described seeing in Dante Coleman's eyes long ago on that hot summer night.

But like Scooter said, she'd probably seen the last of them. They wouldn't dare show their faces on the B60 again; she'd have the bus driver radio the police in a heartbeat. Juanita frowned as she revisited the depths of her rage. Why was she always the victim? If they showed up again, maybe she'd take care of them herself. Maybe she'd just handle her business. And maybe she'd borrow Uncle Herbie's Leatherman pocketknife and cut a couple of Latinos some brand-new assholes.

′ ′ ′

"Sure has been hot lately," Scooter said in a weak attempt at casual conversation. Although cool air filtered through from the ventilation system upstairs, beads of sweat dotted his nose, and his back felt clammy and damp. He covered the tremble in his hands by punching his personal access code into the Ident-a-Tron panel of the state-of-the-art stainless-steel banking vault.

"Yep," he repeated into the mausoleumlike silence. "It sure has been hot."

Mr. Steinberg didn't answer. He'd already entered his access code and activated the security camera, and now stood slightly behind Scooter as he punched three repetitions of twelve digits into the soft rubber keypad. Several combinations of different identification numbers were required to access the main vault, and as the head teller Scooter was privy to two such codes. A few seconds after the last digit had been entered, a red light at the top of the door blinked twice and signaled the release of the electronic locking device.

Mr. Steinberg brushed past Scooter to open the vault's heavy outer doors. As he passed, his trailing hand slid almost imperceptibly across the seat of Scooter's linen pants.

Scooter turned sharply, a questioning look on his face. Heat rose from his collar, which suddenly felt much too tight. There was no doubt that Mr. Steinberg had rubbed against him accidentally, but the intimate touch had flustered him.

Scooter stole a glance at his boss. If Mr. Steinberg was aware of the way he'd jostled him, he gave no notice. He never even turned around to acknowledge or apologize for the contact. Instead, his face was unreadable as he swung back the weighty doors and stepped into the interior vestibule.

An additional security feature of the Ident-a-Tron system required that a spin-type lock release the vault's inner doors within sixty seconds of opening the outer doors. Listening for the signaling beep, Scooter hurried over to swing the dial, first left until it landed on his classified number, then right, and then left again. Thirty seconds later Mr. Steinberg repeated this procedure using his own private combination, and the inner doors were finally unlocked.

The airtight vault had a dank, musty smell that reminded Scooter of his grandmother's sickroom. He hated it down here. For some reason, small enclosed spaces made him uncomfortable. He hurried over to the file cabinet where the weekly report forms were kept. Normally Doug Mason was responsible for filling out the forms, but Scooter had been thoroughly trained. As long as Mr. Steinberg didn't goose him again, he was sure he could complete the transactions.

When Steinberg moved to inspect the safe-deposit boxes, Scooter bent over the low file cabinet and searched the manila folders for the proper form. Not a single word had passed between them, but Scooter could feel the tension in the air.

Scooter located the correct form and filled out the top portion. It felt good to write his name in the box labeled CERTIFYING OFFICIAL. The way he was moving up in the branch and in such a short period, who knew? One day he might just make it out on the main floor as a selective service representative. And after that? Maybe even an account manager.

It took more than an hour to count down the vault. No words were ever exchanged; figures counted and confirmed were the only sound. Finally, Scooter signed off in the required box and passed the form over for Mr. Steinberg's signature.

For a brief moment their fingers met.

Scooter was stunned as Mr. Steinberg's pinkie finger snaked out and lightly trapped his own. Squeezing. Pumping. Amazed, he was frozen in place, unable to withdraw his hand. Instead, he looked up to find Mr. Steinberg staring down at him with an unmistakable look smoldering in his heavily lidded gray eyes.

Heat swirled around Scooter's loins.

Mr. Steinberg was married with two small children! Was he imagining the intimacy of his touch, or was his straight-laced boss making a pass at him? And right in range of the security cameras?

Panic overtook him. It could be a setup. He licked his lips and snatched his hand away. His black pen clanked to the floor and rolled under the counting table. He took a small step backward. Unable to meet the magnetic pull in Mr. Steinberg's eyes, instead he allowed his gaze to travel the length of the older man's trim physique. The front of his pinstriped trousers appeared full and tented.

His own manhood leaped and stiffened. Scooter stammered, "Um. Umm, I think that's it, sir." He coughed nervously as he backed out of the vault, vainly attempting to cover his rising erection. "I think we can . . . I mean if you don't need me anymore I'll go back upstairs and finish the payroll. That's if . . . um . . . if we're finished."

Mr. Steinberg's face softened. His rosy tongue snaked out to trace his pale lips as he stared first toward Scooter's bulging groin, then back up into his employee's embarrassed eyes. "We're finished," he said finally, his voice thick with something that was certain to tease Scooter later that night in his dreams. "Yes, Socrates. We are finished . . . for now."

CHAPTER 10

"I got it, man! Guess what?" Conan burst through the doors of the heavy machinery shop. He was more than an hour late but pumped with excitement. His damp shirt was wrinkled and disheveled and the cuff of his pants had come undone and drooped lazily over his Nike tennis shoes. "Look, *hombre,* I got it!" He thrust forward the bright-red knapsack for Jorge to see. "Yo, *amigo,* who woulda thunk it? I ran that skinny white boy down! You should've seen how fast he was moving! I mean, he must've been some kinda fuckin' track star or something, 'cause he was moving faster than your grandma at a crack convention! Man, he almost ran my ass all over central Brooklyn, he . . ."

Conan suddenly fell silent, confusion spreading across his handsome features. "Yo, man," he stammered, his face flustered with dying traces of excitement, "why you pulling heavies? How come you're working at my station?"

Jorge continued to work. His powerful arms moved rhythmically, throwing levers and adjusting pulleys. Without turning, he shrugged and replied in Spanish, "I dunno, man. You know that nigger has it in for Latinos. I tried to tell him you was out there trying to get some chick's bag back for her, but he didn't give a fuck. You know how they are. They don't even give a fuck about each other, so you know they don't care about us." He stepped down from the concrete platform and faced his friend. Sincerity creased his forehead. Concern shone in his eyes. He pulled off his heavy work gloves. "Williams said to tell you to clean out your locker and get the fuck outta here. Said he don't even wanna see your ass; he's gonna mail you your last check."

Jorge slid his hand under his apron and reached into his pants pocket. He came out with a crumpled pack of Newports. "C'mon, *hombre.*" He threw his arm around Conan's shoulder and turned his baffled friend toward the exit. "I'll walk out with you and get a smoke. But don't worry. I told that fathead fuck I was gonna complain to the head shed about the way he canned your ass."

"Canned me? He can't fire me!" Conan jerked away from his friend and took two steps toward the supervisory section. He whirled around to face Jorge. "I was helping somebody! Didn't you tell him I jumped off the bus to help that girl?"

Jorge raised his hands innocently. "I told him, man, I told him! But he didn't give a fuck. Believe me, I told him."

"Well, we gonna see about this shit—"

"*Hombre,* I wouldn't go in there if I was you. He was mad as hell and he said he doesn't wanna talk to you."

"I don't give a fuck about what he said, he's gotta—"

"Well, do you give a fuck about what your friend here said?" Chance Williams pushed through the doors. His bulk was swollen with anger and his dark eyes flashed.

Conan blurted, "Look, Mr. Williams. I'm sorry for coming in late, but I had to help her. Dude snatched her bag and see"—he held up the red knapsack—"I ran after him to get it back. He even sliced my arm!"

Chance turned to face Conan, but his eyes bored into Jorge. "Oh, you're not the one who needs to be apologizing. Your friend here"— he nodded toward Jorge, who had struck a match and stood calmly puffing from a cigarette—"your so-called Puerto Rican *pizo,* just told me he left you in bed this morning with your dick in your hand! Said you blew him off when he tried to drag your lazy ass outta bed, even offered to do your job better than you could ever do it—"

Jorge exploded. "You lying motherfucker!" He flicked his lit cigarette toward his boss and advanced upon the larger man with fury flashing in his eyes.

"Ohhh . . ." Chance's handsome face broke apart in a wide smile. He hitched up the legs of his pants and crouched. "That's right . . . you bad." He stood his ground and taunted Jorge, beckoning him forward with mitt-size hands. "Bring your ass. C'mon, Chico, act like you know so I can show you how we get down Bedford Stuyvesant–style!"

Jorge did not retreat. Nor did he advance. He remained rooted. Scowling. Sweating. Conan held up his hands in a gesture of peace, then turned to his friend. "Yo, man. You told him what happened, right?" His brown eyes searched Jorge's. "You told him where I was—and about the white guy on the bus, right, man?"

"Hell, yeah, I told 'im!" Jorge snarled. He thrust his fist toward Chance but made no move to attack the larger man. "Fuck him! He's a goddamn liar anyway. You heard that shit he said about getting fired if you're late. Everybody heard him!"

Chance fought to control himself before turning to Conan. "Look. Yes, I said if anybody came in late he would be fired. It's my new rule; I said that shit and I meant it. But that policy was instituted with assholes like your friend here in mind. I had no idea where you were, or what you were doing. I still don't. But according to your homey here, you were slacking off at home. Waxing the old wormie. And for a small raise, he was willing to take over your position—even if he had to step over your unemployed body to get it."

Chance paused and let his words sink in before continuing. "Now, Jorge is right on one point. The policy is what the policy is. However, as the shift supervisor I have the authority to override that policy. I don't know what happened, but I can see you've been cut. If you wanna step into my office I'd be willing to hear you out while I bandage that arm."

He held up one hand. "But first, let me give you a word of advice." Again, his eyes bored into Jorge. "Just because a knucklehead can speak Spanish and grin, don't mean he's worthy of being your friend." He lifted his chin, aiming toward Jorge, who stood panting with pure venom. "If I were you I'd cut that driftwood loose. You won't be missing anything. He's going nowhere fast."

///

"You heading straight home, *amigo*?" Jorge and Conan stood side by side at the industrial-size sink, their arms covered in oil and lubricants up to the elbow.

Conan didn't answer. It had been a long day, and he was glad it was finally over. Cleaning and lubricating the machinery valves was a dirty job, and it usually took two or three repeat washings to get rid of the gooey mess. Careful to avoid the area surrounding his bandage, Conan poured company-supplied Lysol straight from the bottle and generously lathered himself, vigorously scrubbing his hands and forearms with a small nailbrush. He repeated the procedure four times, methodically soaping and rinsing in silence.

Jorge finished washing and left Conan still lathering at the sink. He used several coarse paper towels to dry himself off, then went into a stall and shut the door. The trickling sound of water breaking water filled the air as Jorge hummed a popular Latin tune. The toilet flushed, and Jorge called out over the noise, "So what's up, man? You bouncing home or what?"

Conan was silent. There were no words to express how he felt. All day he'd fought an inner turmoil stuck high up in his chest, constricting his breathing. Although Jorge had been behaving strangely lately, Conan couldn't think of an excuse that would allow him to buy, swallow, and accept such bullshit from the friend he considered a brother. Loved like a brother.

While bandaging his arm, Chance Williams had replayed his earlier conversation with Jorge. Immediately, Conan had wanted to fight. Wanted to fuck him up. Not Jorge, but Chance. He'd wanted to call his supervisor a lying son of a bitch. His mind wanted to reject the words his boss had spoken. Wanted to bum-rush the heavyweight engineer, trip him up, and knock his goddamn lights out. Punch him dead in the mouth and make him take back the lies his lips were spreading. But he didn't. Couldn't. Because in his heart of hearts, Conan knew Chance Williams had spoken the truth. It was Jorge who was the liar. It was his friend who had deceived him. Betrayed him. Slandered him.

Chance had seen the rising tide of anger in Conan's eyes and moved Jorge into another section of the heavy shop. Pissed, Conan had continued to stew and simmer the entire day, but at least he hadn't been forced to be in Jorge's presence.

Until now. Jorge stood waiting. Waiting for an answer.

Conan bent over and cuffed the hem of his pants. He straightened up in time to glimpse his friend slip a tiny blue tablet into his mouth for the second time that day. The first tablet had disappeared on Jorge's tongue very early that morning as they stood at the bus stop. And now another pill went sailing down the chute. Lately Jorge seemed to suck on the tablets like they were breath mints.

"Well?" Jorge was still waiting.

A lump formed in Conan's throat. "Yeah, I guess I am."

Jorge clapped him on the shoulder. "Whassup, *amigo*?" His lips spread apart in a grin that failed to bank the storm in his eyes. "Why you act like the fuckin' cat got your tongue? Snap out of it, *hombre,* and let's go find that fine honey Lourdes *tiene um culaso*! I mean, that ass is pie-yah! I got a trick I wanna show her tonight—"

"Look, man," Conan met Jorge's gaze straight on. "You go. You go on and do whatever the fuck you gotta do. But leave me out of it. I ain't down with your program. After that foul shit you pulled this morning . . . I just"—he shook his head—"I ain't feeling you right now."

Jorge's laughter echoed. "C'mon, *amigo*! I know you didn't fall for Chance's bullshit this morning! Oh, you gonna take the word of some *negro mentiroso* over my word? The word of your brother? *¿Tu eres mí hermano, mi pana?*" Jorge stared, all the friendliness gone from his face, his eyes hardened into tough, angry pebbles.

"He don't have no reason to lie, my man."

"What?"

"You heard me. Mr. Williams ain't got a reason to lie. He has nothing to lose and nothing to gain. Why would he lie?"

Jorge exploded. "Why the fuck," he bellowed, and kicked over a large metal trashcan, "why the fuck would I fuckin' lie? Huh? Answer me that, you stupid son of a bitch!" He pounded his fist against the door of the stall. It swung sharply on its hinges before slamming against the back wall. "That's the problem with *los meslados sin identidad* like you! You go against your own kind for a measly fucking buck!"

He pointed a finger at Conan. "But I tell you what. You wait and see who's there for you when you got snot running outta your nose and tears coming outta your eyes. When you having crazy dreams and pissing in your fucking bed! See who you come crying to then. Me or that square-necked nigger you all of a sudden so tight with!"

"You need to leave that acid alone, man."

"What?"

"That mesc. It's fucking you up. You tripping, *hombre.*"

"I'm tripping? *You're* tripping, you nightmare-having, pissing-in-the-bed *crying* motherfucker!"

Conan warned, "You crossing a line, man."

"No! You're the one who's crossing a fucking line!"

Conan stared into Jorge's eyes. There was a small grain of truth embedded in his friend's harsh words. After the accident there had been many nights when he'd awakened in a cold sweat. Flushed, gasping, fighting his sheets in the midst of some sort of panic attack. It had been Jorge who immediately after the crash had taken to sleeping in Thor's bed, who had been there to comfort him. To remind him that even though he'd jerked the wheel, it had been an accident. To beg him not to punish himself by reliving that fateful night over and over in his dreams.

But still, Jorge's behavior had changed a lot over the past few weeks. Always wild and impulsive, he'd suddenly become highly volatile. Aggressive. He barely slept at night; instead he hung out until all hours, sometimes not creeping into bed until dawn. Conan suspected his erratic behavior had something to do with those tiny blue pills he was always swallowing. Popping tabs, they called it. Tripping. Well, his *amigo* was certainly tripping now. Tripping hard.

When Conan finally spoke it was in a weary voice, heavy and anguished. "No, Jorge. That's where you're wrong. The line was crossed when you lied on me instead of looking out for me."

"How many times I gotta tell you?" Jorge held his arms wide, pleading. "*I didn't lie.* I told that motherfucker you was out there trying to help some *chica.* He made the rest of that shit up." His manner became calm and sincere. "Look, I swear on *mi madre.* On *mi madre*! I did not lie. C'mon, man. You gotta believe me."

Conan paused, then nodded. Jorge seemed earnest. He even

sounded a lot like his old self. Belligerent, but believable. He accepted his friend's outstretched hand and dapped him a solid five; yet as they exited the washroom and walked toward their lockers, Conan knew something just as sure as he knew his own name: Not only had Jorge lied on him earlier that morning, his *mejor amigo* was still lying now.

CHAPTER 11

"**H**ow'd you do on your test?" Scooter asked. His Thursday afternoon class let out later than Juanita's, so they rode separate buses home and used the Friday morning commute to catch up on the previous day's happenings.

Juanita shuddered.

"C'mon, Nita. You're such a brainiac. I bet you got a flipping A-plus!"

Juanita rolled her eyes and shifted in her seat. The morning sun scorched her exposed back through the open windows of the B60, and her walking shorts felt sweaty and uncomfortable against the plastic bucket seats. There was no way the instructor would have the exam graded and recorded today. With over a hundred essays to read, Juanita hoped it would take him at least a week to return the dreaded blue books.

"I don't know about that," she replied doubtfully. A small frown creased her forehead. "More than likely I bombed. Hell, without my notes I was straight-up Leema-Leema-Mike-Foxtrot."

Scooter laughed. "Yeah, lost like a motherfucker!"

Juanita gave him a tired smile. She'd tossed and turned the entire night, finally rising from bed and creeping into the dark kitchen at three A.M. In the slice of light provided by the interior bulb of the refrigerator, Juanita stood with the door ajar and methodically consumed half of a beef roast, two plates of leftover mashed potatoes, a large bag of Wise Onion & Garlic potato chips, a twenty-ounce Pepsi, and three Breyers fat-free yogurts.

It was almost five A.M. when she finally crept from the bathroom. Emptied. Purged. Careful to wipe away all traces of her mess, the early-morning birds testified as witnesses to her shameful act, and with a sore throat and bloodshot eyes, she'd returned to her bed.

Yet sleep had continued to evade her, and instead she'd lain there with her eyes wide, reliving the fear and anger of her ordeal and trying to figure out a way to come up with enough cash to replace her stolen books. With only a few weeks left in the summer term, it seemed like such a waste of money to repurchase what her auntie had already worked so hard to buy, but there was no way she could pass her classes without studying from the texts.

"Don't worry about the books, Nita," Aunt Hattie had tried to soothe her. "The important thang is that you weren't hurt none. There may not be money 'round here for new cars or fancy clothes, but there will always be a few bucks we can scrape together for schoolbooks."

Aunt Hattie promised to give her the money that afternoon, but it pained Juanita to even consider accepting it. Her aunt had always worked hard to provide for her. From the time Juanita could remember, Hattie had scrubbed other people's floors and ironed their fancy sheets to furnish her with the basic necessities of life. But Juanita had not been spoiled. Aunt Hattie believed in education first, frivolities second. She'd seen too many extravagances in the affluent homes she cleaned. Niceties did nothing to strengthen and reinforce the love, respect, and discipline that were the ties that bound a family. There were some things that money just couldn't buy, and frivolities, Aunt Hattie said, were something her niece could do nicely without.

"Damn!" Scooter elbowed her. "Look! Here comes the Frito Bandito. Grab your purse, Nita. Those thieving-ass Reekins just got on the bus!"

Juanita's hand fluttered toward her tiny bosom. Aunt Hattie had insisted she slip a few dollars into a cut-off stocking and tuck it securely away in her bra. Since her breasts were too small to conceal even a tiny bulge, she'd safety-pinned the tight bundle to the side of her bra under her right armpit.

"Look at 'em," Scooter said. The handsome pair were making their way through the crowd and heading in their direction. "They got the *nerve* to get back on this bus after that Jesse James shit they pulled yesterday! I oughtta yank the goddamn emergency cord myself." He reached out and put his arm protectively across Juanita. "Girl, wrap that purse strap around your arm. I hope you got on some comfortable shoes, 'cause we might have to kick us some ass up in here today!"

Juanita sat silently, fear and apprehension boring through her gut. The men were advancing. She glimpsed the top of their heads as they bobbed and weaved, slowly approaching the back of the bus. One sun-streaked blond, the other coal black.

She glanced around. Aside from Scooter, she knew there was no help to be found on the bus. The same passengers who had allowed these men to rob her couldn't be counted on to protect her now.

She would have to save herself. And possibly save Scooter as well. She slid her hand into her small purse and felt the comforting weight of cool metal in her palm.

I don't know karate, but I know ka-razor!

She had discovered it way down in the bottom of an old cedar chest. It had a little rust on it, but it would do. And Uncle Herbie would never miss it.

With sweaty fingers, Juanita pried the blade partially free of its protective sheath. She'd never handled a switchblade in her life, but under the circumstances she could become a fast learner. Besides, the way white folks slashed each other up on television, it looked easy enough.

After all, that's what knives were made for.

Cutting meat and cutting ass.

, , ,

Juanita stared into the eyes of the dark-haired fellow who planted his feet, held one arm behind his back, and stood towering over her. The muscles in his other arm coiled lazily as he reached up and grabbed an overhead strap, the six-pack of his abdomen bulging through his T-shirt with distinct definition.

"Que pasa?"

She scowled fiercely, refusing to be the first to break eye contact.

"Como estas jovencita? Busque tu bolsa por ti. Corri detras de ese blanquito y te lo busque."

"Don't be talking all that Neuyor-Reekin shit to me."

"Huh?"

"Speak English if you're talking to me!"

"Ay dios mio! Usted me esta diciendo que no sabes hablar o entender el espanol?"

"What? I told you I don't speak no Spanish!"

Laughing, the blond guy shoved his friend. "I told you!" he snapped. "She ain't no goddamn Latina! She ain't even Italian or Irish! She's just a nigger, *hombre*. Just a plain old greasy-ass *nigger*."

"Nita," Scooter ordered, "cuss this pineapple slam the fuck out."

Juanita was on her feet. Her hand snaked out of her purse and slipped behind her back, gripping the pearl-handled switchblade, confident that she could defend herself.

Standing toe-to-toe with the blond guy and balancing against the movement of the bus, her mouth flew open to challenge the racial epithet that had been hurled at her. But then she froze.

Nigger.

No one had ever accused her of that one before. She'd been described in a whole lot of other terms, but no one had ever thought she was black enough to be called a nigger. Let alone a *plain old* nigger. With or without grease. Suddenly she felt good. Damn good. She couldn't even bristle at his stereotypical use of the dreaded N-word. He could have called her a black *cucaracha* and that would have been all right, too, because if an asshole like him saw black when he looked at her, then he damn sure saw straight.

"Greasy nigger? And you're jealous, right?" She laughed and put her hand on her hip. " 'Cause I *am* a nigger!" She raked her eyes over her own body all the way to her toes. "I'm nigger down!"

///

"I'm sorry," Conan said for the twentieth time. "Please ignore him. My boy is stupid. Crazy! He doesn't know what he's saying. He's on medication and he can't control his mouth sometimes. Here." He pulled his hand from behind his back and held out her red knapsack. "I got your book bag back for you. I chased that white boy down and got it back. He got your money, though." Conan shrugged. "But when he tossed the bag, I went back and picked it up."

"Sheeeiit!" Scooter rolled his eyes. "Damn, man. You can't come no better than that? You and that white boy rolled off the bus like Batman and Robin! Tell that 'I was trying to catch him' shit to somebody else. Hell, working at Chase Manhattan, I deal with tens of thousands of dollars every day, and I know a criminal when I see one!"

"Oh, so you think I was down with that shit?"

"I *think* I'm a fine-ass Denzel Washington–Gregory Thompson–Maxwell–looking somebody. I *know* you were down with it."

Conan looked at the girl. Her school identification card had read Juanita. Juanita Lucas. But it seemed Jorge was right. She looked Puerto Rican, and her name sounded like it could be Latina, but she spoke no Spanish, and her tone and diction were decidedly African-American.

He asked her, "What do you think?"

She tilted her head and stuck out her lip.

Damn. All of that running for nothing. And then he remembered.

"Well, how do you think I got this?" He pointed to the bandage on his arm. "You saw me yesterday, right? My arm wasn't bandaged then, was it?"

Her exotic eyes renewed their doubtful cast.

"All right, then." He ripped off the bandage that his mother had reapplied that morning. The fresh wound was exposed, its edges raw and angry against the tanned hue of his forearm. "How the hell do you explain this? I ain't brave enough to have cut myself. And besides"— he chanced a small smile as he passed her the knapsack—"if I was down with it, would I be stupid enough to get back on the same bus and ask for your telephone number?"

Jorge howled. "Man, what the hell you want her number for? You heard her! She admitted it! She's not a Rican, *amigo*. She's black, man. *Black.* And ain't no black chick got no business giving you your digits!"

Conan searched Juanita's face. He liked what he saw. Liked the sound of her name on his lips. He didn't care what nationality she was. What color. Orange stripes with violet polka dots would have been fine. He just wanted to get to know her. To be in her presence.

She gazed back at him, and he almost thought he detected a softening of her chin. A slight settling of her shoulders. Just once he prayed that Jorge was wrong.

Just this once.

"555-4742." She treated him to a large, perfect grin. "And you can put that in your memory bank and stash it."

She turned to Jorge and scowled. "And you, *amigo,* can put it in your shoe and beat it."

CHAPTER 12

"So where did he take you?"

Juanita's sneaker-clad feet seemed to tread on clouds. A tender smile played along the corners of her mouth as she rode the receding waves of her magical night. She tied the laces of her navy blue Nikes and slipped a knotted silver chain over her head. A lone house key dangled from the chain and nestled above her pert breasts.

"Well?"

"We went to the movies."

"And?"

"And what?"

"Don't play games with me, Nita." Scooter's tone was sharp. Bitchy. He lay sprawled across Juanita's unmade bed with his hands behind his head, his fire-red shirt bright against his medium-brown skin. It was Saturday and they were going to the weekly skating affair at the Empire Roller Rink. Scooter had arrived early and was antsy and surly. Obviously miffed.

"It was no big deal, Scoot," Juanita placated him. Her words came out sounding like sunshine; her eyes conveyed her joy and she basked in the aftermath of her very first night on the town.

"Humph!" Scooter sat up straight. "No big deal? You meet a hot tamale after he steals your bag on the bus, and the next thing you know you're giving him your number and he's taking you to the movies the same night!" He rolled his eyes and sniffed. "Heffah wearing perfume now, too."

Juanita rubbed a glob of Blue Magic into both palms and raked her fingers through her hair. "I keep telling you, he didn't steal my bag, Scooter! He chased that crazy guy and got it back—that was a pretty bad cut on his arm. You saw it yourself."

"Yeah, right! His friend probably sliced him because he tried to sneak off without upping his share of your moolah. You're way too gullible, Nita. It was too damn convenient for him to get your bag back but not your cash."

Juanita paused with her hairbrush in midair and sighed. "Scooter, I only had four dollars. They could have split that chump change six ways to next Sunday and still come up broke. Besides"—she renewed her strokes, her wavy hair crackling with static electricity and flying out behind her—"it was my textbooks that were important. I'm just grateful he was able to get them back for me."

"How grateful? It takes a helluva lot of gratitude to make you go out with a guy on the same night he asks you." Scooter rose and walked over to Juanita's dresser. He snatched up a bottle of Johnson's Baby Oil, sat back down, and vigorously oiled his arms and elbows. "And you still haven't answered my question. Where'd Hector-the-hatchet-killer take you?"

Juanita sighed. "Conan," she said dryly. "The Barbarian. The Re-Show Theater. This week they showed *Forrest Gump.*" She admired her swinging ponytail in the mirror, unaccustomed to the raw weight of her hair against her back. "Afterward we walked over to Central Park, took a short carriage ride, and talked. And then we came home. That was it."

"Humph. Like I said. It's hard to believe you sat through that movie again out of gratitude. Went out with him at all out of gratitude."

Juanita shrugged. It was hard for her to believe it, too. In the span of twenty-four hours she'd accomplished quite a few firsts. She'd gone on her first date. Taken her first horse-drawn carriage ride. And defied her auntie's will for the very first time ever.

Conan lived about fifteen minutes away by foot, not far from Tilden Projects. They'd walked all the way to the Rockaway Avenue el station and rode the number 3 train into Manhattan, barely catching the special reshowing of *Forrest Gump*. Sitting in the cool, darkened theater, her nervousness vanished. She felt natural and free as her laughter swelled and mixed with the waves resounding through the audience. Conan, with his arm draped loosely over the top of her chair, also seemed to be enjoying himself.

At one point, Juanita had mentally tuned out the movie, the crowd, and even Conan. Elated, she smiled and hugged herself. For the first time in a long time, she felt normal. Just like anyone else. Despite her auntie's misgivings, she was out on a date with a fine guy who not only seemed to enjoy her company, but actually thought she was pretty.

And all night long, Conan had found ways to compliment her. He behaved like a perfect gentleman, and for once she didn't feel too fat, too fair, or too freaky. She was just a normal sistah enjoying a night out on the town, and she felt cozy and warm in her brief moment of happiness.

After the movie they strolled under the vibrant stars. They exchanged tidbits of their lives; she shared a few stories from her childhood, confessed how much she loved Scooter, and confirmed that he was her very best friend in the world. She even told him about her natural mother, how Patrice "Puddin" Lucas had died in childbirth and left her sister and brother, Aunt Hattie and Uncle Herbie, to raise her only child.

Conan was sympathetic, but pointed out how lucky she was to have family who loved her enough to raise her as their own. He apologized once more for his friend Jorge's crass behavior and said that although they were not related by blood, Jorge had lived with the Lopez family for many years.

Conan also told her he had a twin. Or rather, he used to have one.

"What do you mean you used to have a twin?"

"He was killed."

"Murdered?"

"I guess you could say that."

A pulse in his temple beat wildly. She used the tip of her finger to trace the path of a long, jagged scar that ran from the point of pulsation, slipped behind his right ear, and came to rest at a spot between his earlobe and jawbone.

"What happened to you?"

He took her hand and gently lowered it. He squeezed once before letting go. "It was nothing." His voice was somber and quiet. "It was nothing, and I don't like to talk about it."

There was no way she wanted to put a damper on the evening by probing for answers. Answers she had not earned a right to. Juanita smiled her understanding and suggested they stop for ice cream. To hell with her weight. With her hips. She was having such a good time, she'd get rid of those unwanted calories later.

When they reached Fifth Avenue, Conan jumped into one of several horse-drawn carriages. "C'mon." He offered his outstretched hand. "Let me help you up." Juanita giggled and reached for his hand, praying her weight wouldn't topple him from the cart and send him crashing down to the pavement. But there was security in the grip of his fingers, raw strength in his muscular arms; and, from the way she felt herself responding to him, perhaps sweet comfort there as well.

Juanita closed her eyes and reveled in pungent scent of horses and the rhythmic clomp of trotting hooves, basking in the glory of the night. With one heart, she and Conan laughed and whispered and floated blissfully along together, enjoying their very own magic carpet ride under the watchful lights of the city, around the peaceful perimeter of the park.

✦ ✦ ✦

"Did he at least bring you home? All the way to the door? Did Aunt Hattie get to meet him?"

Juanita stirred from the cradle of her sweet memories and turned to face Scooter. She'd almost forgotten he was in the room. She blinked rapidly, the afterglow of her rapture evaporating like fool's dust.

A troubled look fell across her face.

"Meet him?" she snorted. "She liked to scare him half to death."

Aunt Hattie had blown a wire. Short-circuited a fuse. Flat-out gone berserk. When Conan called and invited her to the Re-Show, both Aunt Hattie and Uncle Herbie had been ecstatic. Her first real date!

For once, she'd have someone other than Scooter to hang out with! But the moment Conan stepped into the apartment, the festive mood had dissipated.

"Believe it or not, Aunt Hattie had a tantrum," Juanita confessed. "Well, actually it was more like a shit fit or a kick-ass conniption." She grimaced as yesterday's storm swirled through her mind.

"You had to see her, Scoot. She flipped the script like she had a multiple personality disorder or something! Seemed like just the sight of Conan sitting on her sofa flipped her out."

"Did she go off?"

"Did she?" Juanita shook her head. "I could have died. Here this guy comes to my house for the first time and my auntie is running around acting a pure-dee fool."

Scooter looked puzzled. "Why'd she trip like that? She met him before?" He gave a short, harsh laugh. "Don't tell me Hector snatched your Aunt Hattie's purse, too!"

Juanita shuddered. "Not funny, Scooter." She flung herself down beside him on the bed and buried her face in embarrassment. She wiped her eyes on the soft, thick comforter and inhaled the sweet aroma of Downy and Tide before speaking. "It was just crazy! The moment Aunt Hattie saw him she swelled up and snatched me into the bathroom! Talk about Martha don't you weep, Mary don't you moan? She shoved me down on the toilet seat and clamped her whole hand over my forehead. 'Heal!' she kept shouting. Her words seemed all mixed up and jumbled—like she was having a Holy Ghost fit and speaking in tongues."

"Honey, *hush!*"

Juanita grimaced. "I shit you not. She was hooping and hollering and praying about my carnal corruption at the hands of those wicked Mexicans and Puerto Ricans!"

"Girl, *no!*"

"Yes! She must have thought I was my mama 'cause she kept calling me Puddin. I'm telling you, I had to fight my way out of there!"

Scooter squealed in disbelief. "Fool! You fought your auntie?"

"Well, I didn't really fight her, but shit was I scared! I've never seen her act like that before. Even Uncle Herbie couldn't get through to her. So I waited until she went to wipe the sweat from her face, then I jumped off the stool and ran out the door. Me and Conan hauled ass out of there, and don't ask me why, but for some reason I looked back. Scoot, I almost cried when I saw her standing there, trembling from head to toe and foaming at the mouth like a Saint Bernard."

"But why? Why would she trip like that? Just because a guy finally asked you out? I thought that was what she wanted!"

"Yeah, she did. But evidently she wanted the guy to be black. Or green, or even blue. But damn sure not Hispanic. She hasn't said much to me since last night, other than to make me promise never to see another Puerto Rican or Mexican or Dominican for the rest of my natural life."

Scooter frowned. "Damn, Nita. Your auntie is *that* prejudiced? I never knew that."

Juanita shook her head sadly. "Me neither. I guess I never really had an opportunity to see it before now; it's always been just you and me, and you know how much she loves you. But still, I have a right to pick and choose who I want to be with, who I want to get to know, don't I?"

Scooter nodded. A few days earlier he might have played the race card and sided with Aunt Hattie, but after his close encounter of the steamiest kind in the vault with his white branch manager, he wasn't so sure if race held any validity in affairs of the heart. Or in affairs, period.

Juanita continued. "You know yourself," she said. "Aunt Hattie always told us to love everyone, regardless of their race. She and your grandma taught us that humanity has no color; we are all children of God and part of His kingdom."

"Well," Scooter said, sighing and rising to his feet, "I guess she never figured the paler members of His kingdom would come knocking on her door asking to date her baby girl. But don't worry, Nita. Aunt Hattie'll be okay. We're coming up on the millennium. Things are changing; she'll come around. Grab your skates. We're gonna be late."

Juanita kneeled on the bed and gazed up at him. "So you agree with me? I should be able to date whoever I want as long as he's decent and he treats me right? Even if he's Puerto Rican?"

CONQUERING CONAN / 107

Scooter pulled Juanita to her feet. He couldn't have cared less about Conrad or Conan or whatever his name was. Besides, who could really verify that this guy was legit? On the up-and-up? The way he'd stepped to Nita on the bus seemed sho nuff oily. Thank God nothing more could come out of it. Aunt Hattie had forbidden it, and Nita wasn't fool enough to defy her auntie twice. Next time she called herself raising up on Aunt Hattie, she was likely to get the taste slapped out of her mouth. Nah, there was no chance of Nita dating the shady Reekin again. Why not make her feel good about it even though it couldn't last?

"Yeah, I agree. Even if he is Porta Reekin. It's all about who makes you feel good about yourself, and judging by the way you're grinning and smelling all sweet, I'd say you're feeling pretty damn good." He hugged his friend tightly and then held her out at arm's distance. "Girl, look at you! Got your hair all down your back looking like a high-yella Chilli from TLC! You need that. Need to feel good about yourself for a change, instead of always worrying about something or the other. . . . That happy smile really looks good on you, so God bless the Porta Reekin so-and-so who put it there!"

"You really mean that?"

"Yeah. I really mean it."

"Good!" A grin danced in her eyes. "Because he's meeting us at Empire in thirty minutes to join in on our Saturday-morning skating affair."

CHAPTER 13

Conan slipped from bed while the stars were mating placidly with the moon. Soundlessly, he pulled on his gray sweats and tied his Reebok running shoes. Jorge snored lazily nearby, one arm flung haphazardly over his head, the other buried down the front of his bright-red boxer shorts.

The tranquillity in the lull between twilight and dawn belied Conan's inner turmoil. The night had not passed gently. His dreams had been plagued with visions of broken glass and twisted metal, the smell of burning rubber and spilled fuel, the image of his brother's head, crushed and misshapen, one eye horribly detached and staring accusingly up at him. . . .

He shook his head, blinking away his night terrors and taking comfort in the solidity of the walls painted a serene sky blue, the small color television on its wobbly stand, and jovial posters of Jennifer Lopez and Oscar De La Hoya Scotch-taped to the closet door.

He crept from the apartment in silence, taking care to twist the doorknob without making a sound. The click of the tumbler falling in place as he locked the front door seemed to be the only noise in the building. As he passed the Andrewses' doorway, he paused to straighten their plastic doormat and push it flush against the bottom edge of the threshold. Mrs. Andrews didn't see well, and he wouldn't want her to trip and fall, or worse, Pushie to stumble over the mat with his walker.

Outside, the streets were empty, the parked cars coated with dew. Conan breathed deeply and set about awakening his sleeping muscles. He worked from his neck down; rolling his head, rotating his shoulders, gyrating his hips, extending and flexing his quads and hamstrings, stretching his calves, and finally, massaging the tendons behind his ankles.

Free weights were his poison of choice, but the way his lungs had burned after chasing down the bag thief proved it was time to vary his workout and get some cardio going.

He started out in a slow jog, heading toward the school yard on Lott Avenue. He ran without thinking, crossing Linden Boulevard against the light, leaping over curbs and avoiding soft patches of dew-soaked grass. He purposely cleared his mind; consciously prevented himself from thinking of her, of how she looked, the way her perfume licked at his senses and left his knees rubbery and weak, the easy way she smiled, the generosity in her wide green eyes.

An hour later, Conan was back in front of his apartment building greeting the rising sun; drenched in sweat, heart revved up a hundred beats, his mind heavy with thoughts of Juanita. After stretching and walking in large circles to cool his muscles, he sprinted up the stairs and began his weekend weight-lifting routine. Nothing heavy, just two sets of reps using very light weights to keep his muscles limber and alert. He'd just finished a set of preacher curls when Jorge's sleep-thick voice disturbed his peace.

"¿Que pasa? Why so early, amigo?"

"It ain't early. You just like to lay around all day."

Jorge rolled over and squinted at his alarm clock. "Man, it's not even seven-thirty. You know we always sleep in on Saturdays!"

Conan lowered the weights without effort. He looked over at his brother's bed, the bed that Jorge had claimed for himself the night of Thor's death, and sighed. "Not this Saturday, man. I got something else to do."

"That's what you said last night!" Jorge kicked off the striped sheets and staggered into the bathroom. He urinated in a long, hard stream without bothering to shut the door. The sound of the flushing toilet reverberated throughout the still apartment, chasing away the early-morning tranquillity.

"So." Jorge returned to the bed and plopped down heavily. He bounced slightly on the worn mattress. "Tell me what you did last night that was so important, and what you're doing that's so fuckin' important today."

Conan set the dumbbells on the floor and pulled his damp shirt over his head. He stared hard at Jorge. "What? You my woman? I ain't gotta tell you nothing, man. I don't ask where you go when you're not with me."

"Damn, *hombre*! I was just asking! Ain't no need to get your dick outta joint!" Jorge struck a match and held the flame against the end of a cigarette.

"Man, put that shit out." Conan stepped out of his shorts and stood naked before his friend. "You know my moms don't want you smoking in the house."

Jorge ignored him, taking long drags from the cigarette and blowing out large white rings.

"Asshole!" Conan grabbed his towel and stormed from the room. He ran the shower as hot as he could stand it and used large strokes to cover his body with lather. His attention wandered down to his manhood, flaccid under the battering spray of water.

He wondered if Juanita was a virgin. With her sexy eyes and perky breasts, he was sure some dude had already tried her. He was also sure she had resisted. She wasn't like that. She was a good girl. Not like the wild girls he knew, the ones who threw themselves on guys like him and Jorge, and who had no problem with the quick, easy sex. He didn't want that with Juanita. After all the beautiful young women he'd been with, Conan was ready for something more. Something meaningful. Something his heart told him he'd already found in Juanita.

He rinsed the soap from his hair, holding his head back to let the bubbles stream behind his ears. Already she had conquered him. But he would not touch her yet. Vowed to never even kiss her until she knew how much he loved her, how much he wanted to be with her in the right way. And not just as some roll in the hay. She was too good for that. She deserved so much more.

He reached down to wash his member and, to his surprise, found it had grown.

Hardened.

Conan squeezed his eyes shut and mentally recited his thirteen times tables. By the time he reached thirteen times nine his body was washed and rinsed, and his one-eyed monster had gone back to sleep.

"So." Jorge started up again as soon as he stepped into the room. He was perched on Conan's bed, smoking a fresh cigarette, with his knees bent and his bare back resting against the wall. "What'd you do last night? Did you hang out with some *chica*? Which one was it? Lourdes?"

Turning his back, Conan let his towel fall and dried his feet, paying special attention to the crevices between his toes. "Nah. I went to the movies."

"Oh yeah? What you see?

"Forrest Gump."

Jorge made a sucking sound of disrespect. "I can't believe you wasted your fucking cash to see that *gringo* Tom Hanks act like a retard. I thought you were saving your money to buy a headstone for Thor."

Conan whirled around. "Since when'd you start worrying about my money? About my brother?" He threw the damp towel at Jorge, striking him in the head. "If you gave a good fuck about my dollars, you wouldn't have tried to get me fired from my goddamn job!"

"Man, I already told you! Please don't start that shit again. I was trying to help you. That nigger just lied."

Conan backed off and grabbed a stick of Right Guard from the dresser. He rubbed it under his arms. "Yeah, okay. Whatever. Just do me a favor; don't watch my money or my back."

Jorge grinned, a strangely cold gesture that started and stopped at his mouth. "I was watching that darkie when she gave you her number yesterday. Did you take that coon to the movies? I bet she just loved old *Forrest Gump*. She probably got a thing for white boys. You know how them real light-skinned blacks are, always trying to pass for something they really ain't. Shit, you could probably pass yourself. Blue eyes, white skin. She got green eyes and yellow skin. . . . You two must look like a bowl of sherbet together. Hell, nobody even has to know you're Hispanic unless you—"

"Shut the fuck up!" Conan pulled his green polo shirt over his head and stuffed it down in his pants. His eyes flashed. "That's right. I took her out last night, and I'll take her out tonight if I want. As a matter of fact, as soon as I'm done checking on Pushie and Tante Rosira this morning, I'm gonna take her out again."

He bent over and put a small cuff in the hem of his jeans. "So if you got a problem with that, *hombre,* it's your fucking problem."

Jorge jumped up, his eyes pleading. "Yo, man. Where you going? It's Saturday. You know we shoot pool every Saturday morning! Besides, the tournament begins today. You know everybody's gotta be there!"

Conan grabbed his wallet and slipped it into his back pocket. He used a wide-tooth comb to tame his dark curls.

"Oh, so you ain't got nothing to say? You just gonna leave me hanging like that to go out with some bitch? Take her out later! Bennie is still on Riker's, so we can take tops this year! Shit, not a *maricon* out there can beat us, but if we don't get registered this morning and place in the first round, we'll get disqualified!"

"So?"

"So, you willing to just throw it all away like that? What about me? I'm your partner. Don't I count for something?"

Conan threw his bedspread over his sheets and grabbed a Dallas Cowboys cap. He walked over to the door. The pyre in his eyes grew dim. "Yeah, *amigo.* You do. You count for a lot. But I ain't gotta go to the pool hall to get my balls busted. Lately, you've been doing a damn good job busting them right here at home."

CHAPTER 14

"There he is!" Juanita pointed toward the crowd milling around the door. She waved both arms over her head frantically. "C'mon, Scooter, walk me over there. There's no way he'll see me from here."

Scooter snorted and rolled his eyes. "Nita, do you see all these black people? Humph! You can get off this line if you want to, but ain't no way in hell I'ma lose my spot for Ricky Ricardo. We've been waiting damn near an hour."

"Then save my place," she said, keeping her eyes on Conan's bright green shirt in the distance.

"What about when you get back? You know how these fools act when they think you're trying to jump the line." He waved. "Go on if you want to! Just hurry back before too many more folks roll up in here. All these damn lines are working my last nerve . . . a line to get in, a line to pay, a line to rent your damn skates . . ."

Juanita rushed off with Scooter's complaints far from her mind. She couldn't believe Conan was here. That he had shown up as promised. Not many Hispanics came to Empire; the neighborhood was tough and nearly all black. Quite a few times she had been mistaken for Puerto Rican and been taunted by a few brothers with firewater in their guts. She usually ignored them, chalking their mistakes up to alcohol and ignorance. Any fool could see she was black. There was nothing Spanish-looking about her.

Conan stood off to one side, not really in the winding line, but not far from it. His hands were in his pockets while he bopped his head to the reggae beat blaring from the surround-sound speakers. Juanita was surprised at how comfortable he appeared; he didn't look the least bit nervous. With his green shirt and his baggy blue jeans, he fit right in with the rest of the crowd. Except for that stupid cuff he always wore in his pants. She'd have to ask him about that later.

Her strides were long and anxious as she dodged through the crowd. She watched as two high-assed sistah-girls in tight shorts sauntered past Conan and eyeballed his goods, working him over thoroughly from head to toe. Judging by their squeals of delight, high fives, and the rapid fanning motion of their hands, it was obvious that, cuffed pants or not, they approved.

"Hey," she said shyly, approaching him from the side. "I'm glad you could make it."

Conan grinned, his teeth brilliant against his tanned skin. "Yeah, I'm glad too." He coughed. "You look really nice."

Juanita looked down self-consciously. She'd felt daring when she awakened, and instead of a simple pair of blue jeans she'd chosen black stretch pants and a long white shirt.

He added, "And your hair is nice, too."

It was her turn to cough and color rose quickly in her cheeks. "My friend Scooter is holding a spot for us on the line. C'mon. Let's go rent our skates while they still have some left."

Conan followed her over to the rental line. Scooter, his eyes shooting daggers, had advanced two paces closer to the counter. He had his hand on his hip, and his lip was poked out. "Ain't this some shit? All these folks out here standing in line waiting to give away their money, and ain't nobody up there ready to take it."

Juanita gestured. "Scooter, Conan. Conan, Scooter."

Scooter rolled his eyes. "We met, Nita! Remember? I saw the whole thing. I was right there when he . . . um . . . when he stole—when he gave you back your books," he mumbled. "If that's what you still wanna believe."

" 'Sup, man." Conan offered his hand.

They shook briefly, and as soon as their palms made contact, Scooter snatched his hand back and wiped it on the leg of his jeans.

Juanita bristled. "Scooter! What's wrong with you?"

"That's okay, Juanita." Conan soothed her. "It's cool. No biggie."

Scooter cut his eyes at Conan and swung around toward Juanita. "What's wrong with *me*? No, what the hell is wrong with *you*?"

"Don't go there," Juanita warned.

Scooter popped his fingers three times and swung his arm high in the air. "No, baby! You already took it there; up the block, around the corner, and down the goddamn street."

She sighed. "You done bumped your head. Move up, the line is going."

"You're the one who's crazy! Don't tell me what to do!"

"Okay, Scooter. I'm not in the mood to mess with you today."

Scooter swung around and turned on Conan. "Mess with me? Well, *Geraldo* here is damn sure itching for a chance to mess with you!" He turned on his heels and rocked his neck in a hard, bitchy twist before folding his arms across his chest.

The conversation was over.

Embarrassment flooded Juanita; crimson heat crept up her neck and settled high in her cheeks. "I'm sorry, Conan. I apologize for him. I don't know what's wrong with him. Why he's acting like this. I told him you were meeting us here and I thought he was cool with it."

Conan held up his hands. "Hey, it's my bad. You said this was your Saturday thing, and I shouldn't have offered to push up on that. Jorge is pretty pissed with me too. In fact, he would have tossed the place up if you had showed up with me at the pool hall!"

They laughed, the tension dissipating. "Look," he offered, "why don't I just break out and let you two get your groove on like you usually do? That's fair, right? We can always hook up later."

Juanita's eyes grew wide. "No! I mean . . . don't leave. Scooter gets like this sometimes, but it doesn't last long. Besides, he really likes you. He told me so this morning."

Conan chuckled and touched her hair. "Well, if that's how he acts when he likes somebody . . ."

More laughter. More awkward grins. Hands thrust into pockets and held behind backs.

"I'd like you to stay."

"Would you?"

"Yes, I would."

His grin was a hundred watts strong.

He shrugged. "Whatever you want, baby. That's why I'm here."

CHAPTER 15

Jorge leaped from the bed and stormed around in circles. Spittle flew from his mouth as he cursed and kicked at Conan's discarded towel, then swept his massive arm across the water-stained dresser. He smiled as the football memorabilia hit the floor: trophies, cards, and pendants, memoirs of Conan and Thor's feats on the playing field.

He stooped and retrieved a wood-framed eight-by-ten photograph lying atop the heap of rubble. Three youthful faces smiled up at him beneath the cracked glass. Twin faces with eyes of cobalt, and a third face with a golden cowlick peeking from his cap.

He stared at the face in the middle. His youthful reflection. Conan's mother had snapped the photo ten years earlier during a winter vacation in Rochester, New York. Each of the boys wore multicolored ski caps and bulging, down-filled jackets. Each of them also wore a smile, although Jorge's never made it past his red-tipped nose.

He swore aloud and flung the picture across the room. Glass shattered against the wall and rained down in a glistening heap on the floor. Shit like that is what pissed him off. Just the sight of the picture sent him over the edge. As usual, Conan had wanted to stand in the middle, in between Jorge and Thor. From the time they were kids Conan had always tried to stand out. To get the center spots for himself. Pushing his way to be the one people always noticed first. And Thor. What a fuckin' bitch! Always crying about something stupid. Running to tell his father on Jorge whenever he accidentally bumped him or elbowed him or pushed him down the stairs. He'd hated Thor. He only pretended to like him for Conan.

But sometimes Jorge thought Conan liked Thor best. He was always taking up for him. Stroking his ego. Defending the little faggot. Whenever Jorge suggested they do something really down together, Conan made sure his brother was invited along too. Like he couldn't make his own friends!

Things were definitely better with Thor gone. Much better. Yeah, Conan cried like a little faggot every other night, but he usually chilled out by morning. His guilt had him all tangled up in grief. And why not? He was so fucking spoiled! Used to having every goddamn thing. Didn't know what it felt like not to have anybody. What the fuck did he have to cry about? He had a good job, his mother, his best friend, and even his real fucking father! Jorge grimaced. And now it looked liked the Top Cat even had a girlfriend!

His eyes narrowed under his sloping brow. He opened the bottom dresser drawer and unrolled a dirty tube sock, then extracted a small tin of foil, removed a tiny blue pill, and dry-swallowed it. Sitting on the floor, he closed his eyes and waited for the feeling to flow. He drummed his fingers on the worn linoleum. He was starting to get tired of Conan. Fucking him around like that on the day of the tournament. Every Saturday for the past three years had been dedicated to shooting pool. He usually tagged along while Conan checked on that twisted, broken-down veteran, Pushie Andrews, and then went to visit Victor's elderly aunt, Tante Rosira. And then the two of them headed straight to the pool hall. Even after Thor died, they'd still played pool. And on today of all days, his *hermano* had left him high and dry to hang out with some nigger bitch with *un culo nargas grande.*

Jorge lit a cigarette. The last one in the pack. He squeezed his fist. If he had enough money he'd split this scene in a heartbeat. He was sick of this setup. Grace Lopez walking around him with her pleading, sad blue eyes. Conan's raggedy-ass old man, Victor, with his stupid rules and noble attitude. Shit! Victor liked to bitch about him not contributing any money to the family, when it was him that needed a better job! A fuckin' mailman! Wasn't it his fault the man of the house got paid in peanuts? What? Twelve, fifteen dollars an hour? How was a man supposed to take care of a family on that?

Money. The problem was always money. He needed a solid hookup like that faggoty gay-bird on the bus. The skinny black kid who hung with Conan's bitch. If he could hustle up enough greenbacks, he'd hire a fishing boat to Puerto Rico and make a killing transporting blow. Then he'd cut it up, cook it, package it, and hire a few niggers to sell it on the streets as crack.

Money. That was the only way to get from under the rock of shit that had landed on his head. If he waited around until he saved up enough dough working at his slave-wage job, he'd be as old and broke-down as Victor before he could roll out.

Nah, he had to figure out how to get some dollars quicker than that. Besides, he had a feeling his days were numbered at Grayson Field. Either he was gonna have to take that nigger Chance out, or be taken out himself. He put his head back and laughed, the sound chilling in the empty room. Picture that shit! A *gringo* taking him out! A nigger *gringo* at that! He thought about Bobby, his mother's boyfriend. That foul motherfucker. The only thing niggers were good for was sucking his prick. Other than that, he had no use for them.

Especially the old ones. Niggers like Pushie Andrews and his fat-fuck wife, who carried enough chitterlings, mothballs, and old-age smells to kill a horse. He knew Pushie got a veteran's check each month, and probably Social Security too. Conan was all the time running downstairs taking care of them like they were family or something. He probably thought Pushie was gonna leave him some dough when he kicked the bucket. Jorge opened his mouth wide and laughed again. Everybody knew Pushie was mental. He had flashbacks from toeing that landmine in Vietnam, and even when he was in his prime he drank more wine than a little bit. Was probably still signing his entire check over to the West Indian man in the liquor store, and would be until they shot his old ass and put him in the ground.

His humor restored, Jorge searched through the lone closet and pulled on a pair of Conan's navy blue Dockers. He kneeled down and cuffed the hems. When he stood up straight again, the pants were slightly short, but he left them that way. He rummaged in a drawer and found a blue-and-white Barry Sanders jersey. Conan's favorite. He turned to the mirror and ran his fingers through his hair. His short blond curls felt feathery and light. He studied himself. Blond hair was for bitches. If his hair were a little darker, he'd look just like Ricky Martin. That fake-ass former Enrique Morales who had changed his name to trick people into thinking he was a *gringo*. Yeah, Ricky could sing, but there was something sissy-looking about his face.

But black hair, that would be something. If he dyed his hair and his mustache, he'd look legit. He studied his profile and grinned.

Damn straight. He'd look just like Conan.

/ / /

Hattie grasped the chicken by its hind legs and held it up in the air. Large droplets of water fell from the carcass and splashed into the murky sink below.

"Okay, Herbie. He's cleaned and singed, now you cut him up."

Herbie leaned heavily on his walking stick and made his way over to the sink. Tangled veins, bloody arteries, and yellow gobs of chicken fat were pushed neatly off to one side. A chipped porcelain bowl held a scrawny neck, a lump of liver, a tendon-laden gizzard, and a peculiar-shaped heart. He covered his trach opening with his index finger. "You want the drumstick cut away from the thigh?"

"Please."

Herbie examined the wooden knife rack sitting toward the back of the counter and selected a long-blade butcher knife with a scalpel-sharp cutting edge. With his left hand braced against the chicken's legs, he sawed through its breastbone, then split and quartered the bird with swift, even strokes.

"If the job was left to me," Hattie spoke in an admiring tone, "I'da cut off both my thumbs and still be trying to hack that poor yardbird to pieces."

She used a paper towel to pick up the discarded fat and goo, then sprayed the entire area down with a mixture of Clorox and water stored in an old spray bottle. With that done, she lifted the lid on a two-quart broiler and checked her simmering pieces of smoked turkey, then swirled her finger around in a plastic container full of black-eyed peas that were soaking in cold water.

"I'm fixin' all this for Nita," she said aloud.

Uncle Herbie grunted heavily and split a wing apart from its connecting breast.

"Just feel like I ought to do something special for her on account of how I treated her yesterday."

"Why not jest 'pologize?"

" 'Cause I ain't sorry! You know I gots to protect that chile. You thank I need to be sorry for trying to keep her safe and whole?"

Herbie coughed as a phlegm-filled mass of fluid was forced from his lungs. "I thank you need not wurry yo'sef so much about that thar gal and let her live a li'l bit while she young."

"She living!" Hattie grabbed a dishcloth and began wiping down the kitchen table in small, tight strokes. "Living 'bout as much as she need to!" She put her hands on her ample hips and spun around to face her older brother. "Herbie, that boy is *Spanish*! Probably Mexican! I don't want the likes of him hanging round my Nita! Humph! Look like you would be the first somebody to run him outta here!"

"He ain't done nuthin' wrong, Hat. He jest a boy. That's all."

"Just a boy? Have you gone fool? Them animals what got hold of me and Puddin was 'jest boys' too, huh?" Tears rushed to Hattie's eyes. After all these years, her anger had resurfaced with a vengeance. Just the sight of that Conan boy with his wavy hair and olive skin, his sinister Mexican looks, nearly sent her into shock. Her long-buried scars ripped open afresh, pain and guilt seeping from them like pus on a festering wound.

Herbie set the knife in the sink and rinsed his hands. He tore off a paper towel and dried them before speaking, "Look a here, Hat. Gal, you gots to let the past rest. You cain't live your life hatin' them boys. It'll kill you. It'll kill Nita." He shuffled closer to his sister and touched her arm.

"I promised you a long time ago that I would never leave you. That after what happened that night I would always protect you. When you brung that itty-bitty red baby home, that promise stretched out to cover her too." He coughed violently, hacking spittle into his crumpled paper towel until he recovered.

"What happened to Puddin is done. Ain't nuthin gon' bring her back. If I could do it all over again, Lawd knows I'da been a different man that day. A better man. I ain't never gon' forget what you went through 'cause of me, how you and Puddin suffered, how much you both sacrificed for me."

A tear slid down his cheek. "It was me who brung them boys in the house, Hattie. Me. I thought they was my friends, my band brothers, and that's a fact gonna haunt me till the day I die. I carries that burden wit' me every day, Hat, and I'ma take it wit' me to my grave."

Herbie wiped his eyes and nose with the back of his hand before continuing. "Don't let our sins rest on that gal's shoulders, Hat. For the first time in her life she got sumthin' more'n us and Scooter. That boy may be Porto Rican. He may be Mexican. He may even be Cuban. But he ain't had a nickel in our quarter."

His voice became firm. "It weren't him what hurt you. Weren't him what took Puddin. Jest like all us coloreds ain't the same . . . all them Spanish cain't be the same neither. They got some good ones too. Lawyers, science men, and yeah, even musicians. Maybe he one of the good ones."

Hattie stared at her brother. She knew his love for Nita ran as deeply as hers, and his grief over Puddin's death was just as immeasurable. But Herbie was wrong and Hattie didn't truck well with fools. Herbie had been knocked out. Inoculated from the pain and humiliation his sisters had been forced to endure at the hands of his drunken friends.

No, Herbie could go to shit. He hadn't seen those evil dark eyes hovering in the air as her body was nearly ripped in two by the legion of depraved Mexicans attacking and devouring her flesh. He hadn't felt the searing humiliation of being spread apart and having her every orifice probed and violated with common household items from her own kitchen.

Herbie, in his merciful slumber, had been spared the task of watching fourteen-year-old Puddin, her breasts full, her hips saucily lush, taken savagely from the front and rear at the same time. His eyes had been shut against the naked terror in her face, the tremble in her voice as she sobbed and begged and pleaded, "Help me, Hattie. Help me."

Herbie had not been held down and forced to bear witness to his sister's pitiful anguished screams, moans, and then whimpers while her last breath was squeezed from her throat as her rapist reached an explosive, roaring climax.

No. Herbie hadn't cowered beneath the loathing and hatred in their father's eyes as he ranted and raved and accused his eldest daughter of enjoying and even provoking the grisly attack. His flesh had not been burned raw when their father spat on her and called her a tramp, the lowest kind of whore, a lying Jezebel, holding her down and screaming while their neighbor, Mizz Rosalee, shoved the hot coat hanger deep inside her privates, killing whatever would grow there as he asked, "Jes how much a' that stank pussy did them boys git from you, anyway?"

No, siree. Herbie's memories had stopped the moment his throat was cut and his skull was bashed in. Them drunken Spanish bastards would have done her a favor had they bashed her head in too.

Tears spilled from her eyes and she shook her head. Hattie spoke quietly in hurt, hushed tones. "See, that's where you wrong, brother. That's where you wrong." She pointed one gnarled and trembling finger toward her own face. "After what these eyes done seen, the pictures these-here eyes can still see today? Brother, believe me when I tell you: The only good Spanish boy is a dead one."

CHAPTER 16

Moist heat filled the crowded elevator car. Its occupants were packed in sardine-style, front to rear. Juanita stood sandwiched between Conan to her front and Fontaine Fredricks from the eighth floor to her rear. She had a dilemma; it was either press her breasts against the hard muscles of Conan's back or endure the repulsive jiggle-jangle of Mrs. Fredricks's gut.

Her skin crawled as she chose the latter. It was better than allowing her body to touch his in such an intimate way. Her auntie had taught her all about chastity and self-respect. Although Mrs. Fredricks's bosom felt like warm water balloons, there was no way she wanted to rub against a young man who seemed to respect her.

The elevator doors opened on the fourth floor and several people spilled out, relieving her of her discomfort. There was silence in the car, and folks busied themselves looking at the floor, the ceiling, or the lighted indicator. Anywhere except at one another.

Finally, it was her floor. She nudged Conan gently in the back.

" 'Scuse me," she muttered, stepping past several boys her age. She knew every one of them; they'd all been raised right in this building, but they hardly ever spoke. When they were kids, they'd given her a fit about her weight and eyes, and when they were really fired up they snatched at her bun and made her hair spill down her back. All of that stopped after Dante Coleman. After what she and Scooter put on him, not one of them had dared put their hands on her or talk shit to her face. She'd gotten herself a rep.

"Casper got her hair out today," one of the guys said as they stepped from the elevator car.

"Yeah," said another. "She got a chump motherfucker with her too. He best get ghost before dark!"

Juanita hurried from the car. She glanced at Conan and was surprised at how calm he appeared. Self-confident and assured. His gait was measured and leisurely; he walked like a man who was in no hurry.

As the elevator doors slid closed behind them a boy yelled, "Fuckin' half-white sellout!"

What the hell was wrong with them? Couldn't they see she was just as black as they were? Juanita wanted to either clamp her hands over her ears or scream back at them, but wasn't about to let Conan think she was sweating any of it. Instead, she gave him a bright smile and stopped in her tracks.

"Um . . . right here is cool. You don't have to walk me all the way to the door. Maybe you should take the stairs down and get back home."

Conan tapped her arm lightly. He walked over to the Plexiglas window overlooking the project playground and leaned against the waist-high sill. "I thought you had a good time."

"I did."

"Then why are you trying so hard to get rid of me?"

She blushed. "I'm not . . . just don't want anything . . ."

He motioned to her. "Don't worry about me. I can take care of myself. C'mere."

Juanita moved closer and joined him at the sill. They looked out over the project scenes: the iron horse as it rumbled past on the elevated tracks; the laughing children playing the lyrical games Juanita had longed to join when she was a child; the young street toughs huddled together for courage and security.

Conan rocked back on his heels. "I feel like I'm still rolling on skates."

She giggled. "Me too. It takes some getting used to, but you did pretty good considering it was your first time."

He patted his buns. "Yeah, right! I probably won't be able to sit down for the next three weeks!"

They laughed again, and then silence stepped between them.

Juanita looked down at his feet. "Why do you cuff your pants like that? It looks pretty crazy."

A cloud passed over Conan's face. "To honor my brother. We were identical twins, and when we were kids my mom always dressed us alike. Thor was picky about his clothes, and in order to keep his stuff separate from mine he tore the tag out of his shirts and cuffed the hem of his pants. When he died I just sorta picked up the habit."

"I'm sorry. It looks a lot less crazy now that I understand why you do it."

Conan nodded.

"What's your middle name?"

He looked startled. "Damn! Who woulda thunk it? Nobody ever asked me that one before. It's Matthew."

"Matthew? That's not Puerto Rican!"

"Well neither is Conan. I'm only half Puerto Rican. My mother is Irish. Irish Catholic, raised in England. She met my father when he was in the Army stationed in Germany, and she was a teenager living there with family friends. They got married and he brought her here, and she's never been back to her homeland. Matthew was her brother's name. If you haven't figured it out yet, my mom is a Marvel Comics nut. Always has been. Can't you tell? That's why she gave me and my brother such crazy names. Thor John Lopez and Conan Matthew Lopez. Can you believe it? I guess that was better than naming us Spider-Man Jose and Batman Eduardo. Now, what's your middle name?"

"I don't have one."

Conan burst out laughing, but the laughter died on his lips when he saw she was serious. "What do you mean you don't have a middle name? Doesn't everybody have one? You know, like when they give you a second name to honor some old dead relative or something? Everybody does."

Juanita looked at her shoes. "Everybody except me. The only dead relative I know of is my mother. And her name was Patrice even though they called her Puddin."

"Puddin, huh? Well, why'd she name you Juanita?"

"She didn't. My auntie did. I have no idea why."

Conan looked puzzled. "Haven't you ever asked?"

"No."

Her voice was sad. He reached out and smoothed her hair.

"What's this?" He rubbed his fingers together, surprised.

"Hair grease!"

"Hair grease? For what?"

She laughed. "For my hair, silly!"

His face went blank. "Why do you do that . . . you know . . . put grease in your hair?"

Juanita sighed, "It's what black people *do*. Our hair is not as oily as white people's hair, so it requires a little extra help. Hair grease makes it shiny and easier to manage." She giggled. "It's a black thang . . . you wouldn't understand it."

He cast her a doubtful look. "Your hair looks almost the same as mine. I'm not white, and I don't grease my hair."

"That's because you're not black either! My hair might not look all that black, but my soul sure is. And that's where it counts." She gave him a tough smile. "I guess I'm saying it loud: I'm black and I'm proud!"

"Okay, okay . . ." He held up his hands in a gesture to ward off her wrath. "I like black girls, Juanita. Can't you tell?"

She grinned. "Have you ever dated one before?"

His eyes were earnest. "No, but I always wanted to. I've always admired the way black women seemed so strong and capable. So damn fine. Like they either have it all together or know how to get it there."

"So why haven't you ever asked a sistah out? You scared to come out of the closet and admit you have a thing for dark meat?"

"See there." Conan chuckled. "It ain't even like that. I'm here with you, right? There just isn't a lot of that going on in my neighborhood. I mean, my mother and father are one thing, and there's an old black guy in my building, Pushie, who has a Mexican wife, Miss Angelique, but other than that—oh yeah, Jorge's stepdad was black too, so there are a few mixed couples that I know of, but not many."

"I see."

"Like I said, though. Black women seem strong . . . sometimes in ways that other women aren't. I really admire and respect that in them, but maybe that's why there aren't a lot more Puerto Rican men with sisters on their arms. Not too many of them can handle the challenge."

Juanita agreed. "Most black women are capable because they have to be. Strong for the same reason. Certainly not because we don't need men. It's just that with society and the media constantly telling us what's beautiful and what's not . . . and a lot of our own men buying into that shit and believing it . . ." Juanita frowned. "I've always wished I had darker skin. Not that I don't look black, 'cause I know I do. Just wished I could look even blacker. I'm dying to get twists in my hair."

Conan pushed. "Are you . . . you know, mixed with something?"

"Yeah." She laughed. "Gin and juice."

His smile was warm. "No, it's just that you don't really look like your aunt or uncle, and to tell you the truth, when I first saw you I thought you were Latina."

"I don't know exactly what all I am," Juanita admitted. "I mean, I know I'm black. Straight up African-American. That's obvious. But who knows what other blood I have running through my veins? And really, who the hell cares? I'm a black woman and that's all I really care about. The funny thing is, I don't look a thing like my mother, either. I've seen pictures of her, old black-and-white snapshots of her as a child. She was tall and built, had a real sistah-girl figure. Her skin was deep chocolate and her smile was awesome. It's a shame we don't have any pictures of her taken after she was thirteen or so. I would loved to see what she looked like as an adult. Or maybe even see how she looked when she was pregnant with me."

"Maybe you look like your father."

Juanita sighed and turned away. She ran her fingers across the nape of her neck, her eyes downcast. "I don't know. I have no idea who my father was. We don't talk much about those things in my house. It makes my auntie too sad for me to even mention my mama. Her baby sister. There's so much I don't know. . . . I guess it hurts my Aunt Hattie to talk about it because my mother was far too young and she died way too soon."

Conan reached out and took her hand gently in his. He squeezed her fingers lightly and then released them.

"Well." He swallowed hard. "Try to feel good about what you do know. We're all just one nation under a groove anyway. You might not know what all's inside of you, but at least you know you've got a little bit of chocolate."

Juanita's smile was brilliant. "And you, Señor Lopez, you've got a touch of sangria."

⁄ ⁄ ⁄

Their conversation lulled as the sun began its descent. The elevator clicked softly and rhythmically as it moved up and down the shaft. Being close to Juanita had desire leaping through Conan's veins. In a moment of weakness he leaned in toward her, his lips aching for just a sip of her sweetness. He was inches away, but already his tongue imagined the secrets of her mouth. The sweet warmth of her wetness, her sensuous lips and her gentle kiss.

Juanita stood still, her eyes half shut, her teeth visible through her parted lips. Her white shirt was molded to her skin, her nipples hardened into tiny pebbles. He moved closer and she closed her eyes, enraptured, delicious shivers of anticipation racing across her face. Like a baby bird welcoming food from its mother, she raised her lips, eager to accept a taste of his love.

Conan's back stiffened. His eyes flew open. Her breath was on his face. Her eyes were closed, yet trust shined through. And she was beautiful.

Damn! He had to maintain his control. He had to get her into her apartment. Under the safety of her auntie's eagle eye. He was dying to pull her into his arms and feel her softness against him, but Conan was mindful of his vow and knew he shouldn't be close to her for another moment.

Already he held her in the highest esteem. Had the utmost respect for her. Yeah, he wanted to be with her. Wanted to know every inch of her, but he wasn't interested in having just her body. He could get sexed down anywhere and any time. He wanted her mind and her heart.

"C'mon," he said gently, stepping away from her and leading her toward her apartment. "It's time for you to go inside. Your aunt might be worried about you."

Juanita hung back, slightly embarrassed. Every inch of her felt good; a beat pulsated between her legs that made her want to wrap them around his back. Why had he stopped? Her eyes hungrily roamed his physique. Conan had awakened something in her that was ready to spring free.

But he was right. She should be ashamed of herself for keeping boy company right out in the hallway. And there was no doubt that Aunt Hattie was worried. She was almost five hours later than usual. Scooter had left the skating rink halfway into the Saturday morning affair, but she and Conan had lingered, walking through Lincoln Terrace Park and skimming rocks on the tiny pond.

Conan walked ahead of her and stopped in front of her door. He turned to face her, his eyes hungry but restrained, and said, "Juanita. I want you to know how much—"

The apartment door flung open and Aunt Hattie stepped out.

"Nita! Why ain't you come home with Scooter? I know good and durn well I told you not to see this boy again!" Hattie shook her finger in Conan's face and he backed up, stunned by her rage and her fear. "You ain't welcome in my home, ya hear? You ain't welcome! Next time you come 'round here, I'ma call the cops to come for you! You stay 'way from my baby, you low-down slimy rascal! You stay 'way!" Hattie bared her teeth and narrowed her eyes; her fingers were clawlike as she hissed like a snake, "Or I swear. With God as my witness, I swear! Just like Daniel slew that lion, I swear I'll tear yo' ass from stem to stern with my own two hands!"

'''''''''''''''''''''''''''''

CHAPTER 17

The weekend seemed to melt away into Monday, and for a moment there was a peaceful lull in the after-the-weekend check-cashing frenzy at Chase Manhattan Bank.

"The Madison Group's payroll is complete, Evvie. Gwen and Connie are at their stations, and I'm heading out for lunch."

Evvie was entering account numbers into a ledger. At the sound of Scooter's voice, she smiled and peered over the top of her wire-rimmed bifocals. "Go ahead, Socrates. Eat something healthy. Dinner this Friday will be matzo soup and whitefish."

Scooter made a quick trip to the men's room and washed his hands. Money was filthy, and the countless bills he handled during the course of an average banking day left a grimy coating on his hands that made him itch. Applying a thin coating of Vaseline to his clean hands, he joked for a moment with Jesse Muhammad, then left the air-conditioned bank and stepped into the noonday heat of downtown Brooklyn. It felt good to be outdoors enjoying the sunshine. The endless sky shimmered ocean blue and the clouds seemed to have gone on vacation.

He strolled easily, swinging his arms and rolling his narrow hips. In his charcoal-gray gabardine slacks, gray-and-burgundy striped tie, and starched, short-sleeved white shirt, he looked every bit the image of a young, upwardly mobile black man on the move.

He passed several elderly ladies sitting on a bench, feeding bread-crumbs to dozens of hungry pigeons. "Good afternoon, ladies," he called out. "Y'all are sure looking good today!" Titters of laughter and a chorus of hellos pierced the air, the old women happy that the hand-some, well-dressed youngster had taken a moment to acknowledge them.

Scooter continued on his stroll, peeking into decorated windows and eyeing the bargain merchandise displayed on racks along the streets. Businesses of all types sprouted in this heavily traveled area. Scores of shops lined the vibrant streets, and a savvy shopper with a few bills could make quite a killing. The store owners were mostly Korean immigrants, and while most blacks hated giving them their business, the competition was heavy and it kept the prices low.

A familiar aroma wafted through the air, and Scooter followed his nose into Sal and Joe's Pizzeria. He placed three crisp dollar bills on the counter. "Can I get a slice with extra cheese?"

Feeling generous, he dropped two coins into the tip jar and took the piping-hot pizza from the clerk; he shook flakes of garlic and crushed red peppers over the blistering cheese before folding the triangle in half and wrapping tissue paper around the crust. He blew on the tip, then bit into the crust and tore a long ream of melted cheese from the top. Chewing noisily, he wiped the greasy drippings from his hands before resuming his strut down Fulton Street.

Ten minutes later he found himself standing outside of Albee Square Mall. He stopped to check the wares of several street vendors along the curb.

"Five dollars, my man. Get your oldie-but-goodie tapes and CDs right here for five dollars. We got the Whispers, the Chi-Lites, the O'Jays, Sly and the Family Stone, Blue Magic, the Persuaders, Brenda and the Tabulations, First Choice . . ." The young black vendor wore a T-shirt depicting scenes from the Million Man March.

Scooter glanced at the shirt and felt an immediate kinship with the hustling brother. He worked hard for his duckets too, and was proud to have been in Washington on that historic day. He'd stood side by side, shoulder to shoulder, hand in hand with the men of this country who were his African brothers, united in struggle for social and economic empowerment. Never mind that he was gay. Sexual orientation didn't matter when it came down to sisters and brothers doing their thing in their rightful place in society.

"Right on, my man." He pulled a ten-dollar bill from his wallet and purchased a Blue Magic CD and a copy of *Birthday,* one of his all-time favorites from New Birth.

Scooter walked on and browsed the wares of another vendor. Jewelry, scented incense, socks; an assortment of everyday items lined the crowded table. A glitter of gemstone caught his eye, and he reached down and touched an exquisite crystal elephant trimmed in gold.

"Damn," Scooter breathed. The piece was elegant and creative. It sat in a green felt box and sparkled up at him. Juanita loved elephants. She collected them. After opening her day care, her dream was to eventually attend a major university where she could pledge Delta Sigma Theta.

"Hey, my man!" Scooter held the elephant in the air, the sun sparkling off the fine crystal and casting its beauty to the breeze. "How much you want for this?"

"That's twenty-five, but for you, my brother, I'll let it go for fifteen."

Scooter fished in his back pocket for his wallet and froze.

Bells and whistles clanged in his head. He'd forgotten! He wasn't even speaking to Juanita, let alone buying gifts for her flaky ass!

"Sorry, bro." He pushed his wallet back down. "Maybe another time."

It hadn't taken much for him to forget!

To hell with "wide-ass" Juanita "back-that-load-up" Lucas!

Suddenly the glaring sun was obtrusive instead of soothing. The city heat seemed to have deposited a coat of grime on everything in sight. The mozzarella left a foul taste in his mouth.

It wasn't that he was jealous of Juanita's new friend. Why should he be? Lord knows she'd never had a real friend other than him during her whole life. Perhaps it was time for both of them to branch out. But she still had a lot of nerve inviting that joker to the Saturday morning skating affair. For as long as he could remember it had been just the two of them; him and Juanita, holding hands and skating, learning new moves and dance steps, falling to the floor in laughter, and getting right back up to try it all over again.

She should have asked him if she could bring Conan along. But no. She had invited the asshole first, and *then* told him about it.

And talk about pitiful on wheels?

The spastic idiot had stayed sprawled on the floor more than he was on his feet. With the devil riding him, Scooter had skated past them a time or two and clipped Conan's skate blades, sending the Reekin *and* Juanita crashing to the scratched wooden floor.

And it served them right. They both deserved it. He'd seen the way dude looked at her. And how Juanita had looked back at dude too! Not once did she tug on her shirt the way she usually did when she was worried about her fat rolls showing or her hips looking too wide.

Not!

Juanita had actually glowed. Looked comfortable. Leaned all close to the guy, holding on to his arm like it was an inflatable raft and she was drowning in spit! No. She had too much damn nerve ignoring him like that after all the years of him being her only friend! Some damn friend she was. He wasn't even eating at her house anymore. Had refused to speak to her on the bus. Not that she'd noticed. These days she stood up talking to her new Don Juan all the way in. Let *him* buy her a goddamn elephant!

Scooter stormed back the way he'd come. The city streets had lost their attraction. The vibrant colors now seemed dull and faded. He pulled a pair of sunglasses from his pocket and slapped them on his face. He was crossing east on Nevins Street and heading straight for Chase Manhattan when he was jostled from behind.

"Watch it!" he whirled, enraged by the stranger's clumsiness. "Watch where the hell you're . . ." He snatched off his sunglasses and to his surprise, the man he faced was not a stranger at all.

"Uh . . . hey."

"Whassup."

"I didn't know who the hell had bumped me."

"My bad. I tripped."

Scooter averted his gaze, unsure of where to put his eyes. There was something unsettling in the way the man stared at him.

"Well . . . um . . . that's okay. It ain't no thing."

"Yeah."

Scooter coughed, although he had felt no real need to. "All right, then. I gotta go. You know. Gotta get back to work and shit."

"Me too. I work at Grayson Fields, over on Jackson. You work in a bank, don't you?"

Scooter laughed, impressed. "Damn, you got a good memory! Yeah, I work at Chase Manhattan. I'm a um . . . a supervisor and stuff like that."

"Yeah? Well, that ain't all I remember about you, man."

A half grin froze on Scooter's face. The man combed his body from his eyes to his shoes and then back to his eyes. Then he smiled, and dimples that were much deeper than Scooter's creased his tanned cheeks.

Scooter hesitated. "What else you remember?"

His voice was low and sensual. "I remembered you had some pretty lips. Yeah. You look like you might be able to do a little somethin'-somethin' with them big pretty lips."

Scooter's mouth ran dry. His blood ignited and his heart hammered in his chest. Against his will, his penis leaped.

Embarrassed yet emboldened, he shifted his weight to one leg and let his hand fall and cover his crotch. "Something like what?"

"I tell you what. Lemme bounce with you for a minute. I'll walk you back to your job and tell you what I think. I remember a lot about you, but for some fucked-up reason I can't remember your fuckin' name."

"It's Scooter. Scooter Morrison."

The young man extended his hand and Scooter felt himself respond in kind.

"Yeah . . . Scooter, that's right. I'm Jorge, man. Jorge Corona."

﹀ ﹀ ﹀

"So what kinda supervising you do at Chase Manhattan?"

They walked side by side along the congested sidewalks.

"Well, mostly I'm a payroll supervisor. You know. I cash large checks for businesses so they can pay their employees from their locations instead of giving everyone time off to cash their paychecks. When I'm not doing that, I supervise the paying and receiving tellers."

Scooter stole a glance at Jorge and liked what he saw. Dude was fine! He thought of Juanita and felt a momentary pang of guilt, but hell, what was good for the gander was damn sure good for the goose. You could cook them both in the same sauce. Besides, if Juanita didn't mind being called a greasy nigger, who was he to complain?

"I'm about to make supervisor myself," Jorge reported. "I hooked my boy Conan up with a job at Fields, and that bastard almost got me fired. But the shit backfired on him, and now he's about to get canned and I'm about to be promoted."

"I thought you two were friends?"

"Yeah, we used to be, but that fucker's been playing me too close. He's gotta learn to respect my space."

"Yeah, I know what you mean. I had to cut Juanita loose too. She was sucking up all my air."

"You gotta know how to back a motherfucka up offa you."

Scooter smiled. *Get a ruff-neck gotta get a ruff-neck!*

Jorge's singsong accent and bad-boy image were a definite turn-on. Or rather a turn-up, since Scooter was already turned on. He envisioned his dark skin naked against Jorge's bronze tan.

Jorge asked, "So how long you been working at the bank, my man?"

The way "my man" rolled off the Latino's tongue sent a delicious shiver through Scooter's stomach. Jorge's piercing eyes and dimpled grin fascinated him to no end. Flecks of golden hair stood out on his tanned arms. Scooter allowed his gaze to travel the length of Jorge's physique: wife-beater shirt over tanned, powerful shoulders; trim, tapered waist; taut stomach, six-pack abs; baggy jeans, nice ass. Damn! A booming system!

"So, how long?" Jorge repeated.

"Umm . . . umm, I been there for about six months, but I'm in college, so I only work part-time."

"Oh, you a college boy, huh? I hear you college boys do some freaky shit in those dorms."

Scooter smiled and licked his lips. Sexual tension crawled over him like a raging fever. He didn't want to read into Jorge's words, but the way dude kept staring at him and the heat of his touch as their arms grazed lightly were enough to send him spiraling off into fantasyland.

"We don't have a dorm," he said, chuckling. "I live at home with my grandfather, and as old as he is, ain't nothing freaky happening up in that camp!"

Jorge laughed and clapped Scooter on the back. His hand trailed downward and lingered at the small of Scooter's back. "Well, if you ever wanna get your freak on, you can bring your girl over to my crib and chill. My people don't give a shit if my friends come over and crash the joint."

Scooter stopped. Somehow they were standing in front of the bank. A big part of him wished they were at least a ten-mile walk away. He lowered his gaze. For a long moment neither of them spoke. Jorge broke the silence.

"I live on Parker. Come on over and bring your girl."

Scooter coughed again and met Jorge's eyes.

"I don't have a girl."

Jorge grinned. "Neither do I."

′ ′ ′

Back inside the cool interior of Chase Manhattan, Scooter squirmed on his stool and shuffled a stack of hundred-dollar bills. Although he was giving it his best shot, there was no way he could keep his count. His thoughts drifted and wandered. Dude was fine! His lunchtime stroll had worked him into a perpetual state of excitement. Suddenly there was so much happening in his life!

Juanita wasn't the only one in hot demand these days.

Yeah, he'd been wounded by her betrayal, but then again she didn't know everything there was to know about him, either. She knew he liked boys; they'd talked about that years ago and it had never been an issue. Even as kids they liked to flip through the pages of black magazines, and damned if they didn't think the same guys were cute. They even planned which ones they'd dream about at night and then compared details in the mornings. Dreaming and wishing were as far as things had ever gone, though. They were both virgins, Scooter knew, but he at least was not proud of that fact.

All weekend he'd been dying to tell her about Sol Steinberg and their meeting in the vault. But after the way she treated him at the rink, ignoring his 'tude and focusing on Conan, barely acknowledging him when he announced he was leaving—he had no intentions of sharing his secret fantasies with her again. *Never let your right hand know what your left hand is doing.*

Or revealing his sudden sexual appeal to two very different men.

No, Juanita wouldn't understand his attraction to either Sol or Jorge. And that was okay, because he was not about to trust her with his most private feelings.

Especially his most recent feelings for the hot-blooded Jorge. Scooter smiled and slid a row of quarters into a paper holder. Jorge hadn't been satisfied with just walking him to back work. He'd actually come inside the bank and escorted Scooter over to his window. It seemed as though every employee on the banking floor stopped to look at the two men when they sauntered in. The easy way they walked, shoulders brushing, heads close, was a sure giveaway that they were "together."

On the way to the teller area, Jorge scooped up a handful of peppermints from a crystal dish on the customer service counter and offered one to his new friend. "The next time you want something to suck on," Jorge told him, "I got something much bigger and much hotter than a peppermint."

Scooter closed his eyes and rolled a remnant of the spicy red-and-white confection around in his mouth; his tongue swirled violently, massaging and stroking the candy passionately. He caught himself performing pseudo-fellatio, and heat rose to his cheeks.

He placed the roll of quarters on top of the stacks of bills, stuck the entire wad in his cash drawer, and slammed it shut. He spun the dial in circles and mused about the crazy direction his life had suddenly taken.

His peppery thoughts crisscrossed between Sol Steinberg and Jorge. He was truly working both ends of the spectrum! Sol was whiter than baseball and apple pie, almost puritanical in a rigid, upstanding way.

Who would have suspected the corporate manager of having a distinct craving for chocolate? Ever suspect him of being gay?

And Jorge. Totally opposite! B-boy. Dangerous. Exciting. Rock hard, street tough, and living the thug life.

Scooter was suspended in a delicious continuum: Sol represented prominence and power, and Jorge, a deadly and forbidden animal magnetism. Scooter shivered. And they both wanted him.

His penis throbbed, aching to be touched.

He stood and adjusted himself in his briefs. He was ready, more than ready, to cross that bridge into physical love. He'd promised Jorge he would meet him at his friend's crib in a few days, so there wasn't much more he could do about that.

But Sol was available. On the premises right now. He lifted the telephone receiver and punched in an extension. After two rings the phone was answered on the other end.

"Sir," he whispered sensually, "there's something in the vault that needs your immediate attention."

He looked across the banking floor and smiled. Their eyes locked.

Sol breathed heavily. "I'm on my way." Scooter watched as the branch manager rose from his desk and strolled coolly toward the back stairs.

He popped another peppermint into his mouth, grabbed an empty cash bag, and headed down to the vault.

CHAPTER 18

For the first time in her life, Juanita was on punishment. She was too old to spank, but after Saturday's scene in the hallway with Conan, Hattie had grounded her for a week. Shoving the meal she'd been preparing into the refrigerator, Aunt Hattie ranted and raved and forbade her to even speak to Conan, and had promised Juanita she'd call the police on him if he ever darkened her doorway again.

That evening Aunt Hattie had retired to bed early, muttering under her breath with her Bible clutched in her arms, leaving Herbie and Juanita to fend for themselves for dinner. All day Sunday her aunt had remained in her bedroom, fasting and deep in prayer, but to Juanita's surprise, she'd stepped off the elevator Monday afternoon and was greeted by the delicious smells of roasting chicken and candied yams.

"Oh, Auntie!" She dropped her book bag and hugged Hattie around the waist. "You cooked all my favorite things!"

Hattie grunted something under her breath about mannish, disobedient children deserving to eat bread and water, then disappeared into her bedroom, anger stiffening her shoulders and running ramrod down her back.

Even with the tension lingering in the air, Juanita ate up a storm.

She washed her hands and fixed heaping plates for herself and Uncle Herbie, the juices in her empty stomach rumbling in anticipation of the hot meal.

In addition to the candied yams and roasted chicken, Aunt Hattie had baked a large pan of macaroni and cheese and stuck her toe in a mean pot of turnip greens. Corn bread, cranberry sauce, and an icy pitcher of fresh lemonade rounded the meal out nicely, and not only did Juanita eat every morsel on her plate, she used her last corner of corn bread to soak up the drops of pot liquor from her greens.

"Whew! That was good!" A bubble of air rushed from her lips, and she blushed and covered her mouth with a napkin. "Oops! *Excuse* me! I am *full*."

Herbie glanced from Juanita's plate to her eyes, and back again. He was surprised at the volume of food she'd consumed, and his eyes silently questioned her over the remnants of their meal.

Ignoring him, Juanita drained the last sip of lemonade from her glass and sucked the melting shards of ice before crunching them noisily between her back teeth. Pouring the last bits of ice into the sink, she went through her normal routine of clearing the table and putting the food away in plastic storage containers, then she stacked the dishes on the counter and ran hot water in the sink, adding a bit of powdered Tide to the cascading water until the bubbles threatened to spill over the sides of the sink and drip down to the floor.

"Go 'head, Uncle Herbie," she called over her shoulder. "Why don't you go on back with Auntie. I'll wash and dry tonight." Humming softly to herself, Juanita sank her arms up to the elbows in the warm, sudsy water and methodically washed each dish, pot, glass, and spoon, stacking them neatly in the wire drain to dry.

When she was done, she took a clean dishcloth from a drawer beneath the silverware bin and dried each piece, putting everything away in its rightful place. Peering around the kitchen, she used the damp cloth to wipe off the countertops and the stove, then ran it across the dining table and the seat of each chair for good measure. Finally, she rinsed the washrag in hot water, then wrung it out thoroughly and hung it over the spigot to dry.

It had been nearly half an hour since Juanita had taken her last bite of food, and she felt damn good. She was proud of herself, proud of the fact that she'd enjoyed a delicious meal without experiencing the slightest amount of discomfort, and even now, she felt pleasantly satiated and replete.

She turned and saw Uncle Herbie standing in the doorway.

"Hey! You scared me! I thought you were watching television with Auntie."

Herbie frowned. "No, Neet. No television. I thank it's time you and me had us a minute."

"About what?" Juanita sucked her breath in, concerned. "Something wrong with Auntie? With you?"

"No, we fine. Hattie'n me still going strong, thank the Lord." He pulled out a chair and motioned her into it. "What I wants to talk about is you."

Juanita was genuinely puzzled.

"You know, Neet. That man upstairs is sumthin' else. He put each of us here for a different reason and to serve a different purpose. Not everybody is meant to do the same thangs, or live the same way, or even look the same."

She nodded her agreement, although she was still in the dark. It wasn't often Uncle Herbie got deep and philosophical, and when he did she sure as hell wanted to be able to hang right with him. "That makes sense, Uncle Herbie. You're saying everybody is an individual, right? That we're all unique."

"True, so true." He reached out his dark, work-scarred hands and threaded his fingers through hers, their hands like contrasting piano keys.

"Juanita, you got to be happy wit' yo'sef, baby. You gots to stop holdin' something up as your goal that you cain't never reach. Some of us ain't meant to look like others. Back in the days of slavery, gals like you had to be built strong and sturdy. Had to evolve thataway in order to carry the race fo'ward. That couldn't have been done if y'all had a' weighed a hundred pounds and went around bein' funny wit' food."

"What do you mean, Uncle Herbie?" Juanita asked. "I'm not sure I get what you mean."

Herbie turned his head and coughed, then shrugged. "Be happy wit' yo'sef, baby girl. You smart, you healthy, and you strong. Everythang a black woman needs to be. Don't allow them white folks what controls the TV and stuff to mess wit' your head and tell you how you oughtta look. You learn to 'termine that for yo'sef, and the whole world will be yours."

"But what—"

He cut her off with a raised hand. "I know what you been doin', Neet, and I'm here to tell you that if'n you love yourself hard enough, you don't have to."

She sat at the table long after he'd gone, mulling over his words. She respected Uncle Herbie's counsel, and he was right, of course. He and Aunt Hattie had been giving her lessons in self-love all of her life.

Juanita crossed her arms and lowered her head to the table, ashamed she'd been found out and ashamed that Uncle Herbie had discovered just how little she thought of herself. She didn't know what in the world had possessed her to do something so stupid and so dangerous. She'd read an article in *Seventeen* about people who tried to lose weight by purging, and on a whim had decided to try it. Well, she'd been doing it off and on for almost two months, and although she was getting used to do it, actually beginning to feel like she needed to do it, she hadn't lost a damn pound.

She knew what she had to do. She needed to lift some mental muscle. To bulk up in the self-esteem and self-love department. Resolved, she turned out the kitchen light and headed toward her bedroom, passing the bathroom on her way. She paused at the open door, staring at the toilet bowl and trembling despite herself. Stepping into the small room, she closed the door behind her and stared first into the mirror above the sink, then again at the closed lid of the toilet bowl. Her throat opened and her fingers crawled up her neck and toward her mouth.

No, she told herself firmly. No, she would not. There was no reason to, anyway. The food had been great: lovingly prepared. Besides, just like Uncle Herbie said, black women were built sturdy for a reason. There was nothing wrong with her body. She was healthy and carried her weight well. Not everyone was supposed to wear a size five and look like a supermodel.

Inching toward the toilet, a wave of nausea buckled her and she panted heavily, her newly formed habits fighting for survival. Swallowing against the tide rushing toward the back of her throat, she gasped, sinking to her knees into her customary position. Tears slid from her eyes as she fought to retain her stomach contents. She watched in horror as somebody else's fingers lifted the porcelain lid from the toilet seat. Gulping and heaving, somebody else's stomach contracted and squeezed, seeking to rid itself of undigested fats, proteins, and carbohydrates.

Fighting with every ounce of her will and determination, Juanita climbed to her feet. She stripped off her clothing and stood naked, tiny chill bumps spreading out on her exposed flesh. Steeling herself, she started at her toes, lightly touching them at first, then massaging deeply, seeing them for the first time as the beautiful appendages they actually were. "I love you, toes," she whispered, her words heavy with sincerity, her heart swelling at the sight of the ten little stumps that enabled her to walk freely.

Her hands moved up her legs, praising her thighs and blessing her hips, admiring the narrow grooves of her stretch marks and sanctioning her imperfect flesh. She rubbed her stomach, cupped the pulp of her ass, and cried hallelujah at the rise of her breasts, massaging and appreciating and valuing every inch of what God had bestowed upon her as though seeing her blessed body in all its splendor and glory through fresh new eyes, and loving it completely and without reservation for the very first time.

/ / /

Jorge swore as he hid behind the panel of thin blue curtains and watched Conan from their bedroom window. He drummed his fingers impatiently on the sill and scowled as he waited for his *hermano* to disappear from view. Conan had messed up another Saturday morning to go hang out with that black chick, Juanita, and Jorge would not forget it. His tongue felt thick and acidic as the final traces of his blue candy dissolved in his mouth. *Let him run behind that tramp,* he thought. Pretty soon Conan would see. In a few weeks' time, *everybody* would see just how stupid he was. Taking sides with a dumb bitch instead of your brother could get you in big trouble.

As Conan rounded the corner and disappeared from view, Jorge jerked on the frayed cord of the paper-thin window shade. The string snapped off in his hand, and he tossed it to the floor. With a slight smile playing along his lips, he walked into the kitchen and lifted the telephone from the receiver. Punching in the digits he'd memorized, he waited for a response on the other end.

"Hello?"

"Whassup?"

"Ain't nothing. How you doing?"

"Better when you get here."

There was a slight pause.

"Umm . . . you think it's safe for me to come over there? I mean, is it okay to be in your house in the middle of the day?"

"Nah, stupid. You ain't coming up in here. I'll be looking out the window for you. When you get to the door downstairs, just do like you did before. Press the top right button and I'll buzz you in. You know the setup: Come all the way up the stairs to the last floor. I'll meet you on the landing above the stairs that leads to the roof."

There was a cough on the other end of the line.

"What time you want me to come?"

"What fuckin' time am I calling you?"

"Okay, okay! But I gotta take care of my grandfather first. His nurse ain't due to come in today. After I get him fed and dressed, I'll be on my way."

"You better be. Don't make me wait too long."

Jorge replaced the receiver on the hook turned around. Grace Lopez stood staring at him with an unreadable look in her eyes.

"¿Que pasa?" he asked her. Lately he spoke to her only in Spanish. After all of the years she'd lavished him with her love, he knew his days were numbered in her home. To mock her, he refused to address her in English, refused to communicate with her at all unless it was in Spanish, a language where he clearly had the upper hand.

Grace's blue eyes bored into him as though she was reading his very thoughts and found them to be distasteful.

Jorge brushed past her, stormed into the bathroom, and locked the door. He grabbed a wet washcloth from a hook near the sink and rubbed it over a fresh bar of Ivory soap. He'd been working Scooter over for weeks, and as he soaped between his legs he remembered the feel of those splayed lips as he thrust himself halfway down Scooter's throat.

The more he dogged and degraded Scooter, the better Jorge felt. He enjoyed slapping Scooter's love-wet face with his sticky member, forcing him to crawl on his hands and knees and lick his privates.

And every time he allowed the boy to go down on him, Jorge upped the ante and added a twisted new dimension to the game. And Scooter loved it. He begged Jorge to fuck him. Screamed for it. But Jorge refused, even with a condom; instead he used Scooter's mouth like a pussy, satisfying himself over and over again and forcing Scooter to explode untouched inside of his own pants.

Jorge was straight, but there was a method to his madness. He was no switch-hitter; didn't swing both ways. He loved having sex with chicks and only fucked with men when it served a purpose. For the past few weeks he had sexually and mentally dominated Scooter to the point where there was nothing the boy wouldn't do for him. Nothing. No matter how sick or depraved his demands, like a damn fool Scooter gladly complied. Jorge chuckled and zipped his pants. Scooter was lucky he even bothered to wash it before shoving it into his mouth. At this point he knew that, whether it was clean or not, Scooter would take it any way he gave it to him.

He went back into the bedroom he shared with Conan and rifled through a pile of dirty clothes on the floor. He held up a pair of Conan's baggy blue jeans and a bright green shirt. After a tentative sniff at the underarms, Jorge pulled the shirt over his head and pulled on the jeans. He fed his own belt through the pant loops and then bent over to recuff the hems.

As he stood up he caught a glimpse of his reflection in the splotchy mirror on the dresser. He eyed his blond hair and moved in closer. From deep inside his bottom drawer he extracted a bottle of hair dye and smiled. The model on the box sported a head full of thick jet-black hair. And soon, Jorge knew, soon he would too.

/////////////////////////////

CHAPTER 19

Rico sat on the stoop eating fat purple grapes from a plastic sand-wich bag as Conan approached the building. He'd watched the young man get off the bus and walk wearily in his direction, and even as he popped the chilled grapes into his mouth with lightning speed, Rico's brows were knitted with tension and a storm brewed in his eyes.

"What's the word?"

Conan shrugged without answering. It had been a long day at the plant, a long workweek; in fact, he'd put in overtime on Monday, Wednesday, Thursday, and even today, Friday. And he'd worked hard for his money too. With Chance heading off on vacation and the sum-mer orders picking up, he'd barely taken a break to use the can or grab a bite to eat during his eight-hour shift. And to make things worse, Jorge had skipped work on a payday, which was weird in and of itself. He hadn't been in his bed when Conan awakened for his morning weight workout, and when he failed to show up at work to get his check, Conan had become even more puzzled.

Rico asked, "So, what's good?"

"It's all good, man," Conan replied. He paused with one foot resting on the slate-gray steps and hunched his shoulder to wipe at a trickle of perspiration inching down his face. He patted the shirt pocket that held his weekly paycheck. "Gotta slave away in order to make these papers, so I guess it's all good."

Rico stared warily, his eyes narrow, his chest straining like he was struggling to contain himself. "You doing anything else to make those papers, my friend?" He nodded toward the building behind him. "I mean, as far as I know you *are* still the type of cat who works a real job for his money, am I right?"

"What's up? You know me, Rico. I work for mine every day. What are you saying, *amigo*?"

Rico pushed the bag filled with tiny grape seeds into his front pocket. He stood in a wide-legged stance and folded both arms across his chest. "What I'm saying is," he sneered, "the ambulance and the police just left here. The meat wagon came for Pushie and his wife, and the paddy wagon came for you."

"What?"

"Yeah, you heard me right." He dropped his arms. When he spoke again, his voice was as quiet as death. "Some asshole did a push-in behind Angelique Andrews this morning when she opened her door to bring in Pushie's newspaper. She didn't get a good look at the guy because he kicked her face in before he beat the shit out of her and stole the last of Pushie's VA money out of her bra."

Conan was bowled over at the anger in Rico's eyes as he continued. "Some sick motherfucker stuck his hands up that old lady's dress! Felt on her privates and put his fingers in her underwear! Pushie was so upset they had to take him out of here too. I think he might've had a heart attack."

Conan held his hands up and backed away a few paces. "Hold the fuck up." All the blood drained from his face as his tongue darted out to wet his lips. "You accusing *me*? I know you don't think *I* had something to do with that shit! I love Pushie Andrews *and* his wife! Why would anybody think it was me? *They know me.* Both of them could tell the cops it wasn't me!"

Rico shook his head. "It had to be somebody who lives in the building. The doors down here were locked and nobody remembers buzzing anyone in. Pushie was stuck in the bed and couldn't reach his walker, so even though he heard his wife screaming, he never saw what happened. Mrs. Andrews got her face kicked in so fast and caught so many haymakers that she never saw the guy's mug either. Whoever the fuck it was, he attacked her as she opened her door to get the paper. You know she can't hardly see, but she told the cops that the last thing she remembered as she bent over was a pair of sneakers coming at her. He was wearing blue jeans and had a cuff in the hem of his pants. And based on that, they're looking for you."

Conan looked down at his Nikes. His baggy blue jeans were splotched with drying traces of oil and Lysol, but the cuffs in the hems were neat and pressed.

"I didn't do that shit, Rico. I swear." His voice shook. "I worked today! I worked the whole fucking day long."

Rico shook his head again and looked at Conan with sadness in his eyes. "I guess that's your story so you're sticking to it, huh?"

"What do you mean?"

"The cops called your job, man. The secretary in the main office said you called in sick real early this morning. Said you didn't even wait for the plant to open, you just left a message on the answering machine. They didn't even have a replacement to pull your shift for you."

"I was at work, Rico!" Conan pleaded. "I swear to God!"

"You got proof? If so, I'll take you down to the police station to straighten this out."

"*Fuck!*" Conan slammed his fist into his open palm, fear and disbelief creasing his face.

"There's one more thing," Rico told him. "Mrs. Andrews told the cops she heard her attacker laughing right before she passed out. The sick bastard was laughing when he told her to let her husband know she'd gotten her kitty scratched by a Top Cat."

✐ ✐ ✐

Jorge stood before the open refrigerator door, cramming his mouth with cold rice and chickpeas straight from the pot. Working his jaws and smacking loudly, he reached for a carton of vitamin D–fortified milk and turned it up to his mouth, washing down the rice with long swallows. Wiping his lips on the back of his sleeve, he reached back into the coolness, retrieved a crimson-colored apple, and took three gnashing bites before replacing it on the shelf.

The front door opened and slammed, and Jorge jumped, then braced himself as he heard Conan's heavy footsteps storming through the apartment. "Hey, *amigo,*" Jorge called out cheerfully. "The D-T's was here this morning. You know they was lookin' for you, my man."

Conan stood in the doorway, blocking out the light from the hall. The ride with Rico to and from the Seventy-third Precinct had seemed endless, and the memory of his three-hour grilling stoked his rage.

"And why the fuck was they looking for me, Jorge? Huh? Answer me that!" He stepped toward Jorge and jammed his finger in his friend's face. "I just left the fucking police station. Me and Chance Williams were both there. Whoever did that shit to Mrs. Anderson must've called Grayson Fields this morning pretending to be me so I wouldn't have an alibi. If it wasn't for Chance and a few other guys at the shop vouching for me, my ass would be in jail right now!"

Jorge was silent, but a smirk lurked behind his veneer. He tossed a lock of golden hair away from his eyes and met Conan's rage head-on. "Yeah? So did you do that shit or what?"

Conan exploded. "I was at work, motherfucker! You know I was at work!"

Jorge feigned surprise. "Hey! How am I supposed to know where you go these days, *amigo*? Huh? You don't tell me shit no more! You hang out with all kinds of people I don't know nothing about." He shook his head. "Nah, man. I don't know where the fuck you were when that old bitch was getting her panties bunched."

"So where were *you*? Huh? You sure were ghost today on payday, and you didn't even sleep here last night."

Jorge shrugged. "I spent the night out with my new friend. I wasn't nowhere near here when that shit went down, so don't look at me."

Conan nodded slowly, barely controlling his rage. "But I *am* looking at you, *hombre*. You best believe it. I'm looking straight at your lying ass."

′ ′ ′

Scooter stood over the bed and swallowed pangs of guilt. Ever since he'd begun seeing Jorge, he'd been neglecting his grandfather big-time. Just so happened that Jorge wanted to be with him today, and once again he was responding to his lover's beck and call. He felt like shit. Leaving Jeo home alone and running out at any time, day or night, just for a taste of Jorge's dick. But at least this time the nurse was coming to fill in for him and his conscience was somewhat soothed.

"I have to go out for a little while, Granddaddy, but Miss Sam is on her way." He'd already washed and shaved his grandfather, and dressed him in a fresh set of pajamas. He spoke loudly into the old man's ear as he patted Jeo's cheek and fluffed his pillows. "I won't be long," he promised, "and when I get back I'll let you beat me in a game of checkers."

Jeo attempted a weak smile, but all he managed to do was break his grandson's heart. "I guess I be here," he whispered, the strain of those few words etching itself in his sagging face. Scooter bit his lip and patted Jeo's cheek again before hurrying from the room. Sometimes the smell of his grandfather's disease-wracked body was enough to choke him. The stench of sickness or blood seemed to touch a memory buried in the safety of his subconscious mind. A memory so horrific that even now, attempting to recall it caused his throat to clog with terror.

He slipped from the apartment and hurried down the hall. As he passed Juanita's door, he averted his eyes and lowered his head. It had been weeks since he'd gone over to eat breakfast with Aunt Hattie. Weeks since he'd discussed the neighborhood happenings with cool Uncle Herbie. Weeks since he'd done anything remotely productive in school. And weeks since he'd spoken to, or even acknowledged, his used-to-be true friend.

He walked to the bus stop, where he stood waiting with two elderly ladies and a teenage girl. Ordinarily he would have struck up a pleasant conversation with the older women; after all, flattering old ladies was his specialty. But not today. It was Saturday, and normally at this time he was skating circles around Juanita.

It seemed like eons ago that his life was simple enough to enjoy a day of skating. Juanita still seemed to enjoy it, though. He'd seen her and her shadow head for the bus at the usual time. She'd even begun leaving earlier on school days. Jorge told him that Conan went in early too; it seems he was bucking hard for a new position and apparently he was kissing the boss's ass and going in early to earn brownie points.

Scooter searched for the bus. There was no way in hell he was making up first to Juanita. She was the one who abandoned him. Not the other way around. If anybody needed to apologize for busting up a lifelong friendship, it was her. She let that asshole come between them and now look at what he'd done. Scooter rolled his eyes and frowned.

How stupid could Juanita be? Jorge had already told him that his suspicions were correct; Conan was a goddamn thief; he had indeed been down with that white boy who'd snatched Juanita's book bag. Jorge told him that when Conan found out there were only a few bucks inside, he came up with that phony-ass scam to make Juanita think he liked her. Jorge also told him all about Conan's temper, his arrest record, and how he liked to dabble in drugs. How he lost all of his ex-girlfriends because he liked kicking their asses left and right. He'd even beaten up an old lady in his own building. Kicked the shit out of her and stole her money. Scooter had been ready to go to Conan's ass on this one. Straight up let him know that if he put his hands on Nita he'd get fucked up for real. But Jorge had been a voice of reason. Thank God, he was looking out. He'd convinced Scooter that Juanita wasn't really in danger, and suggested instead that he write a note dropping a dime to Aunt Hattie about Conan, just in case.

The bus finally arrived and Scooter brushed past the two old women and stepped on. He plopped down on one of the two remaining seats and watched the scenery pass by. He was excited about seeing Jorge. Excited and nervous at the same time, because he was going to have to tell Jorge he couldn't help him out. As much as he loved him, he just couldn't do what Jorge had asked. Scooter didn't really know what to think. How to think. Whenever he was near the guy it seemed like all of his willpower drained out through his nose, leaving him wide open and vulnerable to Jorge's demands.

In the beginning, Jorge had promised they'd be able to use his friend's apartment and get down in a real bed, but so far they'd only had oral sex in stairwells, both in his building and in Jorge's, although just two nights ago Scooter had gone down on his Latin lover in the backseat of a friend's car. That night they'd spent their first night together, curled up in the backseat of the broken-down Lincoln, and the next morning just as the sun was coming up they'd snuck into Scooter's apartment, where he closed Jeo's bedroom door and fixed Jorge a mountainous breakfast of ham, eggs, and grits.

Scooter was so happy to have Jorge there that as soon as they entered the apartment he'd promptly done just as he was told without asking a single question. Jorge had wanted to play a joke on Conan, so he'd asked Scooter to call Grayson Fields and leave a message saying Conan Lopez was taking the day off and would be in to pick up his check on Monday. After that he'd snuggled spoon fashion behind Jorge on the living room floor, and fallen asleep watching cartoons. When he awakened an hour later, Jorge was gone.

Scooter realized he was in a bad way. It was weird, but while he was sucking and pulling for all he was worth and Jorge was calling him a nigger, a bitch, a low-life dick-sucking ho, and a slut, he was turned on beyond his wildest imagination. It was only after he left Jorge that he felt bad about the things he had done. When he went home with his face sticky, his knees sore, and dried cum in his hair, something inside nagged at him and told him things were not quite right.

Maybe he was a whore. A slut. For certain he was a dick-sucker. Scooter frowned. And not just Jorge's either. Ever since the day he'd stumbled upon Jorge on the streets of downtown Brooklyn, Scooter's life had been filled with funky gay sex.

That was the very afternoon he'd invited Sol Steinberg down to the vault and had his first taste of male-on-male love. They'd ducked behind a small partition in the vault's vestibule and Scooter had gone down on his knees like he was preparing for prayer. Even now he felt himself becoming aroused as he recalled how Sol had gripped his jaw and rubbed his hands all over his head while he pounded and moaned and cried out, "Bill . . . Oh my God, Bill!"

Scooter had no idea who Bill was, but just the sight of the powerful banker standing before him in his socks and shoes with his five-hundred-dollar pants and silk drawers pooled in a jumbled heap around his ankles turned him on. He felt such power when he blew

Sol. What control he had over the older man who seemed to love the feel of him, the smell of him, the taste of him.

It was with these thoughts in mind that Scooter ran from the bus stop and hurried to meet Jorge. Maybe today Jorge would take him properly. He was saving that particular cherry for him. Scooter had already taken Sol several times from the rear, but never had he been taken himself. Somehow he knew that treat should be reserved for Jorge. Besides, the white man's penis was too small to make his debut booty-bump a memorable experience.

But Jorge! Sweet Lawd, Jorge! Nothing could compare to the size of his Latin lover.

At the entrance to the building Scooter pressed the top right button and waited to be buzzed in. With a furtive glance over his shoulder, he slipped through the doors and headed up the stairs. At the top floor he looked to his right and saw a pair of sneakers and the lower half of a man's legs. Scooter knew the small landing led upstairs to the roof.

With his groin throbbing, he tiptoed toward his partially hidden lover. As he watched, Jorge's pants and nylon boxers fell down around his ankles and lay in a crumpled pool atop his sneaker-clad feet. He could see his lover's bare legs up to the knee.

"Come on up here," Jorge commanded. "And handle your goddamn business."

Scooter giggled and asked, "How'd you know it was me?"

" 'Cause," Jorge growled in a low voice. " 'Cause I can smell your sweet ass."

CHAPTER 20

One week later, Jorge pushed through the heavy doors of a Span-ish bodega wearing a nylon muscle shirt and matching biker shorts. The bright sunlight outside barely cut through the grimy three-quarter-length windows. The lopsided display shelves were laden with candles of all sizes, handmade señorita dolls, and a medley of patron saint statues.

He blinked, allowing his eyes to adjust to the dim interior where a faded poster of the legendary Roberto Clemente covered a wall be-hind the counter. The aroma of rotting fruit broke through clouds of sweet incense burning in a small brass pot.

This was his fourth stop of the morning, and while his spiel had been artificial and stilted when he'd attempted to collect from Chavez Cleaners, by the time he'd left Cisnero's Bakery and El Barrio Boxers' Gym, his speech was smooth and polished and most of all, it was very convincing.

Wearing his brightest, most engaging smile and swaying to the Afro-Cuban bebop of the long-dead Chano that drifted in from a back room, he approached the young, dreamy-eyed girl sitting behind the counter reading a worn copy of *True Confessions,* her eyes glued to the pages, her lower jaw rotating rhythmically.

Jorge's chest swelled and each ripple of his six-pack bulged through the thin fabric of his shirt. With a swagger that was sensual and sure, he pulled the phony receipt book from his sock and leaned his muscular forearms on the glass countertop.

"Hey, sexy."

She wore a tangerine-and-peach-colored tank top, the creamy crowns of her full breasts bulging from its neckline. Her legs were crossed at the ankle and propped up on a case of Goya Coconut Milk, and she reluctantly dragged her eyes from the pages of her magazine and looked up with a frown. Her jumbo pink hair rollers were the exact same shade of the bubble gum she tossed around in her mouth. She poked out her lips, annoyed at the prospect of leaving the hellish lives of the magazine characters and returning to the reality of her own.

Jorge grinned, his dimples flashing. Nonchalantly flexing each muscle, he turned sideways to allow her a better view of his physique in profile.

"Can I help you?" She spoke slowly, the pink gum colliding against her teeth and tongue, and sliding around inside her mouth like a load of clothes in a spinning dryer. Her jaw went slack as her eyes crawled over his muscles, savoring each peak and marveling at the specimen the gods had sent to bless her hungry eyes.

Jorge chuckled inside. He had her. Before he even opened his mouth he could visualize her hand digging into the cash register to support his noble deeds.

She repeated, "Can I help you?"

"Nah, *chica*. You can't help me, but you *can* help uplift your neighborhood by assisting the Community of Colors recreational program."

Her voice was light and breathless. "What I gotta do?"

"Just place a small pledge for our annual walkathon next Saturday during Old-Timers Day. We're raising money to buy used computers for the kids at the center."

"The center?"

He nodded. "Yeah, you know. The Community of Colors Cultural Center, on Riverdale Avenue." The air was stifling in the store, and he propped one foot against a wooden crate filled with ripening mangoes teeming with swarms of tiny fruit flies.

She smiled and swung her feet down to the dusty floor. There was a womanly fullness to her belly, and her hips were seasoned and lush. "Oh, okay! You're down with that old dude Rico and them, right? My daughter is six and she goes there to the afternoon reading program. What section you work in? I think I mighta seen you there before."

Jorge chuckled and leaned in closer. "I do it all, baby. I read to the kids, help the old people with their bills, mentor some of the young heads. I seen you down there before too. Looking all fine and shit. Your daughter's name is um . . ." He squinted his eyes and snapped his fingers several times.

"Jacqui!"

"Yeah, Jacqui. She looks just like her beautiful *mami* too." He placed the receipt book on the counter and opened it up to a blank page. "So how much can you give?"

"Give?" She backed up slightly, her eyes searching his face. Perspiration dotted her top lip. "How much I gotta give?"

"Well," he said, his voice a mixture of heavy cream and honey, "this is the deal: How much do you wanna help out? Your daughter is reading now, right? And that's probably because of the volunteers like me who run the center. So just imagine how smart she could be if there were computers in there that she could work on every day.

"The way this works is, you gotta pledge a certain amount for every mile I walk. Say I walk ten miles, and you pledge . . ." His eyes traveled upward in thought. "Say you pledge five, maybe ten dollars for each mile. That means you give me about fifty dollars now, and if I can't walk that far, I bring you back your change."

"I don't know. . . ." She looked at his beefy arms and stood to get a better look at his tan legs bulging through his bright-yellow biker shorts. "What if you walk more than ten miles? You look pretty buff to me. Like you can walk all damn day with those pretty thighs you got. What then? I'ma owe you some more money?"

Jorge put his head back and laughed, then treated her to a look of passion in his steady gaze. "*Chica,* if I walk all day, it'll only be to get back here to you. You won't owe me a dime. But I tell you what. If I walk more than ten miles, I'll owe you a date."

Brightly painted nails went to her throat as the *True Confessions* magazine slid to the floor. Plastic curlers bobbed and shook as she giggled and nodded, already reaching into the cash register and counting out several bills.

Jorge quickly scribbled out a receipt, then tore it from the book. He leaned over the counter and briefly pressed his lips to hers. "I'll be back, *mamasita.* You keep it warm for *Papi,* okay?"

She squealed through pursed lips and beamed, and as the handsome hunk stuffed her money into his sock and pushed through the door and back out into the bright sunlight, she looked down at the receipt in her hands and smiled.

It was signed, *Top Cat.*

/ / /

It was Old-Timers Day in central Brooklyn, a beautifully warm Saturday afternoon on the last weekend in July. Juanita stood huddled in the safety of the lobby, enjoying the drifting aroma of hot charcoal and lighter fluid, yet out of sight of the teenagers milling about on the porch. Music blared from radios that were too heavy to lift; card games, jump ropes, and beer coolers were out in full swing, and blankets and lawn chairs covered almost every patch of grass on the grounds of the concrete jungle.

It had been hard getting out of the apartment and away from the suspicious eye of Aunt Hattie, and although Juanita did not enjoy telling lies, it felt good to be off punishment and back outside in the fresh air. And good to have a guy in her life. A guy who thought she was all that, and two bags of Wise Onion & Garlic chips!

Dressed in a sheer red blouse with a black leotard beneath it and a black flair skirt, she glanced through the scratched Plexiglas window, hoping to catch a glimpse of Conan walking up the tar-paved path. Outside, Queenie was smoking a joint, while Sheila stood rocking a baby stroller and holding court with some of her old crew. Almost all of the girls her age already had at least one baby, and they spent their days sitting around on milk crates gossiping and cluttering the porch with Fisher-Price walkers and Graco strollers.

Kendra and Mutter were missing from the group, though. Kendra was on Riker's Island charged with setting fire to her boyfriend's car while he was still in it, and Mutter was upstate in a residential program called A Better Chance, earning her high school diploma and hoping to win a scholarship for college. Her mother had caught pneumonia and died shortly after having her twelfth child, and Mutter's aunt had taken over the care and raising of the Jeffries children. Even Aunt Hattie had had to admit that with the exception of the pothead Queenie, the stern-faced, bowlegged woman had done a hell of a job. All of the girls were finishing high school, with two, Pig and Shirley, already off in college. Each of the Jeffries boys had gone into Job Corps and learned a trade.

It was hot and muggy in the lobby, but Juanita really didn't want to stand on the porch and wait, even though time and familiarity had improved her standing among the crew. She'd pretty much established herself after what she put on Dante Coleman, earning their admiration and respect, but never their friendship. By the time she was thirteen she'd had to whip Sheila's ass up and down the stairs— twice—and had once even stood toe to toe with Kendra. They didn't try her anymore, but neither did they embrace her. So she hung back in the shadows, praying for Conan to hurry, peeking out the window every thirty seconds or so.

Her heart leapt and she hurried from the building as soon as she saw him approaching the walkway. "Hey, everybody." She greeted the sisters standing around, taking care to look directly into Sheila's eyes and give her special props by way of a personal nod. She maneuvered around the mess of strollers, pausing to rub the head of a baby here and coo at a baby there. Bouncing down the walkway with the sounds of "Hey, Needa" ringing out behind her, she met Conan at the end of the path with a big grin plastered on her face.

He was dressed simply: jeans, a crewneck white shirt, and pair of high-top leather work boots.

He grinned. "Hi, Juanita. You look nice."

"You too. I mean . . ." She blushed. "I mean, hi, you look nice too."

Conan suggested they take the bus over to the center. "It's really not too far to walk, seeing how nice it is and all, but the sooner we get there the more time we'll have to read to the kids."

✒ ✒ ✒

The Community of Colors Cultural Center was bustling. Children ranging in age from four to twelve were scurrying around, jumping from one activity to another.

"Juanita." Conan grabbed her hand and pulled her over to a handsome man who wore a CCCC T-shirt and a pair of faded blue jeans. "This is Rico, the founder and director of the center. Rico, this is my good friend Juanita."

Juanita's hand was enveloped in a welcoming grasp, and Rico smiled at her warmly. "Hello, Juanita! Very happy to meet you. Top Cat speaks very highly of you, and I thank you for volunteering to help out with the children!"

She stared. "Top Cat?"

Conan and Rico laughed. "Yeah. That's what we call him around here."

"And why is that?"

"Well." Rico draped his arm around Conan's shoulder and gave him an affectionate but manly hug. "He does so much good around here, helps out so much in the neighborhood, that next to me, Conan here is *the* Top Cat!"

Juanita smiled, not really getting the joke and not really caring. All she knew was that she liked this Rico guy. Liked his open smile and the way his eyes crinkled in the corners. She liked the fact that he thought so much of Conan too, which confirmed her belief that she was one very lucky girl to have the attention of such a down-to-earth, good-hearted man.

Conan led her into a large air-conditioned room that was colorfully painted and had posters and drawings taped to nearly every surface of the walls. The perimeter of the room was lined with low shelves stacked with scores of used children's books. The floor was covered in soft mats in red, blue, yellow, and green and had a miniature-size overstuffed armchair in the center of the mats.

"Okay," he said with a smile. "Now you get to see where I spend most of my free time." He gazed around the room, his eyes beaming with pride. "You know, when me and Thor were little kids, my mom used to take us on the bus all the way downtown to the big public library. We even had our own library cards." He kicked a wooden wedge beneath the door to prop it open. "All of the kids I read to are between four and six, just the right ages to be taught the wonders in the world of books," he said, ushering the noisy children inside. "Sometimes a good book can snatch you out of your own life and give you an even better one in its place."

Juanita stood back as the children poured into the room and took a seat on the multicolored mats. Several kids stopped to hug Conan as they passed, and a few of the older boys jumped in the air and slapped him a high five, calling out, "What's up, Top Cat?" in greeting. Watching Conan interact with the rowdy kids made her feel warm and tingly. They certainly didn't call this the Community of Colors for nothing. There were almost twenty children in the room, and Juanita noticed that while many of them looked Hispanic, a fair number were clearly African-American, and there was even a set of Asian twins, two cute little black-haired girls wearing matching red dresses.

"Good afternoon, boys and girls." Conan stood in the midst of the seated children, beaming at each of them as if they belonged to him.

"Good afternoon, Top Cat!"

"It's good to see you all came back this week! Remember, today we're reading *White Socks Only,* by a wonderful lady named Evelyn Coleman, but before we get started I'd like to do something a little different." He turned and beckoned Juanita forward. "Guys, I'd like you to meet a good friend of mine. Her name is Miss Juanita."

The room erupted in whispers and giggles.

A small girl wearing a faded jumper and mismatched socks stared into Juanita's eyes. "She so pretty," she declared, then promptly stuck her third and fourth fingers into her mouth and reached up with her other hand to twist her braids.

"Hey, Mister Top Cat," a brown-skinned boy called out. He was in a bright shirt and designer jeans, a fierce crease running down the front of each pant leg. His grin was impish, and Juanita saw that he'd lost his two front teeth. "Is that your gurlfren'?"

The children giggled even harder, their eyes wide and knowing as they shared conspiratorial looks. A long-legged Hispanic girl with glasses began chanting, "Top Cat and Juanita sitting in a tree, k-i-s-s . . . hmm, hmm, hmm!"

Juanita found herself laughing aloud right along with them; all eyes were on Conan, including hers, waiting for his response.

He held his hands up in the air good-naturedly, chuckling softly as he asked for their silence. "Okay, okay! Now y'all show Miss Juanita some love. Let's all clap for her and show her how happy we are to have her here."

Small hands clapped happily as the children elbowed each other and clowned around on the mats. Conan winked at Juanita. "Shhhh . . . everybody hit the mats! Let's get started!"

Juanita sat cross-legged on the floor. From her position she viewed Conan in profile, marveling at his fine bone structure and chiseled, rugged good looks. His voice was animated and full of emotion as he read from the children's book about segregation and oppression. Engrossed in the story, he seemed to slip into the character and become the young girl who took off her shoes and drank from a whites-only fountain in the South.

Conan was winding up the story, telling about the part where Chicken Man came forward to drink from the fountain, when the door opened and Rico gestured frantically. Behind him stood a teenage girl with thick glasses and two long plaits in her curly blond hair.

"Come out for a minute, man. Abbie here will finish up the story for you."

From the seriousness of his expression, it was clear that Rico meant business. His brow was furrowed and Conan's face was a mask of questions, but he rose from his chair and signaled for Juanita to follow him. "What?" she mouthed, but he shook his head and shrugged as if to say, "Beats me," as they followed Rico down the hall and into his cluttered office.

Seated on a faded sofa pushed into a corner of the small room was a young Hispanic girl with bleached hair and long acrylic nails. She frowned beneath the heavy makeup she wore, and a gold key dangled in the valley created by her cleavage.

Rico ushered them inside. "Is this him?"

The girl stood and shook her head. "Uh-uh. That ain't him. I'm talking about the one who reads to the kids. To my little girl, Jacqui. You know, the real cute guy with the slammin' *culito* and the curly blond hair."

Conan balked. "Yo, Rico. You mind telling me what this is about, man?"

"Two days ago I got a call from somebody at the bakery who wanted information about some walkathon they heard we were having. Yesterday I got three more calls, from people who told me they pledged a lot of money on one of our walkers and wanted to know the route he'd be taking and what time they could come down to cheer him on." Rico pushed a stack of papers off the corner of his desk and sat down. "Now today, this young lady brings her daughter in to attend the reading group and tells me she also pledged money on this bogus walkathon. Supposedly to the guy who reads to the kids on Saturday afternoons."

"But it wasn't this guy!" the girl protested. "This is the wrong one. I wanna see the other guy walk. The one who got my fifty dollars!"

Conan looked from the woman to Rico, and then to Juanita. "Hey. I don't know what she's talking about, but you heard her. It wasn't me. I never took no fifty dollars from her or nobody else. I'm a reader, not a walker!"

Rico stood and walked over to the small window. He turned to face Conan with a look of genuine concern clouding his face. "I believe you, man. I really do. But check this out." He took a small slip of folded paper from his desk and spread it out. Glancing over Conan's shoulder, Juanita saw that it was a cash receipt. The kind you could buy in a booklet from any office supply store. "Somebody is shaking down the business owners in this neighborhood, and while this asshole might be signing your name"—he held out the receipt to Conan and pointed at the signature on the bottom—"he's using *my* good name and the reputation of the Community of Colors Cultural Center to steal from our people."

Juanita bit her lip and stared as Rico paced a few steps before slamming his hands down on the mess upon his desk. "Damn, man! First that shit with Pushie's wife, and now this. . . . I don't know how to tell you this, but you might wanna be careful. Looks to me like somebody has their own criminal agenda and gives less than a damn if you get locked up for it."

The young woman popped her gum and sashayed over to Rico with her hand on her hip. "Does this mean I don't get that date he promised me?"

"I'm afraid so. We don't even know who the hell this guy is."

She blew a big pink bubble that surrounded her peach-toned lips and stuck to her nose before bursting. "So can I get my money back?"

Rico reached into his pocket. "Yeah, lady. You get your money back." He peeled off five tens and handed them to her, then held up his hand as Conan began to protest. "Don't worry, *amigo*. I'm gonna find out who this chump is, and when I do . . . let's just say I'll take my fifty dollars out of his ass."

CHAPTER 21

J uanita knew what she was doing was wrong, but she was power-less to check herself. After helping Conan at the center the day before, reading to the children and greeting their smiling parents, her heart felt ready to burst. No smiling sistah-girl or brother-man dressed in work clothes had ever come to pick her up from day care. Never had she squealed in delight at the sight of her parents with out-stretched arms, or pushed her face into a mother's skirts and breathed in the lingering traces of her perfume.

Watching the happy little girls leave the center with parents whose facial features matched theirs was a painful reminder of all the days when she'd spent hours before the mirror; examining her features for a hint of the dark-skinned girl called Puddin in the photo. Watching the children was a reminder of just how much she'd missed. Scooter had been happy to lie to her over the years and tell her she had Aunt Hattie's lips and chin, but Juanita knew better. His parents were dead too, but at least he had the same skin tone as his grandparents and even had his grandfather's cowlick and dimpled cheeks.

Juanita looked like no one. With her wide green eyes, wavy hair, and low-slung behind, there was no one she even remotely resembled in her family, and by the time the last parent had run through the center's doors five minutes before closing time, breathless and apologetic, her eyes were brimming with tears and she was determined to find her own answers. To uncover those mysterious details that Hattie wouldn't, or couldn't, share with her. To discover who she looked like.

Conan had immediately picked up on the source of her sadness and had given her some sound advice. "Talk to your aunt, Juanita," he urged. "Find a way to communicate that doesn't hurt her so much. Really, baby. There are things you need to know."

Communicate with Aunt Hattie, hell. Not when it came down to her parents. Juanita trembled at the thought of what she was about to do, and she almost picked up the telephone to call Scooter. He was the only one who could relate to how she felt. Not only was he her best friend, he too was an orphan and the only person who she could be totally sure of. She missed him and was ashamed of how she'd been ignoring him since meeting Conan. She made a mental note to give him a call and let him know how she felt, but first she had to get through the next few hours.

Minutes earlier, she'd faked a headache and a sore throat and stayed in bed with her head beneath the covers while Aunt Hattie and Uncle Herbie prepared for services at church.

"Here." Aunt Hattie stood over her wearing a floppy white hat and holding a steaming glass of cloudy water. "I mixed you some hot salt water to gargle with. Just roll it 'round at the back of your throat for as long as you can stand it, then spit it out."

Juanita begged off, telling her aunt her head hurt too much to stand, let alone walk into the bathroom to gargle, and after muttering a few garbled sentences, she slid deeper beneath the soft pink blankets.

The elderly pair had finally left for Sunday services, but not before Aunt Hattie had urged her to try to get up and fix herself a cup of hot herb tea. And now, a full ten minutes after the door had been slammed and locked, Juanita stood in her aunt's lavender-and-rose-colored bedroom searching her closet for the evidence she knew had to be there.

Using a metal stool, she hunted on the top shelf, feeling blindly in the darkness until her fingers brushed against a leather box. She stood on her tiptoes and strained, yanking and grasping until the box was free in her hands. Juanita jumped easily to the floor, then sank down on the full-size bed that was covered tightly with a lavender paisley bedspread and pried the lid off the brown hatbox.

Eagerly, she searched through the faded documents inside, disregarding light bills, rent receipts, a few old lottery tickets, and Uncle Herbie's discharge papers from his brief stint in the Navy. She also found a faded photo of a stern-faced black man who looked just like a younger Uncle Herbie but was dressed in clothing straight out of the olden days. The strong physical resemblance this man held to her aunt and uncle was apparent, even if there were holes in the photo where his eyes should have been. It looked almost as if someone had taken straight pins and poked his eyes clear out through the back of his head.

There were a few other items in the box, a rusted Singer sewing stapler, a pair of funny-shaped Cat Woman glasses, a few rolls of thread, a stale package of Violet candy, and a half-used tube of Fixodent. There had to be more stuff somewhere, Juanita was sure of it. Carefully, she replaced the lid on the box and, standing on the stool once more, pushed it back into its former spot on the high shelf. Her eyes settled on Hattie's nightstand, but her search there proved just as fruitless. The only things she found of interest were her fifth-grade report card and an old obituary program from the funeral of Scooter's grandmother Dot Morrison.

On a whim, Juanita pulled open the cabinet doors to her auntie's prized highboy. It was made from stained cherry wood and had delicate hand carvings on its legs, down its sides, and along its base. The only things Aunt Hattie stored in there were cherished possessions: a box of gold-plated flatware, laced tablecloths, soft rose-scented towels, and hand-sewn quilts. They almost never had occasion to use any of these treasures; there was never any need. They never had company—in fact, besides Conan, no one other than housing maintenance or Scooter and his family had so much as stepped foot in their apartment in more years than Juanita could remember.

She ran her hands along the heavy fabric of the quilts, enjoying the feel of the patched segments of material beneath her fingers. Aunt Hattie claimed that she, her mother, and Juanita's mother, Puddin, had sewn many of the quilts when she was a young girl back in Tennessee.

Juanita fingered the edge of a quilt, then moved on to the rectangular-shaped box of fourteen-carat-gold-plated flatware Uncle Herbie had sent home from Japan. She untied a knot of twine from its top, then lifted the pinewood lid and marveled at the rows of butter knives, forks, and spoons that glittered atop a bed of burgundy velvet cushioning. Aunt Hattie had told her if push ever came to shove and she was broke, she could always pawn a few pieces of this flatware and pay her way out of a bind.

After several long moments of admiring the fancy pieces, Juanita began lowering the lid, then froze with her hands suspended in mid-air. There, on the inside edge of the box, right next to the gleaming knives and beneath the burgundy cushion, was a sliver of brown. A sliver so tiny, she almost didn't see it. Had never seen it when admiring the flatware before.

She glanced at the clock, then quickly carried the heavy case over to Aunt Hattie's bed and carefully pulled each fork, knife, and spoon from its sheathed holder. She extracted the serving spoon and the golden spatula, then pulled the entire sheet of velvet cushion from the bottom of the box. Suddenly the room felt warm, and her head felt like it was filling with helium, floating her to the ceiling. Rubbing her damp palms on the edge of her nightgown, she pulled the brown envelope out of its resting place and read the words that had been written in large, shaky letters.

To be opened only upon my death. Hattie Dell Lucas.

The envelope was taped closed, but there was no way she could stop herself. With the utmost care, Juanita pried the yellowing edges of tape away from the paper, getting most of it off without a hitch, but pulling off telltale strips of brown in one or two spots. Her fingers trembled as she slipped her hand inside the envelope and pulled out a stack of five or six sheets of paper, a few newspaper clippings, and a stack of old photos secured with a big red rubber band.

Her body seemed to float on air as she spread the photos across the bed and began reading from a sheet of official-looking paper at the top of the stack. She'd skimmed the first two paragraphs before the enormity of her discovery struck her, and by then there was no turning back, no stopping the feeling of horror and despair that consumed her spirit and overtook her soul, and certainly no stopping the river of tears that seemed destined to forever flow from the abyss that suddenly yawned endlessly and beyond measure from the center of her heart.

, , ,

It took her over an hour but she did it. After visually devouring every document Aunt Hattie had hidden away in the envelope, committing the details to memory, and studying every photo, Juanita padded into the kitchen, barefoot and still in her nightgown, and opened the double compartment at the bottom of the hutch cabinet. There, she took out graham crackers, a half-eaten bag of pretzels, four Twinkies, an Entenmann's Marble Loaf pound cake, a full box of Lemon Cooler cookies, a Drake's Devil Dog, a small bag of salted peanuts, and a can of fried onions.

She used both hands to stuff the contents into her mouth, cramming and smearing the food around her lips, the moisture of her tears rendering it sticky until every scrap was in her stomach. Even then, the nineteen-year lie sat bloated and heavy, cannonlike in the pit of her gut. She tore off hunks of the pound cake, licked the Devil Dog wrapper clean, and even held the empty pretzel bag up to her mouth, the salty remnants dissolving acridly on her tongue.

Engorged, she sat for a moment, then opened the refrigerator and gulped down the better part of a quart of milk straight from the red-and-white cardboard container. That done, she picked up every wrapper, every shred of evidence of her feast, and placed them neatly into a plastic trash bag, which she tied at the top then pushed into the back of the hall coat closet, where boxes of winter items, hats, mittens, and scarves, were usually stored.

She walked unsteadily toward the bathroom and bent over the bowl, embracing the familiarity and the comfort of its coolness, finding solace and pleasure in the amount of control she was learning to exert on this special part of her life.

She lifted the lid and swept her fingers around the insides of her mouth, and as the weight of the lie was expelled with the torrent, she reveled in the sensation of ridding herself of all that was wrong, bad, different, and amiss in her life. While the contents of her stomach flowed past her lips and splashed down into oblivion, she rejoiced in the act of ridding herself of herself.

✦ ✦ ✦

"Gal, if I done told you once, I told you a hundred times! You don't fool around like that and step outside of your race! And where you thank you going? It's just about the middle of the night! Way too late for you to call yourself walking these mean streets like somebody's floozy! If you need some air, just stick your head out the windah!"

Hattie fumed as Juanita continued to dress unhurriedly, coolly applying lotion to her arms and legs, taking care to rub the creamy cantaloupe-and-melon-scented moisturizer into the crevices between her toes. She smoothed down her light-blue sundress, searched her cluttered closet, and pulled out a pair of low-heeled sandals, then began brushing her hair with long, sure strokes.

Hattie snorted loudly. What in the devil had gotten into Nita! For the past few days she'd been stomping around the house with a storm brewing in her eyes and defiance in her step. Slamming doors and flouncing about like a two-year-old! Her tone was rude and curt; she refused to eat anything Hattie cooked, but every morning her trash can was full of empty cake wrappers, cookie boxes, and half-eaten bags of chips and pretzels. When Hattie asked about it, the chile got fresh and told her it was none of her business what she ate! She even had the nerve to swell up and run her mouth off at Herbie! Such attitude! Seemed like the fool gal had gone outta her pea-pickin' mind over that Mexican trash!

"Nita, I'm *talking* to you! At least have the decency to make like you listenin' when I speak to you!"

"Calm down, Auntie. I hear you. You're talking loud enough for the dead to hear you."

Hattie's eyes bulged. She balled her fists to keep them from trembling. Her voice shook with rage.

"Gal," she breathed, "I don't know who you thank you talking to, but you take that high-handedness with me again and I declare I'll lay you out on this here floor! Don't let your mouth write a check your ass can't cash!"

Juanita yawned and gave her a bored look.

"You got the devil in you, Miss Thang. You need to stay 'way from that boy is what you need to do. We heard 'bout him almost killing that old lady what lives in his building. If'n he can brutalize an old woman right there where he live, what you thank that boy will do to you?"

"He's a man, Auntie. A man. And a gentleman too. Besides, his name was cleared in that whole break-in mess. His boss gave the police a sworn statement that Conan was at work the whole day, even during the time when that old lady was attacked. They don't know who it was yet, but somebody definitely tried to set him up."

Hattie snorted. "Hmph! Setup, my foot! You know them Spanish stick together! It's a piss-poor frog what don't praise his own pond! His boss would probably say anything to protect one of his own."

Juanita stared hard at her aunt, her hands on her hips. "His boss is *black*, Aunt Hattie. As black as they come. And Conan is innocent." She dismissed Hattie with her hand. "They've already proven that. You really should get to know him. He's such a nice guy! He's taken me to the movies three times, we went skating twice, walked around the park a few times, and he's even taken me out to dinner once. In all of that time he has never, and I mean never, disrespected me or made a pass at me; he has never even tried to kiss me, although once I really wanted him to and I could have sworn he wanted to kiss me too—"

Hattie's hand flew to her chest. "Run that by me again? Kiss you? You wanted that trash to *kiss* you?"

"Auntie, please—"

"Don't you 'Auntie, please' me! I been living on this here blue-and-green earth just a little bit longer than you, and you best believe I done seen my share!" Her voice softened in desperation. "Baby girl, them Mexicans ain't to be trusted! Now, I'm only telling you this to spare you a lot of pain. To spare you! You know how them Spanish grocers like to cheat coloreds—taking they food stamps and only giving them half the face value. They refuse to put prices on they goods, and when we walk in the door they charge us whatever high price comes to they head! Just look at the way they treat they own wimmens . . . keeping them pregnant all the time and fighting them in the streets! Gal, you better watch—"

"I better watch what?" Juanita exploded. "Watch *what*?" She dropped the hairbrush and faced her aunt. "Everything you're saying happens with black folks too! I'm tired of judging folks and being judged because of stuff I don't control. All my life I've been teased and beaten up because of my hair, my eyes, my skin—I never fit in anywhere! Not with white people and sometimes not with a whole lot of blacks either! It's always Juanita is too light, too fat, hair too long, eyes too green, lips too big, nose too thin, hips too wide. Folks sit up in church and preach about the love of Jesus. Well from all the pictures I've seen, Jesus don't look a hell of a whole lot like any of us! Black folks worship a man whose skin is white, his eyes are blue, and his hair is light blond—but you profess to love him more than you love yourself!"

"Chile," Hattie warned, sucking cool air in between the spaces in her teeth. "You betta shet yo' blasphemous mouth! You betta hit yo' knees and ask the Lord for forgiveness, ask him to heal yo' broken tongue!"

Juanita snatched her purse from her bed and took a step closer to her aunt. "Tell me something, Auntie," she said quietly. "Before I shut my mouth just tell me one thing: Who in the world is my mother?"

Hattie stiffened, then turned her head and closed her eyes.

"I been in your highboy, Auntie. I know it was wrong, but I went in there looking for the answers you refused to give me. And guess what I found, Auntie? Guess what I found?"

Hattie turned her back. This was a moment that she had feared, had dreaded, for years. Against Herbie's advice she'd woven an intricate web of deceit around Juanita. Tried to cocoon her in a protective layer of lies that would soften the blow of her existence. Fabricated a fairy tale she thought would satisfy the child, and now it seemed as if her house of lies was about to come crashing down.

Somehow she found the strength to turn around and face her niece.

"I found a death certificate, Aunt Hattie, and the name on it was

Patrice Lucas. Said she died when she was fourteen. From strangulation. In 1942. I wasn't born until 1979."

Her face seemed to crumple and cave in on itself. "So who am I, Auntie? Who am I?"

Hattie pulled Juanita in her arms. Tears rolled freely down her face and dripped into the girl's hair. "You a child of God, Nita. A baby that got born from a mother and a father who loved you so much they gived you to me." Hattie tried to pull Juanita closer, but the girl tore herself from her arms.

"That's probably a damn lie too! All these years you've been lying to me about Puddin! Telling me she was my mama! Making me think it was something wrong with me for looking like a green-eyed fat yellow freak when everybody else in the family was beautiful like normal black folks! Well, just who do I look like, Auntie? Huh? Tell me, Aunt Hattie!" Juanita screamed loud enough to bring the walls tumbling down. "Who the hell do I look like?"

Hattie wept. "Baby, please . . . don't."

Juanita sneered, her features forming a hideous mask Hattie had never seen before. "I don't care about your tears, Auntie. I've cried enough of my own. Until you stop lying to me and tell me the truth about who I am, I don't have to listen to you or anybody else. I have a right to know who I look like. No, I *demand* to know who I look like."

Hattie sank slowly down to her knees and clasped her hands together in prayer. The very hands that had washed clothes and scrubbed floors; hands that had cooked meals and cleaned toilets; they'd patted backs and wiped noses. And now all they could do was fold over themselves in supplication and ask for forgiveness.

"Your mama, chile," she whispered to the empty room, because Juanita was no longer there to hear her. "You look just like your sweet li'l ol' mama."

Rise up, Hattie Dell!

"Big Momma?"

Now ain't the time to falter! Stand up, gal, you did what you had to do!

"But I lied, Big Momma. Now the chile gon' end up hatin' me and her mama."

How can you get hate from somethin' built with love? The gal wasn't ready then. She ready now. Finish it up, Hattie Dell. Finish it up!

A few minutes later, Hattie rose to her feet and shuffled from the room. Each of her earthly years showed in her face, and the twisted roads she'd traveled rode high on her back. Wordlessly, she limped past Herbie, who had witnessed the scene but chosen to remain silent, and stepped inside her bedroom. Hattie sat on her lavender bedspread and picked up the telephone. Her fingers dialed the number that over the years had become seared in her memory.

The receiver was lifted on the third ring.

"Hello?"

Hattie's voice shook. "Honey?" she said softly. "It's time. Yes, Lawd, sugar. It is time."

CHAPTER 22

Juanita raced down the dark streets, the wind at her back and her partially brushed hair billowing out behind her like she was a love-struck model on the cover of a romance novel. Tears stung her eyes as sobs of self-pity tore from her throat. She passed through the projects quickly, and although she'd forgotten her wristwatch on her dresser, it had to be way past midnight judging by the way the busy streets had thinned. She forced herself to focus on nothing but the rhythmic motion of her legs taking her as far away as possible from the apartment she shared with those two impostors.

Winded, she slowed to a trot and began taking notice of her surroundings. The shape of the neighborhood had changed. The tall, high-rise projects gave way to low-income apartment buildings and tenements. She slowed further to a half walk, half run, clutching at a white-hot pokerlike stitch that lanced through her side.

A chill in the night air swept mercifully over the parts of her that boiled, and helped cool her. Her hair floated around her face, clinging to her cheeks and mouth like stringy wisps of cotton candy. She pulled the damp curls away from her face and plaited a loose braid at the back of her neck.

Home was far behind her. The two-story attached row homes in this area were in even worse condition than the projects where she lived. She walked quickly, darkness cloaking the shadows and providing shelter to her fears. Aside from a few noisy dogs, not even a car swished past to disturb the stillness, and the only movement she saw was a stray alley cat struggling to knock the lid off a garbage can. Where in the world were all the people? She had a fleeting image of *The Twilight Zone* and rubbed her arms to comfort herself.

She passed an abandoned warehouse and a boarded-up building owned by the telephone company that had once provided jobs by the hundreds for local residents. Ahead on her right were a few high-fenced lots piled tall with rubber tires and hubcaps, and an Associated Supermarket that was closed for the night. She jumped as a dog barked and snarled from a nearby yard, then skirted a few dented trash cans that should have been pushed to the curb. With her sandals clicking, she stepped off the sidewalk and onto the smooth tar of the street.

Juanita glimpsed an illuminated grocery store sign with a Pepsi logo off in the distance and her heart leaped. She picked up her pace. She could ask for directions inside, or maybe even use the telephone and call Conan. He'd come for her. She was sure of it.

Disappointment fell over her when she reached the corner. A bright orange CLOSED sign was displayed in the window. She could see into the store's interior through the slatted theft-proof gates. Deserted.

Okay, she told herself. It was time to come up with plan B. She peered around for a street sign. If she knew what street she was on she'd be able to find the nearest avenue and work her way toward a bus stop. Parker Road, the green-and-white sign read. Parker? Didn't Conan live on Parker? Juanita stopped in her tracks and put her hands on her hips. If she remembered correctly, Conan said he lived at 315 Parker Road. She peered at a house nearby. The lopsided gold numbers displayed above the doorway read 393. The streets were still deserted.

She moved on again, counting the house numbers out loud, the sound of her own voice bringing her small comfort. As she crossed the street into the next block, she was relieved to see activity and hear other voices at last.

"*¿Que pasa, mamacita?*" a man called out a window to her. Juanita ignored him and kept walking, hurrying down the street counting the house numbers. She stopped in front of building 315. It was a three-story brick apartment building, and although it looked old, there were clean glass panes in the large metal door and an intercom system that served as security. She stepped up to the door and paused with her finger over the pad of lighted doorbells. Comacho, Gomez, Rodriguez, Andrews, Jackson, Carr, and Lopez. Which one? All the names sounded Puerto Rican except three. Was it Conan Rodriguez? Nah, that wasn't it. Conan Comacho? Juanita shook her head. Suddenly it clicked.

Conan Matthew Lopez! Yes! She pressed hard on the top right buzzer and was surprised when it resounded almost immediately and the automatic lock disengaged from the door. She entered the building cautiously. Someone had taken great pains in its maintenance, as the black-and-white checkered floors were clean and she could see her reflection in the chrome and brass borders of the fixtures.

There were two apartments on the ground floor, one on the left and the other on her right. Potted plants and brass-rimmed mirrors lined the hall, and the apartment doors sported a coat of fresh paint. Juanita crept up the marble stairs, holding on to the thick wood banister and following the lively sounds of Latin music that blared overhead.

As she passed the second-floor landing and neared the third, a female voice called down, "Lourdes! Is that you? Damn, *chica*! Hurry up! You're keeping the fellas waiting, girl!"

"Umm . . ." Juanita cleared her throat. "No, I'm not Lourdes. My name is Juanita. I'm looking for this guy . . . Conan . . . Conan Lopez."

"Wan-eeta?" replied the voice. "Who the fuck is a Wan-ceta?"

At the top of the stairs she found herself face-to-face with a stunning, dark-haired Puerto Rican girl wearing cut-off jeans and a belly shirt. Her full breasts jiggled beneath the thin material of the shirt, and her shapely legs looked like she worked out regularly with weights. The smell of roasted peppers and seasoned poultry wafted out of the apartment.

"I'm Juanita. I'm looking for Conan. Does he live here?"

The girl tossed her teased mane and rolled her eyes. "Yeah. He lives here. I'm Mercedes and I practically live here with him." She turned on her heels and pushed through the apartment door yelling for Conan in Spanish.

Juanita followed, stepping into a living room filled with lit incense, and peered through the semidarkness. *There's a party over here,* she thought wryly, bombarded by the smell of spicy foods, dancing couples, and loud music. She caught a glimpse of Jorge, who was locked in a passionate kiss with a tall skinny girl sporting a short, tapered hairstyle.

Conan emerged from a back bedroom with a questioning look in his eyes and surprise on his face. He wore a red-and-blue Barry Sanders shirt with the number 20 in large blue lettering, baggy blue jeans, and what looked like a brand-new pair of stark-white Nikes with a royal blue swoosh.

"What's wrong?" He rushed toward her, his eyes searching her face.

"I'm sorry," Juanita blurted. "I didn't know you had company or I wouldn't have come . . . especially so late."

He shrugged. "I don't have company. It's my *tante*'s birthday so we invited a few relatives. You okay?" He reached out to take her hand but stopped short. Every eye in the small room watched him, curious about the strange woman who'd shown up on his doorstep.

"I'm . . . I'm okay," Juanita stammered. "I just thought . . . I was in the area, so I stopped by." She lowered her eyes, knowing how silly she must have sounded. All conversation in the room had ceased; the foreign, animated chatter was cut short. She detected open hostility in quite a few pairs of flashing female eyes.

Conan spoke. "What's wrong, baby? You're shivering. Here." He led her over to the couch. "Sit right here and let me get you something warm to drink."

Juanita sat on the edge of the multicolored floral sofa. The plastic slipcovers felt cold and alien on the back of her thighs. Scented candles were lit upon high shelves, and houseplants thrived in large hanging pots and sprouted from bright ceramic vases. Several couples stood poised in the middle of the living room floor. The furniture had been pushed aside, and the lights dimmed. The music started up again, and the couples seemed to melt into each other's arms. A slow

Spanish ballad wafted from hidden speakers, and thankfully everyone's attention returned to the music. Juanita smoothed her hair and continued to look around.

The walls were adorned with family photos, including one of Conan, Jorge, and a boy who must've been Conan's brother, Thor. There was such a complete resemblance between the brothers that the only way Juanita could tell them apart was by the haunted look in Thor's eyes. That same look that sometimes showed itself in Conan's. There were also statues of Jesus nailed to the cross, and various depictions of the Virgin Mary. The apartment had an impoverished but immaculate look that was common to her own home, and the ornaments and furniture, though old, seemed to have been selected and arranged with care.

"Here, baby." Conan returned and handed her a mug of sweet hot tea. He sat down next to her and draped his arm around her shoulders.

Juanita sipped the tea and enjoyed the comforting weight of his arm on her back. It was rare for Conan to touch her. To hold her hand, even. And he had called her baby. Not once but twice. Her emotions came down hard on her and tears slipped from her eyes.

"Tell me what happened, Juanita." His voice was soothing, his Hispanic accent lilting and pronounced.

"I . . . I went off on my auntie. I went rambling through her papers and saw something I shouldn't have. . . ." She winced. The memory of her scathing words and the way that she'd violated her aunt's trust were a blow to her stomach. Fresh tears cascaded down her cheeks.

Conan passed her a box of Kleenex from an end table and she blew her nose gratefully. "You wanna talk about it?" he asked softly. "Will that help?"

Juanita shrugged. She was no longer sure if anything would help. She should have gone to Scooter. To someone she knew she could trust. She felt uncomfortable under the curious glances of Conan's family, and that Mercedes girl kept poking her head into the living room and checking her out.

"I don't know. Maybe nothing can help me." She stood abruptly. "Look, I gotta go. I shouldn't have come here, barging in on you and your family, forcing you to explain our friendship—"

"Relationship."

"Relationship? What about Mercedes, who practically lives here?"

Conan laughed. "She practically does! My Tante Rosira is her grandmother. Her parents live in New Jersey, but it's boring over there, so she likes to hang out around here."

Juanita shrugged. "Whatever. Me showing up like this really put you on the spot, and I'm sorry."

Conan rose. "You don't have to apologize, Juanita. I'm glad you came. Glad you came to *me*. Let me get a jacket for you and we can go for a walk. You hungry? We have plenty of Spanish food."

She shook her head. Although the food smelled delicious and she had not eaten since her binge and purge the night before, she felt no hunger. No desire to fill her stomach.

"No. Thanks, though."

She waited awkwardly near the front door while Conan went for a jacket. The slow ballad had given way to a blaring, upbeat Afro-Cuban salsa, and the couples on the floor gyrated their hips and stomped their feet in a whirl of frenzied motion. A cacophony of Spanish lyrics assaulted her ears, and she cringed from the onslaught of unfamiliar noises.

"Are you okay, dear?"

Juanita spun around to see a neat, well-dressed older woman with a warm smile. Her dark hair was streaked with bits of gray, and above her slight smile were the saddest blue eyes Juanita had ever seen. The woman wore a simple black dress and small gold hoops dangled from her earlobes.

"Yes," she blurted, then remembered her manners. "Yes, ma'am, I'm fine."

The woman extended her hand and Juanita accepted it to shake, but instead found her hand enveloped in a soft, welcoming embrace. She stared into the woman's eyes and felt an instant kinship. This had to be Grace Lopez, Conan's mother. Her mouth crinkled merrily at the corners and her eyes were the exact same shade of blue as her son's.

"I'm Grace. Grace Lopez. It's too late for such a pretty young lady to be out alone. Conan will take you home, but you're welcome to

come back again. Anytime. As you can see"—she smiled and tilted her
head to one side in a gesture of friendship—"like my son, I welcome
you into my home."

Juanita could only stare mutely at the smiling woman, from whom
kindness radiated like perfume. This is where Conan got his sensi-
tivity, his peaceful nature, and his loving smile.

"I'm Juanita, Mrs. Lopez. Juanita Lucas. I'm sorry for coming here
so late, but I was walking in the neighborhood and somehow wound
up here."

Grace Lopez patted her hand. "Well, you came to the right place. I
trust my son, and if you are his friend, then this was the right place for
you to come. Is there anyone you need to call? Will your mother be
worried about you?"

"I'm about to take her home, Ma." Conan returned and kissed his
mother's cheek before draping a jacket around Juanita's shoulders.

Juanita released Grace's hands reluctantly. She accepted Conan's
jacket. It was the same color as the shirt he wore, and had the number
20 displayed in red across the back and embroidered on the front
breast pocket as well.

"Thank you," she whispered, as much to Conan as to his mother.
In response, he reached over and planted a tiny kiss near the base of
her jaw, beneath her ear.

They walked silently, the darkness of the night a comforting veil of
serenity. The quiet streets no longer menaced Juanita. With Conan by
her side, his strong shoulders and sturdy build protecting her, she felt
as safe as a newborn baby.

Baby. The thought of an infant brought her fresh pangs of despair.
She'd been an infant once. Probably abandoned and taken in by her
auntie's mercy. Her heart renewed its ache.

"C'mere." Conan stopped and leaned against a parked car.

He pulled her to his side and offered her his shoulder to lean on
and she gratefully accepted it.

"I hurt my Aunt Hattie," she sobbed. "I hurt her real bad."

"You hurt her? How?" he asked. "I'm sure you didn't hit her,
right?"

"No. Not with my hands. But I hit her just the same. I kicked her and punched her and slapped her with my ugly words. For the first time in my life I saw my auntie cry. As much as she loved me and sacrificed for me, and it was me who brought tears to her eyes."

Conan rubbed her hand. His touch was even more soothing than his mother's.

"Why?" he asked.

"My mother . . ." she croaked against the hardness of her words. "She isn't my mother."

Conan stared. "What do you mean, Nita? I don't understand."

She took a deep breath. "It's what I was trying to tell you earlier. . . . I went rambling through my auntie's papers and I saw my mother's— I mean Puddin's—death certificate."

Conan stood up straight. "I thought Puddin was your mother."

Juanita sniffed. "I did too. But the death certificate said Patrice Lucas died in 1942. When she was fourteen. Somebody s-s-strangled her! She was only fourteen!"

Conan was quiet. He held her hand a little tighter.

Juanita searched his eyes for understanding. "Don't you see what that means? She died thirty-something years before I was born! Not in childbirth like they always told me! I thought it was me who killed her, but s-somebody choked her neck! She was only fourteen—she couldn't have been my mother. There's no way it could be possible!"

"Then who is?"

Juanita swallowed hard and leaned against him for strength and comfort. "I don't know, but that's what I have to find out."

///////////////////////////////

CHAPTER 23

Darkness blanketed the alcove where Scooter choked and gagged as Jorge slid his wet organ in and out of his mouth. His head was jammed against the wall as Jorge gripped his cheeks with both hands and pounded away like there was no tomorrow.

"So you thinking for yourself now, bitch? Huh?"

Scooter gasped and tried to shake his head but could not dislodge his grip.

Jorge's hips bucked wildly as he raised himself up on his toes and pumped solidly down Scooter's throat. "You gonna think? Or you gonna do what the fuck I tell you to do? Huh? Huh, motherfucker? Huh?"

Scooter coughed and gagged but Jorge had no mercy. A sharp crack split the air as Jorge's palm whipped across his face. Tears fell from Scooter's eyes as Jorge battered him with every thrust and stroke.

It was only a matter of time before Scooter gave in. His lips were sore and bruised, his jaw ached, and blood seeped from his nostrils. Although he felt light-headed and dizzy, he didn't dare try to jerk away from the hurting Jorge was putting on him. Besides, his own penis was rock hard, and the part of him that was needy and vulnerable hoped that maybe today would be the day Jorge agreed to accept his most precious gift.

He went to work on his lover with renewed vigor, doing everything he could to please him and bring a swift end to his delicious torture. But Jorge seemed to have no interest in completing the sex act. He kept it going at a frenzied, rigorous pace until Scooter thought he would surely choke, maybe even die.

"Esss!" he shrieked in surrender, squealing around the massive love muscle jammed into his mouth. "Esss!"

Jorge slowed his stroke slightly.

"You ready to do what the fuck I tell you to do?"

"Esssss. Eeease. Essss!"

Jorge plunged himself deeper and renewed his gyrating, thrusting motions. But this time, instead of holding back, he let himself go, and the moment Scooter felt his mouth flooded with warm sticky fluid, he let himself go too.

/ / /

Hattie finished scrubbing the kitchen floor, then pushed the bucket in a corner and sat in Herbie's window seat to wait for it to dry. She watched the children playing outside and wished there were some way to protect their innocence from the harsh realities of project life.

She heard a key turn in the lock and strained to listen to the murmuring voices on the other side of the door. She knew who it was. Nobody but Juanita and Herbie had a key, and since she'd just washed the floors in Herbie's room while he lay in bed asleep, it could only be one other person.

"Hi, Auntie." Juanita pushed through the door, still trying to remove her key from the lock. Hattie knew Juanita hadn't been alone. She'd heard his voice, and couldn't believe the boy had the nerve to walk up to her door again, but that would have to be dealt with later.

Juanita took two steps forward and froze in position. "Oh," she said sheepishly. "The floor is wet! I'm sorry, Auntie. I'll go back over it with the mop."

Hattie shook her head quickly. "That's all right, sweetie. Don't worry none about it. It'll dry directly."

Hattie made her words come out low and soothing. A couple of weeks had passed since her niece confessed to looking through her papers and finding out the truth about Puddin's death, yet other than a tearful apology for her disrespect, Juanita had been reluctant to talk about it and had chosen to remain silent and push the incident under the rug.

Hattie had lived long enough to know that silent didn't hardly mean fixed. She knew the initial storm had passed, but if the issue was left unresolved there'd be smaller, more powerful residual storms in its wake.

It was time for them to talk. To tell her baby the God's honest truth. Hattie rose and took Juanita's hand. She led the puzzled girl into the living room and sat her down on the high-backed sofa before she spoke.

"Baby," Hattie began, "I know how hard it's been for you over the years . . . being raised by two peoples old enough to be your grand-folks, getting teased all the time by them no-count gals 'round here 'bout your hair and them beautiful green eyes . . . growing up thanking you to blame for your mama's death—"

"I don't fault you for any of that, Auntie," Juanita interrupted. She leaned her head against Hattie's shoulder and sighed deeply. "I was wrong for going through your papers. I've been lucky to have you and Uncle Herbie in my life."

"Yes, you were wrong for rambling, that much is true. But I was wrong for lying. For not telling you the truth from the very beginning. Alls I ever wanted was to protect you, to spare you the pain of growing up feeling like you didn't belong to nobody."

Hattie pursed her lips as a faraway look crept into her eyes. "I was there, baby. The day you come into this-here world, I was right there. It was the evening of May the second, 1979. Back then, I worked for the Jacobsons, and lemme tell you, they was some mighty ornery folks. I was fixin' to clean up some old mess the Missus had done made, and I heard this funny noise. Like a cat what done got caught by a whole mess a dogs."

Hattie watched Juanita's eyes widen and sparkle a particular shade of green. "I ran upstairs to find out who was making all a' that racket and that's when I found them."

"F-found them?"

Hattie nodded. "Your mama and daddy was trying they best to get you born. There was blood everywhere. The floor, the bed . . . that beautiful white carpet the Missus was so proud of. Ruined. But alls I could see was my sweet baby girl. My Lola. Suffering so, but trying her best to be brave."

Juanita squeezed Hattie's hand. "Lola?"

Hattie nodded again, slowly. "That's your mama. Lola Jacobson. Your daddy is Pierre Johnson. They gived you to me to raise."

"But why?" Juanita cried.

Hattie pressed her lips together. "Nita, I done the best I could by you. From the moment I agreed to raise you, Herbie and I lived strictly for you. Now, I ain't looking for no prize or no special reward, 'cause I did it all out of love."

She waved her hand, warding off the words that were forming on Juanita's lips. "I know you have a whole heap a' questions and I pray to God you get a whole heap a' answers, but, honey, some thangs just ain't for me to tell. For you to get the best understandin' of why thangs was done the way they was, I thank you better hold off and ask your mama."

"Ask my mother?"

"Yes, baby. Your mama. She wanna see you."

Juanita broke down sobbing in Hattie's arms. As Hattie stroked her baby's hair and rubbed her back, she prayed to God that she and Lola had done the right thing by Juanita. She knew it hadn't been easy for the child living amongst the elderly and abandoned by kids her own age. She suspected early on that no matter how much hair grease Juanita packed in her hair, or how much she imitated those silly-looking gals on BET, with her green eyes and fair skin she would have to accept herself for who she was if she hoped to find peace in her life.

"Come on, Nita. Pull yourself together." Hattie gathered Juanita close and planted a big kiss on her forehead. "I sure hope them tears are tears of joy, because you one lucky girl to be loved by so many folks on this-here earth!"

Juanita gave a semi-smile.

"Now, gone in there and wash your face and blow your nose. I made plans for us to meet Lola this Friday night at Sammy's Steakhouse over on Mott Place. That gives us almost a week to get ready, and as slow as you are, chile, you gonna need it!"

Hattie watched as Juanita rose from the sofa. She saw the questions raging through her, and later, she knew, there would be some anger. Some pain. An attempt to assign blame where none was really due. She prayed Lola was strong enough to deal with her daughter's sorrow.

As much as Hattie loved Juanita, her love for Lola was also ever strong. After Juanita's birth, Lola had gone on to graduate from high school and college, and although she continued to live on Long Island, not far away from the home where the saga began, she commuted to upper Manhattan three days a week where she worked as a top executive for some big-time marketing firm.

Hattie grunted. Lola musta owned the whole darn firm the way she kept the money rolling in. From the time Juanita turned five, Hattie had received a monthly check from Lola that was bigger than any she'd ever earned at one time. She was proud of the fact that aside from the time Juanita had her tonsils out, she'd never used a red cent of the money to raise her. She figured that when she took the job on, it was without the promise of a dime, and after the first few years she got accustomed to budgeting and doing without. There'd been no need to dip into Juanita's pot of gold.

And even when Juanita was accepted into college, rather than go to the bank and withdraw her tuition, Hattie took a second job and made Juanita go to the library and look up scholarships and grants that she might qualify for. Thus, the bulk of Juanita's money remained intact, safely earning interest in a long-term CD and two mutual fund accounts.

Hattie planned to surprise Juanita with a fat check when she graduated from Huntington. Her baby would not have to go begging no bank for a minority businessman's loan. Her mama had provided for her over the years, and if the good Lord was willing and the creek didn't rise, Juanita would be able to finance her dreams with cold hard cash.

Hattie folded her hands across her chest and momentarily closed her eyes. It felt good to have the burden of a twenty-year-old lie off her back. She couldn't wait to see Lola's reaction when she saw how lovely her daughter had turned out. To see Juanita's reaction when she saw that those wide hips and green eyes didn't just drop out of the sky. No, they was given to her. Given to her by a sweet little Jewish girl who loved her enough to bring her forth into the world, swathed in fear and crazed in pain, with Hattie at her knees and her daddy by her side, in the second-floor bedroom of a sprawling mansion in the lily-white suburbs of Long Island.

,,,,,,,,,,,,,,,,,,,,,,,,,,,,

CHAPTER 24

Scooter pushed through the revolving doors twenty minutes earlier than usual. It was a dog day, and the temperature promised to spike well over the ninety-degree mark before noon. Oblivious to the weather, he was dressed to kill, but today, in addition to the permissible short-sleeved white shirt, Scooter wore a double-breasted gray houndstooth jacket with a pair of black gabardine slacks.

"Hey, my man!" Jesse Muhammad dapped Scooter a solid five. "You sure stepping early today!" The middle-aged security officer moved back and inspected Scooter from head to toe. "Stepping clean and stepping light, too. What's wrong? Your dogs got to barking in them old 'yassuh massa' shoes?"

Scooter looked down at his casual penny loafers and forced himself to smile. "Yeah, bro. I guess you're right. Had to give my corns a break, you know?"

Jesse roared. "Boy, you done finally figured it out! Trying to please the white man will not only give you corns, it'll give you bunions, and hammertoes, and ingrown toenails. . . ." He chuckled. "If you don't leave that nasty swine alone, it'll give your fool behind a heart attack too!"

Scooter left Jesse laughing at his own jokes and walked briskly to his station. With his back to the security cameras he unpacked his small tote bag and checked his front pocket for the item he'd placed there that morning.

With nothing left to do except replay his plans again and again in his mind, fear washed over him in great big, gut-twisting waves. He'd seen a late-night show on channel eleven where a guy had pulled off something pretty much like this, but that was TV and this was real life. His life. There was so much that could go wrong. Just one fucked-up move could cause a chain reaction that ended with his black ass being sent straight to jail. In fact, if he was caught they'd probably put him under the goddamn jail.

The risks made Scooter dizzy. He lowered his head to his desk and closed his eyes, willing himself to breathe normally.

"Good morning, Socrates! What brings you in so early?"

Scooter sat up quickly and nearly toppled from his stool.

"Um . . . Hi, Evvie. How's it going?" He smiled thinly at the elderly woman and pinched his own thigh to keep it from trembling. He was messing up already! He should have stuck to his normal routine.

"It's going good for me, son," Evelyn replied, concern clouding the merriment in her eyes, "but you look like hell, if you don't mind my saying so."

Scooter turned his charm up a notch, brightening his smile. "Oh, I'm fine," he reassured her. "It's just that my grandfather hasn't been sleeping well lately with his cancer and all. . . . It gets pretty hard when he calls for me in the middle of the night."

Evelyn took his hand. "You poor boy. It's a remarkable thing you're doing for your grandfather. Not many young men your age would be half as dedicated to an elderly family member as you are to your grandfather." Her eyes went misty. "I just hope that someone takes care of me when I'm older and can't do for myself."

She patted his cheek. "Open up on the regular line this morning, would you? Connie just called in sick and Gwen said she'd be a few minutes late." She smiled again before returning to the banking floor.

He let out a long sigh. The slightest mention of his grandfather's name was enough to evoke sympathy from his coworkers. Scooter felt terrible about exploiting Jeo's terminal illness, but most of what he said was true. Between the old man's moans of pain, the horrific smells emanating from his cancer-ridden body, and the frightening terrors of his recent hazy dreams, his nights *were* pretty tiring.

He frowned. There used to be a time that he felt safe and warm. A time when his life was simple and the love of his grandparents and Juanita was enough to sustain him. He didn't know when it all changed. When, like a drug addict, he began desiring more and more of what he knew he shouldn't have.

He rose from his stool, fear pushing his melancholy away. The clock above his station read 8:59. Scooter grimaced. It was a good thing he was studying drama in school. A good thing he was a damned good actor. Facing what lay ahead today would require pulling out all the stops. He was going to have to act up a storm. Act his ass off and give an Oscar-winning performance.

The clock struck 9:00 and Jesse unlocked the doors. Scooter slid the CLOSED sign away from his window as the first customers streamed up the snaking line to the teller stations. He took a deep breath and swallowed, determined to get through this even if it killed him.

"Good morning, Mrs. Domingo." He smiled at the elderly Hispanic woman standing before him. Her curls were snowy beneath her black pillbox hat, and in her gnarled hand she clutched a bright green savings account passbook. "How can I help you today?"

/ / /

It was now or never. All morning long he'd been in and out of the men's room. Stone fear had him trotting back and forth, but now the last drops of nervousness had been squeezed from his bowels and there was nothing left except cold, stark terror.

Scooter flushed the toilet and walked over to the sink, where he spent a full five minutes vigorously soaping and rinsing his hands. Using his elbow, he pushed down on the dispenser lever to release a long sheet of paper towels.

His reflection scared the life out of him. Fear erupted from his body in the form of thousands of itchy fluid-filled pimples. His face, neck, and torso were covered with the hivelike dots. *I look like a walk-*

ing pepperoni pizza, he thought. He hadn't tangled with this much acne since before he turned seventeen.

For the one millionth time, Scooter doubted his own sanity. Surely he had to be a brand-new fool for even thinking he could get away with such nonsense. The actors in that made-for-TV drama didn't have to contend with any of the extraneous variables that could trip him up, and while he fully expected to be behind bars before supper, he was compelled to move forward with his plans.

"Don't forget what I got waiting for you," Jorge had said to him on the phone in the early hours of predawn. "I know you say you my bitch, but I been hurt real bad before." Jorge's voice had actually cracked with emotion. "I need you to prove your love to me, man. If you fuck this up, then I know for sure I gots to find me another honey to roll with."

Icy terror filled Scooter's heart, but his fear of being caught had nothing to do with it. His dread of losing Jorge far exceeded his fear of prosecution. If there was one thing he had learned over the last few weeks, it was that life without Jorge was pointless. His every waking moment was consumed with delicious thoughts of the brash young man. Never before had anyone filled him with so much anticipation and brought him so much joy. For the first time ever, Scooter was in love. Pure and simple.

He would have done anything for Jorge. Anything.

Besides, the money was for a worthy cause.

A heart operation for a dying old woman.

And if Jorge needed a few bucks to save his poor grandma in Puerto Rico—if a few measly dollars out of the hundreds of thousands stashed away in the vault meant Jorge's sweet grandma would live another day—then Scooter was ready to get down to the wire and go through the wall to make sure she got it.

CHAPTER 25

"Conan," his mother called before entering his room. "Where are all of your clothes? I've done the laundry and I see a few of Jorge's things, but there's hardly anything for you at all."

Conan lowered the dumbbells to the floor, then wiped his neck with a towel. "I dunno, Ma. I'm missing some shirts, and a few pairs of my pants have disappeared." He moved past the bed and peered into the small closet he shared with Jorge, tossed a few items around, and reached down to grab something from the floor.

"Ouch!" Conan stuck his index finger in his mouth. "There's glass in here!" He reached in again gingerly and pulled out a picture frame filled with slivery shards.

Grace sucked in her breath. "That's one of my favorite pictures!" she wailed. "How'd it get broken, and why is it in the closet?"

Conan fingered the wooden frame and sat heavily on his bed, examining the three young faces staring up at him. "I didn't do this, Ma. So it had to be Jorge. He's been acting crazy lately. Doing drugs, lying . . ." He hunched his shoulders and raised his eyes to meet his mother's. "He just don't seem like the same person, Ma. So much about him has changed, like he's mad at the whole world. Including me."

Grace smoothed her son's hair. "I've noticed the same things. It's spooky the way I catch him looking at me sometimes. Twice I started to mention it to your father, but then I changed my mind. You know how your father feels about him."

"Looking at you?" Conan stood, fuming. "What do you mean he's been looking at you? If he *ever*—"

"It's nothing, dear." Grace waved her hand. "He just stares, that's all. But I've been meaning to talk to you. You've got dark circles around your eyes and you haven't been eating dinner with us. I know you have a new girlfriend, and I'm sure she's really special, but tell me, son." She placed her hand gently on his arm. "Are you sleeping at night, or are you still having nightmares?"

Conan sat back down and let his head fall to his knees. He mumbled, "Yeah. Almost every night." The fact that he'd killed his brother was a terrible cargo of guilt. It was only in the last few weeks that a ray of light had been able to touch and ease his heartache.

And it was because of her. Juanita. There was something fresh and innocent about her. The girl was deep and compassionate. She understood loss. She understood his pain.

Grace sighed and sat down next to her son, pulling him into her arms and rubbing his back in large slow circles. "You've got to start healing, Conan. Start accepting what has happened and let it go. It's what Thor would have wanted."

"But I jerked the wheel, Ma! I killed him!"

"That's only what Jorge says! It was an accident, and nobody knows exactly what happened. Look, you both admitted to drinking, and Thor had more alcohol in his blood than you and Jorge combined!" She held Conan close. "Don't ever blame yourself for your brother's death. And don't let Jorge blame you, either. He feeds on your guilt to control you. Jorge is not well, Conan. I've done my best to raise him and love him the same way I loved you and Thor, but after what happened to him, after what his stepfather did to him . . . locking him in that horrible closet for days on end, and then Bonita taking him out and both of them using him for their twisted pleasure . . ." Her voice trailed off, leaving her sentence unfinished.

Conan looked at his mother and saw her eyes sparkle with tears. "Is that why he's like that, Ma? Something happened so bad that Jorge can't love? He can't share? Something that's messed him up so bad he hates the whole damn world?"

Grace took her son's hands. "Son, what happened to Jorge shouldn't happen to an animal. No child should have to suffer the torture Jorge was forced to endure. That's why I've tried to love him all these years. Tried to make up for the wrongs that were done to him." Grace swallowed hard and paused for a long moment. "What happened to Jorge," she finally whispered, "was grounds for murder. If your father had done to you what Bonita and Bobby repeatedly did to him, I'd have cut out his evil heart and waited for the police to arrive."

///

Scooter watched as Sol Steinberg left his desk and walked toward the international banking office. Immediately, he crouched down near his petty cash vault and retrieved the crumpled Sears bag from his right front pocket. He balled the bag up and slid it into the sack containing the large payroll he'd just prepared for the F. W. Wilson Corporation. He knew the security cameras were angled to record the face of the customers and not the feet of the staff, so there was little danger of his being discovered stuffing the bulging cash sack down the front of his jacket. The danger would come much later.

"Gwen." He rushed past his assistant. "I'm taking an early lunch. I won't be gone long. If anyone asks for me, just leave a message at my station and I'll handle it when I get back."

She asked, "Are you okay, Socrates? Is anything wrong?"

Scooter froze. Perspiration dripped from his chin and an odor of fear filled his nostrils. He crossed his arms over the slight bulge in his jacket. "I'm fine, why do you ask?"

"Well." The young woman seemed to struggle to find her words. "It's just that your rash looks like it could be a bad case of something serious, and the way you're perspiring, you may even have a fever." She looked worried. "Are you sure you're feeling okay?"

"I'm fine," Scooter replied and brushed past her station. Damn white people were always digging around in folks' business. His shoes slapped softly against the carpeted walkway as he sped toward the men's room.

Safely inside a locked stall, Scooter removed his jacket and cradled the cash sack. He reached inside, retrieved the plastic Sears bag, and tried to shake out some of the wrinkles.

His heart galloped and his skin crawled with heat. Every pimpled hive seemed to have split and multiplied, and he could feel the warm pus draining and bonding his clothing to his skin. He paused to scratch his back and chest, and then slipped his hand down his pants and dug into his crotch. Terror dried his mouth like the bed of a barren river, and he prayed in silence. *Oh, Lord, please stay with me. Guide me and protect me, Lord. I know I'm just a sinner saved by Your grace, but please, Lord, let me get out of here with this money and make it in time to save that old lady. Amen.*

Strengthened, Scooter wrapped the cash sack in his jacket and stuffed the entire wad into the Sears bag. He unlocked the door and stepped from the stall in time to hear the voices of two men as they entered the rest room.

Scooter jumped back inside and swung the door quietly shut. Like a burglar, he soundlessly slid the latch before placing both feet up on the commode. He crouched there trembling and itching and feeling hot sweat roll down his back and slide between the crack of his ass as the two men laughed and joked near the urinals on the far wall.

Scooter could tell by their accents that the men were from international banking. Most of the staff in that department was from out of the country and had come to America to learn about its international trading system.

When the coast was clear he hurried from the rest room and crossed the banking floor. He walked with his head lowered, doing his best to appear nonchalantly lost in thought. The plastic bag swung pendulum-like from his arm and the undersides of his white shirt were drenched in stale sweat. He could see daylight up ahead. Less than ten paces and he'd be enclosed in the capsule of the revolving door and then safely out on the street.

Eight steps. Just six. Five steps. Three more. Two. Scooter entered the capsule and breathed a sigh of relief. His blood pressure dropped twenty points as he leaned on the glass doors and prepared to exit in a quick semicircle.

The carousel rotated easily for two small paces then stopped. Scooter pushed, but the doors held fast.

His stomach caved in with fear.

He leaned his shoulder against the glass and was prepared to bull-doze through the doors, glass and all, when he felt a heavy hand clamp down on the back of his neck.

"Hey there, boy. What's in the bag?"

Scooter spun around and his bowels nearly went loose. His eyes darted left and right. A warm trickle of urine dampened his underwear and his knees quivered.

Jesse Muhammad's smiled was broad. "I said, young buck. What's that you got in that big old bag?"

The guard's smile was wide and bright, but his eyes were deadly. His hand crept toward the butt of his revolver, and Scooter saw his thick finger crawling toward the trigger housing.

He racked his brain for what seemed like an eternity. He con-sidered dropping to his knees and begging Jesse not to shoot, then spilling his guts and dumping the stolen payroll out on the floor. He would have done just that too, had he not glimpsed the small sparkle in the older man's eyes.

"Um . . ." Scooter swallowed a ball of fear. "Um . . . ah gots me a white man, brother." He showed his teeth as he pretended to shuck and jive. "Yeah, ah gots me a white cracker-man in a white-cracker bag, wearing a white-cracker hood!"

Jesse howled, his broad grin nearly splitting his beautiful black face in two.

"You learning, man! You really learning! I tell you! The white man'll throw a rock up in your shit quicker'n a muh-fuh, won't he? Man, enjoy your lunch! Bring me back a bean pie!"

Jesse's laughter echoed in his ears as Scooter raced down the con-gested Brooklyn streets. He darted through the crowd wildly, glancing over his shoulder every few seconds like a runaway slave.

The stolen bag of money felt like an albatross around his arm. He was sure each glance from a passing stranger was a knowing look from an undercover agent. Scooter knew that in order for his plan to work, and if he meant to stay out of jail, he had to stash the money where no one could find it.

He stood on the corner of the busy intersection and became barely conscious of the pedestrians as they ran helter-skelter along the busy streets. Where was the last place an investigator would look for a bag full of stolen money?

Scooter scanned his horizon trying to decide which direction to take. He was literally flying by the seat of his pants. He'd fallen asleep before the end of the movie, so he had no idea how the dude on TV had gotten away with his caper. This was the only part of his plan he had not worked out, relying instead on a quick solution to occur to him. He squinted his eyes and filtered out the city sounds. He scanned the streets again, this time from a highly reduced perspective.

Suddenly his eyes lit upon something that brought a smile to his face. Scooter wrapped the handle of the heavy bag around his wrist and jogged easily across the street. Safely on the other side, he wiped his forehead and stood looking up like a tourist at the familiar blinking green-and-white sign. It read WELCOME TO FLEET BANK.

/ / /

Twenty minutes later Scooter was back on the street with a key to a safe-deposit box clenched securely in his fist. He sped to the post-office where he purchased a small brown mailing box. He wrapped the key in two sheets of white paper and nestled it inside. Tearing off a strip of heavyweight tape, he sealed the box and addressed it to Mr. Jeo Morrison.

Praying his paper-thin scheme would buy him a little time, Scooter glanced at his watch and saw his lunch hour was almost over. He paid the certified postage on the box and hurried back to work.

Back at his workstation and seated safely upon his stool, Scooter wondered if he'd somehow spend the night in his own bed. If he would ever see Jorge or his grandfather again. He figured three things would have to happen to make this possible: Sol's loyalty must be solidified, Jorge had to show up on time, and Scooter had to put his acting skills to work in the performance of his life.

ol skipped down the stairs whistling the theme song from *Cheers*. More than a week had passed since the last time Socrates invited him down to the vault, and he was hungry for the black man's touch. He'd thought about asking him out to lunch and then taking him to a five-star hotel for a long afternoon roll, but Socrates wouldn't hear of it; he was adamant about being the one who initiated their encounters.

Secretly, Sol liked it that way. He liked giving up control to the young man who looked and smelled so much like Bill but who rocked him from the backside with so much more fervor.

Today was Thursday, cash count day, and after their initial rendezvous he'd changed the vault register and permanently reassigned the cash-counting duties to Socrates. Now they could go down into the vault together at any time and no one would suspect a thing.

Even better, they'd discovered that if they opened the interior vestibule doors and stepped behind them, they'd be out of camera range, but could still hear clearly if someone ventured down the stairs. To a passerby it would appear that they were huddled innocently near the file cabinet where the blank forms were kept, or perhaps reviewing historical documents for accuracy.

Sol chuckled. Life had never been better. Things were actually going well in his marriage. With his own needs being met, he managed to work up enough desire to give it to Blanche at least once a week. The kids were finally doing well in school; his attentiveness to their academic efforts was beginning to show. Even the branch seemed to be running smoothly. Things were much less stressful these days, and he had Socrates to thank for that.

Sol waited near the vault entrance. Socrates would be down shortly. In just a few moments he would unzip his fly and get his horn blown. He rubbed his hands together and smiled.

It was almost impossible to wait!

> > >

Sol was waiting near the vault entrance when Scooter loped down the stairs. "Hi," he said shyly and reached out to take Scooter in his arms.

Scooter squirmed away and gave his boss a seductive grin. Wordlessly, he punched in his code and waited for Sol to do the same. They followed the familiar procedure and were soon inside the vault.

"I missed you," Sol whispered as he pulled Scooter close and pressed his nose to his neck. "You're warm." He leaned back and peered at Scooter with concern. "What's wrong? Did you get hot just thinking about me?"

Scooter smiled with false cheer and nodded. He pulled away from the banker and reached into the vault. He began stacking mounds of large bills atop the counting table. "Yeah, that's it. I was just dying to get down here and get a piece of you." He squirmed a little just to show Sol how turned on he was, then continued to pull the packets of bills from the back of the vault.

"Well then, why'd you make me wait so long?" Sol mewed. His tone was slightly whiny. Almost petulant. Scooter could have sworn he saw the powerful banker pout.

With the counting table covered in neat stacks of prepackaged bills, Scooter pulled the vestibule doors open and moved himself into position, bracing his back against the cash table. "I'm sorry," he said, and began stroking Sol's member as he unbuttoned his slacks, "for making you wait." His boss panted softly, at attention and on the ready. "As a matter of fact . . ." Scooter unzipped his own pants and turned his boss around. He yanked Sol's pants down, exposing his pale buttocks, and forced him to crouch in a deep bend. "As a matter of fact," he whispered, "let's get going right now."

, , ,

An hour later Scooter assisted his last customer and pushed his CLOSED sign against the window. "Gwen, I need you to work the main line while I finish these payrolls. As soon as I'm done I'll open my window and give you a hand."

Gwen looked doubtful. "It's Thursday, Socrates. Don't you have school this afternoon?"

He kept his voice even. "No. The summer session ended two weeks ago. I'll be working full-time until the fall semester begins in September."

Scooter watched as Gwen called customers from the main line and redirected savings-account holders down to the last two windows. He glanced at his watch. It was 1:39. In six minutes his life would change drastically. Quickly, he assembled his props on the counter. Payroll instructions, rolls of quarters, dimes, nickels, and pennies, several empty cash bags, and one burlap cash sack containing several wads of blank paper from a stack beneath the copier.

The clock ticked ominously, the minutes molded in molasses. At exactly 1:45, a light-haired man entered the banking lobby. Jesse had stepped away on his preprogrammed bathroom run, and the young man went almost unnoticed. He approached Scooter's window head down, hands in pockets.

Scooter peered from hooded eyes, pretending to count out blocks of bills as the young man stepped up to his window and motioned with a dark object.

Playing to the cameras, Scooter pretended not to understand. He moved his CLOSED sign aside and leaned closer to the window.

Suddenly his body jerked wildly. He swung his head from side to side and raised both hands in a gesture of surrender. The man at his window kept his head lowered but motioned for Scooter to hurry.

Trembling, Scooter grabbed the bogus cash sack and pushed it through the revolving payroll door. The man quickly opened the partition on the customer side and retrieved the bag before sauntering casually toward the exit.

No sooner did the young man push through the revolving exit than Jesse resumed his position at the door and Scooter, who had clamped his hands dramatically over his chest, reached under the counter and activated the silent alarm. Visibly shaking, he staggered from his station and crashed into Gwen, knocking the heavy white woman from her stool.

Gwen shrieked as they hit the ground in a crash and a tumble. As they rolled along the floor, arms and legs ensnarled, Scooter thrashed and bucked and whimpered his fear, then stared straight into her eyes and managed a terrified whisper. "He was going to shoot me!" Then he clutched at his chest, showed the whites of his eyes, and fainted dead away.

CHAPTER 27

In the midst of Grand Central Terminal, Jorge raged.

Flinging the burlap bag left and right, spilling its contents to the filthy floor in front of the long rows of orange-and-blue rectangular lockers, Jorge spit and swore and cursed the gods for every bad break he'd ever received.

"Fuck!"

He slammed the locker shut, the metal catch flipping back and smashing his index finger against the door. Bright blood spurted from a rupture beneath his nail bed and he shook his hand twice, flinging crimson droplets on the floor and his pants leg, and splattering the surface of the bottom row of lockers. His rage was too powerful for him to worry about his finger. Not when his bag full of twenty-dollar bills had turned out to be a bag of fucking paper!

Pacing along the narrow stretch between the lockers, his feet flew and trampled in the mess of papers, sending them flying. Errant white scraps stuck to the bottom of his sneakers, causing him to slip and slide, but Jorge was filled with a growing ball of fury that gathered speed and swelled within him, obliterating all thought except that which directed him to kill.

Scooter. That lying, stupid, double-crossing black bastard had dared defy him. He didn't know who he was fucking with, that much was for sure. That dick-sucker would surely feel his wrath. Feel his hands around his neck. He would make it so the scrawny bastard never again saw daylight. Never again even thought about screwing over a *cien por ciento Puertorriqueño*!

Jorge flailed his feet at the paper as he attempted to dislodge a piece from the bottom of his shoe. Frustrated, he bent over and saw something that made his mouth go dry. In the midst of the scattered mess was a white envelope with large, flowery writing. His name stared up at him, and he snatched the envelope from the ground and held it up to his eyes; then he ripped into it, grabbed the thin sheet of paper inside, and read the words that were looped all the way down to the bottom of the page.

Dear You,

I know you probably think I cheated you or chickened out on what I said I was going to do. I didn't. Please don't be mad at me, but I just couldn't risk your getting caught carrying the cash (I love you just that much). But don't worry, your grandma will be fine. I got it all under control and the money is in a safe place. Things are going to be really hot here tonight, I'm sure they will have a lot of questions to ask me, but I will try to get home as quick as I can. I'll meet you at your place at around nine. Please don't be mad. I am not backing out. Just a little while longer and your grandma won't have to suffer anymore.

All my love,
Me.

P.S. Rip this up in little tiny pieces and throw them away in a lot of different places.

Jorge finished reading and grinned, his anger seeping from his pores and riding the air on each breath he expelled. Yeah, Scooter had broken rule number one and had an original thought, but he hadn't forgotten who the hell was running things. Who was boss. Besides, in a way, the little bitch was right. How would he have explained that shit if he was caught holding a bag full of cash? His grin deepened into a full-fledged smile. His plans were still on course. All he had to do was stay low, begin his transformation, and wait for nine o'clock to arrive. Scooter would show up with his money and all would be good.

Life would be good.

, , ,

"I tell you, the boy knows nothing," Evvie pleaded, holding a towel filled with ice to the young man's forehead. Socrates sat in the employee lounge, now the internal affairs' interrogation area, surrounded by the two blue-suited investigators, Sol, and Evelyn.

Socrates had recovered from his fainting spell and was being grilled by a tag team of stone-faced men playing good cop, bad cop. Sol cringed every time the boy's large brown eyes filled with terror as he recounted his story over and over.

"Were you aware that the glass you work behind is bulletproof?"

Sol could actually feel his lover's anxiety as Socrates yelped, "Hell no, I didn't know! I mean, that's what you all like to tell us, but hey! How do I know it's *really* bulletproof? You can't prove it by me! I've never had a reason to test it!" Then he broke down crying. "When I saw that big black gun pointed at my face, all I could think about was dying. Me dying and no one left in this world to take care of my grandpa." Tears rolled down Socrates' cheeks and splashed onto his shirt. Sol wanted to cry along with him.

What a difference he saw in his lover. Just a while earlier the boy had taken him brutally from the rear. His body was still sore from the delicious assault. And now it hurt his heart to see Socrates in such pain. He looked almost as bad as Bill had when they'd been discovered, then humiliated and interrogated about their affair.

Sol watched as Socrates hung his head, snot bubbles frothing from his nostrils. The young man's shoulders heaved as he babbled about the big black gun, and dying and leaving his grandfather alone. The older investigator, Bob Mack, a cigar-smoking veteran whose role it was to play mean cop, motioned Sol to the side.

"You want me to take this lying nigger downtown?"

Sol gasped. "Surely you can't think he had anything to do with this! Next to Mrs. Lipswitch here, Socrates is my most trusted employee!"

His face lined and ruddy, Mack leaned closer to the branch manager and spoke from the corner of his mouth. "Look, sir. We see this type of thing happen all the time. Especially with the darkies. They get a little positioning, and then, you know, their natural urges take over. Sticky fingers. They brag to a friend about the amount of money they can get their hands on and suddenly they start devising a way to take some of it home." He paused to let his words sink in. "Now, this hit was no drop in the bucket. A twenty-grand payroll is enough to justify several heads rolling. Don't tell me you can't see this monkey had his hands all over this."

Sol felt an old anger bubbling toward the surface. He was no longer a nineteen-year-old kid at the mercy of the establishment. Today he was a man of power. An influential figure in the banking industry. He may not have been able to protect Bill, but he would damn sure protect young Socrates. There was no way these bigoted assholes would railroad another black man out of his life. Never would that happen again. *He* would decide whose head rolled and whose didn't.

"Mr. Mack, I appreciate the time you and your assistant have spent here, and now both of you can leave. Submit your report through the proper channels tonight, but it's late and my employees need to get home to their families and get some rest. This young man here"—he gestured toward Socrates, who sat with his head resting on Evelyn's breast as she pressed a cool cloth to the back of his neck—"this young man has obviously been severely traumatized and may require medical attention."

"Sir," Mr. Mack protested, a fresh cigar dangling from his lips, "I'm going to have to detail my suspicions in my report. It's highly unusual for branch personnel to dispute our findings. As you know, I'll have to write that up too."

Solomon pulled himself up to his full six feet three inches and squared his broad shoulders. "It's also highly unusual, Mr. Mack, for a senior investigator to conduct an inquiry where his personal biases and prejudices are allowed to impair his professional judgment." Sol moved in close and his voice came out in a deadly whisper. "Don't you ever come back into my branch hurling racial epithets and ethnic slurs pertaining to my employees. The vice president of Chase Manhattan Bank has issued a bankwide policy that prohibits this type of crap, and I can have him on the telephone in five minutes flat. And trust me, it's also highly unusual for him to tolerate his employees being called 'monkeys,' especially since his lovely mother happens to be part African-American and very well connected."

Sol stepped back and nodded toward the door. "Now, you and your sidekick can both get the hell out of here before I put that in *my* report!"

Evelyn grinned at her boss as she held Socrates in her arms. Sol would have liked to have embraced him too, but he knew that would be pushing it. Still, he felt good about himself for standing up for Socrates the way he had. This one was for Bill. He'd finally been vindicated. If anyone else from the Office of Investigations tried to implicate his young lover in this robbery, it would be over his dead body.

PART III

LOVING LOLA

"You look beautiful, baby. Now quit fidgeting and messing 'round wit' your hair. Your mama done seen you as naked as a jaybird, so whatever you wearing will look good to her."

Juanita was dressed in a navy-blue silk dress with a matching quarter-length short-sleeved jacket. It was the tenth outfit she'd tried on and she finally found something suitable. Every other outfit had either been too tight, too short, too long, too heavy, too thin, too whatever. This dress looked good on her, she admitted, so on her it would stay.

Good thing too, because impatience shone in her aunt's eyes. "Gal, I say you look good! Pick up these clothes 'round this-here room and let's get ready to go. Mamas love they children no matter what color they is."

Juanita waded through the pile of clothing strewn on her bed and along the floor and sighed. Although she knew her auntie was right, for some reason she wanted to look her best for the stranger who was her mother; and in a way, that too pissed her off.

She kicked at a pair of blue jeans on the floor and plopped down atop the heap on the bed. "I don't know, Aunt Hattie. All week long I was about to bust waiting on Thursday to get here, and now that it's here I feel kinda funny."

"Funny how?" Hattie paused with a discarded dress in her hand.

"Well, for one thing I feel like bats are flying around inside my stomach and I can't stop running to the bathroom. Then I keep getting mad at myself for wanting to get all dressed up for someone I don't even know, and who, as far as I can tell, hasn't really been all that eager to get to know me."

Hattie laid the dress across the bed and reached out and hugged Juanita to her bosom. "Baby! Please don't talk like that about your mama. You got to give her a fair chance to explain! It was her life, her story, and she got a right to tell it the way she saw it happenin'."

Juanita poked out her lip and frowned. She knew Aunt Hattie loved her birth mother and wanted everything to go smoothly, but she just wasn't sure. For days she'd been so nervous that she stayed up late at night fighting the urge to binge. Last night she'd wanted to raid the kitchen and had instead gone into Uncle Herbie's room and climbed into his bed, snuggling against his wiry back for strength, something she hadn't done since she was a small girl. Uncle Herbie had awakened, but never said a word. He simply reached over his shoulder and touched her face, then swung the quilt over her and went back to sleep. In the morning he'd kissed her cheek and said, "I'm proud of you, Neet. You's a strong black woman. The worl' need more jus' like you."

She struggled from Hattie's arms.

"Promise me you'll give her a fair chance," Aunt Hattie asked. "Just a fair chance."

Juanita bit the insides of her cheeks and agreed. What the hell was a fair chance? A fair chance would have been her mother doing what a lot of other black women did. Keep their children and at least try to raise them. Heat rose in her cheeks and she fanned herself with a flat piece of cardboard from a pack of panty hose. She felt hot and guilty when she had those thoughts. Like Conan said, she should be grateful Aunt Hattie and Uncle Herbie had been there to take care of her. Most abandoned children weren't nearly as lucky.

Juanita turned to her aunt with a soft smile. Hattie looked good in her light-brown dress and multicolored earth-tone scarf. Her near-white curls hung to her shoulders. She wore a pair of high-heeled shoes she'd bought for Dot Morrison's funeral, and she tottered on them just as much today as she had back then.

Hugging the older woman around the waist, Juanita squeezed her eyes shut and promised, "I'm gonna do my best, Auntie. Just like you taught me, I'm gonna do my best."

′ ′ ′

Jorge leaned partway out of the open window. A cool breeze swept over him, chilling him from his damp hair to his toes. He pulled the bright red bandana from his head and checked his reflection in the window glass. It amazed him how different he looked. Black hair did him a lot of justice. He ran his fingers through his ebony curls, then turned to the side to study his profile.

Damn! What a difference a bottle of dye made! He reached into his drawer and pulled out his secret weapon. He fumbled as he snapped open the latch on the plastic case, nearly toppling it to the dirty floor. He stared down at its contents. A wild chuckle spilled from his lips.

Just call me old blue eyes. He laughed behind his hands. He reached inside the case and carefully removed one of the two azure-blue contact lenses. With a steady hand, he inserted the lens over his right eyeball. Blinking rapidly, he did the same to his left eye. Tears streamed from his eyes as his pupils protested the foreign objects, then slowly adjusted.

Jorge walked into the bathroom and pressed his face as close to the mirror as he could. The whites of his eyes were tinged with red streaks, but already they were fading. He stepped back a pace and studied his new self.

Goddamn! he thought, a smile creasing his face. He could play Conan better than Conan could play himself. Jorge took another look in the mirror and marveled at how much the gentleman smiling back at him resembled a Barbarian.

′ ′ ′

Sammy's Steakhouse was packed to the gills with the usual end-of-the-week crowd. The tempting aroma of tender marinated steak cooked to perfection over the open-flame grill made Hattie's mouth water.

She eyed the hungry patrons waiting for a meal. The line snaked out of the door and halfway down the street, but Hattie wasn't quite ready to order yet. She preferred to go inside and claim a table, make the introductions, and then the three of them could leave their jackets at the table and wait in the line together.

She glanced at Juanita and saw the face of a little girl searching for her mother. Lola hadn't arrived yet, Hattie knew, because she'd already visually swept the entire room herself. She felt Juanita's shoulders slump. As much as she'd done for Juanita, Hattie knew she could never fill Lola's shoes, and she took no offense in the child's desire to learn more about her natural mother.

"Come on, Nita." She led her over to a table facing the door. The family at the table hadn't completed their meal yet, but table-hawking was a common practice at crowded eateries in this area. "We'll wait right here for these folks to get through, and that way we can keep our eyes on the door at the same time."

Hattie glanced down at her watch. It was 6:21 P.M. Lola had agreed to meet them at 6:30. She still had a few minutes. Hattie stood next to Juanita and leaned against the wall. She found herself staring down at a cute little dark-brown boy who appeared to be about five. His mother and a man Hattie supposed was his daddy (although you couldn't be sure these days, even if he was paying the child support) were busy talking up a storm about the girl's friend they called Cynthia, while the little peanut-headed boy was busy messing up the good meat on his plate.

She watched as the child poured his fruit punch right onto his plate and mixed it with his potatoes, then began piling the soupy pink mixture on top of his perfectly browned T-bone steak.

Hattie sucked her teeth as her stomach begged for attention. All that good meat gone to waste and there were children over in Africa— hell, in her very projects—who were almost starving. She made a stern face at the cute little rascal and he stopped with his mess long enough to make a face right back at her.

Durn kids these days. Hattie shook her head and rolled her eyes at the mannish little boy. She glanced at her watch. In a few minutes Lola would be officially late. She looked over to see how Nita was holding up and found her baby searching the face of every female stranger who pushed through the door.

Come on, Lola, Hattie mentally begged for Juanita's sake. *Come on and see 'bout your baby, chile. Your baby be needing you bad right about now.* Hattie's feet began to throb. She rubbed her nose and shifted her weight to her other hip. *C'mon, sweet Lola,* she silently begged, *'cause old Hattie be needing you too.*

, , ,

With thoughts of Scooter and the bag of money crowding his mind, Jorge searched his bottom drawer for the bare necessities: Conan's birth certificate, Social Security card, DMV photo ID, and lastly, the two photos Jorge had of his mother and grandmother and the miniature flag of Puerto Rico, unmarred after fifteen years and still in its clear plastic case. He'd already stuffed the clothes he planned to keep—almost all of Conan's jeans and most of his shirts—into a green Army rucksack and hidden them beneath his bed. If he was going to be the Barbarian, he might as well dress like him.

If everything went according to plan, he'd be flying the friendly skies in less than two days' time. First to Florida, then a connecting flight straight to sunny Puerto Rico! He planned to look up some of his father's relatives and get some quick connections. If he was lucky, his old man might still be living on the small island. If not, fuck 'em all. He'd planned his work and now it was time to work his plan. Fuck Conan and everybody else on this low-budget scene. From the money he stood to make, he'd be able to buy this whole building in less than six months.

Lock, stock, and barrel.

The only regret Jorge had was that he wouldn't be able to show that asshole Conan how crafty he was. How much he'd done on his own, without any help from him or anybody else. Jorge swore. He kept forgetting Conan was really a *gringo*. That's why he acted like such a little *perra*. He woulda never had the balls to go through with that shit today. That half-breed would have turned yellow as soon as he walked in the bank, and ended up fuckin' the whole program up! You couldn't expect too much from those *gringos*. Especially one like his ex-*amigo*.

Just thinking about Conan made Jorge itch for a fight. He was gonna have to find a way to nail that smug bastard before he left.

If not, his Latino spirit would never rest. Shit, Conan was lucky he didn't give him a taste of what he'd given Thor on the night he died. It would serve him right to be forced to bow down at the feet of a real man.

A real Barbarian.

Jorge raised the window and leaned partway out. The litter-strewn streets were dotted here and there with groups of playing children and soft-bodied young girls pushing expensive baby strollers. He glanced at his watch and peered into the darkness as far as he could see. It was close to ten o'clock.

Damn! Where the fuck was Scooter?

CHAPTER 29

////////////////////////////

"Baby?" Hattie rubbed Juanita's back gently, trying to awaken her. For the last hour or so she'd been slumped over the table sleeping fitfully. Every so often she'd come awake with a start, sit straight up, her eyes frantic and searching, then disappointment would murk her features and once again she'd rest her head in her hands.

"C'mon, chile. Sit up, baby." Hattie used her napkin to wipe a thin trail of saliva from Juanita's cheek.

"She here yet?" Juanita asked, a groggy hopefulness in her voice.

Hattie didn't answer. Her heart sagged in her chest. She didn't know how to feel. Up until now she'd kept herself numb. Refused to let despair claim her thoughts. For three and a half long hours she'd stared at the door as it opened and swung shut. For the first two hours she'd been nervous and expectant, but as the minutes dragged past slower than pond water, self-preservation kicked in and she stopped giving herself eye strain each time someone stepped inside.

The managers had been wonderful, even if some of the patrons had acted the fool. One old Jezebel in a lopsided wig and a floppy pink hat had the nerve to come over, grab Hattie's arm, and demand she and Juanita give up their table.

"Un-ass the table, Granny! If you ain't gon' eat, then move yo' god-damn feet!"

Hattie cut her eyes at the skinny woman, who had one hand on her imagination and tugged on Hattie's arm with the other and hissed through her teeth, "Wench, if you don't loose my arm I'll snap off your wrist and kick your backbone in!"

Juanita had stiffened beside her as Hattie shifted in her chair. "Ain't it a shame," Hattie asked without a hint of embarrassment, "when your own peoples tear they drawers and make you show your toe?"

After that she purchased two sodas and a large plate of fries. She'd picked at one or two fries and even swallowed down half of the sweet orange beverage, but now the rest of it sat before her. Cold and un-appealing.

"Let's go, Nita. It's almost ten o'clock and they be closing the doors in a minute. I don't know what happened to your mama, but I'm sure there's a good reason she ain't here. Let's go on home and wait. Maybe she done called Herbie and left us a message."

Hattie watched a tiny flame flicker softly before dying in her niece's green eyes. Juanita rose from the table without saying a word, but at a time like this words were unnecessary. The look on her face told a story of a lifetime of unfulfilled dreams and disappointment in abun-dance. Hattie had been prepared to back Lola's every play, but she had no idea how to compensate for the empty, rejected look in her baby's eyes.

As they stepped out onto the street, Hattie opened her mouth to offer a word of hopeful condolence, then closed it again. What was there to say? Your mama couldn't make it? Your mama couldn't come? No, that would never do. While she was sure Lola had her reasons for not showing, Hattie refused to insult Juanita's intelligence by making up some garbled excuse.

She hailed a dark-blue station wagon with a Black Pearl emblem on the side and livery license plates. Hattie slid across the backseat and held Juanita close. The tears came quicker and harder than she ex-pected. She rocked her crying baby in her arms and said the only thing that could really make a difference in the life of a child.

"It's okay, baby. Go 'head and cry it out. Let go of the pain, my chile, 'cause when it's all over you can best believe two things: Jesus loves you, and so do I."

/ / /

"What the fuck you mean, you ain't got it?" Jorge felt a hot rage take control of his entire body. His hand was a blur, echoing through the empty halls as he pimp-slapped Scooter's face.

"Please." Scooter fell to his knees and begged. "Please don't . . . don't."

Jorge drew his Nike-clad foot back to kick, but couldn't. The landing was too confining. Too small to get enough force behind his foot to do the kind of damage he planned to do to the yellow-bellied *gringo* asshole-licking motherfucker balled up on the dirty floor in front of him.

Instead, Jorge pummeled Scooter's head, neck, and back with his fists, his muscles straining, raining down hard on the defenseless man with sledgehammer-like blows.

"Please," Scooter begged tearfully. His cries were muffled and garbled, but Jorge wouldn't have heard him even if he were screaming into a bullhorn.

In a raging frenzy, Jorge swung blow after vicious blow before collapsing against the railing in disbelief. He'd waited all night for Scooter to show. He'd called Scooter's apartment every fifteen minutes and searched from his window like a crackhead looking for one last rock.

At one point he'd decided to sneak over to Scooter's projects, but then quickly changed his mind. Who the fuck knew what kind of situation he'd find there? Scooter's crib was probably crawling with D-T's and Five-O, and even though Jorge's hair was no longer blond, he wasn't stupid enough to take unnecessary risks.

And now, at almost eleven o'clock, more than nine hours after he'd left the bank with a bagful of blank copier paper, this sniveling nigger was kneeling at his feet telling him he didn't have the money? Saying he'd stashed the dough in a safe-deposit box and mailed himself the key!

For the first time in many years, Jorge wanted to cry. Just cry. Something he hadn't been tempted to do since the last time his stepfather touched him. He shook his head wildly. The little *chica* was still at his feet begging for mercy.

"A'ight! A'ight! Stop whining like a bitch and stand up."

He watched as Scooter climbed shakily to his feet. He looked a mess. Sores, open with pus at their tips, dotted his face like freckles. His eyes looked haggard, and blood trickled from his busted bottom lip.

Scooter babbled, "I'm scared, Jorge. I'm fucking scared." He tried to bury his face in Jorge's neck, but Jorge wasn't having it. He shoved Scooter so hard, his back crashed into the wall.

"Man, what the fuck you scared about? They let you go, didn't they? Just stick to your story and nobody will find out!"

"I don't know, man." Scooter dug into his armpits, then scratched his neck. "I got a bad feeling about this. A real bad feeling!" He leaned against the wall and moved side to side, scratching his back like a cat. "You shoulda seen the way those motherfuckers were looking at me! They knew, man. Those people knew I was down with it! I'm supposed to go to headquarters on Monday morning to take a lie detector test and shit, but my boss is looking out for me and said I don't have to go." He stopped scratching and clutched at Jorge's arms, his eyes suddenly wild. "Maybe I should give it back. Or maybe I should just leave the box at the post office. You know? Just not pick it up. That way the key will just be out there. Floating out there wherever the hell they keep unclaimed mail!"

Jorge balled up his fist, intending to knock some sense into the cowering man standing before him, but suddenly checked himself. He *needed* Scooter! Needed the little prick to cooperate! If Scooter refused to pick up his mail, there was no way Jorge could get the key! Get the money! Bad enough he'd have to wait until Monday when the goddamn post office opened, and even then he'd have to pray the service was swift. Plus he'd have to take a later flight! Damn! It was just like a *gringo* to mess up his plans!

Jorge thought hard. He needed to play this game out carefully. He uncurled his fingers and brushed them against Scooter's crotch. "Man, just calm the fuck down and think." There was only way one to get Scooter to do anything he wanted him to. After tonight he'd have the trembling little pussy so whipped he wouldn't even dream of leaving that key at the post office or giving back a dime of Jorge's hard-earned cash.

"Come here, *chica*," he said with a gentleness that was meant to be both soothing and seductive. The way Scooter complied and folded himself into Jorge's arms told him he'd struck the right tone.

He massaged the small of Scooter's back and allowed his hands to stray down toward his lean buttocks. "It's okay, baby. I'm right here." He pulled Scooter close and ground against him forcefully until he felt what he wanted to feel. It was amazing how quickly he could turn the little bitch on. What power he wielded in his dick. Enough power to change a man's mind. He'd changed Thor's, and now he was about to change Scooter's.

For the very first time Jorge's hand touched Scooter through the fabric of his pants. He squeezed and pulled until Scooter's mouth went slack and his eyelids fluttered. There was a lot more to him than there had been to Thor. A lot more.

Jorge took a deep breath and plunged his tongue deeply into Scooter's warm mouth. He tongued him down, pretending he was kissing a girl. Scooter moaned and draped his thin arms around Jorge's neck.

"Uh-uh." Jorge pushed Scooter slightly away and broke the passionate kiss. He reached into his back pocket and pulled out a single latex condom. "Take off your stuff," he commanded, and gyrated his hips in wide suggestive circles.

Jorge watched through heavily lidded eyes as Scooter scrambled out of his black pants and pulled off his underpants. Submissive and obliging, Scooter dropped down to his knees in the manner he'd become accustomed, but Jorge's strong arms lifted the slender young man back to his feet.

"Not like that." Jorge smiled as he turned Scooter around and forced him out of his squat. He rolled the condom down over his own massive erection, then bent Scooter over and rammed against him with brute force. "Like this," he said, as he hammered and pounded and gave his eager young lover exactly what Scooter had been hoping for.

′ ′ ′

Juanita watched as Hattie pulled five wrinkled singles from her bosom and handed them to the cabdriver. Almost as an afterthought, she dug in and retrieved another bill, tipping the kind-eyed man for his service.

Juanita hung back as her aunt slid across the torn leather seat and stepped gingerly from the taxi. Hattie peered into the cab's darkness expectantly.

"I'm not coming, Auntie," Juanita said woodenly. Her emotions were all jumbled and fighting at the pit of her stomach. "You go on ahead. I need to take a little ride. I promise," she reassured her aunt, "I'll be careful and I won't be long."

She braced herself to be hit with fifty-'leven reasons as to why she'd better get herself out of the taxi and march her tail on upstairs, but instead her Aunt Hattie simply nodded. "You got money, baby?"

Juanita swallowed hard; this was so unlike her Auntie. "Yes'm. I have enough."

"You wanna tell me where you going, chile?"

No, Juanita thought. She certainly did not. But with all of her conflicting emotions, she wasn't about to tell her auntie a lie.

"I'm going to him," she said simply, and hoped like hell it was enough. Hattie surprised her again by nodding again and backing away from the taxi without a word.

"Auntie!" Juanita cried before Hattie could turn around. She stared up into the face of her true mother and tried to smile as the water seeped from her eyes. "I love you too."

′ ′ ′

"Three-fifteen Parker Road," Juanita redirected the cabdriver. "And please hurry." She had to get to Conan. There was a tide rising inside of her, a dam of emotions threatening to burst. He wouldn't be expecting her tonight, but that was all right. She and Conan had figured she'd be up talking to her mother for half of the night, too keyed up and loaded with questions to sleep, so Conan had promised to meet her at the bus stop the next day as usual.

"Call me if you need me," he'd told her.

Well, she sure as hell needed him now. How often did your birth mother stand you up for your first meeting? Was there something about her, some deviant, unknown element, that made her own mother despise her? Forget calling. She needed to see him. To touch him. To finally feel his strong arms around her. To finally feel his full lips touching hers.

She was ready to feel Conan's love.

And to give him hers.

The taxi whizzed down the streets and avenues, and before she realized it they were parked outside of the apartment building where Conan lived. She wasn't sure if he was home, but at eleven o'clock on a Thursday night, where else would he be?

Juanita gave the cab driver four dollars. "How much will it cost for you to wait until I'm sure my friend is home?"

"Not a dime, honey," the older man told her. "Just be sure and come straight back and let me know."

Juanita gave him her word as she climbed from the taxi and peered up to the third floor windows. Lights were shining brightly from nearly every room. She searched the buttons and located the one that read LOPEZ. She pressed it hard and waited. A second later she heard a soft buzzing noise and the sound of the lock giving way.

As she ascended the stairs, Juanita remembered the first time she'd traveled this route. That night, her steps had been hesitant and full of fear. Tonight she walked purposefully. Her chest burned with her mother's rejection. There was no way she wanted to lay her burdens on Aunt Hattie's lap. No, she needed Conan.

She climbed the stairs quickly and paused on the top landing to get her breathing under control. As hurt and angry as she was, she still wanted to look cute when he opened the door.

From where she stood, Juanita had a clear view of Conan's apartment. The door was slightly cracked, but the muffled noises she heard seemed to be coming from overhead.

Curiosity flashed through her but she felt fear as well. She tiptoed up the last few stairs and craned her head toward a small landing to her right. Conan lived on the top floor, so this landing must lead to the roof.

She peered through the semidarkness, ready to make a mad dash toward Conan's apartment at the slightest sign of static. She hiked her dress up and gathered it around her waist, prepared to run toward the door like a bowlegged thief.

And then she heard a sharp cry.

"Ooooh . . . yeah. Give it to me . . . yes!"

Juanita froze. The voice was eerily familiar. She crept toward the landing and squinted. Up close she made out two pairs of legs. One set, dark, thin, and bare, were exposed to the traces of hall light as they rocked back and forth in pleasure.

The other pair of legs were clad in baggy denim jeans.

Cuffed at the hems.

Atop stark-white Nikes with a royal-blue swoosh.

Juanita watched as the jeans-clad legs buckled and bent, obviously coupling with the brown-skinned person in front of him. Wet, animal-like sex sounds assaulted her ears. Graphic instructions were whispered: *harder, deeper, squeeze it, faster!*

Juanita was frozen. Rooted to the spot. There was no way she could move, no way she wanted to believe her eyes and ears and validate a scene so wretched. And then a gutteral, lust-filled voice yelled out, "Who's the Barbarian, huh? *Who,* goddammit?"

"Youuu . . . ouch . . . ohmygod . . . you!"

It was her best friend. Shrieking in ecstasy.

For the first time in weeks, Juanita's stomach heaved and bucked, unaided by her sweeping fingers. Scalded by an ocean of tears, she retched and swooned as she scrambled down the flights of stairs, yanked open the heavy glass doors, and flung herself into the taxicab waiting at the curb.

CHAPTER 30

Hattie paced, drenched in a panicked sweat. "You see her, Herbie?" She leaned over her brother and peered out the window and into the darkness.

"How you let that baby go ridin' by huhself in a taxicab, Hattie? I cain't believe you done no fool mess like that!"

"Don't you chastise me, Herbie! You keep that shit up and you gonna make me lose my religion on you!" Hattie wrung her hands as a low moan rolled off her lips. "She said she was just gone for a little ride. Said she be right back! How long ago you say the hospital called?"

Herbie repeated for his sister what he had already repeated several times. "It was 'round 'bout seven o'clock. The lady say she was calling for a Miss Lola Jacobson. Said Miss Jacobson was ridin' in a taxicab and they was hit by one of them trucks what deliver frozen food."

Hattie searched his face. "Was it a big truck?"

"Dang it, woman! How I know how big the truck was? How much I care? All I know is my Nita ain't got no bidness out ridin' 'round in no taxicab this time a night by huhself!"

Hattie stared at her brother. She didn't realize Herbie had it in him

226 / CHOCOLATE SANGRIA

to raise his voice like that to her. All these years he'd treated her real gentle-like. Always accepted her moods and her ugly ways without complaint. And now here he was, covering his throat hole and hollering up in her face like somebody's damn fool. She was gonna have to deal with Mister Man later. Right now she had to jump on his bandwagon, 'cause Nita was somewhere out in those streets, and poor Lola needed her and needed her bad.

"Herbie, I'ma let this shit slide on account a' the fact you crazy from wurrying 'bout Nita. But I'm still your sister and you still gots to—"

"Hesh up, woman!" he cried, peering out the window. "Here Nita come now! She jest gitting outta the taxicab!"

"Well, fool, holler at her to hold the cab and wait!"

With one knee-high stocking sagging around her left ankle and her feet teetering in her high heels, Hattie grabbed her pocketbook and hurried out the door and down the stairs as fast as her legs would take her.

Juanita stood leaning heavily against the taxicab. Her face was red and splotched, her cheeks the color of high flames; her hair had come undone, and tears leaked from her eyes in a steady stream.

"Auntie," she moaned. "Th-th-they were . . . I'm sorry. Y-y-you were right. I should have listened. P-p-please."

Hattie closed her eyes and crushed Juanita to her bosom. The poor child was finally allowing herself to grieve.

"Hush, baby. It's okay." Hattie guided Juanita back into the taxicab and slid into the backseat. "Woodhurst Hospital," she instructed the bewildered driver. She sat back and gathered Juanita in her arms. As the cab sped down the streets Hattie stroked Juanita's hair and made little shishing noises of comfort. As Juanita cried bitterly into her breast, she rocked her like a baby in need of a nap. "Your mama didn't leave you," Hattie whispered, "and she didn't stand you up. She was tryin' her best to get to you, baby girl. When the cab she was ridin' in got hit by that-there truck, your sweet mama was on her way."

⁁ ⁁ ⁁

The antiseptic odor of the hospital caused Juanita's empty stomach to pinch and twist. Holding tight to Hattie's arm, the rhythmic clicking of high heels on waxed floors did little to blot out the sound of her pounding heart. Ignoring her discomfort, she swallowed her nausea and clutched Hattie for strength. "Nita," Hattie cautioned. "I don't know what kinda shape Lola gon' be in, okay? Just remember she's your mama no matter how messed up she look."

Juanita nodded mechanically. She'd reached the limits of her endurance. Tiny parts of her had gone numb, as if the area of her brain responsible for self-preservation were shutting down an overloaded switchboard and conserving her limited resources.

"We're here to see 'bout Miss Lola Jacobson," Hattie told the slim black woman seated behind the desk at the nurse's station. She wore her white nurse's hat tilted regally to accommodate her beautiful mass of twisted, natural locks. Her name badge read, FRANCES BLAND, RN.

"Let's see . . . Jacobson." A mahogany-colored finger slid down a list attached to a clipboard. "Oh!" She smiled. "I'm sorry! Lola Jacobson isn't on this list yet. She was just admitted this evening, and since there hasn't been a shift change, our inpatient list is still pending in the computer." She peered at Hattie, and then at Juanita. "Is the woman you're looking for a pretty white lady with funny green eyes and dark brown, almost black, hair?"

Juanita jerked. Only one word penetrated her fog.

White? Did this woman say Lola Jacobson was white? The look on Hattie's face was more than enough to confirm it.

"Look," the young nurse offered. "Miss Jacobson is in stable condition. Even though it's after visiting hours, how about I show you both to her room so you can sit with her for a few minutes before security discovers you and asks you to leave?"

Juanita walked zombielike down the sterile corridor. Her body felt weightless, her feet barely seemed to graze the loam-green tiles. The only thing real was Aunt Hattie squeezing her hand and murmuring soft words under her breath.

Filtered light shafted through the glass window of room 356. The nurse held the door open and Hattie entered first. Juanita hung back, her muscles coiled to flee, her eyes unwilling to face yet another assault.

"Come on, baby." Hattie reached out her hand. "It's gon' be okay, sugar. This here is your *mama!*"

Juanita put her faith in Hattie and took a tentative step into the room. A wild mass of dark curls, hair almost as dark as her own yet textured very differently, lay fanned out in layers atop the bright pillowcase.

"C'mon." Hattie smiled and nodded.

With halting steps, Juanita moved to her aunt's side. She stared into the face of the unconscious white woman stretched out in the bed. Crisscross strips of white tape secured a rectangular-shaped bandage lengthwise across the woman's forehead. Her skin was pasty-colored, not much different from the sheets that were pulled up to her neck.

Juanita studied the stranger's face unchallenged.

An IV tube ran from a pole at the head of the bed to the woman's right hand. A thin plastic tube disappeared into the right nostril of a slender, aquiline nose. High cheekbones were almost lost in the landscape of her face. Thin lips were slightly parted in slumber, and a prominent dimple dented the strong chin.

A sob tore from Hattie's throat. She patted Lola's hand. Juanita continued her silent study, her eyes roaming over the supine figure with a curious but detached interest. She noticed there was no wedding ring on the stranger's finger, but considering the circumstances that meant very little.

As her aunt reached out a trembling hand and smoothed the woman's hair, Juanita watched, fascinated, as her eyelids fluttered gently and then opened wide. Juanita stood, shocked with anticipation, mute with disbelief.

The woman looked around without turning her head. Her eyes moved haltingly as she became aware of first herself, then her environment. Her gaze lit on Hattie and her eyes registered joy; when her eyes caressed Juanita, they registered rapture.

Twin pools of emerald.

Juanita could not bear to blink. As if bonded by some powerful force, the stranger's eyes fused with her own, and to her amazement Juanita discovered that the odd green eyes she'd battled in the mirror for so many years did not belong to a stranger after all.

They belonged to her mother.

/ / /

Jeo Morrison's chest rose slightly, then quickly fell. He panted shallowly and his lips were blue from a lack of oxygen.

"He been calling for ya, ya know," the middle-aged home attendant told Scooter with an accusing lilt in her singsong West Indian accent. "All night de poor man be up moaning 'bout you, child." Fatigue showed in her face as she paused to take Jeo's pulse. Her dark brown curls grazed her stout shoulders.

"I'm sorry, Miss Sam," Scooter whispered softly. The merest of movements sent intolerable waves of pain soaring from his head down to his feet. "I-I-I had to work late. There was a situation at the bank and we couldn't leave."

Samuela Hansome raised an eyebrow doubtfully and looked at her watch. "They only pay me for tree hours, ya know! Ain't no bank me know of keep a man the en-tire night when he grand-pa at home trying to die!"

Scooter fell silent. The weight of his shame was almost too much to bear. He'd been so wrapped up in his own drama, he'd neglected his grandfather when Jeo had needed him most. A burning pain rolled low in his gut and settled near his bruised rectum. He scratched greedily at his arms and neck. Fresh shingles had appeared on his skin in droves, and he longed to use the toilet and clean himself up in a hot, soothing shower.

After kissing his grandfather's forehead, he left Miss Sam standing guard over Jeo and went into the small bathroom at the end of the hall. Every inch of his body throbbed from the intense beating he'd taken from Jorge. Scooter unbuttoned the shirt he'd put on earlier that morning, a lifetime ago, and peeled it from his back. Bits of dried pus and flesh clung to the inside of the shirt.

He unzipped his pants and turned on the tap, eager to drench his inflamed body with scalding water. Wincing, Scooter stepped out of his pants and underwear in a series of tiny movements and then froze. A wave of nausea buckled his knees. Weak, he clutched at the sink to keep from falling over.

He peered down at his underwear. Large amounts of still-moist blood darkened the seat of the once-white boxer shorts. He saw thin trails of watery feces and stiff white splotches of coagulated sperm. He sobbed out loud.

Jorge had brutalized him.

Scooter had been so consumed in the throes of his sexual fever that he hadn't realized how mercilessly Jorge had battered him. Ripped apart his membranes. Torn Scooter's tender places to shreds.

He felt a powerful urge and quickly lowered himself to the toilet. Unbearable pressure swelled at the top of his rectum. His bowels contracted and let go. Bright-red blood spewed from his body and hit the water, splashing back up on his rear and staining the sides of the bowl.

Scooter held on to the commode, gripping the hard ceramic with his last ounce of strength. He considered yelling out to Miss Sam and begging her to call an ambulance, but instead he bit down on his lip and tried to pray.

Dear God, please forgive my sins. I was wrong to lie, to steal, to turn against my family and friends, and to fornicate. Give me the strength to bear my burdens, Lord. Please give me strength.

Sometime later, when Miss Sam was about to leave, she knocked on the bathroom door and, wrinkling her nose at the stench emanating from within, found him there with his hands trembling but still folded in prayer. Scooter was whimpering softly, moaning in pain, and stewing in his own mess.

, , ,

Daylight broke through the clouds and tickled Juanita's eyelids. She stretched fitfully and slowly became aware of her surroundings. A steady bleep came from the heart monitor mounted above Lola's bed. The sound of a heavy cart rolling down the hallway filtered into the room.

Juanita raised her head from the armrest of the small plastic chair and attempted to sit up. Her right leg was tucked beneath her body, and a sharp cramp traveled from her toes all the way up to her hip. She yawned and straightened her leg, then looked over to see how Aunt Hattie had survived the night in her own tiny seat.

She stared in surprise. Aunt Hattie's eyes were wide and clear, moving from the sleeping Lola on the bed back to Juanita.

"What's wrong, Auntie?" she whispered. "You couldn't get to sleep in that hard chair?"

Hattie smiled and crossed her feet. "Baby, I done slept in tougher spots than this. Just didn't want to, that's all. I got my rest watching you and your mama here together in one room."

Juanita yawned again. "You still need to close your eyes and catch a few winks. Maybe I should call a taxicab so you can go home and rest."

Hattie clucked her tongue. "Gal! I bin sleeping every night for over seventy-some-odd years! What harm one night up gon' do me?" She waved her hand. "Ain't no way I'm leaving your mama till I know for sure she fine!"

"I'm fine, Aunt Hattie," came a low voice from the bed. Lola reached out seeking Hattie's touch. "Please . . . come closer . . . I'm fine."

Juanita watched as her aunt struggled to her feet and moved to Lola's bedside. A moment later she joined her there as Hattie buried her dark face against the paleness of Lola's skin.

"I'm okay, I'm okay," Lola murmured over and over as she patted Hattie's heaving back. She turned to look at her daughter. Juanita blushed slightly at the naked love shining from her mother's eyes.

"Juanita . . ." Her voice was a gentle caress, a sigh of happiness. "Please, bring your chair and sit beside me."

Juanita slid her chair up to the bed as she was instructed. Lola gestured for her hand and Juanita slipped her fingers into her mother's waiting grasp.

"I was only sixteen," Lola began without preamble. She stared straight ahead as if seeing vivid images of her past. "Sixteen, but my soul, already my soul was old." She swallowed hard and paused. "Pierre—" She glanced at Juanita. "That's your father. Pierre was twenty-two, but we knew we were in love. We planned to run off and get married the minute I turned eighteen, but as you may know, Juanita, life has a way of hurling stumbling blocks in your path when you least expect them."

Juanita nodded. Her thoughts lit upon Conan. A residual pang of loss echoed through her heart.

"The day Pierre was hired, I knew without a doubt he was the man for me. True, I was just a child, inexperienced and naive to the ways of life, but with all of the love I had stored up inside me it was bound to come tumbling out.

"For the longest time Pierre refused to touch me. It was against his beliefs. He was born in Haiti and raised in a strict Catholic household, and although I was born Jewish, we never really practiced the tenets of our faith in my home. Still, Pierre and I vowed to wait until we were legally married before going all the way. We almost had to—because otherwise my father would have killed him; I was a minor, Pierre was over twenty-one, and of course the ultimate insult was that he was black."

Juanita listened in awe. She was having a hard time accepting the fact that she had been born of a white woman. She'd always envisioned her mother as the strong black Nubian type, a proud African queen. She'd never speculated too closely on her father's race. Because of her skin tone she'd figured he was either a light-skinned black, or maybe even an American Indian. Never in her wildest dreams had she figured the unknown man who fathered her to be of Haitian descent. And Jewish? Her own mother a Jew? Didn't they penny-pinch on Delancey Street and cheat hardworking black folks out of their money?

Lola continued softly. "It took me four months to get to him. Four long months of teasing him and touching him and using every ounce of my considerable feminine wiles to break him down. Four months to pierce his armor of self-control."

Lola shook her head slightly and frowned. Her eyes were sad and faraway. "See, as much as I loved him, I hated it that he could resist me. Hated that he could push me away when I tried to drive him crazy with my willing love. At first he said he could never marry a white woman, but eventually that changed. In my heart I knew he loved me just as deeply as I loved him, but the child in me needed immediate validation that I was wanted. Physical proof of how much he desired me."

Juanita barely breathed. She pursed her lips and took small sips of air so as not to disturb Lola's reflective mood. This, she knew, was the untold story of her life.

Lola's eyes were fixed on an invisible spot on the wall, and her tone was flat and open. She spoke calmly and without pretense, laying herself bare. Naked. Exposed.

No apologies, no excuses, only the simple truth.

"For most of my life I'd been ignored. Ignored by my parents, ignored by my relatives, ignored by a world I did not understand. My parents were pretty well-off. Okay, I'll say it. They were rich. Still are. On the surface there was nothing I lacked. Materially, that is. But sometimes money is the last thing a child needs. Every child deserves to have someone who thinks they are the smartest, the prettiest, the best doggone thing in the world. It was only after Aunt Hattie came that I began to learn about love."

She gave Hattie a weak smile.

"But after a while, even Aunt Hattie's love wasn't enough. When I discovered I was pregnant, immediately I fell in love with the thought of having a child. A part of me and a part of Pierre. Someone to love me unconditionally, proof that I was lovable and deserving of love.

"I hid my pregnancy for eight months. I had always been heavy, so everyone thought I was simply gaining more weight. Pierre begged me to see a doctor, to get vitamins and checkups to make sure you were healthy, but I refused. You see, I knew how far my father's hand could reach. Any doctor I saw within a hundred miles would have examined me quietly, then dialed my father's number before I could get out of their office.

"I decided to keep my condition secret. From everyone. Even Aunt Hattie. Pierre felt terrible. Terrible for not being strong enough to wait. Terrible because he was helpless. He made me take long walks and eat properly while I was pregnant, and we planned to steal some money from my parents and run away to the city a week before you were due. I would check in at a local emergency room to have you, and when you were old enough to travel we'd leave for Haiti and live with his mother until we got on our feet. You were named for her, you know."

Lola smiled. "Pipe dreams, huh? Just goes to show you that the decisions you make at sixteen are not usually based on reality or founded in practicality." She turned to Juanita and searched her face. Seeking, Juanita knew, but seeking what?

"But babies have a way of coming when they get good and ready. When I went into labor, a whole month early, I had no idea what to do. Pierre tried his best to help me, but I was hysterical. Just crazy with pain. My parents were having a dinner party and the house was full of guests. There was no way they would have understood their sixteen-year-old daughter dragging down the stairs trailing blood, clutching her stomach, and asking for permission to go to the hospital and have her baby."

She chuckled. "I don't think Mother would have appreciated me interrupting while the adults sipped their Merlot." Lola glanced at Hattie and smiled, her eyes crinkling. "That's where Aunt Hattie came in. If it wasn't for her I don't know what we would have done. What I would do now, even. Aunt Hattie helped me give birth to you, and when I asked her to keep you, to take you away from the cruelty of my mother's house and raise you as her own, she agreed.

"She was accustomed to covering for me. Used to giving me the extra kisses and hugs she knew I needed. The extra bits of food to hold me over when my stomach pinched with hunger from one of mother's attempts to make me diet, the extra attention I needed when I couldn't get anyone else to listen to me, the extra pampering and flattery I needed when I looked into the mirror and hated the person looking back at me.

"Yes, Aunt Hattie always seemed to have a little extra something in her apron pocket for me. It seemed only natural that she would have more of the same extra when it came down to caring for you."

For the first time since she'd entered the room many hours earlier and looked down into the face of her birth mother, Juanita felt her heart fill with compassion. A surge of emotions overpowered her and she dropped her head to her chest. The culmination of heartaches and betrayals and revelations stunned her. Her shoulders shook with tears. Tears for her mother and the loss of an innocent love, tears for Aunt Hattie for being both strong enough and black enough, and for having enough extra love in her heart, to come to the rescue of a green-eyed little white girl; and finally tears for herself. For Scooter. For Conan. For love. Tears for the death of a friendship, the betrayal of trust, and the demise of a promise that could never be kept.

,,,,,,,,,,,,,,,,,,,,,,,,,,,,,

CHAPTER 31

"You know, Juanita," Lola said. She was sitting up in bed eating a small bowl of chilled pears in clear syrup. "After all of these years, I still love your father." She paused with the spoon in the air. "The great thing about it is he's happy now."

"How do you know?"

Lola gave her daughter a secretive smile. "Because he told me. He's back in Haiti and married to a beautiful Haitian woman, but when you graduated from nursery school in '83 he was right there. In the audience. Crying huge tears."

Juanita looked at Hattie for confirmation.

Hattie nodded, "Yes, baby. That's true. He was here for your junior high school graduation and for your baptism too."

Juanita frowned. "Well, why didn't he approach me? Why didn't anyone tell me?"

Lola set the bowl on the nighttable and stared thoughtfully at her plastic spoon. "As much as we both loved you, we agreed not to interfere in your life. When you were a baby I still lived with my parents and had no way to support you. And when you grew older we thought dabbling in your life might confuse things for you. Perhaps make you think you had to choose between us and Aunt Hattie."

Juanita snorted and mumbled, "That would've been a real easy choice!" Her heartache gave way to anger and she stared down at Lola and let loose with both barrels. "Seems to me like my father was just another color-struck brother who got caught with his hand in the wrong damn cookie jar! And white girls like you *always* go after black men! It's a plantation thing. It makes you feel like you're somehow bucking the system, and makes brothers feel like they're almost as good as the white man 'cause they've finally got something that belongs to him! *Aunt Hattie* is the one who took care of me! Worked like a dog scrubbing white people's toilets just to feed and clothe me!" Juanita's eyes bored into Lola's without a drop of mercy. Her voice was icy. "Aunt Hattie scrubbed other folks' floors on her hands and knees to put me through college. To make sure I had what I needed and didn't do without."

She sucked her teeth and backed away from the bed. "So what if you made a mistake and had a baby at sixteen? You weren't the first girl to do that and you won't be the last! Other women survive teenage pregnancies without giving their kids away! Maybe you should have kept your legs closed the same way I have! If you thought you could just run me some bullshit cockamamy story and I'd sit here and say, 'Poor Lola,' and throw my arms around you and welcome you into my life, then, lady, you thought just like Nellie, and I hope like hell you know what Nellie thought!"

"She thought cat shit was jelly." Hattie sighed. "Yeah, chile. I knows me some Nellie. I ain't as old as you seem to thank I am. Ain't as crazy, either. Now, if you thank you gonna stand here and cuss your mama like that in my presence, then you the one got another thank coming! I *know* I raised you better'n that!"

Lola spoke quickly, "It's all right, Aunt Hattie—"

"Like hell it is! Ain't no child of mine gonna go 'round cussing grown folks! Especially if they her mama!"

Juanita felt her anger subsiding. Aunt Hattie was fired up and ready to knock her into the middle of next week.

"Now, it's true." Hattie softened her tone. "It's true that Pierre was wrong. He ain't had no business fooling around like that in the first place. He was a man, and Lola here was just a chile. It's also true that

I worked like a horse to feed you. No one can deny that, least of all me. But your stomach ain't never kissed your spine! All my labors was of love! I scrubbed them floors and cleaned them shitters 'cause I loved my family and that was what I wanted to do!"

She shook a gnarled finger in Juanita's direction. "Note I said what I *wanted* to do. Not what I *had* to do. Now, let me tell it once so I ain't got to tell it no more. Every fifth of the month since the year you turned five your mama has sent me a check for taking care of you. Every month!"

The old woman tossed her head from side to side and raised her hands in the air.

"I chose not to touch that money. I chose not to! It were my choice to make and I made it! Sure, there were a couple a times when things got tough and me and Herbie couldn't press a thin dime between us. Once or twice I was forced to dip into your money. But not much. And I always put it back. I been saving it for you, gal. For your future. For your dreams. When you finish your studies up at that there college, you gonna be able to get yourself a day care center! By God's grace, the sweat off my back, and the generosity of your mama and your daddy, you gonna be able to walk in that door and throw down your money and buy yourself a real live dream!"

Hattie put her hands on her hips and pursed her lips. "Now, you get yourself over there and hug your mama! 'Pologize too! You ain't missed out on nothing! You been loved! Folks been working all they life for you! So gone over there and address your mama real proper-like, Miss Thang, before I take this here strap off of my purse and whip your ass until it ropes like okra!"

                                                * * **

"Damn!" Conan muttered under his breath. "Where the hell are all my clothes?" He slid hanger after empty hanger across the metal bar in his closet, then searched through the contents strewn on the dark floor. Turning away from the closet, his eyes scanned the room. He knew it was useless, but he knocked the lid off his pot-belly-shaped wicker clothes hamper and dumped its meager contents to the floor. Searching through the dirty clothes, he found underwear, socks, and one or two shirts he seldom wore. A pregnant cockroach waddled out from beneath a pair of Jorge's work pants, but otherwise there was little else there.

He gathered the dirty clothes in his arms and dumped them back into the hamper, then brought his heel down and stepped on the roach, grimacing as yellow goo squirted from her side. He reached back into the hamper and used one of Jorge's socks to wipe up the mess, then threw the carcass and the sock into a far corner of the room.

Conan frowned as he stood before their six-drawer dresser. At one time he and Thor had shared the space, three drawers each, but when Jorge moved in, their mother had insisted that the dresser be split three ways. Conan and Thor had given up one drawer a piece, and each boy ended up with two. It was right after Thor died that Jorge had dumped out the bottom two drawers, pushing Thor's clothing into a dark corner of the closet and keeping four drawers for himself. Conan hadn't minded. His grief and his guilt had been too naked and intense to squabble over small things.

He bent over and pulled open one of Jorge's drawers. He was surprised to find it nearly empty. The next drawer was also devoid of clothing, filled instead with old issues of *Playboy* and *Penthouse* magazines. Conan tried the bottom drawer, and held his breath at the rising stench emanating from within. The drawer held mounds of dirty tube socks, and Conan was just about to slam it shut when something caught his eye.

He reached inside and pulled out a receipt booklet, its cardboard cover bent and stained. Several pages had obviously been written on and torn out, but there was no doubt about what he'd found. Pushing the booklet into his pocket, he rushed from the apartment and sped down the stairs.

On the first floor, he pounded on Rico's apartment door, barely controlling his anger as the evidence burned in his pocket. Rico answered the door wearing a sleeveless white T-shirt, jeans, and black leather slippers.

"Rico! Look what the fuck I found!" Conan pulled the booklet from his pocket and handed it to his friend.

Rico studied the thin pages, rectangular white sheets with light blue writing. He held them up to the light, attempting to discern the impressions left by a ballpoint pen. After careful examination he frowned, then slapped the booklet against his palm. His eyes were dark.

"Where'd you find this?"

"In my room. In Jorge's drawer."

Rico nodded. "Looks like you found the thief, man. Let's go get him. Let me put on a shirt and run upstairs to check on Pushie, and I'll be ready to roll. Are you gonna call the cops, or am I gonna call 'em?"

"No." Conan shook his head quickly. "Let's not call anybody just yet. Lemme talk to him first. See what his story is."

"C'mon, Conan." Rico's entire body protested. "Goddamn, man! How many times does this guy have to fuck you around? It was him! You got the proof right here, man!"

"I know, I know!" Conan held out his hands. "Look, he's probably around the corner. At the pool hall. Lemme run down there real quick. You know, check out a few spots and see if I can find him. I'll bring him back here and we can grill him together, and if you ain't satisfied with his answers then I'll call the cops on him myself."

"You still dig him that much, Top Cat?" Rico asked gently, his words keen and pointed.

Conan looked down at the ground, then headed toward the door. "Yeah, man. I dig him enough."

CHAPTER 32

The sun was riding high in the cloudless sky by the time Hattie and Juanita left Woodhurst Hospital. According to Lola's doctor, her injuries amounted to nothing more than a concussion and a few bruises, and he promised she would be discharged sometime Monday morning. After spending the night and half the morning listening to her mother fill in the blanks of her life, Juanita was plagued with mixed emotions, the most prevailing being a deep sense of forgiveness. For everyone. Lola, Pierre, Conan, Scooter. And even herself.

Lola told her that as soon as she was out of the hospital and had a few weeks to catch up at work, she was packing her bags and hopping on the first thing smoking to Hawaii. She needed a few weeks' vacation and asked if Juanita could use some time away too.

"I'd like to go," Juanita answered, "but I can't leave Aunt Hattie for that long."

Lola grinned. "I see you feel the same way about her that I do. You know, Juanita, for the longest time I hated my parents. Despised them and wished they were dead. When I was a child I often wished I were adopted. Wished some nice family would come and steal me from my parents' home and give me all the comfort they never did."

Juanita listened as her mother spoke, marveling at how different their lives had been. How different they still were. Lola's speech and mannerisms were definitely Caucasian. And even after being raised surrounded by all of that money, her life had still been filled with heartache and loneliness.

Although she'd had a tough time growing up, Juanita's life had been largely filled with love. Filled with hugs and kisses and patience and laughter and all the things a little girl needed to grow up into a secure young woman. She was suddenly ashamed of herself for the way she'd spoken to Lola. Spoken to her mother. Now, instead of being filled with bitterness and resentment over her abandonment, she found herself understanding, and accepting, and somehow loving Lola.

"I'd like you to think about it. Think about the vacation," Lola said tearfully as she removed a small heart-shaped locket on a silver chain from her neck and placed it in Juanita's palm. She squeezed her daughter's hand. "Aunt Hattie and Uncle Herbie could come along too. Maybe we could even take a trip to Haiti. It would make your father so happy to see you walking off an airplane in his country. He'd give anything to be able to hug you, kiss you, talk to you, and to show you how much he really does love you. Even though he knew you were in a good home, he's always felt guilty about letting you go. In his mind, that single action forever branded him as something less than a man, and since the day he drove Aunt Hattie home and left his baby girl in her arms, he has never been the same. Neither of us had any other children. How could we? They wouldn't have been you."

Juanita didn't answer. She'd simply smiled at her mother and walked out of the door. She needed time to think. To absorb all that had been heaped upon her in such a short time. If there was one thing she learned from her mother's teenage experiences and her own insecurities, it was that people had a right to love whomever they pleased. Black, white, male, female. Whomever.

Juanita and Hattie arrived home to find Uncle Herbie in the kitchen frying up a pan of porgies and stirring a skillet of cornmeal mixed with onions and sweet green peppers. "I figured y'all would be pretty hongry when you got back. Wanted to make sure my gals had sumthin' good to eat." He grinned at his sister and she smiled at him in return. Juanita loved to see them show their teeth in nonverbal love. She felt blessed to have been raised by such loving and humble people as the aunt and uncle standing before her.

Juanita went into Hattie's bedroom and picked up the telephone. Quickly, she punched in Scooter's number and waited for him to answer.

"Hello?"

Juanita nearly hung up.

"Scooter?"

"N-nita?"

He sounded terrible, but it had been so long since she'd heard his voice that joy leapt to her heart.

"What's wrong, Scoot? Did you just wake up?"

"Um, no. I'm okay, I guess. How about you?"

Juanita hesitated. Scooter didn't sound fine. If she didn't know any better she would have sworn he'd been crying.

She asked, "Is Uncle Jeo okay?"

"Yeah," he said quickly. "Granddaddy's the same."

"Well, I just called because I miss you and I think it's time we talked."

Silence screamed through the other end.

"Scooter?" Juanita thought she heard him sob.

"I'm here . . . Nita. Nita, I did something really bad. Something terrible . . . I-I-I . . ."

"I know, Scooter, but I'd rather talk about it in person. Can you meet me at Lincoln Terrace Park?" She glanced at her watch; it was nearly two. "At three o'clock, at the monument near the pond?"

Scooter sniffed. "Okay, Nita. Whatever you say. I'll be there."

, , ,

Juanita hung up and frowned. Scooter didn't sound right. Not right at all. She sucked her teeth. And why the hell should he? He probably felt guilty as all get-out for sneaking behind her back and having sex with someone he knew she loved. Such betrayal by two of the three men she loved most in life really hurt. There was a gaping wound where her heart had once been. But in order for her healing to begin, in order for her to move on with her life, she knew she'd have to release both Scooter and Conan by offering them her forgiveness and giving them the right to love as they pleased.

She picked up the receiver again and speed-dialed another number. The telephone was answered on the third ring.

"Chello?"

Juanita swore under her breath. It was Conan's Tante Rosira. The frightful old woman didn't understand a lick of English.

"Hello, can I speak to Conan, please?"

"Wha? Conan no here! He go out!"

Damn! Juanita thought about simply hanging up, but decided against it.

"Could you tell him," she shouted into the telephone, "that Juanita called, and ask him to meet me at Lincoln Terrace Park at three o'clock?"

"Tell he wha? Conan no here!"

Juanita silently cursed again. She was just about to hang up when she heard a feminine voice speak into the telephone in perfect English.

"Hello? This is Grace, can I help you?"

Yes!

"Uh, hello, Mrs. Lopez, this is Juanita. I was wondering if I could leave a message for Conan. I need to see him . . . um, it's pretty important."

Grace Lopez's tone was warm and friendly. "Sure, dear. I'm on my way out to do a little shopping, but I'll be happy to leave him a note. What's the message?"

Juanita recited her message and listened as Conan's mother repeated it.

"Okay," she said. "Meet Juanita at three o'clock at Lincoln Terrace Park. She'll be waiting at the monument near the pond. Is that all?"

"Yes, ma'am," Juanita answered.

"All right. I'll tape the note to his bedroom door. That way he can't miss it."

∕ ∕ ∕

Emerging from the shadows of an apartment building directly across from where he lived, Jorge bolted across the street, his eyes glued to the corner that Conan had just turned. After screwing the shit out of Scooter, he'd found two local assholes to get him high and had been there in the building all night long, popping pills and smoking his first taste of crack before finally falling asleep in the filthy, narrow crawl space beneath the stairs. With an eye peeled for Conan, he paused long enough to turn his key in the outer door's spring lock, then quickly bounded up the stairs. Confident that he'd not been seen, he unlocked the apartment door, closed it quietly, and tiptoed down the hallway into the bathroom.

He stood over the toilet and urinated in a hot, rushing stream. Shaking his penis twice, he pushed his pants all the way down and sat down on the cool seat, staring into the water between his legs, riding its amber waves. His underpants were crusted with a pungent mixture of semen, urine, and bloody fluids, and the stench of his body rose in a cloud of funk as he tried to remember the last time he'd showered or changed his clothes.

Without bothering to flush, he rose and turned on the cold-water tap, splashing his face and allowing the clear water to trickle down his chin and drip onto his shirt. A tornado swirled through his brain and, bent over the sink, he swayed and rocked, a storm of dry heaves building in the pit of his stomach and threatening to burst forth from his parched throat.

He stared into the mirror and frowned. He was flying high. Wired for sound. Conan's white-and-blue jersey and baggy jeans hung soiled and wrinkled from Jorge's dehydrated frame.

Conan. That *gringo* son of a bitch. It was Saturday and they should have been down at the hall shooting pool and talking shit. Instead, he'd watched as his friend raced down the block and around the corner, probably heading toward the avenue to pick up something for his green-eyed bitch.

Jorge dug into his back pocket and retrieved a ball of tinfoil. His last blue pill disappeared into his mouth and he swallowed without effort. Minutes later, his hands began to shake. His vision blurred, then cleared, and from a great distance he realized that he had probably exceeded his limit. Perhaps he should have waited awhile before downing another tab.

Leaning against the wall, he tied a red-and-white bandana snuggly around his skull. The vibrant colors of the cotton scarf were brilliant, nearly blinding. In fact, all of his senses were ablaze, raw and enhanced. A door slammed in the distance, startling him. A dog tied up in the yard next door barked twice, and he nearly fell to his knees from the grating discomfort. In the kitchen, the telephone rang, jarring him to the bone.

Jorge staggered out of the bathroom and collided with Grace as she rounded the corner, a roll of black electrical tape in her hand. Her breasts grazed his chest and Jorge peered into her cold blue eyes, then raked his gaze down the length of her body. His bloodshot glare took in her charcoal-colored dress, her flat stomach, and her trim, girlish legs. Her ass, he knew, was plump but tight. He leered at the woman who had raised him, enjoying the look of horror that crossed her face.

"Watch it!" she snapped and stepped around him.

Jorge laughed and turned to ogle the jiggle in her hips as she hurried down the hall. "I am watching it!" He was still laughing as he pushed open the door and stumbled into his bedroom. Suddenly he frowned.

Blinking, Jorge moved closer to the door and squinted to read the note hanging at chest level and secured with a piece of black electrical tape. His cheer dissipated like vapors on a wind. Tight anger wound its way around his chest and he clenched and unclenched his fists.

Meet that nigger bitch in the park, huh?

That's why everything was all fucked up now! Because of Conan and that fuckin' girl!

Before she came barging in on his program, everything had been everything.

Fury rocked him on his feet. The pain of Conan's betrayal was dim compared to the rage Jorge wanted to hurl in Juanita's path. His head buzzed. His eyes glazed over as brilliant colors flashed and danced in his peripheral vision.

Juanita. It was time to handle that greasy bitch once and for all. Who was she to come between brothers? Between *amigos*? *Yeah,* Jorge thought, and yanked the bandana from his head. He'd take good care of that black whore. Give her the same thing he'd given that bitch-ass Thor, and then he and Conan could go back to being brothers. Back to being solid friends.

He swore and ripped at the scrawled note, then turned on his heels and stormed from the apartment. Blindly, he stumbled down the hall. Strobelike flashes pierced his brain as the acid surged in his bloodstream. A rainbow danced wildly before his eyes. The old man next door sneezed and Jorge flinched. Downstairs, Mrs. Vegas in 2-B cackled at a wisecrack from Alex Trebek, and the fillings in his teeth wailed. Soft moans of pleasure drifted from an apartment to his right, and instantly his penis became hard.

Yeah, Juanita. I'ma take care of that bitch, he silently vowed. He stood at the top of the landing and laughed. He could see it now. Feel it now. And if Conan didn't like it. . . . Jorge fought through his haze and focused on a vision of his ex-friend.

If Conan didn't like it, then he'd take care of him too.

CHAPTER 33

"**H**ow long you gonna be gone, Nita? I promised your mama we'd go back to see her this evening."

Hattie was seated at the table in her favorite pink duster, sipping from an I LOVE NEW YORK ceramic mug full of steaming black coffee. Haggard lines creased her face and she complained of swelling in her feet. Juanita bent and kissed her aunt gently on the forehead. A heart-shaped trinket dangled from Juanita's neck. She was freshly showered and her hair, back up in a severe bun, was still wavy and damp. Butter-flies beat furiously in her stomach and her breath kept catching in her throat, but she forced herself to act natural for Hattie's sake.

"I won't be long, Auntie. I have a few loose ends to tie up, and after that I'm coming straight back home. Go ahead and lie down for a lit-tle while. Will you be ready to leave by, say, five?"

"I'm ready now," Hattie replied, stifling a yawn.

Juanita smiled weakly and turned toward the door. She tucked her white T-shirt into her waistband. Her gold-and-white ankle-length skirt swept gently around her bare legs.

Hattie peered sleepily through one eye. "Gal, you betta tell some-body where you going before you walk outta that door!"

Juanita paused with her hand on the knob. "Oh! I'm sorry, Auntie. I'm walking over to Lincoln Terrace. If you need me I'll be near the monument at the park."

, , ,

Jorge continued down the stairs, gripping the railing for balance. Tumbling over his feet, he moved like a kite without sails, searching for a wind to lift him into oblivion. At the sound of voices near the second-floor landing he slowed cautiously. Forcing his fog to clear, he paused with his back pressed flat against the wall. It was Rico. That motherfucker. Coming out of Pushie's apartment. Was probably in there balling Pushie's fat old lady with the dirty pussy.

Jorge fumed and stumbled down the stairs toward the older man, his balance skewed, his vision off-center. "Hey, motherfucker." He stood before Rico, his eyes blazing, his lip curled upward.

Rico looked up, surprised at Jorge's new look. Not only was the young man sweaty and covered in grime, there was real danger in his eyes and he swayed in a wide-legged stance.

"Damn. Nice hair. For a minute I thought you was Conan. But I guess that couldn't be, huh? Especially since he's out there looking for your ass." Rico shook his head and squared his shoulders easily. "It wasn't bad enough what you did to Pushie's wife, was it? No, you don't only finger old ladies, you go out there and steal from your own people and try to get your best friend locked up for it too!"

Jorge stared, his face a hardened mask of fury and rage. He stepped up close and spoke through his teeth. "Yo, Rico. Mister King of the Fuckin' Community! You stupid motherfucker, you! I remember all them days you called the cops on *mi madre* and got her locked up. Got my mother thrown in the pen out on Rikers, didn't you? You fucked up my family, man." He advanced, his intentions clear, and continued, "Always running up in my mother's face. You thought you was a bad motherfucker back in the day. Let's see how bad you are now."

Rico folded his arms across his chest, but his eyes darted toward Pushie's doorway, as though measuring the distance to safety. He could have sworn he saw movement at the peephole, and took comfort in the fact that he was not truly alone with this young man, who was obviously flying high.

"Look, Jorge. I only tried to help you. It was Bobby I called the cops on. Not your mother. The only reason they arrested her was because she kept protecting him." He held out his hands. "She just kept letting him do those terrible things to you. She let him—"

"Don't talk about my mother!" Jorge lunged, scooping Rico up in a wrestling move he'd learned from TV, one palm gripping Rico's crotch, the other clutching his neck. Crazed, Jorge lifted Rico high above his head, then hurled him down the stairs. He raced down behind him as Rico's body spiraled and slammed into the marble, his head cracking against the steps, his nose spurting blood, his bones snapping audibly, until finally he came to rest in an awkward heap on the bottom landing.

Jorge panted and raged above the broken, unconscious man. "It was Bobby!" he screamed, kicking Rico in the ribs and stomping his face over and over until some small part of his brain registered the growing screams and shifted into survival mode. Doors were opening and curious faces were peeking out of apartments. A chorus of "Who's that?" and "I'ma call the police" floated down the stairs and somehow penetrated the fog surrounding his brain.

Without a backward glance, Jorge fled the apartment building, his fury not nearly spent. He was just rising to his peak, just getting where he wanted to be. His hands were aching to squeeze the shit out of somebody. Next on his list was Juanita. And then he'd hunt down that little bitch Scooter, and if he didn't have his goddamn key . . . Well, he wouldn't let himself think any further than that. Because to do so would mean the destruction of all he held dear. Without the money to finance his dreams, he was chained to this ghetto. And if he was chained to the ghetto, then Scooter and Juanita would both be buried in it.

✝ ✝ ✝

Mercedes greeted her cousin at the door dressed in a skintight white Lycra cat suit and little else. Fat tears spilled from her eyes smearing twin streaks of mascara on her cheeks.

"Conan! Oh my God! The ambulance just left here!"

"¿Que pasa? A donde esta mami y Titi Rosira?"

Mercedes sniffed. "They're fine. Out shopping." She took his hand. "Conan. It's Rico. Somebody beat the shit out of him and threw him down the stairs! People heard yelling and screaming, and when they looked out of their apartments Rico was lying at the bottom of the stairs . . . bleeding. He was unconscious at first, but he came to as they were putting him in the ambulance."

Conan staggered backward, the raw weight of her words knocking the air from his lungs. Rico. Who would want to hurt the one person in the world who truly cared about the people in this community? His mind dared not search for possibilities. He turned and raced toward his bedroom.

"Are you going to the hospital?" Mercedes yelled at his back.

"Yeah! I gotta get my . . ."

Conan paused at his bedroom, staring at the closed door. Black electrical tape was stuck to the remnants of what appeared to be a note. The entire bottom half had been torn off; apparently snatched down. Conan recognized his mother's neat, flowery handwriting.

Meet Juanita at three o'clock

Meet Juanita? The rest of the message had been ripped away. His mind raced. Meet her where? Conan looked down and saw a red bandana on the floor near his feet.

Jorge!

He dug his fingers into his scalp. What to do? Meet Juanita *where*?

Calm down, he told himself. He checked his watch, his chest heaving. It was nearly 2:15.

Motherfucker!

He slammed his fist into the door. Three of his knuckles split, leaving tiny droplets of blood on the white paint. Ignoring the pain, Conan paced the floor. He had to find out where Juanita had gone. Find out where he was supposed to meet her. He had to get to her before Jorge did, or there was no telling what would happen. He squeezed his eyes shut against the horrible images racing through his mind. Behind his closed lids he saw a broken body lying at the bottom of the stairs, but instead of the body having Rico's face, it had Juanita's shattered smile and clouded green eyes.

No, he comforted himself. Jorge wouldn't hurt her. Jorge knew how much Juanita meant to him. His old friend wouldn't do that to him. Wouldn't dare fuck with his heart like that. But there were too many vivid memories of Jorge's twisted nature for him to ignore. Too many episodes of Jorge's anger and jealousy that, these days, seemed directed at him.

A fleeting memory of a pained look radiating from Thor's eyes flashed in his mind. Conan rushed past Mercedes as he flew from the apartment. "W-w-wait!" she cried as he skidded around the corner and out the door. His heart pounding, he took the stairs three at a time. Once outside on the open streets, he raced in the direction of Juanita's projects, praying that he would catch her at home.

Conan realized that the last time he'd run at such an all-out pace was the day he'd chased the thief to get Juanita's bag back. It seemed like another lifetime. A lifetime of loneliness, grief, and sweat-drenched nightmares. A lifetime without Juanita.

Conan skirted children jumping hopscotch and shooting skelly. He jumped over garbage cans and darted between parked cars before opening his stride and taking to the streets.

Someone called from an open window, "Yo, man, who you runnin' from?" Conan ignored the voice. He blocked out all stimuli and concentrated on getting to the projects as fast as he could. His breath came easily, like a well-oiled machine: inhaling when his left foot struck the ground, and exhaling on his right.

He put himself in a mental zone and stayed there until he found himself panting and wheezing, standing before the concrete tower where Juanita lived with her aunt and uncle.

His watch read 2:44.

Conan jogged up the five flights of stairs, and fatigue was not an issue. With his hand on the wrought-iron doorknocker, he prepared himself to face Aunt Hattie. The last time he'd seen her she'd cussed him out and threatened to rip him apart with her bare hands. He knocked twice, hard. Then three more times in rapid succession. He hoped Aunt Hattie's fingers were tough and strong, because there was no way he was leaving her apartment until he knew exactly where to find Juanita.

/ / /

"Betta be the dangone po-lice bamming down the door like that!" Uncle Herbie leaned on his walking stick and shuffled over to the front door. He peered through the peephole and immediately unlocked the deadbolts and flung the door open wide.

Conan stood there swaying, his dark hair plastered to his skull, sweat rolling down his face and into his eyes. "Hattie!" Uncle Herbie screamed, his finger pressed to his throat, his terrified eyes searching Conan's face. "OhmysweetLawd, *Hattie Dell!*" Uncle Herbie reached out and grabbed Conan's upper arm in a viselike grip.

"What you doing here? Where is she?" he demanded. "What done happened to her?"

Conan's hopes sank. He'd missed her. He shook his head. "I don't know, Uncle Herbie. I think she's in trouble, though, and I need to find her fast!"

Hattie appeared in the doorway, panicked.

"What you want? Nita's gone!"

There were tears in his eyes as Conan pleaded. "Look, Aunt Hattie. I know what you think about me. I know you think I ain't good enough for Juanita and you might just be right. Maybe I'm not good enough for her, but I love her, and I've got to find her!"

"Hold up!" Hattie balked. "Nita's in trouble? How you know that? Trouble is what she gonna be in if she don't stop fooling around with the likes of you!" She moved to close the door. "Scoot back, Herbie. This boy best get away from my door and leave my baby alone!"

Conan shoved the door open and pushed his way into the apartment.

"Get out!" Hattie shrieked, pounding her fists on his chest. "You get your filthy self outta my goddamn house!"

"Hesh up, Hattie!" Uncle Herbie held his walking stick high in the air. "Woman, you jes hesh the hell up an' let the man speak! He say he know sumthin' 'bout Nita, and I, for one, wants to hear it!"

Conan held both hands up in the air, palms out. His eyes were wild but earnest. "The last time I had a feeling like this," he began, swallowing hard, "was the night my brother died. We were drinking at a bar and Thor walked off and disappeared. I knew he was drunk and couldn't take care of himself, but I was so into my own thing and what

I was doing that I ignored him and kept right on grooving." Conan wiped at the tears that were falling freely from his eyes and struggled to continue. "Thor came back about an hour later. He'd been with my friend. My friend Jorge. I saw something in my brother's eyes that night. Something that didn't look right, but I wanted to keep partying, so I ignored it." His shoulders slumped. "I planned to ask him about it later, I really did. But later never came."

Conan stared into Hattie's eyes. "My twin brother died that night, Aunt Hattie. Killed in a car accident that I probably caused, but I can still see that something in his eyes. I see it almost every night in my dreams." He squeezed his eyes shut briefly. "I never found out what happened to Thor. He never got a chance to tell me, but I think my friend Jorge had something to do with it. The same Jorge who might be after Juanita right now."

Hattie's skin turned pallid. Her lips moved but no sound came out.

"What makes you think Nita's wit' yo' friend?" Uncle Herbie whispered, terror in his voice.

"There was a message from her. My mother left me a note, but half of it was ripped away. The only person who would have done that was Jorge. I think he got the message that was meant for me! All I could make of the note was to meet Juanita at three o'clock—"

"The park!" Hattie screamed. "Nita said she was gonna be at the monument in Lincoln Terrace Park!" She clasped her hands to her cheeks. "Git out there and find my baby!" she cried, pushing at Conan's back as he fled the apartment and raced down the hallway. "Wait!" Hattie yelled.

Conan stopped in his tracks and turned to face her.

She stared at him for a moment and then corrected herself. "You go on out there and find *our* baby!"

Conan nodded and disappeared down the stairs.

CHAPTER 34

A warm breeze tickled her arms as Juanita strolled through the crowded park. A steel-drum ensemble grooved to a funky Caribbean beat on one of the raised circular stages, and a crowd of onlookers had congregated to enjoy the sounds.

Juanita sighed. Just two weeks ago she and Conan had walked along this same path after spending a Saturday morning skating. The bottom of her skirt brushed lazily across the tops of her sandal-clad feet. A plump squirrel ran out onto the path and froze. Her approach seemed to startle him and he darted back to the tree line and the relative safety of the lush green shrubs.

Juanita walked onward, skirting a grassy clearing where children played freeze tag and Frisbees sailed gently through the air while dogs ran around in circles, playfully nipping small ankles and fleeing bottoms. A few weeks ago this tranquil scene would have filled her with joy, but now she hurried along with her head down. Nearly everything about that time in her life had been a lie.

She crossed a narrow wooden footbridge and approached the monument from the east. Two elderly women tossed morsels of bread to a gaggle of Canada geese that were skimming the murky waters near the shore of the pond, and several families sat on blankets enjoying a late-afternoon picnic spread. Close to the path, a circle of young boys swung bats, hitting a big red ball back and forth between them. A young couple huddled together on a cozy bench, their heads pressed together, sharing a book whose title Juanita could not make out. Juanita averted her gaze from the love emanating from the pair as she stepped over a pink tricycle that had been abandoned on the footpath.

Not long ago she'd hoped for a future of sharing books, cozy picnics, and star-filled nights with Conan. A future of tricycles and doll babies and toys of all sorts scattered throughout a home they'd fill with laughter and children. She clenched her teeth on her bitterness and dashed dreams. She'd come here to give Scooter and Conan her blessings, and she resolved to do just that.

As Juanita neared the tarnished monument of Ulysses S. Grant, she searched for signs of Scooter; she prayed Conan's mother had given Conan her message and he would have the courage to come to her. Mosquitoes and diamond needles swarmed lazily over the still pond. Two of the three benches at the foot of the monument were empty, and on the other sat a teenage white boy dressed in a McDonald's uniform. The bill of his visor was pushed down on his forehead, and he swung his leg at the knee as he spoke into a yellow cell phone.

Juanita moved to take a seat on an empty bench, and that's when she saw him. He stood near the northwest corner of the monument. Although his back was to her she recognized his gleaming black hair and broad, strong shoulders. He was dressed in yesterday's clothing; a pair of baggy blue jeans and his Barry Sanders football jersey, the number 20 standing out prominently in blue against the white background of the shirt.

Her eyes rested on his Nike sneakers as she rounded the monument and approached him. She shuddered. The last time she'd seen him he'd been wearing the same clothes except, of course, his knees and legs had bucked and bent, pumped and pounded, as the man she loved did unspeakable things to her best friend.

Juanita covered her mouth, nauseated at the memory. She hurried to speak before she could break down and cry.

"I'm glad you came. I was wondering if you would even show up."

He remained still, his wavy black hair bending slightly in the breeze. Juanita took a deep breath and dug deeply into her heart.

"I, umm . . . saw you and Scooter. I mean, I was coming to your house to tell you about my mother and I saw you two . . . on the stairs." She gathered fistfuls of her skirt and squeezed her eyes tightly, praying that when she reopened them Conan would have crossed the small space between them with a rational explanation as to why her crazy eyes had lied to her. To explain why she couldn't have seen last night what she thought she'd saw.

She opened her eyes to his back. He stood silent and immobile, his hands thrust into the pockets of his baggy jeans, the cuff at the bottoms showing the underside of the denim material.

Juanita swallowed. "I asked you to come here to tell you that I don't hate you. I don't hate Scooter either. While I was at the hospital with my mother I learned something. I learned that love has no boundaries. No limits. All of us are free to love whom we please. It's just sad that you didn't love me enough to be honest with me. To tell me how you felt about my best friend." Her voice snagged and a stray sob escaped her. "I loved you, Conan. Even now, after what you did to me, the way you hurt me, I still love you. So why?" she begged tearfully. "Why didn't you just tell me you liked men? There's nothing wrong with you being gay. I could have accepted that. Why did you pretend to love me and let me love you if you knew it was really Scooter you wanted?" She stared at his unmoving back, mocking and unfazed. "Answer me, goddammit! After what you did to me, the least you can do is look at me when I'm talking and answer me!"

Silence. A curious pigeon waddled over to investigate. It pecked at the ground and after finding nothing of interest, flapped its wings and soared over to the low branches of a nearby oak tree.

"Why can't you face me, Conan? Didn't you love me at all?"

Clap. Clap. Clap. Clap. Clap.

His large hands came together in a slow rhythmic cadence.

"Way to go, *bitch*. What a fuckin' performance."

Juanita's mouth flew open as he spun around and faced her. Her heart plummeted as she stared into a pair of bloodshot, bogus blue eyes. A wild look contorted the once-handsome face, now haggard, evil, and streaked with filth and snot.

"I still love you!" he mimicked, and laughed. "Yeah, you fuckin' love him, all right. I hope you love that *gringo* motherfucker enough to die for him, 'cause that's exactly what you're gonna do." He stepped toward her. "You shoulda known better than to try to mess up a good thing between brothers."

Juanita swallowed hard and tried to keep her voice from trembling. "W-w-where is Conan? What are *you* doing here?"

Jorge advanced. "We were *brothers,* you greasy black bitch!"

Juanita stole a glance over her shoulder. The small boys were still swinging at the big red ball, but the picnicking families were too far away. They'd never hear her, even if she yelled, and the two old ladies would be of little help.

"Hermanos!" Jorge screamed. "Until you tried to take him from me. Didn't that mean anything to you? Huh? What the fuck could he have wanted with you when he already had me?"

Terror stole Juanita's voice and snaked down into her gut. The kissing couple had closed their book and were strolling away in the opposite direction. She thought of the teenager dressed for work at McDonald's. She calculated the distance to the far side of the statue.

"Don't even think about it, bitch!" Jorge closed the small gap between them and grabbed her shoulders. His splayed fingers dug into her flesh, and Juanita felt naked power surging through his hands.

She winced as Jorge swung her around, slid his thick forearm around her neck, and clamped her in a chokehold. Roughly, he bent her backward, forcing her down to the concrete.

Juanita lay sobbing in the cool shadows of the monument, her tender flesh cushioned by cigarette butts, broken glass, and colorful bits of trash. The melodic clanging of the distant steel drums slithered through the air, contrasting the fear in her voice with their peaceful, radiant chimes. "Please . . . don't," she begged, struggling as long strips of material were ripped away from her lower body. She gagged at his nearness, at the rotting stench rising from his body. "My God . . . please don't."

"You can't have him, you stupid bitch!" With one hand, Jorge wrenched her wrists high above her head and squeezed, grinding and pressing his knees between her legs. He lifted her white shirt and bent his head to gnash and tear at her tiny breasts.

Juanita shrieked as his teeth sank into her flesh, ripping her skin. Jorge brought his head up violently, crashing into her nose, silencing her. Juanita sputtered and gasped as warm blood spurted from her nostrils, trickling down her lips.

"That's right. Scream again, *gringa*! I like that shit. It turns me on." Jorge unzipped his pants, freeing his throbbing, eager erection.

Pushing against him, Juanita fought and drew her legs upward until her knees touched her chest. She squirmed and bucked and dodged his probing penis.

Jorge laughed and clamped his hand over her mouth, the heel of his palm crushing the bridge of her battered nose. "You want it up the ass? Yeah, all a' you *gringos* like taking it in the back. Ask your friend Scooter how good I gave it to him the other night."

Juanita's shrieked into his dirty palm. It had been Jorge! Not Conan! Jorge!

He ground himself against her softness, her thin white panties the only barrier between them. He chuckled at the realization in her eyes. "Yeah. It was me. Me who fucked Scooter, me who fucked Thor, and me who's gonna fuck you." He slid his hand between their bodies and yanked the crotch of her panties aside. "Open up, bitch. Open up and get beat down by a real man!"

Juanita struggled to bring her knees together. His thrusting weight pounded her. She screamed as the tip of his penis slipped through her outer lips and jarred her delicate, tender hymen. Fire burned between her legs as he jammed again and again, doing his best to penetrate her.

"God . . . please help me," she gurgled in pain and fear.

"He belongs to *me*!" Jorge roared and tried to hammer his maleness between her squirming legs.

Tears of rage and desperation flowed from Juanita's eyes. *Lord no,* she begged. It wasn't supposed to happen like this. She was pure, saving herself for her future husband. "Please . . . please . . ." she moaned. And then she felt him rear backward, arching his muscular back and withdrawing his hips, preparing to rob her of what she held dear. Juanita squeezed her eyes shut and raked her fingernails across his forearms, resigning herself to the inevitable, anticipating the pain. And then he fell atop her, his body weight crushing her, the air knocked from her lungs. His face was against her neck, but strangely, his hips were no longer thrusting, his penis no longer stabbing.

"Nita!"

Jorge's weight was rolled from her body, and through her tears Juanita saw Scooter looming above her wielding a child-size baseball bat. He dropped to his knees.

"Oh, Nita! I'm so sorry, baby." Gathering the tattered remnants of her skirt, he covered her body and rocked her in his arms. "This is my fault! I never should have listened to him. I was so jealous! Jealous of you and Conan, and like a fool I believed in Jorge!"

Juanita wept. "It's okay, Scoot. I don't care what happened or how jealous you were. I love you and we both made some mistakes. But it's over now. It's all over. You saved me, Scooter. This time *you* saved *me*."

Scooter shook his head, tears streaming down his rash-covered cheeks and dripping onto Juanita's face. "It ain't over for me, Nita. It's never gonna be over for me. See, I fucked up my life. I really fucked up this time."

Juanita winced as pain radiated through her battered nose. "No, Scooter. Nothing's been done that can't be fixed. Don't talk like that. Everything's gonna be okay."

"You don't understand, goddammit! I stole the fucking money! The payroll! I stole the bank's payroll to give it to *ugh*—"

Scooter rocked forward and grimaced, his eyes rolling up in his head. He arched his back and turned his head. "He s-s-stabbed me, Nita! That motherfucker done stabbed me!"

Juanita watched, shocked and mesmerized as a bright red stain appeared on Scooter's yellow shirt. The blood soaked through on his left side and spread under his arm and across his chest. She crawled to her knees and lowered him to the ground, their roles and positions suddenly reversed.

"Yeah, I stuck that little bitch. And I'll stick him again," Jorge breathed, "if he don't give up the key!"

Juanita was dizzy with fear and grief. She looked into Jorge's eyes and saw they were dazed but still deadly. Scooter's blow to Jorge's head had taken him down, but not out. She had to buy them both some time.

"W-what key, Jorge?" She could not keep the tremor out of her voice. "What the hell are you talking about?"

He closed his fist and punched her in the face. Her head whipped back as agony flooded her nose. "Don't play with me, *puta*. You ain't gotta know shit!" He stepped over Juanita and lifted Scooter by the back of the shirt. He flung him into the soft grass. Scooter landed faceup, his arms outstretched, his face a mask of pain and fear. Jorge sneered and turned back to Juanita. "All you gotta do is open up and let me finish handlin' my business!"

Juanita scooted backward as Jorge moved in on her, his stench wicked, his eyes filled with a sick, crazy glare. He meant to have her, and this time, she knew, he wouldn't be stopped.

She braced herself, refusing to submit to fate, prepared to kick and scream and scratch and bite for all she was worth.

"Don't move, Jorge. Just don't fuckin' move!"

Conan!

His black curls, much darker than Jorge's dyed hair, glistened like chips of coal against the horizon, and his bronzed arms bulged in his muscle shirt; the blue of his eyes was more brilliant than the cloudless sky.

He looked every inch the Barbarian he'd been named for.

Jorge stopped and smiled.

"Get the fuck away from her, man." Conan's words were low and chilly. "This shit is between *men*. Between you"—he pointed—"and me!"

Juanita shrieked, "Conan, he's got a knife! He stabbed Scooter—he's got a knife!"

"So what?" Jorge chuckled and tossed the switchblade to the ground. It thudded to the pavement, its long blade glistening red in the sunlight. "I don't need no knife to fuck up my *gringo amigo*." He held up his hands. "What you wanna do, Conan? Or should I say Co-pussy? Who's the fuckin' Barbarian here? The way you been crying over this dirty bitch, it sure as hell ain't you!"

Juanita cowered as Conan lunged and clipped Jorge at the knees, slamming him to the ground. They wrestled and fought, fists flying, as she crawled over to the grassy area where Scooter lay sprawled awkwardly on his back. Bright specks of blood frothed on Scooter's lips, and almost his entire shirt was red with blood, only the collar and right sleeve retaining any of its sunshine yellow.

"Somebody call an ambulance!" Juanita stood and screamed, forgetting her bruised and aching nose and even the tussling men as she jumped up and down and waved her arms. Two little boys stood staring. One held a large red ball, the other a small bat. As Juanita screamed and flailed her arms, they took off running away from the monument.

In the distance she heard other children playing. The two old ladies had vanished. Even the ducks seemed to have waddled away. "Hold on, Scoot," she begged, her eyes a river of emotion. "Just hold on. Help is on the way."

Scooter lay quietly, a garish scene playing itself out behind his fluttering eyelids. He saw a woman: soft brown skin, short curls framing her heart-shaped face, flecks of red splattering her cheeks, neck, and arms . . . and the glistening knife clutched in her hands. *Mommyyyy don't . . .* Plunging again and again into the body of a man. A thin, bespectacled man who could recite his alphabet backward and who always smelled of Soap-on-a-Rope and English Leather.

Scooter watched from four-year-old eyes as the woman set the knife on the coffee table and slipped into her shoes, leaving dainty red footprints on the carpet as she walked out of his life. In a haze of filtered light he saw his father prone at his feet, bloody and torn as he dragged himself toward the sofa whispering, "Call . . . Daddy . . . help." Scooter saw his Garanimals-clad self rooted to that worn sofa, sucking his finger and staring down into his father's open eyes as the shadows across the floor lengthened, then disappeared, the darkness protecting him from those dead eyes until the room filled itself with light from the new sun and the cycle of dark and light replayed itself four times more. And then there was the smell. The smell that had perched itself on the edge of his consciousness, the same smell that was sliding into his nostrils and down the back of his throat once again.

He opened his eyes and moaned, "Nita . . . I think . . . I think my mama killed my daddy."

"Ssshh. Hush. Don't talk, Scooter. Help is coming!"

"Nita . . . the money I . . . stole is in a safe-deposit box . . . I mailed the key to my grandpa." A bright stream of blood sputtered from his lips. "Turn it in, Nita."

"Sshhh . . . don't talk, Scooter." Blood bubbled from a hole just above his armpit and seeped through the tear in his shirt. Juanita pressed her torn skirts over the crimson pool and prayed for a miracle.

She caught sight of the blade lying on the path. What if Jorge went for the knife and stabbed Conan? And then her? She hated to leave Scooter's side, but fearing the worst she scrambled across the cobblestones on her hands and knees and grasped the long, serrated blade gingerly between two fingers. Turning away, she flung it as far as she could into the low brush.

She rushed back to Scooter in time to see Jorge, his fists raised in the air, sitting astride Conan's chest. His fists made loud smacking sounds as he beat Conan down without mercy.

"You're such a fuckin' pussy!" Jorge screamed between blows. "You, your old man, *and* that punk-ass brother of yours!" Wild laughter escaped his lips. "You wanna know something else, Mister Top Cat? Mister Badass-motherfuckin'-Barbarian?" Jorge howled. "*I* jerked the fuckin' wheel that night, asshole! I got rid of that whining motherfucker! It was *me,* you stupid son of a bitch!"

Juanita's heart almost stopped beating. Cursing his rage, Jorge lifted himself partway up and brought his forearm down hard on the bridge of Conan's nose. An audible snap whipped through the air.

Conan went still and stared up at Jorge. "You . . . killed Thor?" Disbelief spread over his features as he shook his head, slinging blood. "*You* did it? On purpose?" His face hardened into a mask of rage. "Jorge, no!" he yelled. "He was my *brother*!"

Jorge froze as the impact of his crime hung in the silence.

He grinned and split the air with a triumphant cheer. "Yeah, motherfucker?" He put his head back and clutched his crotch with both hands. "Thor might have been your brother, but the night he died, I made him my *bitch*!" Peals of laughter spilled from his mouth. Swept up by the wind, they rushed through the trees as the birds took flight and dark clouds eclipsed the sun.

Conan raged, bucking like a bull until Jorge was slung to the ground.

Lying on his back, Conan exploded with a guttural moan so agonizing, so torturous, Juanita covered her ears to blot out the madness.

And then he was on his feet. Swinging, stomping, kicking, battering Jorge, who had balled himself into a knot and lay bleeding but squealing with hysterical glee. Conan roared and lifted Jorge's body high in the air, he raised his leg and brought Jorge down hard, his spine snapping across the iron of Conan's thigh.

A scream burst forth from Juanita's mouth as Jorge tumbled to the ground like a sack of old shoes. He lay prone with his arms outstretched, his bloody face serene, his legs twisted in a jumbled heap.

Conan raised his foot over Jorge's exposed throat.

"Don't do it, or you'll have to go down with him."

The policemen drew their weapons and circled Conan.

"No . . . please," Juanita pleaded, her hands stretched out to two cops. The young guy in the McDonald's uniform gestured wildly toward Jorge as other park dwellers rushed over to witness the scene.

Conan remained positioned for the kill. His muscles tensed, his face glowing with fury. A crowd was quickly forming and sirens wailed in the distance, moving closer.

"It's okay, son." One of the patrolmen spoke quietly. "Step aside. Whatever he did, it's over now. We'll take it from here." His grip was steady on his pistol, but his voice was soothing and compassionate.

Conan aimed at Jorge's throat. His shoulders tensed as he gasped, "He . . . he killed my brother. . . ."

Murmurs rose from the growing crowd, some urging Conan on toward his revenge, others urging him toward restraint. "Killed your brother?" a stylishly dress black man asked. "Take that motherfucker out! An eye for an eye!"

Juanita begged from her knees. "Please, baby." She crawled the distance between them. "Don't do it . . . it won't bring Thor back. Jorge's not worth it, baby. Think about us. I love you, Conan. And I need you too."

Conan lowered his foot to the ground. Jorge lay still on his twisted back, this time out for the count. And then the sirens were upon them.

The flashing lights of a police-escorted ambulance greeted them as the red-and-white vehicle sped across the grassy field.

Juanita leaped to her feet. Scooter! She raced to him and fell to her knees. He was unconscious. Pink froth bubbled from his parted lips. Wet and halting, each wisp of air fought to enter his lungs, then struggled to be free of his body. Juanita wept. This time there might be no saving Scooter. Cradling his head, she planted tiny kisses on his eyelids and murmured her love.

Nearby, Conan towered above the unconscious body of his former friend and spat down into his face. Then he walked away without a backward glance and reached for Juanita. "Come on, baby. Move back so they can take care of him." He pulled her to him and held her as the EMS workers rushed to Scooter's side.

Juanita shivered as a female paramedic—a sister—clamped an oxygen mask over Scooter's face and cut away his shirt to examine his wound. Her fingers seemed sure as she poked an IV needle into the back of Scooter's hand and threaded it through his vein, and then a clear tube with a small accordion-like device on its end was pushed into his chest. Juanita watched as the other attendant, a balding white man in his late forties, prodded Scooter's wound, then sat back on his heels, shaking his head.

"What?" Juanita yelled, panicked. "Is he gonna make it?"

"I don't know," the paramedic said. "But if you ask me he's one lucky somebody! Looks like the blade went in at a weird angle—almost straight through his back. From the blood on his lips and the way he's breathing, I'd say he probably has a nipped lung." He pulled over a portable stretcher, and he and his partner gingerly lifted Scooter and placed him upon it. "Don't worry, lady. We'll get him to the ER, where they'll take a couple of X rays and run some tests."

Relief flowed through Juanita as she and Conan watched the pair lift Scooter's stretcher onto the ambulance. To her dismay, they loaded Jorge's unconscious body inside as well, although one of the officers handcuffed him to the stretcher first.

"Ma'am," a patrolmen called, eyeing her ripped blouse and blood-soaked skirt. "You're going to need to come down to the station and file a report. Are either of you hurt? Do you need to see a doctor? We can take you down to Woodhurst in a black-and-white."

Battered but grateful, Juanita and Conan declined his offer, and as the sirens wailed atop the ambulance that would carry Scooter and Jorge to the hospital, Conan pulled Juanita into the safety of his arms and felt the full heat of her body for the very first time.

"I love you," he whispered as he held her against him. He stroked her arms, caressed the small of her back, the swell of her hip; his fingers loosened her bun and tangled themselves in her hair, then gently and without regard for the crowd that continued to stare, Conan lowered his head and took from her mouth his very first taste of chocolate; and Juanita, in turn, parted her lips and accepted a sip of sangria.

EPILOGUE

/////////////////////////////

"**H**ur'up and wipe off that counter, Nita. Then I want you to take out the trash. You sure my hair ain't sweated back too bad? Scooter, you ain't still smelling that fish what Herbie fried last night, is you?"

Scooter shook his head. "No, ma'am."

Juanita sighed. She'd never seen Aunt Hattie so nervous. True, they had never done this before, and yes, she too wanted things to go perfectly, but Aunt Hattie was treating this dinner like it was the last coming of some great messiah. She'd spent two full days scrubbing the tiny apartment and had even sent Juanita to the library to get a book that promised to teach her to speak Spanish in five easy lessons.

Dipping the checkered dishcloth in soapy water, Juanita obediently polished the countertops until they shone, then draped the rag over the edge of the sink and tiptoed across the kitchen as she prepared to take out the half-full bag of trash.

"Gal, quit stomping 'cross the floor! Them cakes already got too much coconut juice running through that batter. You keep on marching through here like a herd a' elephants they gonna be a mess for sure!" She glanced toward the sink. "And don't jest leave that rag hanging like that! Fold it up neat-like. Make folks thank we trifling!"

Barely controlling herself, Juanita waited until Hattie bent over to check another pot, then rolled her eyes at Scooter and tied a knot in the plastic trash bag. Titters of laughter filled her ears and their eyes locked over the heat of the kitchen.

"What's so funny Scoot? Be glad your arm is in a sling or else you'd be taking out this trash instead of me!"

"No, I wouldn't."

"Yes, you would!"

"Yawl hesh!" Hattie snapped. "All that durned racket when we fin'ta have important company! Makin' me lose my concentration—" Her face crumpled as she snatched the lid from a hot pot with her bare hand. Ignoring the hissing steam and the sizzling pops, she poured a cup of cold water over the bubbling concoction, stirring furiously as she scraped the spoon against the bottom of the pot and muttered under her breath.

"Lawd ha' mercy." She frowned into the pot. The odor of burnt beans overflowed in the tiny kitchen and Scooter hurried over to the window and pushed it up high. Cool air rushed in, sending the light tendrils of smoke trailing upward and spiraling toward the window.

"That's okay, Aunt Hattie," Juanita reassured, pinching her nostrils and noting the crestfallen look on her aunt's face.

"It jest oughtta be," Herbie rasped. He fanned his hands in front of his face, waving back the smell of burned beans and scorched yellow rice. "We got nuff food up in here to feed the whole daggone buildin'!" He stood shakily and surveyed the spread covering the dining table and cluttering every spare inch of flat surface in the kitchen. "Yardbird, beef roast, fried plantains, black-eyed peas, fresh spinach, Spanish beans and rice, cabbage . . . I hope like hell it ain't the Pope comin' up in here to visit, 'cause wit' all this gassy food you got going he likely to blow his fool self up and set them thar white robes a' his on fire, Hat."

Hattie scowled at her brother, but above her frown her eyes were anxious. "I jest want them to feel comfortable-like, Herbie. I ain't got much idea about what-all Spanish folks eat, so I tried to fix a little bit of everythang I could thank of."

Turning to Juanita, Hattie smiled. "You know, my mama useta cook big for company like this down in Tennessee. Lucas wimmens can put on the hog, and that's a natural fact!" Her smile waned as her tired eyes swept over the kitchen. "I can't even remember the last time we let anybody up in this old apartment. Even now I'm shamed for folks to see it."

Her eyes judged the kitchen, taking in the sight of the grease splatters covering the flat oatmeal-colored wall behind the stove, the curling yellowed edges of wallpaper unraveling in strips near the door, and the curtains billowing from the window, clean but clearly having seen better days. Her slippered toe nudged a loose square of linoleum near the stove that, no matter how often Herbie glued it down, stubbornly folded back on itself in protest.

"Well," she said, sighing. "The rice and beans done burnt, the cake probably ready to fall, and if Mister Roast was gonna be decent enough not to yank out folks' teeth, he woulda had to come outta that Crock-Pot almost an hour ago." She wiped her hands on her apron and replaced the lid on the beans and rice. "I guess this'll be fine, though. Alls we can give them is alls we got. Lawd knows it's coming from the heart."

"Amen," Herbie said, and Juanita and Scooter echoed their agreement.

*, *, *

The knock on the door was a hesitant staccato.

"Lord." Hattie snatched off her apron and fled toward the rear of the apartment. "Y'all let 'em in while I put on some lipstick!"

Scooter laughed. "Lipstick? Why you tryin' to improve on perfection?"

Herbie stood leaning heavily on his walking stick as Juanita opened the door, swinging it wide. Conan stood before her, a fading half-moon below his right eye, a simple smile on his face. Beside him was his mother, Grace, and just behind them stood Victor Lopez.

"Hi," Conan said, and held up the large pan covered with a brown paper bag. "The food is still hot."

Juanita blushed. "Hello, Mr. and Mrs. Lopez." She stepped back and waved them into the apartment. "Here." She took a warm pan from Grace Lopez's hands and Uncle Herbie held the door open until

Victor, carrying a bag filled with fruit juice and soda, was inside. "Let me help you with this."

Herbie greeted Victor and introduced himself, and Grace smiled at Juanita. "I hope we aren't too early. It's so good of your aunt to invite us over, and Conan's idea of a potluck was great. Where should we put these things?"

Juanita ushered the trio into the kitchen and made room for the additional pans on the crowded countertops. Uncle Herbie was stacking the beverages in the refrigerator when Hattie entered the kitchen.

"Hello, everybody!" She grasped Grace's hands and beamed at Victor. "I'm Hattie Lucas, and you two must be the folks of this-here fine young man what helped save my baby's life. I'm so grateful to him . . . to all a' you . . ." Hattie's eyes misted as she stared at Conan, then she pulled a crumpled handkerchief from her pocket and blew her nose.

Juanita hugged her aunt's waist as she led her over to a straight-back chair. "Everything is okay, Auntie. I'm safe now. We all are." She pulled out two more chairs from the table and motioned for Grace to sit, then took Conan's hand and led him into the living room, where Scooter waited.

Herbie coughed and covered his trachea hole with his finger. "Ball game on in the back, Victor. Gots me an extry chair in my bedroom if'n you cares to join me."

Alone in the kitchen, the two women sat briefly, then busied themselves uncovering pans and arranging plates and glasses on the small table.

"You know," Hattie said softly as she positioned a setting of gleaming gold silverware next to each plate, "I been on this earth almost twice as long as you, and it makes me feel good to know that I still gots the heart to listen and the mind to learn." She turned to face Grace, who gazed at her with openness and respect. "I been wrong, Mrs. Lopez. I done wrong too."

Hattie smoothed an imaginary wrinkle from the edge of the starched tablecloth, then forced her hands to be still by clasping them together. "A long time ago something real bad happened to me. Happened to me and my baby sister, and all these years I been carrying in

my heart a load of hatred and mistrust of some folks because of it."
Her voice dipped slightly, but her chin remained strong and her gaze
steady as she stared into Grace's clear blue eyes.

"Bit by bit, though, I'm learnin'. Learnin' to leave the past in the
past, and instead look at people for who and what they might be *today*."
Hattie reached out and took Grace's hand in her own. "I wronged
your boy, sugar. I looked at your male chile and I saw every evil ghost
from every nightmare I ever had. Didn't matter none that he was a decent boy, a chile what was raised right and proper. Didn't matter at all
that he never hurt nobody or that his heart was in the right place. I
judged him, and I wronged him. And I wronged my Nita too. Now, I
done already asked God and them chirren for they forgiveness, and
ain't but one thing left to do, and that's to ask you for yours."

Grace stammered. "Me? Why? You've done nothing to me! If
Conan has already forgiven you, Mrs. Lucas—"

"Miss. Miss Lucas. I ain't never been married. Gave up that possi-
bility the night my hope died. Listen." Hattie sighed deeply, and every
year of her life surfaced on her face. "I had me a momma once. A
daddy too. Everythang what gets done to a chile has some bearing on
the parent too, whether they realize it or not. Your chile hurt, you
hurt. Jest that simple. Maybe that's why my daddy done me the way
he did. Maybe he was jest too hurt. So when I trespassed 'gainst your
boy for being part Spanish or Mexican or Porta Reekin or whatever it
is you and your family is, I trespassed on your ancestors and mine too,
'cause they both suffered toiling in this country and not a lick of difference was made between 'em by the folks who hated us all. So, Mrs.
Lopez, I humbly ask for your forgiveness, and hope you see fit to give
it to a stupid old lady who jest keeps livin' and learnin' more and
more, look like by the hour."

Hattie found herself enveloped by a pair of thin but strong arms.
"I'll forgive you on two conditions."

"What's that, Mrs. Lopez?"

"One, you forgive me for burning the chicken wings I tried to fry
for your family, and two, you call me Grace."

Hattie chuckled before standing back and enjoying the merriment
dancing on Grace's smile. "I thank I might be able to manage them

few little thangs if you can forgive me for burning up that big old pot of Spanish rice and beans and messing up my ca—"

Clapping her hand over her mouth, Hattie yanked open the oven door. Mindfully, she grabbed a pot holder and pulled the cake pans from the oven. She stared at the concoction of crusted brown goo, smoldering in a concave mess. "Lawd have mercy! My cakes done fell in!"

Grace stared at the crispy lump in the pans, then covered her mouth to stifle a giggle. Hattie's laugh came from her belly, and as the women gazed at each other over the hardening goo, it was clear that they were celebrating more than just a simple moment of laughter. They were celebrating a moment of shared humanity.

Wiping at her eyes, Hattie asked, "Did you know there's a girl name Ellen Ochoa who was the first Spanish astronaut?"

"No, as a matter of fact, I didn't."

"Well, that's not all. Some migrant farmer who call hisself César Chávez got a medal of freedom from President Clinton too. And that Oscar De La Hoya? Put a hurtin' on Sweet Pea Whitaker he ain't gonna never forget! I mean he tore that tail up something terrible. . . ."

/ / /

In the living room, Juanita sat on the small sofa sandwiched between Scooter and Conan, enjoying her men as they watched ESPN.

"Man, golf ain't even really a sport."

Scooter balked. "And why not? They work up a serious sweat walkin' all over those greens."

"That's because it's hot out there, not because they're athletes."

Reveling in their warmth and security, Juanita snuggled deeper and reminded herself of how lucky she was. She had a wonderful aunt and uncle, a new mother, a man who loved and respected her, and the affection and camaraderie of her closest friend. And next month, when she and Conan visited Haiti, courtesy of Lola, perhaps she'd add a father to her list as well.

"Tiger is da man!" Scooter shouted. "He's the brother who raised the bar!"

Conan laughed. "Brother?"

"Man." Scooter waved his good arm. "Brother, cousin . . . I don't care if he calls himself a Cablinasian or a cannibal. Those fried chicken and Old English jokes don't mean a damn thing when he's out there eating their asses up! As good as he is, they're gonna be begging for some hot sauce to go with them collard greens!"

Juanita nodded. Scooter was sounding a lot more like his old self: chatty, opinionated, and filled with spunk. It had taken quite a bit of crying and convincing, but she had finally persuaded him to forget about the whole banking incident and let sleeping dogs lie. For the time being.

"C'mon, Scoot," Juanita had pleaded. "You sent the money back and quit your job. What purpose would it serve to turn yourself in? You never tried to profit from this. Yeah, you were wrong, but you were trying to help an old lady have a second chance at life. Your intentions were good, and that should count for something. Besides, the real thief, the real monster behind all of this, is in jail where his crazy ass should stay for ninety-nine years and one black night. Maybe he'll get some help while he's in there too."

Juanita had begged him, rationalizing his crime away for weeks, and finally Scooter had allowed himself to be somewhat swayed. But Juanita knew he didn't feel good about it. "Let's just see what happens, Nita. I can't promise I won't turn myself in, I just need a little time to think this thing through. Even if they never figure out who sent back the money, even if Sol can keep covering for me, when Jorge goes to trial it might all come out anyway, and I'm prepared to deal with that. To face up to it. I hurt a lot of people at that bank. People who cared about me and believed in me, and no matter what you say, I'll never feel good about that."

His shoulders slumped and Juanita knew it was because of Sol. He'd told her about his relationship with his boss, and how much it had hurt the banker when Scooter had resigned his position. "I really hate that I hurt him, Nita," he'd complained. "Hate that I used him the same way Jorge was using me. At least one good thing has happened in all of this. He came out to his wife, and they're both in counseling."

Scooter's remorse was real and palatable, and Juanita had truly felt his pain.

And even now as he sat beside her, bickering back and forth with Conan, whose company he seemed to really enjoy over the past six weeks, there was still something in Scooter's eyes that gleamed with apprehension and unease. Juanita shivered. She knew he'd committed a serious crime, but the thought of him rotting behind bars because of one stupid lapse in judgment scared her down to the bone.

"Man, later for you." Scooter waved his good arm at Conan and rose from the couch. "I'ma go check on Granddaddy, and when I get back, you best be prepared to get beat down in some bones."

As the door closed behind him and the sounds of womanly laughter tinkled from the kitchen, Conan pulled Juanita into his arms and kissed her full on the lips. "We did it, baby. We built ourselves a bridge out of love. Check us out . . . me, here in your house . . . holding you. My mother in the kitchen." He lifted his chin. "My dad back there with Uncle Herbie." He kissed her again. "One nation under your roof! Damn, *mamacita*! Who woulda thunk it?"

Juanita kissed him back and grinned. "Beats me, *papi*. Who woulda thunk it?"

CHOCOLATE SANGRIA

A Reader's Guide

TRACY PRICE-THOMPSON

Reading Group Questions and
Topics for Discussion

1. Why are the neighborhood children so mean to Juanita and Scooter? What do Juanita and Scooter do to protect themselves from such cruelty? How does their bond become stronger and more complex as they grow older?

2. Hattie is the epitome of the strong, self-sacrificing black woman. What made her this way? How did the murder of her younger sister shape her views of Hispanics? What did she see in Lola that touched her heart? Why did she agree to raise Juanita?

3. Juanita experiments mildly with bulimia in *Chocolate Sangria*. What effect do Juanita's weight and appearance have on her self-esteem? Are her efforts to make herself appear as "black" as possible understandable? How confusing and dismaying might it be for her to look through her family photo album and not see anyone who remotely resembles her? Is our self-identity determined by our physical features and our environment, or does it come from within?

4. Each of the main characters in *Chocolate Sangria* suffers tragic experiences that influence events over the course of their lives. How might Scooter's early trauma have affected the choices he makes later in life? Should he have turned himself in to the authorities for his role in the robbery?

5. What is Uncle Herbie's role in *Chocolate Sangria*? What is the origin of his sense of obligation and responsibility toward Hattie and Juanita? How helpful is he in providing balance to Hattie's biases? In providing positive reinforcement as Juanita struggles to accept her weight and body type?

6. The role Conan plays in the death of his twin brother and the guilt he experiences as a result are powerful and intense. Is Conan's guilt a factor in his allegiance to Jorge? Why?

7. How did the sexual abuse Jorge suffered as a child affect him? Is Jorge gay or simply an opportunist?

8. At the conclusion of *Chocolate Sangria,* Scooter is at a crossroads. What direction do you think his life will take?

9. What are the similarities and differences in the way Scooter uses Sol Steinberg and the way Jorge uses him?

10. In *Chocolate Sangria,* people of color share limited resources and a common community, but intraracial prejudice is experienced on many levels. Why? Is it realistic to think that two people, despite their different races and family pressures, can love each other and stay together happily?

11. Which is more important to Juanita and Conan's lasting love, their commonalities or their differences? How does the diversity in their ethnicities bring them closer together? Does being pro-black mean you must also be against other races?

12. Which of the characters in *Chocolate Sangria* do you identify with the most? The least? Which is more important to human relations, tolerance or respect? What are the biggest challenges you face in tolerating, respecting, or accepting others who are very different from you? What would it take for you to overcome those challenges?